THE HEIGHTS

A **LIZ BOYLE** MYSTERY

KATE BIRDSALL

The Heights
A Liz Boyle Mystery™
Red Adept Publishing, LLC
104 Bugenfield Court
Garner, NC 27529
http://RedAdeptPublishing.com/

This is a work of fiction. Names, characters, places, and incidents either are the product of the author's imagination or are used fictitiously, and any resemblance to locales, events, business establishments, or actual persons—living or dead—is entirely coincidental.

---

1.   https://StreetlightGraphics.com

For my mom

I had melancholy thoughts...
a strangeness in my mind,
A feeling that I was not for that hour,
Nor for that place.

— William Wordsworth, The Prelude

CHAPTER 1

The assistant prosecutor and I are just sitting down to prep for a trial that's supposed to start tomorrow when Lieutenant Fishner slams through her office door, red-faced, her gray-blond hair a mess.

"The shit has hit the fan. We'll be lucky to avoid riots. Get over to the East Side Shoreway twenty minutes ago, Boyle—they need you. Officer-involved shooting of an African-American juvenile who may or may not have been armed."

I don't know what she means, exactly, when she tells me that I need riot gear and to pick it up downstairs because the fifth district ran out an hour ago. My partner went home early, so I'm flying solo.

"I guess we can do this later."

Becker nods. "Text me when you're done."

It's fortunate that I follow procedure and keep a tactical uniform, complete with a bulletproof vest, in my work locker, that it still fits, and that I wear combat boots every day of my working life. It means I don't have to mess around too much, not that I'm in any hurry to get to where I need to be. There won't be much I can do there, anyway, other than watch my city come unglued.

I change alone in our dingy locker room. As I pull the blue Cleveland Police baseball hat down on my head, I catch a glimpse of myself in the mirror: there I am, Special Homicide Detective Elizabeth Boyle, badge number one-seven-six-one. I turn away and run a hand across my forehead. My thirty-eight years are right there, every one of them etched onto my face. They're in the silver strands that are making their way into my dark-red hair. They're in the way I carry myself, I guess, now that the swagger has fourteen years of actual police experience behind it. The years are both in me and on me, and yet, with this uniform on, I almost feel like I used to: like I have no idea what I'm doing, but I'm about to do it, anyway.

I did five years on Patrol and three as a sex-crimes detective before I took this gig. These days, I'm in a unit that solves murders that appear to be sexually motivated, at least most of the time. We also get calls on high-profile cases, since putting the word "special" in front of "homicide" suggests something more than sex crimes to the public, something more than tracking down violent idiots who leave their DNA all over crime scenes and murder victims. I suppose it could have something to do with our 80 percent clearance rate, but I'm not so sure.

Feeling like I have no idea what I'm doing makes me nihilistic, which isn't an especially endearing trait of mine. But I'm going to act like I do know what I'm doing and hope that I learn something. It worked, way back when.

I throw my regular clothes into my locker and move to the sink to wash my hands. I suppose I look more well-rested than usual, but we'll see how long that lasts. I dry my hands then shove the door open and step into the hallway.

Five minutes later, I'm even more cynical when I climb into a zone car with Marcus Morrison, a guy I went to the academy with and haven't seen in a while. He looks like he's taken the bodybuilding to a new level—the veins on his sizable forearms are visible.

"You coming with me, Boyle?" When I nod, he asks, "What are you riding with me for, anyway?"

"Fisher told me to ride with Patrol. Here you are. Call it serendipity. Where's your partner?"

"Already there. I just came back for another Taser and my helmet. Where's *your* partner?" He holds up the Taser as if I won't believe him otherwise.

I would rather be riding with Tom Goran. He understands my need for silence. "Goran went home hours ago." *Another Taser, since we aren't under investigation by the Department of Justice for using Tasers too much already.*

"Been a long time since I saw you in BDUs," Morrison says, looking over at my navy-blue cargo pants and chuckling. "You got what you need? Where's your plastic shield? You know homeboys be *dangerous*, 'specially to nice white ladies like you." He keeps laughing, even elbowing me at one point as if I should be laughing, too, and I try to figure out what's funny.

"A twelve-year-old got shot. How can you laugh at any of this?" I ask the window as he pulls out of the parking lot. The Kevlar vest cuts into my left shoulder, and I try to loosen it through my navy-blue shirt.

"What, cause I'm black, I shouldn't laugh? That's exactly why I can laugh at it. You know what I'm saying. I know you do."

I don't ask what he means by that. Probably something about the fact that, since I'm gay—I finally told him the last time he asked me out—I get to laugh when assholes make dyke jokes.

He'd been cool about it, said he wouldn't talk a bunch of smack to the rest of the department. At this point, I'm not sure I would care, because it's not as though it's a huge secret. Marcus had seemed relieved that my rejection wasn't personal and asked if we could be friends and if I wanted to go golfing with him sometime. I said no but that I'd go to the shooting range with him so we could relive our glory days and see if I'm still a better shot than he is. It hasn't happened yet. I'm pretty sure I'm still a better shot. "What the hell went down, anyway?"

"Reports that a kid waved a gun at a couple guys out in the fifth district. They took him out. He's at MetroHealth. Nobody knows yet if he's gonna make it, and people are filling the streets, blocking intersections. Brass is worried about looting and shit. I guess there's video from a couple places."

I nod as he accelerates onto Ontario.

On the way there, Morrison tries to make small talk about the brain-bender of a case I worked last spring, the one that ended with me getting a commendation after saving my brother from a psychopath. I don't really have much to say, because I'm trying to focus on what needs to happen right now and what might happen tomorrow in the courtroom, and I don't want to get sidetracked. So I give a series of "yeah, uh-huhs," and Morrison seems to get the drift.

We pull up near the Shoreway about twenty minutes later. I glance at my watch—it's almost nine thirty—then push the door open. I can see why Fishner wanted me to ride in a cruiser—no other cars are getting through the barricades, not even unmarked police cars. I glance around and spot my partner's blue Chrysler, his personal vehicle, behind the barricade in the grocery store parking lot. I sigh in relief.

"You got a radio?" Morrison asks.

I pat the radio on my left hip and slide its earbud into my left ear.

"We're on channel twenty-one. All of us, just for this. Body cam?"

I nod and glance down at the eye affixed to my shirt. I pull out my phone to text Tom Goran: *Where are you?* "I'm staying back," I tell Morrison. I don't even know why I'm here. It's been a long time since I wore a uniform, and I've never been in riot-standby mode—I'm a detective, not a member of the SWAT team. Blue and red swirls coat the asphalt and the decrepit old brick buildings. I take a deep breath and blow out the exhale as if it's smoke.

The scene appears to be nonviolent. People—families, men and women and children—line the street leading to the park. Some sit on stoops outside of the long-shuttered and graffiti-covered storefronts, and some lean against the crumbling bricks. A few look out of their open apartment windows, and some have gathered up front, against a bigger barricade—a line-of-cops kind of barricade—where a woman with a bullhorn leads the crowd in chants.

A man's voice comes through my earbud, telling us that we are to allow people to take all the cell phone video they want and that the media is everywhere. *Don't do anything stupid. Don't get punchy, now. Just be calm and let the people assemble, and let's show everyone just how kind and gentle we all are.*

I've never experienced guilt before over being a cop, but that's exactly what happens as I make my way through the crowd. I'm not afraid of people in general. I don't walk around wondering what kind of criminal acts any one of them might be planning, because doing that is a fast track to burnout, alcoholism, or eating the gun. But I can't help the palpable sadness, the anger that surrounds me. Beyond the signs proclaiming that black lives matter, beyond the balled-up fists, beyond the rhythmic chants and the tearful songs... Past all of that, there's some kind of deep-seated sense of injustice and a sense that it's happened *again*, as opposed to this being the first time, along with the feeling of visceral rage that comes out of being powerless.

I might be afraid of what'll happen tomorrow, after I give that testimony. I might be afraid that I won't be in this club anymore, the one that I've called home for almost fifteen years. And I might be afraid that, at this moment, that could be okay with me.

Near the front of the crowd, a teenaged boy wearing only a T-shirt in spite of the October chill is shrieking at a stone-faced male cop. "You shot my *brother*!" he wails. "My *brother*! And then you *left him there*! And then you arrested my *sister*! You *beat her*! She was just trying to *help him*! What the fuck? What the fuck?"

The cop says something to him, and the boy escalates. He makes two fists, and the cop steps forward, holding his baton, his other hand on his Taser. The energy between them crackles like static electricity, and I know exactly what's going to happen.

No. I instinctively take several steps in their direction, pushing through the crowd, who recoil as though I'm radioactive.

Just as I make it to the uni with the baton and hold up a hand, silently begging him to stand down, the woman with the bullhorn comes up next to the kid and takes his arm. He breaks down with tears and snot and everything. He holds onto her as if he's a little boy, balls her jacket into his fists, and sobs, his face contorted with the kind of grief that's recognizable only if it's familiar. "My brother. My sister," he cries into her shoulder, and the hot heaviness of my own tears stings my eyes. She whispers something to him, and they move away from the front of the line. I take another deep breath and step away.

Channel Three's camera catches it all on video.

I move to the back of the crowd, where I stay for a while, just watching and hoping to everything holy that this doesn't escalate into some kind of nightmare out of Gotham City.

Fishner calls right as I'm deciding to get the hell out of here. "Leave. Meet with Becker," she says in a weary voice. "Patrol has everything under control. We need to back off. They're not violent."

"Okay," I reply. *"They're not violent." Does she mean the protesters or the cops?* Some sensation that I can't name uncoils in my chest. I've been working on this, and I should be able to name it. But I can't.

"You need to be fresh in the morning for court."

I hope she doesn't give me a pep talk. She's been all happy about my willingness to put my ass on the line and break the blue code of silence. I wait and listen.

"You need to know that I think—I know—you're doing the right thing. I also know you're not interested in department politics, but what you're doing tomorrow needs to happen." I hear her close her office door. I'd recognize that squeak anywhere. When I'm silent, she keeps going. "If more people spoke out about the kinds of things that too many of us find ourselves getting into, the department would be better for it."

It sounds as though she's talking about more than my little appearance in court, and I wonder how long she's been planning this spiel, but I let it go. "Thanks," I mumble, half hoping that I'm still part of "us" after tomorrow and half wondering what I'll do if I'm not.

I can't find Morrison, and I'm too tired to talk to anyone, anyway, so I call my partner, who hasn't responded to my text, to check in. He's leaving, too, and tells me to meet him by the Chrysler in the grocery store parking lot.

I lean on the hood for five minutes before I see him ambling my way, in his BDUs just like I am, looking as sad and tired as I feel. He raises his right hand at me when he catches my eye and speeds his gait.

"You ready to get out of here?" Goran asks after he spits his gum on the ground.

"You know it." I force a smile. "Nice haircut. Having the sides short like that hides all the gray."

He winks at me.

Halfway back to the station, he clears his throat as if he's going to say something, but then he stays silent.

"What?"

"What?" he replies.

"Tom. What?"

"I just don't want to see you screw yourself." He jabs the space between his bottom incisors with a toothpick.

I stare at the dashboard. "This doesn't have anything to do with tomorrow, does it?"

Out of the corner of my eye, I see him flick his gaze at me as he switches on the turn signal. "Screw Grimes. It's not about him. He was out of line. And he's a scumbag. We've all heard about it."

I turn to face his profile and watch the tic in his strong jaw. If I'm staring at him, Goran has to answer me. "What, then?"

"Just, well, I've heard stuff. I just want you to be safe."

"You want me to be safe," I repeat. "You seriously think that—"

His phone rings, and he looks grateful for the interruption. He pulls it out of his pocket and taps it. "This is Goran." He scratches the side of his face. "Uh-huh, yeah. Okay." He hangs up and slides the phone back into his shirt pocket. "One good thing about these damn itchy uniform shirts"—he makes brief eye contact with me—"is that the phone just fits right in. Let's go get a drink."

I send the assistant prosecutor a text telling her that I'll be back in twenty minutes. "I have to meet with Becker first. It shouldn't take long."

CHAPTER 2

I meet Becker in the conference room. She has files spread out all over the table and crime scene photos queued on her iPad, which she's connected to the projector. She asks me, again, something about the knife that I'm not supposed to mention, and she keeps doing that thing where she asks the same question sixteen different ways, just to see if my answer changes.

"Tell me exactly what you saw when you arrived at the scene," she repeats, her hands in a pyramid with the fingertips together. Her French manicure looks fresh.

"I walked into the house after Patrol called and found her body there." I point at the crime scene photo, dated July of last year—the photo that I took when I arrived. The answer doesn't change with me, not when it comes to this kind of thing. "Patrol found Mr. Reynolds in a second-floor bedroom, in his boxers, covered in blood and rifling through drawers. They then detained him. Goran and I made sure that the first floor was secure, then I went upstairs while he worked the grid."

"And the murder weapon?"

"I thought I wasn't allowed to talk about the murder weapon."

Her hands drop to the table. "You're not going to *mention* the murder weapon, but I need to hear it again. The defense might bring it up, try to pin the mishandling of evidence on you."

"Oh, that's just what I need. I still can't figure out why *we* aren't mentioning it," I grumble.

"Liz. Please."

We're not mentioning it because the way we handled the knife reveals another incompetent cog in the machine that is the police department that employs me. I almost—*almost*—feel bad about it. "Fine. I observed Mr. Reynolds wrap something in what looked to be a pillowcase and throw it from the bedroom window. After he did that, he called me—and I quote—'a motherfucking white pig bitch' and then came at me with what I thought was intent to harm me. I sidestepped him then restrained him against this wall." I swipe through the photos until I see the flowered wallpaper.

Julia tucks a piece of her long copper hair behind an ear. "At any time, did you or any of the other officers on the scene use excessive force?"

"They're going to object to that. I can only speak for myself. I'm not Internal Affairs or whatever special task force we're using these days."

She just stares at me, her blue eyes searching my gray ones for something.

"I did not use any force whatsoever. I handcuffed Mr. Reynolds, advised him of his rights, and told the patrol officers to escort him downstairs and put him in the back of the zone car. Nothing more."

She watches me through her newish tortoiseshell glasses. "You know you're not on trial here, right?"

I sigh. "Of course I know that. But you have to understand, I'm not just some witness. I'm a cop, and this is borderline rat territory. It's a big deal, Julia."

She picks her pen up from the table and bites the cap. "You're doing this because you have to." She shuffles a folder around. "Everyone knows you'd rather stay out of it. You're doing the right thing."

"Yeah, well, the guy's gonna lose his job and maybe serve time. Doing the right thing feels like shit."

"Probably not as bad as not doing it would, given the extent of the injuries."

She has a point there. I consider the medical report that said Reynolds ended up with a broken nose, a broken collarbone, and a concussion.

She gets back to business. "Did you notice whether he had any injuries at that time, before he was taken downstairs?"

"At that time, no. But he was covered in what was later determined to be his grandmother's blood."

"How about later?"

I run my hands through my chin-length mop, try to squeeze the tension out of my neck, then let my hand drop to the table. My big watch clacks against it, and it startles me. I glance at it and watch the second hand click twenty-four times. "Later, after we took his clothes into evidence, swabbed the blood on his skin, all of it, I noticed that he had a bloody nose, a contusion on his forehead, and bruising on his neck."

"When and where was this?" She knows the answer. Lawyers ask questions only if they already know the answers.

As much as it irritates me, the prep can't hurt—I'm not looking forward to being on the stand this time. "When I questioned him about the stabbing and the earlier rape of the neighbor. In the interview room. It was early the next day, at approximately six o'clock."

She scans my face. "Did you witness anyone else using excessive force at the scene?"

I flinch because perjury isn't my thing. I'm practicing for a real trial, not the trial of Shareef Reynolds. He's already pleaded guilty to stabbing his grandmother thirteen times over a twenty-dollar Timex watch after he raped the grandmother's neighbor. No, I'm practicing for the trial against officer John Grimes, so I decide to play it straight. "I witnessed Officer Grimes place Mr. Reynolds into a choke hold."

She nods. "Was this before or after you handcuffed him?"

I clear my throat and adjust my black button-down. "After."

"Was this the kind of choke hold that the department trains offi-cers to employ?"

"I have no comment about that."

She rolls her shoulders back. "Think about your credibility. Of course you have a comment on that."

"At this time, the department does not allow any kind of choke hold, and it was certainly against procedure to put an otherwise-re-strained man into such a hold." I don't care for legalese, but that's how we have to sound in court, like the mindless drones that we're supposed to be.

"And you did what in response?"

"I told Grimes to stand down and that he needed to get his shit together—I mean, I suggested that he take a moment to regroup. Then I took Reynolds down to the car myself and called my lieu-tenant regarding the fact that we had Reynolds in custody and were bringing him in."

"Did Officer Grimes say anything to you following your demand that he stand down?"

"Of course not. I have rank."

"Liz."

"He suggested, under his breath, that I not tell anyone what I saw him do." I start jiggling my leg.

"Did he threaten you in any way?"

I let out the breath I'd been holding. "He said he would have me, quote, 'gang raped by a bunch of, uh, N-words,' because 'fucking dumb bitches have no place being detectives' and that he 'knew my kind, anyway.'" I smooth my jeans. He could probably organize some kind of attack, but it's more likely that he's full of shit.

"Did he say 'N-words'?"

"No." I flinch again and look away, feeling my pale skin blush. I don't use that word.

"You're going to have to say the word on the stand."

"I know."

"You're here in spite of the threat," she says, her face softening.

"Are we still practicing?" I push my chair back from the table, and my left eye starts to twitch. "Look, I wouldn't be here at all if his partner hadn't registered a complaint and named me as a witness." I consider what I'm saying. "If the guy, Reynolds, hadn't been jacked up all the way across town and back. I mean, who the hell knows what happened to him in that zone car. Off the record? You don't get a bruise like that on your face from being in a choke hold. You don't get a bruise like that and a broken nose unless someone punches you in the face."

She looks interested, so I keep going. "I hate to say this, but this whole thing... It's just... I'm not a rat." I make my leg stop jiggling and lean forward in my seat. "I would have dealt with him in my own way. On my own time. I sure as shit wouldn't have gone to IAU, and we wouldn't be here, like this, right now." I would have launched an off-the-books investigation on him and figured out how to get him to dig his own grave. I know enough people on that beat, and they respect me enough to give me information. It wouldn't have been hard—the guy isn't a genius.

"But think about those things he said to you, not to mention the things he did to Reynolds. The things his partner says he routinely does in the course of arrests. Not even arrests, just in general. Do you want him representing you to the public? Should cops like him exist?"

I take a deep breath. "The things he *said* are part of the job. A lot of us say horrible shit all the time, about anyone and everyone. The things he *did* are another story."

AFTER I FINISH WITH Becker, I change into my regular clothes, and my partner and I end up at Sammy's, our usual dive bar. Goran keeps looking at me as if he wants to say something, as if he's holding back. But I don't take the bait, even when he gives me his even, steely-eyed cop look. I change the subject, and we talk about his wife, his kids, and his new gas grill that he got on sale because summer ended over a month ago.

He wants me to come by this weekend—we're off Saturday and Sunday this week—to break it in. "Before it gets really cold," he says. "Even though you know I'll be out there in January." He grins and mimes burger flipping.

I don't say whether I'll come or not. "I'm taking my brother to the Browns game on Sunday." I empty the last of the pitcher into my glass.

"Come over after. Perfect timing. Bring Chris. Bring whoever you want. This grill is huge." He holds his hands about four feet apart. "It's my dream grill," he says like he's in love.

We laugh, and I don't tell him that I'm not sure I can do anything this weekend, that I might have to stay home alone because anxiety is needling at my core, that I'm ashamed and guilty and all kinds of other things because of what I saw tonight and have to do tomorrow. I drain my glass and shove my chair back. "C'mon, Goran. You need to get home to the girls."

He stands, throws money onto the table, and pulls on his jacket. He opens the door for me, and we step out into the cool October air.

"You want me there?" he asks as we walk to our cars.

"No, don't worry about it."

A homeless woman starts to ask for money but then sees the gold shield on my left hip. I give her five dollars, anyway.

"Bless you," she says. "Have a blessed day."

"I'll be there tomorrow." He pops a piece of Doublemint into his mouth. "We all will." He names our whole squad. "Fishner, Roberts, Sims, me. We'll all be there."

I think about protesting then realize I'm smiling.

CHAPTER 3

Friday morning comes quicker than I would like. When my alarm goes off to tell me to get my ass out of bed, I have the kind of gritty, cottony-eyed feeling that comes from that weird deep-but-restless sleep. At least I sleep now. It's kind of a big deal.

Before I get out of bed, I listen to the two new voicemails from the calls I ignored last night, one each from my friends Josh and Cora. Both wish me luck today, and Josh reminds me that even though I'm a terrible friend—he means it in an endearing way—I'm not *that* terrible, and I'll do great, and let's all get together later. It seems they have plans for some social activity involving me. I have to admit that knowing I have people helps. I send them each a thank-you text.

I pour the first of the coffee then flip on Channel Three. The bright-eyed anchor, who today is wearing an equally bright tie, comes on the screen next to a picture of cops in riot gear. I turn up the volume.

"Today we're covering the Cleveland Division of Police's swift response to yesterday's events." It cuts to footage of the line of cops and the people marching in the street. "Following an officer-involved shooting of a person who appears to be a twelve-year-old who had a gun at Kerruish Park, residents took to the streets to protest," he says in voiceover, "but thankfully the protest was nonviolent." It cuts to police ID photographs of the two officers who were first on the scene, one of whom fired a bullet into a kid. "Micky Palmer, a twenty-year veteran of the force, and Bryce Richardson, a rookie, have both been suspended with pay, pending investigation."

I remember Palmer, who seemed like a good guy when I was a rookie in the districts. Richardson still has baby fat on his face—he can't be more than twenty-two.

They're probably with IAU right now or with the special new task force that investigates our use of lethal force. Maybe both. I'm supposed to talk to the Department of Justice people next week about various things that happened last year. It's all smoke and mirrors, and we all know it. I push it out of my head because there's not room right now.

The news cuts to footage from last night's press conference with the mayor, the police commissioner, and the chief. The mayor says violence will not be tolerated in the streets of Cleveland. He makes a plea to the camera for his "African-American brothers and sisters to come together in nonviolent demonstrations and vigils for the boy." The commissioner is stone-faced, and the chief shifts back and forth on his feet, wincing like his shoes are too tight when the commissioner says, "Cleveland will not be like the other cities in which violence has dominated the news. We are committed to peace and to protecting that peace. Fundamentally, we are peace officers."

Somehow, the fact that the kid is on life support at MetroHealth gets buried. It's all about the cops, what the cops did right, what the city is doing right, and how *right* every single one of us is.

The anchor promises to keep us posted with new developments then moves on to a story about yet another cop, Joe Mattioli, who is scheduled to appear on some popular morning show. Mattioli, a retired Cleveland homicide dick, wrote a book about his time on the force and his wife's tragic murder. Now he's all over the media, smoothing his tie and preening and grinning and telling his sad cop stories.

People say they hate cops, but they love the idea of us enough that his book's been on the bestseller lists for weeks. Last I heard, he'd sold the rights to Hollywood so that some famous director can make his dramatic turn away from superhero movies with Mattioli's story. Apparently, it's a big deal that he's coming back home tomorrow. The anchor plays up that he's going to make an appearance at a suburban bookstore.

I read the first half of the book when my mom gave it to me for my birthday back in August. It didn't grab me, so I stopped after briefly wondering if any actual cops could read the whole thing or if most of us would just as soon read romance novels or comic books or something else in our off time.

I toss the remote control onto the coffee table and avoid tripping over Ivan, who meows his dissatisfaction, on my way to the kitchen for more coffee. Then I hit the shower.

I don my charcoal-gray court suit, apply my eyeliner more carefully than usual, and toss my cop gear into my messenger bag with my laptop. I scarf a banana and a spoonful of peanut butter over the kitchen sink, pour a cup of coffee for the road, and head to Julia Becker's office.

ONCE I'M ON THE STAND, the questioning goes pretty much the way Becker and I predicted, at least at first, and I feel as terrible as I thought I would when I have to repeat what Grimes said to me. I watch him doodle on a notepad, and I swear he chuckles when I get to the threat. I try to avoid looking at Maliq Sims, the newest member of our squad, then I feel bad about that too—I know I'm skirting his gaze because I had to say that word in open court. He probably hears it a lot, and I like to think he expects more of me than to use words like that.

It goes from bad to worse when Jeff O'Connor, Grimes's big-deal defense attorney and a huge turd, gets a wild burr up his ass and decides to bring up old stuff. "You're familiar with uses of lethal force, am I right?" he begins.

Right away, I know where he's going, and I concentrate on not fidgeting with my watchband. I study the face, and sixteen seconds tick by.

"A couple of years ago, I think it was in January," he says, and it hits me like a fist to the sternum. He looks through his notes and nods. "Did you shoot and kill a man named George Arsalan in a Tremont alleyway while you were on duty? In fact, aren't you scheduled to meet with Department of Justice investigators to discuss your own use of force"—he pretends to look at his notes again—"next week?"

I'm not surprised. Of course he would bring it up, because he's just that kind of guy.

Becker tries to look poised. "Objection," she says. "Relevance."

I glance at Lieutenant Fishner and the guys, who sit near the back. Goran sets his jaw and gives me the tight nod that means "You got this." Sims and Roberts, the other guy on our day-shift squad, stare straight ahead.

Fishner gives me a look, but I can't tell what it means. O'Connor turns to the jury and goes on some pathos-driven diatribe about why my history of violence and hypocrisy and blah blah blah are all relevant to my credibility as a witness, and Grimes gets a smug expression on his face, which I would like to punch. I gaze at my boss and wait for the judge. I don't look at the jury.

"Overruled," the judge says. "Answer the questions, please, Detective Boyle." She looks down her nose at me.

I take a deep breath and hope no one notices, but no one will, because I'm not easy to read in these kinds of situations. "Yes," I reply. My voice sounds hoarse. I clear my throat. "I did. And yes, I'm scheduled to meet with a Department of Justice investigator next week." *It will be pro forma, Julia told me. Don't worry about it. The DOJ isn't going after cops anymore.*

Becker blinks at me, and the left side of her mouth twitches. I'm surprised we didn't go over this.

"And you did not face criminal charges, am I right?" O'Connor asks. "In fact, you returned to active duty"—he pretends to look at his notes again—"just six weeks after you murdered that man, am I correct? With absolutely no charges, no loss of income, nothing. And you received very little media coverage, am I right?"

Something inside me chills into the kind of cold that might never get warm again.

Julia slams her hand into the table. "Objection! Detective Boyle did not 'murder' anyone. She was found innocent of any wrongdoing in the official investigation and faced no criminal charges. This is public record, as are the facts that Arsalan was Caucasian and the leader of a child pornography ring and that he posed an immediate lethal threat to both Detective Boyle and her partner, in addition to any innocent bystanders who may have been in the area."

The judge sustains the objection and tells the jury to disregard the word "murder."

I don't look away from O'Connor. I don't blink.

"Is there anything else in your jacket, your official police record, that the jury should know about before they decide whether to take your testimony seriously?" He gives the jury a sympathetic look.

Becker objects, but we both know police jackets are damn near impossible for anyone on the outside, even lawyers, to get. Sustained. O'Connor has no further questions, thank everything holy, and Becker stands up for redirect.

The questions are gonna be about the shooting. I'm gonna have to talk about it, here, in this room with these people, with a cop on trial who really did assault a man who was in handcuffs and posed no threat. And okay, yeah, he killed his grandmother and raped a neighbor, and I get it. It makes me angry too. But that's why we have the court system. We can't just go around hitting people, slamming them into floors, doing horrible things that we think we'll get away with just because we always have.

I blink fast a few times and see all of it. My "official police record," my unofficial one, my whole jacket, Arsalan pulling a Magnum .45 and firing, me shooting him as he put three bullets into a trash can less than two feet away from my partner. There's every twisted thing I've ever done, my whole life story, and the question the department shrink asked me, way back when in that first psych exam, about whether I would bring my traumatic experiences as a kid and young adult to work with me. There had been worry and sleepless nights as I relived all of it and pretended it wasn't happening. Someone signed off on me, anyway.

Possible mental instability, it might have said. I realize my hands are shaking, so I place them flat on my thighs.

Killing that man in the alleyway. I take a deep breath and wait for Becker to begin.

The whole weird, seemingly never-ending thing with the creep from Internal Affairs.

There's probably a mountain of paperwork in that file.

Quite a few commendations sit in there, too, and promotions all the way up to detective-one, but that doesn't matter now. What matters is that something just clicked inside my brain, and I look around and notice that the light is sharper, somehow, than it was before. *I can't wait to get out of here. I need to go to the gym. See my friends. Try to enjoy my weekend—*

Becker brings up the commendations. She asks several questions about what, exactly, I saw Patrol Officer John Grimes do at that scene and nothing about how I killed Arsalan before he could take out my partner and maybe me, not to mention the two civilians in the alleyway. There's nothing about the nightmares, the guilt, the therapy, or the antidepressants, thank everything holy. She doesn't ask me if I call what I did "murder."

I answer each question with the kind of smooth confidence that we practiced, and no one brings up the Reynolds murder weapon or the way Patrol botched the evidence handling at the scene. My answers seem to pacify everyone in the room other than Grimes and his attorney. Two of the women on the jury nod and make sympathetic noises when I describe Reynolds's injuries as they see a picture of his face on the screen.

On my way out, as my boss and my partner and the other guys surround me and murmur their support, Grimes turns to me and points. He mouths the words, "Don't forget what I said," and I stare at him until his sneering face becomes a blur, a flesh-colored smear in my otherwise-crisp field of vision. Goran steps toward the other man then stops and drops his big hand onto my shoulder, reassuring me instead.

As the door to the courtroom swings closed, Becker calls her next witness, Patrol Officer Devon DuBois, a young black woman who put her ass on the line to complain about Grimes in the first place.

What I did *was* murder. But it was justified. I had no choice, and I can't let it define me anymore.

BACK IN THE SQUAD AFTER lunch, I keep noticing how sharp everything still looks and how, if I stare at something long enough, it starts to look like it's vibrating, so I pay attention to behaving like a normal person. We're working a case involving a floater that washed up about a week ago in the Cuyahoga River. It's the worst kind of body, because they get gross, bloated, and mushy in the water. I'm trying to run down social media leads and planning a trip to visit the victim's parents in Akron when we receive word that Freddie Perkins is dead and that the videos—one shot by the man who called 911 in the first place when he saw Perkins with the toy gun at the park, and one surveillance video from the park people—show that the rookie jumped out of a still-moving cruiser and shot the kid in the belly before asking any questions.

The video also shows that neither cop tried to administer first aid. In fact, they stopped Perkins's older sister from doing just that by restraining her on the ground then arresting her. *What the actual fuck? Who does that?* I squeeze my eyes shut then let them pop open again.

I look at my watch and see that it's time to leave if I want to get to Akron and up to Cleveland to see Dr. Shue, my therapist, on time. I tell Fishner that I have to go, that I'll tie up everything with the floater on Monday, and to have a nice weekend. Then I head down the stairs and out to my car, which starts up right away in spite of its age.

AT SOME POINT, AS I'M giving my shrink the download about everything, right after I tell her that I still feel less-than, fragmented, the opposite of whole, she gazes at me over her chic glasses and asks, "Who told you that you *should* feel whole? Who ever told you that anything would be any way at all?"

I stare at her, blink slowly a couple of times, then change the subject in the way that I do, and then time is up, and I leave, still ruminating. Nobody ever told me that anything would be any way at all.

On my way home, I pull into the gas station and pop the tank open on the black Passat that I love even though it's old now.

As the gas whooshes into the tank, I answer the question and then laugh to—at?— myself.

I told *myself* that things would be a certain way.

After I shot—murdered—that guy, I went nuts, like really nuts, for a period of several months. And I'll be damned if I'm going to go nuts again just because I had to think about it today.

Maybe that's the medicine talking—the brain pills I fought taking until I sat on the edge of my bed and seriously considered suicide late one night a few months ago, even planning how I'd do it. Or maybe I'm just learning how to behave like a normal human being.

MY DAYS OFF GO BY IN a blur. Friday night, I'm out with Cora and Josh and his partner, Jacob, and the next thing I know, I'm at Cora's house, and it's one in the morning, and I'm drunk, and she is, too, and we end up in bed somehow. Saturday, we wake up, and we're both off work, so we go feed my cat and sift his box. Then we go to breakfast and to the grocery store before we hang out for a while in her nice backyard. It feels good, as if time hasn't really passed, as if we're the same as we always were.

But we didn't speak for a long time. We broke up a year and a half ago in a decidedly dramatic, depressing way, and our relationship will never be the same. I blew it.

At one point, I say something about Heraclitus and his river—she's always loved that guy and his weird aphorisms.

She gathers her thick dark hair and pushes it over a shoulder. The wristband of her sweater slides back to reveal part of her full tattoo sleeve. "Everything flows."

I ask her to go to Tom's with Christopher and me after the game tomorrow. She smiles her phosphorescent smile and tells me that it'll be okay, and yeah, she would love to go to the barbecue. I want to know if last night meant anything or if this is still just a friends-with-benefits thing, but I'm too afraid to ask, because I already know the answer. *We'll just keep doing this until one of us gets into a relationship with someone else, and I suppose that's okay.* I give her a hug and leave and keep the dinner date I've had for a while with my now-sober mom.

Mom and I talk about the creative writing class she's taking and how awesome sobriety is and how great her life is now that she's not drinking and eating painkillers all day, and she doesn't ask about me—she never does—and I avoid reminding her of all the horrible bad things she did for the twenty-five years she was a fall-down drunk. I pay for dinner then go to the gym then home, where I play guitar for a while and surf the internet for longer while I drink a six-pack a little too quickly. Then I go to bed before I have time to think anymore about being called a murderer in open court. I need to get some sleep so that I can entertain Christopher tomorrow.

CHAPTER 4

H ardly anyone looks good in orange. That's my thought at half-time.

The call comes in as I'm waiting in line for the bathroom.

The woman behind me, whom I've been imagining as somebody's grandma even though she's probably only Fishner's age, fifty or so, sighs. "We're gonna be here for hours!" she laments. I smell the beer on her breath when I turn to reply.

"Looks that way." I nod.

She rolls her eyes.

My younger brother leans on a railing about fifty feet away, waiting for me. Christopher said he was going to try to find a place to smoke, but I know that no such place exists here anymore.

I catch his eye and flash him a grin.

I hesitate before yanking the buzzing phone out of my pocket. *Lt. Jane Fishner*, it says on the screen. I flex my jaw. I've been on call for two months straight.

It vibrates in my hand, again and again. I don't answer it, but I don't dismiss the call either, because Fishner knows how many rings it takes to get to voicemail. It stops, and I take a deep breath and gaze back at my brother, who shoots me a quizzical look. I wiggle my eyebrows at him, and he grins. He's taller and bigger than I am—six two, two twenty or thereabouts, to my five nine, one sixty. He's wearing a Browns baseball cap over his blond hair, and even under the hat, he looks like he's just been to the barber. He's growing back his reddish-blond beard. On the way here, he said it gets cold out there in the early mornings, and the beard will keep him warm.

26

Christopher doesn't mess around. He'll say straight up that he's a garbage man, sanitation worker, whatever. There's no shame in that, because it's the best job he's ever had, and he seems to enjoy it most of the time. It beats doing dishes at a restaurant like he used to do, and we have the love of dawn in common.

My phone starts buzzing again as soon as I get it back into my pocket.

We end up with a lot of overtime. Fishner, who is right on track to be Captain Fishner one of these days, is right when she says we're understaffed—we could use two, maybe three more detectives. Some report came out a couple of months ago that says violent crime is down citywide, but it's never looked like that to me.

I guess the brass figure we're happy for the OT money or something, but today, I'd rather spend time with my brother then go to Goran's barbecue.

It's not lost on them that Goran, Roberts, Martinez, Sims, and I are good at what we do, individually and as a squad. Goran and I both got promoted to first-grade detective at the beginning of September, in spite of my little run of misbehavior last year. Nothing changed except our pay grade, though Fishner has joked that the next step is sergeant and we should both think about it, because she could use a detective sergeant, and if one of us gets it, they might hire more guys for the unit.

Sergeant comes with a lot of time at the desk, and being a detective these days is already too much desk work for my liking. There are too many screens and not enough people, too much sitting and not enough moving.

When she calls a third time, I figure I have to answer. She wouldn't blow my phone up like this unless it was a big deal.

"Boyle," I say out of habit.

"I need you at Lake View." She sounds out of breath.

"What, the cemetery?" I squeeze my eyes shut then let them pop open. The bathroom line is finally moving forward.

"How soon can you get there?"

I map the route in my head. "Little under an hour."

"Quickly," she says. "This is really, really bad."

"Isn't that sort of outside our jurisdiction? And bad how?" At least half of Lake View Cemetery is technically Cleveland Heights, and I don't want to get into some turf war right now, today, this week, or ever again, especially given that Cora is a Heights detective and the last thing I need right now is some kind of jurisdiction complication.

"Nope. Our side. Really. This is bad. I'm sorry, but I need you and Goran on this—unless you want me to hand it to the sheriff's department."

"I'll be there in an hour," I reply. *Nothing against the sheriff's department, but no way.*

She hangs up, and I put my phone away.

About six months ago, a few people were held up at knifepoint in the same cemetery by "gang members," or so the media called them. They turned out to be a couple of dumb kids looking for weed money. Everyone got freaked out and started saying that the Cleveland-Cleveland Heights border was getting scary again, like it was in the eighties. It's not a bad neighborhood, though. Some would call it nice. I call it gentrified.

At least none of my dead relatives are buried at Lake View. Not that I've visited them in fifteen years, anyway. Maybe twenty. And probably never again.

I remove my hat and rake my fingers through my hair. I step out of line just as my turn to pee looks imminent. The beery grandmother turns to me. "Go get 'em!" she says, and I'm not sure if she means the Browns or me.

People start to filter back to their seats. A big LCD screen at the end of the concourse tells me the second half starts in four minutes. I watch the seconds tick by instead of looking at Christopher, who isn't going to like that I have to leave.

I walk toward him, appreciating both his physical presence and the fact that he seems to be doing okay these days.

"Look," I begin, "I'm sorry."

He crosses his arms, and I meet his eyes. They're pretty in the sun, light blue with a ring of gold around the pupils. They look like our dad's eyes did, not like my mom's and my creepy silvery-gray ones.

He flexes his jaw.

"That was Fish—my boss," I say, squaring my posture to mimic his. "It's bad." As if that will make a difference to him. As if it isn't always bad.

He looks at me in the way I've looked at him in the past, with the slow Boyle blink and a pouty set to his full mouth. A combination of anger and disappointment flashes behind his eyes, then he shoves it away. He jams his hands into his pockets.

"I have to go," I say. "I'm sorry."

Another minute ticks by. People push past us to get down to their seats—it's two minutes to kickoff. "You care too much about murders," he says in a matter-of-fact way. "What about the rest of us?"

I don't have time to argue with him, so I sigh and gaze over at the bathroom line, where the grandmotherly type is finally through the door.

"At some point, Liz? You're gonna have to stop this shit," my brother says.

"It's—"

"'It's my job.'" He mocks me. "I know it's your job. But at some point? You're gonna have to stop this shit." His gaze is unwavering.

"I'm gonna go back to my seat and watch the rest of the game. I guess I'll take the bus home." He says this in a calm, even voice. He turns to walk away.

I grab his sleeve. "I'm sorry. I'll make it up to you. We'll get dinner this week, okay? We can invite Mom too." I attempt a smile.

"Whatever you have to tell yourself."

I let go of his sleeve. *You never step in the same river twice.*

"Be careful," he calls over his shoulder.

I lean on the railing and watch him stand in line for a couple of minutes. He comes away with a hot dog and a beer. He applies ketchup and mustard to his dog then disappears down the stairs and to his seat. He doesn't look at me.

I push off the railing and trot down the concrete ramp. It's all but deserted now. The crowd cheers from above, below, and to the side of me. I glance over, trying to get a visual on the scoreboard. A big steel beam blocks my view, so I listen to the announcer, who says that Cleveland has returned the kick and is now on the other team's thirty-yard line.

It figures I'll miss the one game they win. "Back in the Saddle Again" starts blaring through the loudspeakers. By the time I get to the bottom level of the stadium, the only people in the concourse are workers. I smile at the one who makes eye contact with me.

A gust of wind blows down off the lake and against the right side of my face. I slow to a fast walk and turn into it. *All right, Boyle. Refocus. Put your cop hat on.*

As if you ever take it off.

On my jog to the car, which I'd paid twenty-five bucks to park, I wonder what I'm going to encounter at Lake View. It's not like Fishner to be cryptic on the phone.

I fire up my car and tune the radio to the game. The first thing I hear: fumble, recovered by the other team and returned for a touchdown.

Welcome to Cleveland.

CHAPTER 5

I swing by my apartment for my cop gear.

I keep the jeans but ditch the hat, run some water through my wavy auburn mop, and don my Garrison belt, holster, service Glock, and handcuffs in their leather case. I slip the shield into its belt clip and trade the orange Chuck Taylors for a newish pair of tactical boots that I need to finish breaking in, the denim jacket and Browns hoodie for a nicer shirt and my leather blazer. I brush my teeth to erase the smell of beer. I only had two, but I can't show up at a crime scene reeking of booze. Not anymore.

My place in Coventry is close to the cemetery, and even if I'd rather be at the game, the fact that it's gorgeous outside isn't lost on me. At least I'm not chasing some domestic-violence-committing, wife-murdering lunatic through the woods in the sleet or the snow or whatever Northeast Ohio might have to offer in late October.

By the time I get there, about forty minutes after my brother walked away from me, the light outside is starting to change. It's got this hue that one of my college literature professors used to talk about. I don't remember the context now, but I do remember that he was generally pretty excited about boring seventeenth-century chronicles of people's lives. He'd said that this time of day is called "the golden hour," when poets write nature poems and photographers like to take landscape pictures. Even the gritty urban decay in much of the city looks pretty in the right light: the concrete, the steel, the belching factories all take on a slightly different cast. Even the graffiti glows.

I glance at the clock on the dash as I ease past a couple of news vans and through the iron front gates of the cemetery. A white marble Virgin Mary holding an infant Jesus gives me a placid gaze on my left. They're both wearing crowns. Statues like this used to fascinate me when I was a kid. I would stand there and stare at them until I thought I could see them breathing—they're scattered all around here and most other cemeteries—until my mom would call for me to hurry up, saying don't disrespect the dead and let's get over to visit your sister and your father.

The service area, which someone has blocked off with yellow crime scene tape, consists of a small gravel parking area and three outbuildings. The first thing I notice, other than the obvious cemetery maintenance stuff—riding lawn mower, rake, wheelbarrow, some empty urns for flowers—is the nervous little man hovering outside the yellow line, wringing his hands next to a uniform.

Someone has drawn the tape around the buildings and the parking area, all the way back beyond the largest of the three buildings to a place I can't see from here.

It's my first visit to this particular cemetery—which calls itself "Cleveland's Outdoor Museum" and which holds the graves of Rockefeller and President Garfield, among others—even though I've lived a few blocks away since I graduated from college and the police academy in the same summer.

I kill the engine, push the car door open, and jam the key into my pocket. I clip my badge to my lapel and slam the door closed. A uniform sees me and lifts the yellow tape so I can pass through. I sign in on the scene log, under Fishner's and Goran's names.

"What do we have?" I call to my boss, who stands alone near a zone car, before she sees me. She's wearing a green corduroy jacket, and a tan knit hat covers her graying shoulder-length blond hair, which she keeps pulled in a bun most of the time but is down today.

Jeans and hiking boots are not her everyday apparel. Fishner dresses up for work most of the time.

"Body's over there." She gestures west with her radio antenna, but I can't see it from here. "We got the call just after three thirty. That guy there called it in." She tips her head at the guy next to the uniform, who shifts his weight from one foot to the other and gazes at the sky.

"Anyone talk to him yet?"

"Briefly," she says. "He's a groundskeeper."

The gravel crunches under our feet as we walk toward the body. I glance over at Fishner, whose jaw flexes in an erratic rhythm, before scanning the rest of the scene. I start by running my gaze along the perimeter of the crime scene tape and back again. If anything catches my eye, now is the time to back the tape up to preserve it.

Somebody needs to get into that wooded area.

"Only thing we've found yet is the blood trail from there"—she points at the smallest outbuilding—"to there"—and at the body. "A set of tire tracks and two footprints. One a men's twelve or thirteen, the other a men's eight."

"Could be a women's ten," I reply, glancing at my boots then back up to scan my surroundings. I pull my notebook out of my inside pocket and write down what she says before training my gaze on the techs, who inspect the patches on the lawn that are drying to rust-brown.

They won't touch anything until one of us tells them to. "Who's the primary on this?" I ask.

My eyes flick to another crime scene tech, who is taking digital photos of the tire tracks, back to the turf excision, then to the tire tracks themselves. Wide-set, knobby. Probably a truck or an SUV.

"You and Goran." She has some weird look on her face. "I put Roberts and Martinez on the follow-up from last week, and then they'll join you. We need you to close this fast."

I open my mouth to ask why this is any more important than any other murder case, then I catch a glimpse of Goran, who trudges out of the wooded area, looking focused but slightly grumpy. I flick my chin at him and turn around to survey the outsides of the outbuildings again.

Two of them are painted a dark green that blends in with the landscape. A few boards have been replaced on the side of the smallest one—it looks like a storage shed—and they haven't been repainted yet. The biggest is a stone structure that's probably been here since the cemetery opened in, what, the late nineteenth century? I know there's another group of buildings, meant to serve as offices, back near the Euclid Avenue entrance.

A murder of crows carries on somewhere above me, so I gaze up at the tops of the trees, which are starting to lose their leaves into the breeze. Seven of them caw down at us, in silhouette against the blue sky.

Here's the thing. It sounds stupid, but a crime scene really does kick the senses into overdrive. It's all about processing input as quickly as possible, at least at this stage of the game. Maybe I'm just that kind of cop.

Regardless of what kind of cop anyone is, the stark reality is that we get only one shot at a crime scene. One shot. Full stop.

Even from here, I notice the numbered tents next to the tire tracks. *Physical evidence.*

My partner is the kind of detective who will never let anyone but me know what he's thinking until he's sure. He's more methodical. He takes his sweet-ass time to creep around a scene, looking at everything twice. He takes photos of everything. I do that when I can, but I'm more about mental images, quick sketches in my notebook, and gut instinct. Words, diagrams, sentence fragments. Relaxed little chats with people who might or might not have killed someone.

I guess that's why we make good partners.

He comes ambling our way, clad in a disposable white Tyvek jumpsuit. "Happy Sunday. So much for that barbecue."

"Yeah, you too." I turn back to Fishner. "What's the deal there?" I point at the tents next to the tire tracks. "Who is that guy, the one who found her?"

She flips her notebook open. "Paul Greenwade. I talked to him. Groundskeeper, was doing cleanup. He called 911 from his cell. No pulse, obviously." She watches me write Greenwade's name in my notebook next to a short physical description of him. He's still shifting from foot to foot and gazing at the sky.

"Criminal record?"

"Criminal mischief in ninety-nine. Nothing since."

"Anyone else?"

"Nada," Tom replies.

"Anyone touch the vic?"

"Just long enough to confirm that she was dead," my boss says. "Not that there was a question about that."

Fishner leads us past the buildings and down a small embankment to the body. I slide on a pair of latex gloves before pulling back the plastic sheet. This isn't my first rodeo, but I have to work hard not to puke. Goran takes a step back and faces the other way, and Fishner goes glassy-eyed all of a sudden.

"Oh, wow. Do we have an ID?" I scan the battered, naked corpse, a woman who tucked herself into the fetal position before dying, and wonder, not for the first time, what possesses people to do some of the shit they do to each other.

"I think it's Heather Martin," Fishner replies in a low tone. "I recognize the wedding ring. Don't ask."

"Heather Martin, the criminal defense attorney who just happens to work with Jeff O'Connor?"

She nods.

"The rock wasn't stolen," I say. "Not robbery."

"I made some calls," Goran says. "She didn't come home last night. Her husband, Eric Martin, figured she was working late on some big upcoming case of hers."

"I assume you told him not to go anywhere," I reply.

He nods.

"We still need a formal ID," Fishner says. "And I'll handle it with the councilman."

Heather Martin was married to a councilman who also happens to be a big wig with Arbor Health, a major insurance company and one of Cleveland's largest white-collar employers.

I cock my head but don't ask why Fishner wants to handle it, nor do I ask how she recognizes the dead woman's wedding ring, but I make a mental note of both.

"He's a big FOP donor," she says. "The brass is already up my ass on this."

My eyes follow the trail of blood back to the smaller shed before returning to the body. "Full rigor." I glance at my watch. "So we're looking at roughly five a.m. for time of death."

Goran nods.

I gesture to her clenched fists. "Cadaveric spasm." I swallow as a thick, slithering feeling takes my stomach. "Watson on his way?" Our deputy medical examiner usually catches Special Homicide cases.

"Within the hour," Fishner replies.

"What's your read on this?" I ask, my eyes still scanning and ears open. *No clothing. Wedding ring and Cartier watch, still on the body. Expensive blond dye job, based on the graying roots, stained with blood in sections. No obvious weapons in the surrounding area.* I make a note of all of it.

"You need to see the shed," Goran says.

Fishner gazes down at me. "This is going to be a media shit show if it's her." She purses her lips.

I clench and unclench my jaw a couple of times before pushing myself up out of the squat.

"It'll give them something else to report. The brass will feed it to them to divert them from the other stuff."

The other stuff. I don't ask whether she called us in on this because she hopes we solve it and I protect my good name.

"I've got Patrol blocking off the entrances and perimeter. Heights gave us a few patrol officers, too, given the media interest."

There'd been a lot less attention a few years ago, when those two inner-city teenagers were shot and killed here, over by the James Garfield Memorial.

Wealth has a way of making everything capital-I Important. All "media interest" means to me is that my job is going to be harder than it should be.

She glances back and forth between Goran and me. "You two, finish up here. I'll see you back at Justice." She means the Justice Center, the big police complex downtown that holds our squad room on the sixth floor.

"I'll give Becker the update," she says. "We have a search warrant for this whole area already. Let me know if you find anything else."

"Who's here from Crime Scene?"

Goran gestures to a figure standing next to the shed, clad head to toe in protective gear, who waves when she sees me.

Good. I go way back with Jo Micalec, the medical examiner's chief forensic investigator, and I know she won't screw it up.

"We need to get everyone but Micalec out of here. Now," I say to Tom as I stand. I cover the body then take a step back and meet his eyes.

"Yeah, I know." He brings his thick eyebrows together. "Me too. I almost puked."

As I walk to my car for my Tyvek suit, I send Cora a text message telling her that today's barbecue is a no-go because we caught a body.

She replies immediately with a sad-face emoji. I shove my phone back into my pocket.

Goran follows me to my car.

"You got the video camera?" I ask.

He nods.

"All right, you take the spiral, and I'll work the grid. Then we'll hit the shed."

He nods again. "I've got Patrol on the canvass. Who the hell killed Heather Martin?"

"It's kind of part of our job to figure that out, right?" I reply in a joking tone.

He nods. "I'm going to send Roberts and Sims to talk to the husband. Maybe they can get a photo, and we can try to ID her that way."

"Have them ask about that lotus-flower tattoo on her shoulder," I reply, not commenting on the fact that we're both ignoring Fishner's politics. "That'll give us a solid ID."

He pulls out his phone.

In my mind, I establish a grid from the body to the shed. The shed is about fifty feet from the body, and given the dark-red trail between the two, either she was dragged, or she crawled to her spot before her heart stopped when it ran out of blood to pump.

That's just a guess for cause of death—exsanguination, or "bleeding out"—and it's more likely to be blunt force trauma from the looks of it. The amount of blood in the grass is still incredible. Given the extent to which she'd been beaten, cause of death could be almost anything.

Opportunity and motive could be anything, too, especially given that Heather Martin has irritated a lot of people in her thirty-year legal career. I'm sure I'll find out just how many once we get to that part of the investigation.

In my jumpsuit, I head to the body, where I narrow my eyes and take a deep breath as I tower over the inert corpse. Could be a stalker. Overkill like this is common for a stalker—they just go berserk, come completely unglued, and mangle beyond recognition the object of their desires.

There aren't any drag marks. She might have crawled.

It could be a jilted lover. Maybe her husband, or someone to whom she owed money, or someone who wanted money he knew she had. It's not likely to be a stranger. I make a note of my inklings in my notebook, since part of my job is to reconstruct what happened here. No matter how much I think I'll remember that great idea or flash of inspiration, I might not.

The crime scene itself is one of the most important aspects of a murder investigation. It's our first opportunity not to mess it up. Everything we find here has to go into a bag, onto the record, and into the courtroom once—if—we find a suspect and think we can prove that the suspect did it. Not that most cases go to trial, though, because the prosecutor's office is filled with people who love plea deals. Either way, my guess, given the size of the service area and of the cemetery itself, is that we're going to be here for the predawn transition from late to early.

I radio Dispatch for lights and tents, since we only have about an hour of daylight left, and the weather forecast said something about rain.

I walk over to Paul Greenwade, who's still shuffling back and forth outside of the yellow crime scene tape. He looks horrible. I guess most people aren't used to bloody bodies. Either that, or he did it and is enjoying this. My instinct is no, but instincts aren't infallible.

Greenwade is a small man, no more than five five. Soaking wet, he weighs maybe a buck ten. Whoever killed our vic is, if I'm a betting woman, very strong, given how battered her corpse is. Greenwade is wearing well-worn khaki pants—blood, I'm assuming it's the victim's, has gotten onto one leg, just under the front pocket—a green polo shirt with the cemetery logo embroidered on the chest, a light nylon jacket, and brown work boots that look like they've seen better days. No spatter on his clothes.

"Oh my goodness," he repeats several times as I approach. "I already gave a statement. Already gave a statement. Already—"

"Sir, I'm Detective Elizabeth Boyle." I suggest with an outstretched arm that he follow me over behind one of the zone cars. "I just have a few more questions, okay?"

He minces along after me like a baby bird. "I told them already," he says again, avoiding eye contact, his voice robotic.

"Sir, if you—"

"Call me Paul. Call me Paul. Call me Paul." His voice is high for a man. His beady hazel eyes move everywhere at once but never to meet mine; he scans along the yellow tape, up into the trees, back to the shed, to where the body is, down at our feet, and around again.

I take a deep breath. "Paul," I say in a soft voice, my witness voice, the one I use to soothe people, "I know you already talked to the lieutenant. Thanks for that. Would you mind telling me what happened, anyway?"

He crosses his arms in front of his chest and plays with his windbreaker with both hands. "Call Bobbie. With an I-E. Call Bobbie. Bobbie Butler. She is in charge here."

I write Bobbie's name in my notebook and go quiet for a minute.

Silence can be an effective tool, especially with someone who just found a dead body. I'm better than most at employing it to suit me. It gives them time to put it together and think through what they want to say. Or it gives them the space they need to blurt out the thing they just remembered or the thing they forgot to hide. I scan him again: he's probably midforties, given the thinness of his hair, the faint beginnings of crow's-feet at the corners of his eyes, the way the skin on his neck is just starting to separate from the sinew beneath it.

I notice a spot that he missed with the razor, where his beard, sparse and reddish-brown, grows in a dime-sized patch.

"I'm sorry," he says. "I am upset. Upset. Very upset."

"It's okay," I murmur. "Take your time." *Actually, don't,* I don't say. We're losing light fast, and I need to get into that shed. I catch a glimpse of Goran talking to Micalec near the vic. She bends down and photographs the body close up then backs up and gets more shots from farther away.

"I was going to get the weed whacker. The weed whacker is in the shed. I had to work in section three. I went in the shed. There was blood. I dropped my phone and picked it up again. It did not break."

His eyes are squeezed shut as if he's replaying all of this in his head like an old home movie.

"I thought it was a prank," he says in a softer voice, his eyes still closed. "Sometimes people joke with me. I thought someone was joking with me again."

I reach out to touch his bony shoulder, trying to reassure him, and he jumps back as if I branded him. "No." He shakes his head. "No, no, no."

"I'm sorry." I hope that I didn't just force him into silence. *Spectrum?* I write in my notebook.

He still hasn't opened his eyes. He cradles himself with his arms and rocks back and forth. "There was a smell. It smelled like metal. It smelled like hot metal, and I knew it was not a joke."

Smelled the blood, I write in my notebook. *Weed whacker, section 3.*

"So I ran away and tried to call Bobbie, but she did not answer. You smell like beer. Do you have an alcohol problem?"

I wait for him to continue, trying not to think about my new attempts at moderation.

"Then I saw her. I saw her, I saw her." He gets up on his toes then lets his weight drop back to his heels then repeats the action three more times.

"Paul, did you touch the bod—her? Or move her?"

"No. I saw her and called nine-one-one. Then I tried to call Bobbie again. But she did not answer."

"Did you recognize her? Have you seen her in here before?"

He wipes tears out of his eyes and opens them but doesn't look at me. "No. She did not look like a person. I know she is a person, but she did not look like one."

"Do you remember how your pants got dirty?" He doesn't have spatter on his pants. It's more like what would happen if he dropped his phone into a puddle then tried to wipe it off.

"I do not own protective coveralls such as the ones you are wearing and would not have known in advance to wear them. My phone got dirty when I dropped it after I opened the door to the shed. I wiped it on them. They can be cleaned."

I don't tell him right away that we're going to need to take his pants. "Thanks, Paul. Do you remember when all this happened? About what time did you come back here for the weed whacker?"

He stares at a point above my head. "At three fourteen. Three fourteen. At three seventeen, I opened the shed and smelled the hot metal. At three twenty-one, I found her. I called Bobbie in between."

"Was that the first time today you came back here?"

"Yes. I was repainting the gate before that. The black rustproof paint is kept in the office, so I did not come back here because there was no need."

"Do you know if any other groundskeepers were back here today?" I push a wayward strand of hair behind my ear.

He follows my hand then stares at my ear. "No, it is Sunday, and they do not work on Sundays. I am the only one who works on Sundays."

"How many are there?"

"There are fifty-two weeks in a year." He blinks fast several times and shakes his head. "But you know that already. I apologize for insulting your intelligence. There are four other full-time groundskeepers, two of whom are master gardeners. We are well-known for beautiful horticulture. We also employ six part-time groundskeepers and two volunteers. It is somewhat surprising that there are not more of us, given that we are a major tourist attraction. There are also people who work as tour guides during the busy season. You have unique eyes." He says all of this in a single breath.

We'll need to get someone to talk to all of those employees. I almost catch his gaze, but he looks away too quickly. "Do you remember seeing anyone suspicious, maybe a vehicle?"

"Today is Sunday. There is a yoga class on Sunday mornings. A lot of people visit their loved ones on Sundays. I remember seeing Mrs. Mannion with her daughter. And Ms. O'Toole. A man named Mr. Andersen, spelled with two *e*'s. There were also some people whom I do not know." I notice for the second time, as I write down their names, how mechanical and unemotional his inflection is, how he doesn't talk like most people do.

Talk to Mannion, O'Toole, Andersen, I write in my notebook. "Paul, can you tell me if the entrances are locked at night?"

"Yes. I lock the gates at exactly five p.m. at this time of year, and then I practice piano and eat dinner, and then I go to bed. I get up at six and practice yoga on my own, not in a class, and unlock them at exactly nine a.m. so that people may enter."

"Are there other ways to get in? You know, weak areas in the wall, that kind of thing?"

"Yes. There is an area over there"—he points at a hedge behind a group of trees—"that we must pay a dry-stone mason to fix. He is scheduled to fix the wall next Wednesday. It would be easy for someone to get through there. But if there is a tire track there"— he gestures at the track—"it is more likely that someone entered through the service entrance with his or her vehicle." He turns his whole body to face south. "The service entrance is off of Mayfield Road. It is protected by a simple chain-link fence and small lock. It would be easy to remove the lock, open the gate, and drive through."

I write all of it down.

"You are writing down everything that I say." He stares at the pen in my right hand.

"I am. I need as much information as you can give me. You're doing great." I smile, and he watches my mouth.

"In that case, here is a map." He pulls a folded map out of his back pocket and opens it. "I will mark these areas for you." He takes out a green ballpoint pen and shows me where we are on the map. Then he hands it to me. "And I will show you what I found." He digs in a front pocket. "I found these in the driveway before I went into the shed." He removes a white handkerchief from the pocket and opens it to reveal something small and dark red, and a slightly larger silver object. "Would you like to look at them?"

"Yes, please," I say, sliding latex gloves onto my hands.

"You are wearing gloves to avoid contaminating evidence." He watches my movements with rapt attention. "I wear gloves like that when I am painting. They make my hands itch, and I do not like it. They do not make your hands itch, or you would wear a different kind."

It strikes me that my instinct is to talk to him like he's a child, and I'm not sure why it bothers me. "May I look at those?"

He holds out the handkerchief.

I lean forward. "Did you touch these with your bare hand?" I inspect the acrylic fingernail, still intact, and the necklace pendant, a simple circle with "E.M." engraved on it. I flip the pendant over in Greenwade's hand. On the back is a symbol that looks vaguely familiar, like an ornate number four.

"No, I am not stupid. Although I found them before I made the discovery in the shed, I retrieved them with the handkerchief. You may have them if they will help with your investigation."

"Thanks, Paul." I pull two small evidence bags out of my pocket and secure each object. He watches me write the date and time on them then sign across the seals. They could be useless in the scheme of things, but one never knows—they could break the case wide open. "Can you show me where you found them?"

He leads me to the edge of the crime scene tape, along the driveway that leads to the main entrance. "I found the Jupiter symbol, which someone likely wore as a necklace, given the metal loop at the top of it, here." He points at the ground to our left.

I mark it with a tent and snap a photo with my phone, noting the lack of other visible evidence in the immediate vicinity.

"Jupiter represents prosperity and happiness. It is the lucky planet in astrology, which is not really a science, although some people believe that it is." He makes eye contact with me for the first time but looks away before I can read him. "You have been nice to me, and I appreciate it. You have a soothing voice."

I give him a small nod.

He leads me to the other side of the driveway, near the shed. Micalec sees us and raises an eyebrow. Paul glances back and forth then moves about six inches to his left. "And I found the artificial fingernail here." He points at the ground.

I notice that his boots look like a size eight. "Thanks, Paul. Do you mind if we take a couple of pictures of the soles of your boots, get a soil sample?"

"I imagine that you want to link them to that footprint over there. So yes, you may take photographs. That is my footprint. I know that already."

I nod and place another tent. "Paul, where do you live?"

"I live here. Not right here but at the cemetery. That way I can keep an eye on things. My apartment is in the front, next to the entrance, in the stone house above the office."

"Do you have an ID that I can see?" I need to get his DOB, address, height and weight, that kind of thing. Even if Fishner already did, I need it for my records. I'm not getting a guilty vibe from him, but I need all of the info I can get at this point.

He pulls out a Velcro sports wallet and hands me his driver's license. I'm surprised that he has a commercial endorsement, and it occurs to me that I'm being judgmental. I nod, photograph the license, and hand it back. "Is there anything else that you can remember right now?"

"I remember many things but nothing else about the woman who was killed or any strange people lurking around."

"Jo"—I gesture to her—"will be right over with the camera. I appreciate your help. Here's my card." I write my cell phone number on the back. "Call me if you think of anything, okay?"

He stares at the card. "Yes, Detective Elizabeth Boyle, Cleveland Division of Police, Major Crimes-slash-Special Homicide, number one-seven-six-one," he replies, absolutely affectless. "If I think of anything, I will call you. Are we finished with this conversation? I am tired of talking."

"Sure, Paul. Thanks again."

He shuffles away, and I consider how much information he gave me. He's an interesting guy.

Before I pick my way through the grass around the body, I verify with Micalec that she's processed the area and taken photos, then I ask a uniform named Tisch to go to the front office and ask some questions about visitors and the dry-stone mason. Paul Greenwade watches me from his position behind the crime scene tape then retreats after giving me a little wave and nodding at my return smile.

Michael Watson, our deputy medical examiner, arrives and un-folds his basketball-player-sized frame from his Lincoln.

"What's new?" he asks in his deep baritone as we walk over to the body. "Saw you on the news yesterday. Good for you for standing up to that racist prick."

Bile bites like acid in my throat. "Yeah, that sucked," I mutter. "How are you?"

It's getting dark. It's going to be a long night.

"Doing well, thanks for asking." He raises the sheet and winces when he sees the body. "Oh my."

"Yeah, I know," I reply.

"It might be a couple of days"—he turns her onto her back—"until I can open her up. I've got two ahead of her. But I'll go ahead and say homicide." He looks up at me then back at the body.

I scan the dark splotches of lividity that are already fading on her right side. "Sooner the better. Let me know?"

"You got it." He makes a small incision then slides a digital thermometer into her liver. "How you been? You know, with all that's going on?"

"I'm okay."

"Glad to hear it." He slides the thermometer out and examines it, and I look away for a beat. "Let's estimate time of death at roughly four thirty a.m. I'll keep you posted."

I nod, unsurprised that she died roughly when late becomes early. "Any guesses?" I squat next to him, astonished again by the extent of her injuries. "Crime of passion. Anger," I murmur, not unaware of the cliché.

He points a long, gloved finger at her smashed skull. "Off the record, I'd say blunt force trauma, and I'd say *rage* more than anger. But there's an awful, awful lot going on here. We have an ID?"

"We think she might be Heather Martin."

He purses his lips. "Okay." He nods. "Okay." He slides her hands into brown paper bags like the lunch bags I used as a kid. "Did you catch that tattoo on her shoulder?"

I nod.

"I'll keep you posted," he says. "Ready when you are to get her out of here. Public place, and it feels like rain."

I nod and follow him to our vehicles. He gives me a little salute before turning to direct his assistants, who unload a gurney from the medical examiner's van, and I lean against the Passat. I'm rereading my notes when Goran approaches. "Micalec wants you to meet her in the shed," he says, grimacing.

"That bad, huh?"

He nods. "A barbecue would have been a lot more fun."

I glance around. "Where's the L-T?"

"She said she was going to talk to Eric Martin, the vic's husba—"

"Assuming Heather Martin is the vic."

He nods. "She wanted to question him herself."

I narrow my eyes. "She's a weird one."

"Isn't that the truth?"

CHAPTER 6

Micalec works fast, which is a big reason that she's my favorite crime scene tech. She's already photographed everything once. Watson takes more pictures of the body before two of his crew wrap her in a clean white sheet then load her into a heavy black body bag, onto the gurney, and into the refrigerated van.

I take a detour over to a set of uniforms and tell them to get someone out here to set up the tents to protect the scene from the rain. On my way back, I pause at the second footprint outside the largest outbuilding, which looks like a big man's boot print.

The smell of sweet, wet, tarnished copper hits me when I approach the entrance to the shed, following the trail from where the victim lay, inert, never moving again under her own volition.

It's not lost on me that the timing of this case makes it capital-I Important enough to bring our senior forensic tech out to the field. Jo usually supervises regular shifts at the lab.

The shed gives me another reason to gag. Blood, at various stages of drying, covers nearly every surface.

"Oh my god," I mutter as I swallow several times.

Micalec nods. "Yeah, don't barf," she says from the back corner.

I take a step back and out of the path of the floodlight. "Okay, so... She was bound to that chair"—I point at a rickety wooden chair in the middle of the space with my flashlight—"and beaten?"

She nods and gestures at the ceiling. "Spatter up there too."

I train the flashlight beam up to where she points.

"But yeah, look at this." She points at the shiny black rope on the ground near her feet.

I follow it with the light.

"Bound with that, you think?" I lean in and squint at the chair legs. "Nylon?"

"Roger that," she says. "There are marks here where she clawed her way out of the bindings, at the wrists. You saw the bruises, right?" She takes another photo from a different angle. "She'd already lost a lot of blood by then—spatter makes me guess that she was hog-tied, beaten, then bound to the chair and beaten some more." She points around the shed as she talks. "Two pints, maybe a little more. Did you get a good look at her? Looks like she knocked the chair over, maybe hit her head on this." She points at the corner of a workbench. I take a couple of photographs with my phone, duplicates of shots I'm certain she already has, just to capture how I'm seeing this.

When I finally step all the way inside, the thick smell hangs around us like a palpable force, a hard, sharp reminder of life and death and the precarious balance between the two. The tang of blood is stronger than the smell of the gasoline from the overturned can in the corner. The can itself is covered in spatter, along with almost every surface in here.

"I'm not getting many prints," Jo says as she dusts the chair. "And I'd guess most of them are hers."

I nod and remove the necklace from my pocket. "There might be a print on this necklace. Greenwade found it outside."

She squints at it, safe in its evidence bag, then nods and goes back to photographing the spatter.

It's been a long time since I saw a scene like this. Usually people just strangle or shoot or stab each other, and it's, comparatively speaking, clean. Everything here is a complete mess, knocked over, pulled down from the walls, and spattered with blood. It's like a scene in a bad horror movie, and I wish it was. I can't imagine having to fight for my life hard enough to cause such disarray, especially during or after that kind of beating and whatever happened before that beating. But a part of my job is to imagine exactly that.

It looks like she thrashed around quite a bit before he started hitting her. I'd bet that he had her in a choke hold and she kicked with her legs, knocking over these clay pots and tearing that bag of soil so that it spilled on the dirt floor. He somehow got her subdued and tied, but it didn't stop there. Another red fingernail is lodged in the workbench to my right.

"That hers?" I point at a clump of hair on the floor.

"Looks like it. Dyed blond, looks like with the good stuff. Salon color." She takes a picture then bags some wood splinters. "Gray-brown roots. I'm thinking this could be our murder weapon, at least one of them." She holds up what looks like the leg of another chair. She points into the other corner at an overturned three-legged stool, probably from someone's basement.

"Why the hell are there seats in here?" I murmur, more to myself than anyone.

"Tape too. Bondage tape. Only sticks to itself." She picks up a section of what looks like red duct tape and holds it out at a distance for me to inspect before she drops it into an evidence bag. It's red and shiny and looped around itself. It looks like he must have used it as a gag and then cut it off her.

I raise an eyebrow.

"Hey, I know how to do my job," she says with a chuckle, and I follow suit.

We have to laugh. We will find any reason to laugh under circumstances such as these, and maybe now I understand what Morrison was doing in the car the other day. Nothing is funny, not one damn thing, but we're human, and we need to get through the day somehow, and laughing beats alcoholism or abusing our loved ones or firing our service weapons into our brains.

"Pretty common brand," Jo says, squinting at the texture of the tape. "You can get this online, if you want."

"I'll keep that in mind. How about that rope?"

She flicks an eyebrow at me. "Looks like nylon, the kind of rope you can buy anywhere. But see how it's thinner than that regular yellow rope, like the kind you'd tie something to your car with?"

I nod and make a note of it. Maybe that'll give us something.

"I'll run some tests. There are a couple of interesting knots too."

I move slowly through the space, adjusting to the smell and the low light, taking everything in so that I can make a sketch when I leave, just to cement the details in my mind. A collection of tools, including the gas weed whacker, sits in one corner, covered with a bloody tarp. I raise the tarp to reveal a push lawn mower, a backpack blower that looks much too large and heavy for Greenwade, and a selection of hand tools. The tools are clean and seemingly well-maintained; they must have been covered with the tarp when the victim was bludgeoned.

"Did you see this broken vodka bottle over here?" I ask.

She nods. "This is a forensic dream," Jo says as she bags some bloody gravel from under the chair. She levels her gaze at me. "I know you know what I mean."

I glove up then push an orange extension cord out of the way to reveal a stack of metal easels that people use to hold wreaths onto graves.

"I'd be surprised if we don't get DNA off of *something*." She narrows her eyes. "And given the struggle, maybe we'll get some of his blood here. He's got to be injured."

I nod. "Big guy, based on that footprint out there."

"Yeah, I'd say so," she replies.

She follows my gaze to the metal closure on the door.

"Padlock on the door is an old-style lock," she says. "They don't make those anymore. She must've broken those boards and crawled through, after she bled into that pool right there." She points at the floor near my feet.

"So he wanted her to die in here, alone," I say.

"Yes," she replies. "And slowly."

I'M LEANING AGAINST the crime scene van, jotting down my guess at a timeline, when Tisch comes over and talks to me.

"Here's what I got," she says. A piece of her dark hair has come loose from her bun, and she shoves it behind her ear. She doesn't tell me anything new, except for the fact that Bobbie Butler is Paul Greenwade's sister. And yes, Greenwade has Asperger's.

"What about the employees?" I ask.

"Got a list, but no one was here today except Butler and Greenwade. No burials, nothing."

"Visitors?"

"They don't keep track. They're supposed to—people are supposed to sign in, but nobody does. I got the numbers for the three potential wits, O'Toole, Mannion, Andersen. Butler didn't want to give me their info, but I convinced her it was a good idea. You want the really bad news?"

"No, not really," I say with a sigh.

"No video anywhere but inside the memorial and the mausoleum. Something about not wanting to violate people's privacy."

"Fuck it all," I reply, removing my gloves and running my hands through my hair. "Okay." I squeeze the bridge of my nose. "Thanks."

She nods and steps back.

Right as it starts to rain, I see Goran break into a run, heading this way from the wooded area. "I found her purse," he says when he reaches me. "Unis on the canvass?"

"Yup. Let's see the purse. You got photos, right, in situ?"

He makes a face at me.

"Sorry, just checking," I say as he starts to walk away.

"Under the tent," he says. "Get Jo."

The purse, a Kate Spade, contains Heather Martin's wallet, with all of her credit cards, driver's license, and about three hundred in cash, a bag of expensive makeup, a small notebook, and her new-looking phone, which has a dead battery.

We can charge the battery.

We have a preliminary ID.

WE GET BACK TO THE squad room a little after four thirty a.m. I'm wired as all hell, so I forgo the idea of following Tom to the Z—that's what we call the dingy little room with lumpy bunk beds and an old recliner—for a nap. Instead, I put on a pot of coffee before I return to my desk and call the patrol sergeant. "Hey," I say. "Do me a favor and put a call out for Martin's car. It's an Acura something or other. Run the check, yeah? Start at her house. First things first."

"Ten-four, Detective."

I thank her and turn to start the crime board.

I fill in the left side of the whiteboard with what we know so far:

WHO: Heather Martin, defense attorney - *verify ID and find car*

WHAT: Homicide. Martin tied to chair in shed, beaten (maybe with chair leg), bled out before kicking through door, prob. blunt force trauma to head. Crawled down embankment and died @ ~ 4:30 a.m., 10/27.

WHERE: Lake View Cemetery, in back near service area and reservoir. Purse found in wooded area about 200 yards from shed where she was found. (Find out when/where last seen alive.)

WHEN: Discovered by P. Greenwade, 3:14 p.m., 10/27. EMS notified 3:17 p.m.

WHY: ?????

HOW: Blunt force trauma? Exsanguination? Blood droplets next to tire tracks.

SUSPECTS: ????? (Get list of enemies)

OTHERS: Paul Greenwade (disc. body, lives at cemetery, grounds) - found fingernail and platinum (?) pendant, E.M. and Jupiter symbol

Bobbie Butler (manager of cemetery) - confirms no other employees were on-site

Mannion, O'Toole, Andersen – possible witnesses

FORENSIC: tire tracks, footprints (large men's boot, smaller boot), red bondage tape, rope with weird knots, broken vodka bottle, broken chair leg, fingernail, pendant, old lock.

There's not much more to write until we get autopsy results and a handle on the last twenty-four hours of Martin's life, so I print a satellite map of the cemetery, mark key locations, and stick it to the board next to the map Greenwade gave me, a blown-up BMV photograph of Heather Martin that I pulled from the database, and a copy of my scene sketch. I wonder what Fishner has gotten from Eric Martin.

I stare at her face, wonder what she was hiding, and contemplate my ongoing insistence that everyone, at the core, is doing just that, even if we're hiding it from ourselves. At some point, the inevitable exhaustion pulls my head down to my desk, and I fall into a dreamless sleep. I wake up in a puddle of my own drool at about seven then head home to shower, change, and feed Ivan the cat, who I'm sure has eaten my aloe plant and vomited it onto my bed by now.

CHAPTER 7

The next morning, my phone rings while I'm in line at Bialy's for the best bagels in town. It's Mike Roberts, who has been on our squad for a little over three years. He's a good guy, even though he makes too many dick jokes and brags about all the women he bags. He's come through for me in the past, though, and doesn't seem to be judging me about the Grimes thing. "Boyle," I say.

"Hey, two things. One, the Mannion and O'Toole families claim they saw nothing. They were there at completely separate times, and their loved ones are buried far away from where our vic was found."

"I really hope number two is better."

"Oh, yeah. Patrol found Heather Martin's SUV," he says. "Not at her house. Want the address?"

I write down the address in my notebook. "Get more on the people from the cemetery," I say. I flip through my notebook. "Get addresses and prelim backgrounds on Mannion, O'Toole, Andersen for the murder book, just to keep everything aboveboard in case this goes sideways." I remember the knots. "In your follow-up, ask if any of them have a boat, any connection to the navy, anything like that."

Then I call Goran. "Meet me down by Fairfax Park. What bagel do you want?"

"The usual, and what's at Fairfax Park, other than graffiti and needles?"

"Our vic's vehicle. Watson schedule the post yet?" I ask. "Hold on." I order our bagels from Judith, the little old lady who has worked here for fifty years. "The post?"

"Not yet. We need the ID first."

"It's her. We know that already," I say as I pay for breakfast. I smile and mouth a thank-you at Judith as she slides two coffees across the counter then tosses a container of cream cheese into the bag with the bagels. "Did you look at the knots? What are those?" Goran was in the navy for two tours in the first Gulf War—he knows his knots.

"Definitely nautical knots. Weird ones. Hard ones. Fishner know about the car? She's bringing in the husband, 'just to talk.' Let's hope that means 'ID the body.' Roberts and Sims didn't get anything from him other than yes to the tattoo and what they thought was a big sad act. Still no concrete alibi, but maybe the L-T will get one."

"Good question about the car," I say as I push through the front door. "The whole thing about the ring bothers me. Don't you think it's totally weird that Fishner *recognized* the ring?"

"Yeah, they were probably friends back in the day or something. Martin was in the prosecutor's office when Fishner was promoted to detective."

"How do you know that?"

"I was on patrol with Boss Lady. Sad to say, Fishner and I go way back."

I laugh. "I always forget you're old guard. You seem so young and chipper."

He clears his throat. "You're not that far behind me, partner. Don't forget it. What I think is weird is that Eric Martin didn't notice she wasn't home."

"Maybe he did it, and she probably works late a lot. I mean, she's won how many cases in the past ten years? You don't do that without working your ass off."

"Yeah, you'd know," he says. "Talk to Cora lately?"

"Meet me at the park in fifteen minutes." I roll my eyes. "We need to start building a list of Heather Martin's enemies when we're done checking out this vehicle."

"It's gonna be a long list," he says. "She pissed a lot of people off."

"See you soon." I hang up and scarf my bagel in the car. Before I head to the park and since I'm in my own car, the Passat that needs new struts in addition to the clutch I put in it last year, I scroll through my phone until I find exactly the right music: a newish track by a noise-techno-rock outfit from South Dakota, all about the world being divided by concrete and iron, by gender, by people's unrealistic expectations. It sounds grim, but it isn't. It's honest and loud, and it matches my mood this morning.

I arrive at Fairfax, a park in a poverty-stricken, predominantly black section of the near-East Side, about ten minutes later. Two zone cars are parked near a new-looking metallic-blue Acura MDX, and several people are watching from their porches.

Tom's steady footsteps behind me register in my brain.

"Hey," he says. "Where's my bagel?"

I gesture at the vehicle. "I'm gonna go check this out."

He opens my car door and grabs his bagel off the passenger seat. "There in a jiffy," he replies, but I'm already fifty feet from him. Patrol Officer Andrea Colby sidles my way when she sees me.

"What's happening?" I ask. "How've you been?" I scared her once, back when she was a rookie. I almost feel bad about it.

She squares herself into the cop stance that a lot of petite women adopt. "We got word last night to look for the vehicle. Found it here on a regular patrol about an hour and a half ago." She doesn't remove her mirrored sunglasses, and I don't remove mine. "I'm doing all right." She grins and turns her head, and I wonder how on earth she gets her hair into a bun that tight. "Off probation, on days now, new partner."

"It's good to see you, Colby," I say.

She pushes her sunglasses up onto her blond hair. "You, too, Boyle. It's been a while."

"How's it working the third?" I mirror her with my own sunglasses.

"It's rough," she says. "Nothing like the second. It's crazy how different it is over here."

I nod. *The things you see on patrol.*

"Listen, Boyle. I'm glad I ran into you." I half expect her to cross her arms over her chest, but she doesn't. "That testimony you gave. That can't have been easy."

I watch her face, watch the eyebrows come together for a split second, the twitch of her bottom lip.

"And... uh... DuBois and I are close. And she really appreciates what you did. So I guess I appreciate it too."

I smile. "Just doing what I had to." I don't tell her that, if left to my own devices, I wouldn't have.

Colby continues, "Grimes is a terrible person and a worse cop. You wouldn't believe it if I told you the half of what I know. And he threatened Devon too—I'm just hoping he goes away for a long time."

I rub the back of my neck then run my hand through my hair, worrying about DuBois. "Yeah, actually I would believe it. I've seen guys like him before."

"You're probably taking shit from everywhere, so I just wanted to tell you that hardly anyone thinks you're a traitor. As weird as it is, you know, with the blue wall of silence and everything... Well, a bunch of us are glad you did it. It took courage."

I attempt to hide my surprise. "It took a lot more courage for DuBois, but thanks," I reply. "I mean it."

"You still run into Anthony?" He was a homeless witness we had in common.

"Now and again. I kick him a meal when I see him."

Goran slides in next to me and jams the last of his bagel into his mouth.

"Anyway, no sign of anyone in or near the vehicle. It's locked, but we waited for you to open it," Colby says.

"Show me."

We make our way past a couple of other cops and over to the Acura. Colby reaches for the door handle, but I stop her. I narrow my eyes and point through the window. "See that?" I gesture at a thin copper wire that someone has stretched across the front seats, from one door handle to the other.

"Yeah, that looks hinky," Goran says. "Bomb squad."

Colby blanches and hits her radio.

The three of us jog backward from the vehicle. "We need to clear this area!" I yell at the patrol officers nearby. "Move your cars and establish a wide perimeter. Now!" I turn to Colby. "Anybody on the canvass? We need to find out if anyone saw anything."

"Yeah, a woman over there"—she points at the most well-kept house in the neighborhood—"said she saw a man in a hoodie just after six a.m. on Sunday morning."

We'll need to follow up with her. Heather Martin likely was killed just before then.

A voice crackles through Colby's radio, notifying us that the bomb squad has been dispatched and is about eight minutes out. A CDP SUV screeches around the corner, lights and siren on, and pulls to a stop right in front of us. The decal on the side says it's a K-9 unit. The driver, whom I don't recognize, rolls down his window. "The Acura?" he asks Goran.

My partner nods, and the officer jams the SUV into Park then shoves his door open. He crosses to the other side and lets his German shepherd out of the back.

Colby shakes her head. "I can't believe I didn't see that wire."

I nod. "You didn't know to look for it. Now you do."

She takes a breath. "Martha Rodgers," Colby says, reading from her notebook. "With a *d* in Rodgers. I told her someone would be by to talk to her in a bit."

I nod just as the dog begins to bark.

"We need to get this neighborhood evacuated before the bomb guys go in," Goran says.

K-9 Dude walks our way, and I squint at his name tag. "Something in the rear of the vehicle. Bomb guys are gonna see if we can tow it or if we have to check it out here. They're en route."

"Ten-four, Gomez. Anything on the outside?" I walk toward the SUV, staying a good two feet away from it. A small patch of paint is missing from the front bumper, and even from here, I can see dirt coating the undercarriage. I mentally place the car at the first crime scene, and it makes sense. "We need to photograph and print the whole exterior. Maybe we'll get lucky."

"I'll get the pictures and the kit," Goran says. "Wait for the bomb guys, Boyle. I'm not going near this thing." He heads to the Charger, our unmarked duty car, for the camera and our scene kit.

A voice crackles through Colby's radio, and she responds that Special Homicide Detectives Boyle and Goran are on the scene, that the Acura belongs to a vic, and that we need the bomb squad to collect some evidence from the outside of the vehicle before attempting to disarm it. I drop my sunglasses down onto my face and head over to talk to our witness, who is still watching from her porch.

Martha Rodgers, who appears to be in her early fifties, says she rose early to let her dog out. She's got a little enclosed area in her front yard that she gestures to from the porch, where we stand next to a swing and a couple of outdoor chairs, which are chained to the railing.

When the dog starts barking, she tells it to be quiet. She appears to notice the Acura first. "Cars like that don't be coming through here"—she shakes her head—"unless somebody lost or somebody else stole it. If you lost, you ain't gonna park there. You gonna keep driving on out."

"See anyone get in or out?"

"Yeah, after a time. And here's the strange thing. Guy got out the back door."

"The back door on which side?" I ask.

"Passenger. I could see through the glass."

"You saw through the glass even though it's tinted?" I ask.

"Yup. Good eyesight." She points at her face.

"Did you see what the man looked like?"

"White dude, I think. He was all in black. Looked like maybe a motorcycle jacket, but he had a hoodie on, and his face was covered with something."

"Height? Weight?"

"Tall. Over six foot. I don't know weight, though. Big dude, but he coulda just been wearing a lot of clothes."

I consider the large boot print at the scene. "Anything you remember about his clothes? A hat? Anything unusual?"

"Just all black. It was dark. I didn't see him up close."

"Did you hear him speak at all?"

She shakes her head.

"Where did he go after he exited the vehicle?" I ask.

"Well, now, that's a good question. I saw him throw something down that storm drain there behind that police car"—she points across the street—"and then go into the park."

I nod. "Did you look to see what he threw into the drain?"

"Nuh-uh. It looked little."

"How much time would you say passed before the car pulled up and when he went into the park?"

"Maybe about ten minutes. I let BooBoo back inside but stood and watched from the front window. Somebody got to keep an eye on things around here. And look, that van say bomb squad. There a bomb in there?"

"We aren't sure yet. Someone will likely be by in a little bit to ask you to evacuate, just to be safe."

She nods, but I can tell from the set of her jaw that she isn't going anywhere.

"How long have you lived here?" I ask.

"'Bout ten years. It's gone to shit, in case you can't tell."

I look around, taking note of the boarded windows on the house next door. "This neighborhood's always been rough."

She nods and pulls her jacket around her a bit tighter. "Better than where I was at before."

I let that one go. "Thanks for the info, Ms. Rodgers." I hand her my card. "Let me know if you think of anything else, okay?"

She nods.

After grabbing my flashlight from my car, I head to the edge of the yellow tape. "I've got to look in that drain," I tell Goran.

"At least wait until they give us the all clear," he mutters. "C'mon, Boyle. Just follow procedure for once."

I elbow him in the side. "Who pissed in your Cheerios?"

His jaw twitches. "I'm just not interested in going out like this."

"What, you don't want to be blown to smithereens? It'd be a blaze of glory, Goran. We could be legends." I grin at him.

"Not funny," he grumbles.

A stout man in bomb gear ambles our way. He slides back the face shield on his helmet. "You in charge?" *Brown*, his name tag says.

We both nod.

"Someone was banking on stupidity," Brown says. "Bomb that size would have taken out anyone who tried to open the door, but it's not big enough to have hurt anyone more than ten feet from the vehicle. Lucky someone spotted that wire. We're gonna tow it out of here in a few minutes."

"Is it disarmed?"

"No, but if you want to take a look at the outside of the vehicle, that's fine. Just don't fuck with the door handles. I'll get prints for you."

"Ten-four," Goran says.

"Loop Micalec in," I say to Brown, and he nods.

We move to the Acura and photograph it from various angles. I take note of gravel lodged in a tire then slide an evidence bag out of my pocket and secure it. The tires are big and knobby. The outside of the vehicle doesn't tell us much, but maybe the evidence gods will smile upon us and the tread pattern will match what we found at the scene.

"You want to catalog this evidence while I dig in a storm drain?" I ask my partner.

He nods. "I'm sure as hell not crawling on the ground. Go for it."

I chuckle as I make my way to the storm drain.

I kneel on the ground in front of it and hear footsteps behind me. Gomez asks what I'm doing.

"Witness says she saw a man throw something in here."

"Let me get that," he says. "You're going to ruin your clothes."

I stand and thank him, and he gets down on his belly and looks in the drain.

"Something shiny in there," he says. "Maybe a necklace chain? And over there, looks like car keys, maybe? And what's that, some kind of remote control?"

"Don't touch anything," I reply. "We need to get a photo first."

I hand him my phone, and he snaps several pictures before handing it back to me.

"Thanks," I tell him.

Colby is standing near her zone car about twenty feet away, and I gesture for her. She trots over, and I point at the drain as Gomez stands. "Let's get that evidence bagged and over to Micalec in the crime lab."

They both nod.

I take note of the grime on Gomez's uniform then clap him on the arm. "Thanks, man."

He smiles, and I walk back to the Charger. That could have gone very badly, and I say a silent thank-you that no one was hurt. I slide into the driver's seat and flip through my notebook. "Big white dude with lots of clothes on" doesn't give us much, but it's better than nothing.

I pull up the photo on my phone of the objects in the drain and make a sketch of the general layout, wondering what that transponder—Gomez called it a remote control, but it doesn't have any buttons on it—is for. I narrow my eyes and make a mental note to ask Sims, our tech guy, what he thinks.

CHAPTER 8

We get to the squad room about an hour later, and I start digging through records on Heather Martin while we wait for the other guys to get back from lunch. There are enough databases these days, both inside and outside the department, that this could take all day, so I make a list of what I know already and work backward from there. I know that her name was Heather Marie Martin, nee Acker, and that she was fifty-one. Public records check says she married Eric Michael Martin when she was twenty-three, and they had their first child, a son named Julian, two years later. I click over to the prosecutor's records—she prosecuted cases right up until she had him and went back to work a month after he was born. Second kid, a daughter named Elise, came along when she was thirty, and she was back to work within a month again.

There's another hit, one that's more interesting, which suggests that Heather Martin has a police jacket. She was a cop for a very short time, for about two years before she married Eric. Of course, her jacket is sealed, and it's impossible to unseal a police jacket unless the NSA is involved, but being a cop means more potential enemies, even all these years later.

I hit social media to try to find the kids. According to a career website, Julian is a civil engineer for the state of Michigan. Facebook tells me that Elise is a sophomore at Ohio State, where she's in a sorority. Her profile is semiprivate, though, so I don't get a lot.

Then I check cell phone records for their numbers and call each of them. They don't answer. I leave an identically obscure message on each voicemail.

Okay, so Heather Martin. Criminal defense attorney. Partner at Sellers, Martin & Fairbanks, a big-deal downtown firm. Used to be a cop. Former prosecutor who put a lot of bad guys away in the nineties, at least based on the *Plain Dealer*'s records. According to CDP records, she's registered four separate threats since '96, from three men, one of whom threatened to "beat her skull in with a baseball bat," and one woman. I write their names in my notebook to cross-reference against the prison database—if they're still inside, they're less likely to be involved, but every lead is worth checking. Sometimes people are stupid enough to do what they say they'll do, and it ends up cut-and-dried.

The irony isn't lost on me that Martin was a big deal in the prosecutor's office, and now, her partner Jeff O'Connor works for a lot of cops, including John Grimes. I heard two things about him through the grapevine this morning: one, everyone thinks there's a fifty-fifty chance that Grimes will be acquitted, and it looks like the jury will deliberate later this week. Two, the rookie who shot Freddie Perkins just put a ten-thousand-dollar retainer down for O'Connor's services. *Just in case.* I take a deep breath and refocus on the investigation. There's no point in worrying about what-ifs when there's a homicide to solve.

It's possible that Martin and O'Connor had a beef. Maybe she hated that he took those kinds of cases, and she put up a fuss with the other partners. I'll have to look into this. Anyway, all of the high-profile prosecution stuff died down in the late nineties when she joined Sellers and they opened a practice in 2000.

Anything is possible, and good detectives remind themselves of that all the time. The cases we don't close are sometimes because the cops involved are on such a single-minded mission that they miss something or screw something else up. It's just a reality—one that I'm aware enough of to keep O'Connor in the far back of my brain as I keep moving forward, because he probably didn't kill his boss. I might think he's a first-rate A-hole, but that doesn't mean he's a mur-derer.

Defense attorneys piss people off all the time. And if I'm a bet-ting woman, whoever beat Martin to death was pretty pissed off. I make a note to get a list of cases she lost, in case one of the creeps she couldn't get off is out of prison with a vendetta.

I click back onto her profile on the firm's web page. It says she graduated from Michigan Law and worked for the Cuyahoga Coun-ty Prosecutor's Office until she, and I quote, "realized that justice could best be served if she represented the unfairly accused." I scoff at this because she may have represented the unfairly accused, but everyone knows that defense attorneys also represent the guilty, and sometimes the guilty walk away.

Her financial records don't tell me much beyond the fact that she had a hefty retirement account, with her kids as beneficiaries, a joint checking account with her husband that looks as though it's only used for household bills, and a savings account at a local cred-it union with about half a million in it. It looks like they own their house outright, and I see no evidence of car payments. They're finan-cially comfortable, which could provide motive: money.

Social media doesn't tell me much of anything about Heather Martin. Her Twitter and LinkedIn accounts are all work-related, and it doesn't look like she has a Facebook account. I can't find her on any online dating sites, Tinder, or the like. She has a squeaky-clean online profile—it's almost too clean, and it makes me wonder what she was hiding.

I send Julia Becker a text message that says I need what she can get me on Martin's days in the prosecutor's office, just following a hunch. She won't like it—she's awfully rule-abiding most of the time. But we're sort of friends these days, or at least we're not enemies, and she might want to help me out with this one.

"OKAY, WE NEED TO WORK fast," Fishner says for the second time in two days, in our afternoon conference-room briefing, after Goran and I review everything we know—and don't know—with the rest of the squad. "Eric Martin is on his way here now. Roberts and Sims, head out to the lab and see what Micalec has going with the physical evidence from the crime scene, especially the phone. Boyle and Goran, I need to talk to you in my office for a minute about the bomb situation."

I'm squinting at the crime board and trying to figure out why the hell someone would set up a bomb in Martin's car, leave it in that neighborhood, and throw evidence, including the keys to the vehicle and some sort of weird transponder, into a storm drain. At least the bomb squad disabled the bomb. That could have been bad.

"Maybe it was a setup all along," I mutter. "The bomb. Maybe that was the point, to blow up cops. She was collateral damage."

All five of them turn and look at me. Goran raises an eyebrow, and Fishner leans forward onto her hands.

"You know what I mean?" I stand. "It failed, but still, there's a possibility that the bomb was the primary crime and Martin was an unlucky victim." It's not likely, given the extent of her injuries, but we have to consider the possibility. "Even so, Goran, we need to go get a warrant for her house. For her office. We need to talk to her kids—"

"My office first," Fishner says.

I turn to Roberts and Sims. "Did you get anything more on any-one who was at the cemetery the day her body turned up? Who is checking her phone?"

Roberts nods. "Everybody's clean except Anders Andersen." He laughs, but no one else does. "And here's something—he was a bomb expert in the Marines. Can't find a clear connection to the vic, though."

"Micalec and I will look at the phone today," Sims says. "There's a guy over there who's real good."

I add "Talk to Anders Andersen" to my list. "See if Micalec or your guy has anything on the transponder-slash-remote control from the storm drain."

Sims nods, and Fishner dismisses him and Roberts. Goran and I follow her to her office.

The door squeaks closed behind us. Fishner puts on her fake smile, so I remind her that we sent the necklace chain, the weird transponder that looks like it automatically opens a garage door or something, the gravel, and the prints from Martin's SUV to the lab, that Micalec knows the guys are on the way, and that she's prioritized the case.

"What now, L-T?" Goran asks. "Nothing on the inside of her SUV. It was wiped clean. The bomb guys said they were glad they could tow the vehicle, since it wasn't somebody's first bomb. They had to use the robot."

"Motorcycle jacket," I say. "We need to ask Eric Martin if he has one."

"A lot of people have motorcycle jackets," he replies. "And what's more interesting is that transponder."

"Yeah, and that weird key. Looked like a key to a gym locker," I reply.

"A part of why you're Special Homicide," Fishner begins, "is because you're genuinely good cops." She sighs and slides down into her chair. I feel Tom glance at me. "Another part is because you know how to handle high-profile people and high-profile cases. This is one of them, especially given the bomb." She stares at me then at Goran. "Heather Martin has received a lot of threats over the course of her career," she says to him.

"Yeah," he replies.

Fishner makes her rat face. I don't mean it that way—I just mean that sometimes she does this thing with her eyes and lips that makes me think of a rodent. "Get on it. Tread carefully."

Tom shifts on his feet, but we both stay quiet for a beat.

I break the silence. "I'm gonna keep digging into her life, look into these threats, and figure out who her enemies were. We need to search her office, and we need to talk to her husband and all of her associates. We've already wasted too much time. The car thing was on the noon news, and it'll be on again at six, since people love bombs, and they're already on the homicide like bugs on a light. I have a plan. We need to—"

"Let me talk to Eric Martin," she says. "He has very good lawyers, obviously, and I want to get a read on him before we move forward. If he's guilty, we need to charge him sooner rather than later. Carrothers will be here any minute to meet with us. He's probably downstairs now. Do what you can from your desks until I give you the green light. As I said, tread carefully."

"What the hell does that mean?" I ask. "And why is Captain Carrothers directly involved in this?"

"Boyle."

I breathe and try to temper my irritation. "Since when is the captain involved in questioning a suspect? I thought his whole big thing was to play wizard behind the curtain and just take credit for all of our hard work. When was the last time he worked a case?" I want to ask her directly about how she recognized Martin's wedding ring, but she doesn't leave room.

"You're right that it's atypical," she says. "Close the door on your way out."

We walk down the hallway in silence and stop at the vending machine.

"I don't like this," Tom says as he punches a code into the machine. "I mean, why the hell is Carrothers here? Why didn't the L-T answer your question?" He pulls a can of sparkling water out of the machine and thrusts it at me.

I watch his jaw flex and hold out my hand to take the can from him. "Are you all right?" I ask when he's quiet.

He puts more money into the machine. "Yeah." He retrieves a Diet Coke for himself.

We stand across from each other in the hallway and sip our respective beverages. "What's going on, Tom?" I lean my shoulders against the wall, my patented blank-faced-cop mug in full effect.

"Don't look at me like that."

I keep staring at him.

He crinkles his nose as if there's a bad smell.

"Is it work or personal?"

He grunts.

"Goran."

"I just don't like Carrothers being involved in this, especially given Martin's police jacket."

"You've seen her jacket?"

"No, but this whole thing brings up bad times in the department. Things that I don't want to think about anymore."

I raise an eyebrow. "What things?"

"Just things. Don't worry about it. I don't want you to get involved."

"Goran, in case you haven't noticed, I'm already involved. If these 'things' can get us closer to finding out who killed our vic, I'm gonna be super pissed that you didn't share them with me."

He shakes his head. "Not connected. Water under the bridge. I promise."

I make a conscious choice to believe him then push off the wall, and we head down the hallway.

"You write the warrants, and I'll look more deeply at financials," I say. *Follow the money. It often leads somewhere.*

He grunts again.

"It's not my fault that you hate computers," I chide. "And quit pouting like a sad little kid."

He tosses our Nerf football my way without looking at me, his way of telling me he's over it. "Yeah, okay." He opens his laptop, and I do the same.

I'm wading through the rest of the financial records that I can see without a warrant—not many, other than Eric Martin's campaign finances for the last city council election—when Carrothers and Fishner walk by with Eric Martin, whose good cologne wafts around us.

"Afternoon, Detectives," the captain says.

Goran, whose palpable disdain for brass is even stronger than mine, rolls his eyes, and Fishner shoots me the look that means they're going to talk to him in her office with the door open, so we should stay close by and eavesdrop. I walk over to the filing cabinet outside her door and pretend to be looking for something.

Everything about Eric Martin screams money. The suit surprises me: guys in their fifties don't usually go for European-cut suits, but he wears it well because it's tailored for his slim frame. He probably does triathlons. The shoes have to be Gucci or Armani. The haircut was probably a hundred bucks. The watch is a Breitling Chronomatic—I know this because I've lusted after that very watch. I'd never wear it, though. A seven-thousand-dollar watch is too much to risk on the job every day. I would just keep it in its box and look at it from time to time.

Fishner asks him to take a seat at the table for four that sits on this side of her desk, and he does, but not before asking if he should close the door. He makes eye contact with me and holds it for a second too long. I'm not intimidated by powerful people in the way some folks are, so I don't look away. And what I notice is that he doesn't look very sad that his wife is dead.

"Oh no, Eric, it's fine," she says. Her voice sounds strange. It's as though they're familiar, as though they talk all the time. Fishner is one hell of a good actress, though, so maybe she's playing a role.

I catch Tom's eye then ask in a loud voice where the report is for the Koslonski case. I feel Carrothers watching me down the impressive span of his nose.

There is no Koslonski case, so Goran grabs a folder off his desk and heads my way. "Is this it?" he asks as he approaches.

"Have you seen him before?" I whisper out of the corner of my mouth.

He bends down and pretends to tie his shoe. "Yeah, maybe. He looks familiar. But he's city council, right? So he's probably been around."

I open a drawer and pretend to look for another file. Fishner is still talking to good old Eric as if she knows him and they go way back. Tom slides into Sims's chair, which is closest to where I stand, and acts as though he's looking at the murder book he just opened.

I clear my throat.

"I'd really be more comfortable with the door closed, Jane, if you don't mind," Martin says. He stands and heads my way. I don't look at him when he closes the door.

Really, Jane?

"Boyle, look at this." Goran gestures at the open binder on Sims's desk. "What's he doing with this?"

I lean forward. It's the first of three books for Martina Lowell, one of the first cases Goran and I ever worked together.

"He left it on his desk. It's not as if he's hiding it," I say. "And it's not as if it isn't in the database, anyway." Because there is no statute of limitations on homicide, some rookie and a close-to-retirement guy spent about three years scanning everything into a server. It makes research a lot easier, all told, even though I kind of miss the old way, the smell of the creepy old file room in the moldering basement, the handwritten notes, the photographs on photo paper instead of on tablet screens.

"Yeah, so why the hell is he looking at the book? And where are the other two? He's been trying to get into this unit for a long time, and—"

"Chill out, Tom. He's not a bad guy." I gaze at the picture on Sims's desk of him with his wife and daughter. "It's just a murder book."

"You know that's not true," he grumbles as he turns the pages, reading his own handwriting and mine, looking at the old crime scene photos, the pictures of the eleven-year-old's parents. Goran and I were sure that Lowell's father had molested her for years before strangling her, but then he'd gone to trial and walked on an alibi that we think he faked, and we couldn't prove otherwise because the prosecutor's office couldn't ask his wife to testify against him—this was before Becker was our prosecutor, and the old guy couldn't find a workaround.

About two years later, Lowell ended up shooting his wife and then himself in some kind of drunken, depressed rage. We tried to act like that was somehow proof that he'd murdered his kid. We tried to act like that was justice, but we both knew we weren't sure he'd done it, that we were second-guessing ourselves and that, either way, that's not what justice looks like.

Martina Lowell is the one who keeps Goran up at night, the one he can't put out of his head in those dusky sleepless hours.

We all have them. Every single one of us has at least one.

Watson calls a little while later and tells me he's scheduled the autopsy for tomorrow at seven.

CHAPTER 9

A couple of reporters wait outside the exit for us as we head out
to talk to Heather Martin's law partners.

"Detectives Boyle and Goran!" the older of the two says.

How the hell they know we are working this case—as opposed
to any other competent team of detectives—is beyond me.

"It's your turn," Goran says.

"Damn it, fine." I sling my messenger bag, which contains gloves,
evidence bags, and the new iPad that I'm trying to force myself to
use, over my shoulder.

"Detectives, what can you tell us about the brutal, bloody body
at Lake View Cemetery?" the young one asks. I haven't seen him before. "Has it been ruled a homicide?"

"Nice alliteration," I reply. "No comment." I don't mention the
fact that he's a journalist and should know better than to modify
"body" with "brutal" either.

The guy looks surprised that I know what alliteration is. They
both follow us to our car as if they're little kids.

"Can you confirm that the victim is Heather Martin, the well-
known attorney?" the other one, a guy who's worked the Cleveland
crime beat for twenty years, asks.

"No, not at this time." I unlock the car and get in. Goran dramatically slams his door, and I silently curse him for making me talk to
these parasites.

"Wait. Where are you going now?" the young one asks. "Here's
my card. Would you be willing to talk later?"

I don't take the card. "No, but have a great day, anyway." I close the car door while Tom laughs. A year ago, I would have broken the guy in to his new beat by telling him to eff off. But we have to be kinder, gentler cops these days. Maybe it's for the best.

SELLERS, MARTIN & FAIRBANKS takes up half of the thirty-eighth floor of Terminal Tower, a fifty-two-story building right on Public Square, which is one of the things people feel like they have to look at if they're visiting Cleveland. It's not as if there's a long list. The Rock & Roll Hall of Fame is worth seeing once. The art museum is ranked one of the best in the world. The West Side Market is great. Great Lakes Brewery is worth it for beer people—I'm one of those people. Public Square and Terminal Tower are Cleveland icons. Check, check, done, and on to the next Rust Belt city.

I park the Charger in a tow zone, and we get out and head inside after making sure that the media guys didn't follow us.

"You dotted your i's and crossed your t's on those warrants, right?"

He makes a face. "How long have we worked together?"

"Think we'll get anything from these lawyers?"

"I just can't figure out why Sims is looking into Lowell," Goran says. He pokes his gum with a toothpick.

"What the hell? You're still on that?" I squeeze the back of my neck. I didn't even realize I was tense. "It seems like a much better use of your time to wonder why the hell Fishner is interviewing the dead woman's husband *with the captain.*"

He grumbles something that I can't understand.

I hit the elevator button. "Are you gonna obsess about this or just ask him? Think about it. What happened to Martina Lowell kind of matches the MO on the case he's doing court prep for. Maybe he's trying to—"

"I don't like any of this. The whole Sims thing is weird. And what's going on with Fishner?"

"You got me on that last one." *She's been weirder than usual. She never gets this involved. Is she protecting someone? No, she wouldn't do that. She's too by-the-book.*

The elevator door opens, and he motions for me to get on ahead of him. He's such a gentleman.

"At least set a time limit for how long you're going to obsess."

"This whole thing is off, Liz, and you know I'm right. Just cause you seem like you're in a good mood these days—even though I can't figure out why, since you just had to do all that with that racist asshole—doesn't mean shit doesn't smell like shit. When was the last time you even saw Carrothers on our floor, much less in the L-T's office with a potential murder suspect?" He jabs at the elevator wall with his thumb, as if Fishner's office is right down the hall.

"See? That's more like it. But do you need to interrupt me *and* be a jerk? Maybe pick just one." I grin at him, trying to get him to smile. "And such foul language. That's not like you, Tom. You kiss your kids with that mouth?" When that doesn't work, I clap the side of his shoulder. "Maybe you need a vacation. You could go somewhere warm and drink margaritas on the beach. Or maybe a cruise. I could see you on a cruise. You could start wearing Hawaiian shirts." I don't tell him that every time I've slept since I gave that testimony, I've dreamed of being kicked off the force for treason, and I still haven't told him about the prescription that keeps me feeling all right most of the time and helps me sleep at night.

"You're projecting," he says.

"I wouldn't be caught dead on a cruise."

"Take your sunscreen to the beach, then." He makes hard eye contact with me. "Seriously, though, don't you think this whole thing is off?"

"Yeah, I do. But it's still a case, and we've still gotta to try to figure out who killed her, and given the way our brothers in blue have been acting, we should do it fast. Make everyone look good."

He leans back against the wall of the elevator. "Are you really in a good mood, or is it an act?"

"Both," I reply. "There's no point in freaking out, not about this one." I don't tell him how real it feels in the dreams when a hooded executioner leads me to a set of gallows. I don't tell him that I'm aware of how callous I sound, and I don't tell him how much it scares me that I don't really feel anything at all.

"What's your game plan in there?" he asks as the elevator door glides open. He defers to me because I can be very, very good at getting people to talk to me.

"Ask these people what they know and try to gauge what they're hiding. Then use that warrant to search her office." We never know what we'll find when we dig through people's belongings. The question in homicide investigations is whether whatever the person was hiding led to murder.

"You gonna talk to O'Connor, or you want me to do it?"

I fucking hate that guy and would rather never see him again. "We do it together... unless Fishner decides to have Carrothers interview him with her. Then we don't have much of a choice."

That actually gets a smile.

"What do you think she was hiding?" I ask as we approach the frosted-glass door of the law firm.

He shrugs. "Your guess is as good as mine." He opens the door for me. He stops on the way to the reception area and squints at the directory. "Whoa, Liz, hold up." He points at the directory. "Mark Reese."

"So what?"

"Mark Reese was the prosecutor on the Lowell case. Don't you remember?"

"I remember. It's just coincidence, partner. Relax. Let's keep moving." Cleveland is both a big city and a small town, and sometimes it seems as though all the lawyers are connected. In spite of my disbelief in coincidence most of the time, that seems the likely case with Reese.

Goran knits his eyebrows together but follows me through the lobby.

At the reception counter, we ask for either Sellers or Fairbanks, Heather Martin's two named law partners. The youngish woman at the front desk tries to give us a bunch of rigmarole about how we need an appointment. Goran reminds her that we're investigating her boss's brutal homicide, and she goes quiet for a couple of beats.

She still doesn't budge. She purses her lipsticked lips and gazes back and forth between the two of us. She looks as though she likes to go sit on restaurant patios and drink gin and tonics after her mani-pedi. She probably has a tiny dog that she carries around with her in a satchel.

I don't say anything about the warrant. It's better to let people think they're helping before you barge in and ransack the place. The warrant only covers Martin's office, anyway, not the whole firm or any of her files. Attorney-client privilege can be a bitch.

From my position behind my partner, I look down at the name-plate on her desk. "Sheila, where were you on Saturday night, into Sunday morning?" I ask. *Oops.*

Her eyes go wide. "I-I-I was at home."

"Yeah? Anyone with you at home? Can anyone verify that you were there?"

"Are you suggesting that I—" She stops herself from finishing.

"Just asking routine questions," I reply. "We could continue this here, or you could come with us over to the station, or you could let your boss know that we're here to speak with him."

"I'll let Mr. Sellers know you're here."

I don't tell her that she has lipstick on her teeth.

"We'll follow you," Goran says. He doesn't want Sellers getting a jump on anything. Better to surprise him in the act, regardless of what he's doing.

Turns out he's not doing much of anything.

Sellers has a big corner office, one of those that boasts a great view but is actually on the wrong side of the building to see anything other than railroad tracks, gravel mounds, belching smokestacks, and a slice of the Cuyahoga River.

"Detectives," Robert Sellers says from behind his glass-topped desk. He pastes a big courtroom grin on his face and closes his laptop.

Sheila turns to leave.

"Sheila, some coffee, please?" he asks.

She nods and shoots me an evil look.

"She's just an intern," Sellers says, "so I don't feel bad asking her to fetch the coffee." He laughs too loudly, opening his mouth to reveal a set of tiny, catlike teeth. "Have a seat." He gestures to an expensive-looking leather sofa across a glass table from two matching but taller chairs. He stands behind his desk and moves over to that side of the room.

Before he can reach one of the chairs, Tom and I plant our asses in them, leaving Sellers to sit on the low-riding couch.

"Without a warrant, it's hard for me to answer any questions you might have." He sinks into the couch and stretches an arm across the back of it. "And I'm sure you know that none of us can share anything about Heather's clients."

This is not the behavior of a man who is especially broken up over the—what'd the reporter kid call it?—brutal, bloody body, who happens to be his now-former law partner.

"We have one," Goran says. He pulls it out of his inside pocket and holds it out to Sellers, who doesn't take it right away. It's a misguided show of power that seems to be an epidemic these days, especially among well-to-do men.

He finally reaches out and takes it and makes a big show of how he can move in slow motion. "This is only for her office," he says after he reads it over. "Her files aren't in there, anyway. Good." He tosses it on the coffee table in front of him.

"Can you give us a read on Heather Martin over, say, the past month?" I ask.

"Heather was just Heather," he replies. "Hell of a good attorney."

"Anything strange or out of the ordinary?"

"Not that I recall." He stifles a yawn, which almost looks like a real yawn.

"Any threats made to her or the office in the same amount of time?"

"Not that I recall."

Sheila knocks on the door then brings in a bamboo tray with a silver coffeepot, matching cream and sugar containers, and three matte-black ceramic mugs.

"Thanks," he calls to her.

She shoots me a look again, which makes me think I need to talk to her once more before we leave.

"Can you give us your whereabouts on Saturday night, into Sunday morning?" I ask.

"Of course. I was at home with my wife and children. My wife can verify that, because she asked me to turn off the TV at about three a.m."

It's a good lawyer answer, delivered exactly the right number of seconds after I ask. Goran asks for his wife's phone number, and Sellers makes an ostentatious show of looking it up on his giant new smartphone, mumbling something about how quickly technology is changing then faking a laugh.

The questioning goes on like this for over twenty minutes, until Goran and I realize this is a waste of time.

"Listen, Bob," Goran says in his good-cop voice. "I know you can't tell us much. But is there anything you remember? Anything odd at all? Anything out of character?"

"Not that I recall," he says. "Heather was a very private person outside of work. And our relationship has been strictly professional for as long as we've worked together."

I watch Tom make a note in his notebook. Heather and Eric Martin were married for over twenty years. Infidelity doesn't surprise either of us anymore, given that sometimes cheaters end up dead. We stand to leave.

"It's too bad Jeff isn't here," Sellers says to me on our way out, too close to the side of my face for comfort, especially given his halitosis. "I'm sure he'd love to see you again."

"Oh, I'm sure he would. Let him know that we'll be by tomorrow to chat. In the meantime, will you show us Martin's office, please?"

"I'll have Sheila let you in. We've kept it locked."

"Who else has access?" Goran asks.

Sellers levels a steely gaze at my partner. "No one has been in there except the cleaners. I can check the security records to see when that was, if you want."

"Yeah, that'd be great," he replies.

Sellers summons Sheila with a phone call, and she quickly returns and leads us down the hallway, leaving Sellers alone in his office.

Heather Martin's office is on the other side of the tower—the good side. From here, because it's a clear blue sky today, I can see all the way to Lake Erie. I make a mental note that the second named partner has the cushy office and move "verify Sellers's alibi" up on my mental agenda. Martin's office decor is minimalistic and tasteful, with two light-blue walls and two brown ones, nature prints, and good furniture. It's less try-hard than Sellers's space but has the opposite effect. It's a nice office.

Sheila lurks for about thirty seconds too long, so I turn to her. "Thanks so much for your help, Sheila." I walk her to the door, close it behind her, and turn the lock. I'll talk to her again when we're done in here—best to give her time to decide to tell me the truth.

The office is devoid of anything interesting, at least on the surface. There's no trash in the trash can and no paper in the recycle bin.

"How'd she get the prime real estate?" I ask as I slip on a pair of latex gloves. I hand Goran my iPad. "You wanna get the photos?"

He takes the device from me. It looks tiny in his big hands. "Beats me. Maybe she knew where the bodies are buried. Seriously—don't you think it's weird that Reese is here? How long has he been here? Why didn't we know he was here?"

"We did know he was here. It wouldn't even matter if you hadn't come across that murder book on Sims's desk. Let it go. I'm serious—we need methodical Goran today, not neurotic Goran." I hold his gaze until he nods.

"You're one to talk," he mutters.

I start with her desk, a big wooden thing that has no drawers. Her desk is more cluttered than Sellers's, which makes me think she did work instead of just sitting and preening. In addition to a day planner, which doesn't look used, there are pictures of her kids when they were good-looking teenagers, one of Martin and her husband wearing athletic gear and numbers, as though they'd been in some kind of race, and one of a Great Dane holding a giant rawhide bone in its mouth. Her laptop sits on her desk, its charger glowing green. "She didn't take this with her," I observe. "Think this links to their file server?" I flip it open. "Shit, FileVault," I mumble.

"Huh?"

"Apple's encryption software," I reply. "Unless we can hack her cloud account, and if she stored her password there—big if—not even the NSA can get into here. Let's hope Sims gets something on the phone."

"How do you know this stuff?" He takes a photo of the laptop and charger.

I close the laptop and slide it into an evidence bag. The charger goes into a separate bag. "Call it on-the-job training." I have it on my new computer too—it means that no one can get to anything without my password, which I definitely don't store in the cloud. "There's a lot of tech so far."

He waves the iPad around. "This thing takes great photos."

I glance up at him as I kneel to scan the underside of her desk. "What do you think of that transponder? It's weird."

"Probably opens some kind of door or something. Beats me. Micalec'll figure it out."

We make our way through the search. As usual, and to my relief given his paranoia today, Goran takes his time with his photographs. The only interesting things we find, other than the computer, are a burner cell phone and a shiny black business card with a phone number embossed in silver. There's no name or address. And what's more suspicious is that Martin—or someone—tucked the card behind the photograph of her husband, between it and the leather-covered-cardboard backing of the brushed-nickel frame. What's even more suspicious is that the phone contains only one contact number, the same one that's on the business card.

I write the number in my notebook before setting the phone and the card on the desk. Goran photographs them then slides them into separate evidence bags.

"Let's call Sims and have him run a tower dump on the cell towers near here and by her house, while we're at it," I say.

"You do it. I don't want to talk to him right now."

"Dude, are you going to grumble and grunt all day? What is this, opposite day? I'm supposed to be the agitated one, remember?"

That gets a little chuckle. "You call Sims, and I'll call Robert Sellers's wife. Deal?"

Sims ended up in our squad in large part because he's a tech wizard. At one point, he was recruited by the feds but turned them down. He says he's already combing through Martin's text messages. "I haven't found anything out of the ordinary. Mostly her daughter. Typical stuff," he says.

"Of course it is." A case like this never gives easy breaks. "Can you do a dump and get location data?"

"Tomorrow morning at the latest. I'm on it."

"There's a burner too." I give him the number.

"Get it over to me, and I'll see what I can do."

"Last thing—a MacBook with FileVault."

He chuckles. "I'm good but not that good. Let's hope we find a password somewhere."

I mentally cross my fingers, thank him, and hang up.

Goran calls Monica Sellers on speakerphone and verifies that she was home with her husband on Saturday night and that she remembers waking up to ask him to turn off the TV at some point. She knows he didn't go anywhere because she struggles with insomnia and didn't fall asleep again until after six, when he got up to go play squash. She sounds believable enough, but it's hard to tell without seeing her face.

I make sure the door is locked behind us when we leave, evidence in tow.

Goran writes the firm a receipt for what we're taking. We both sign it, and he hands it to me. "I'm gonna go ask Sellers about that security log," he says.

"Do you believe the wife?"

"I think so."

"Sheila, thanks for letting us talk to your boss," I say to the young woman in my fake-grateful-and-contrite voice. I hand her the receipt then write my cell phone number on the back of my business card. "I'm sorry for being short with you earlier. Here's my card. If you think of anything, will you let me know?"

"Come with me," she says without moving her mouth. She leads me past my partner, who just watches, down the hallway, and into the women's room. She shoves the door open then pushes the two stall doors wide, clearly to make sure no one else is in there. It smells like grape air freshener, and the streaks on the mirror surprise me, as does the harsh yellow fluorescent lighting. It doesn't match the rest of the décor, and I can't help wondering if they have another bathroom somewhere for the fancy clients.

"I'm sorry I acted that way," she says, her blond hair greenish under the lights. "I'm just an intern. I could get fired at any time for anything. Let's hope today isn't the day. I swear to God I had nothing to do with what happened to Ms. Martin."

"I understand," I reply. "Just to eliminate you, can anyone verify your whereabouts on Saturday night, into Sunday morning?"

She stares at me. I'm not being cruel. It's just better to get this out of the way.

"Yeah, I was with my boyfriend at his apartment in Shaker," she replies. "I'm sorry I lied before. That was stupid."

I don't say that lying to the police is a bad start to her illustrious legal career. I ask her for her boyfriend's name and number and write it down. I thank her and tell her it's just a formality, then I repeat the same questions I asked Sellers. "Has anything strange happened lately?"

Unlike her boss, Sheila has answers. "Sort of? A guy named Anders Andersen," she says. "With an *e*. He's been calling a lot. O'Connor is his attorney, but he was calling and asking for Ms. Martin. He sent her a letter or something too. It came the other day."

"How do you know it was from him?" A little jolt of adrenaline hits me. Anders Andersen was on the potential witness list. His name came up at the crime scene.

"It had his name and return address on it," she replies. "It felt like maybe photos in the envelope."

"Do you remember anything about that address?"

She shakes her head. "It said 'Anders Andersen, Andersen Restoration,'" she says. "I only remember because his name is kind of hard to forget and because I've always thought it was weird that O'Connor took his civil case."

"When did it come?"

She screws up her nose as if she's thinking. "I want to say Wednesday or Thursday of last week."

I write this in my notebook. "Do you know if Ms. Martin received the envelope?"

"I saw her with it a day or so after it came. She was on her way out and had the envelope in her hand. I remember it because it was one of those manila envelopes, but it was darker orange than most of them. I saw her with the envelope on Friday morning—yeah, it was definitely Friday morning, because it was right after the partners' meeting. He'd been calling leading up to that."

The day before she was killed. I make a note of it. "Did anything unusual happen in the partners' meeting?"

"I'm not sure. I basically just answer the phone."

"Do you know anything about Andersen's case or how he was connected to Heather Martin?" Maybe he was trying to get in touch with her about the case, given that O'Connor has been tied up with the Grimes thing.

"Even if I did, which I don't because, like I said, I basically just answer the phone, I wouldn't be able to tell you. I'm sure you know that."

"Would anyone have Ms. Martin's computer password? Maybe it's written down somewhere?"

She shakes her head. "Of course not."

"Do you recognize this phone number?" I read the burner's number to her.

She squints at the phone then shrugs.

I flip through the photos on my phone and land on one of the transponder. "Any idea what this is?" I hand her the phone.

She shakes her head. "No clue."

"When do you graduate? You a second-year? Third?"

Her eyes widen, and she appraises me. "Third-year. I graduate in the spring."

"Why'd you lie about being at home the other night?" It's a guess, but her reaction proves me right.

Her eyes get even bigger. "No one knows about my boyfriend." She blushes under her makeup. "I do a lot of flirting around here, if you know what I mean."

No, I don't—that could mean any number of things—but I'm not trying to have a discussion about euphemisms with her. "Thanks for the name," I reply. "Good luck with your internship. Stay in here for three minutes after I leave if you don't want anyone to think you were talking to me. And get in touch if you think of anything else, okay? Use your own phone, not the landline here."

I meet Goran in the lobby, and we push through the door in silence.

"Anders Andersen of Andersen Restoration," I say as we make our way down the hallway to the elevator. I jab the button, feeling hopeful about the lead. "There was an Andersen at Lake View. Remember? Paul Greenwade said he'd been there that Sunday, visiting some dead relatives. I guess he sent her a weird envelope and was calling a whole bunch. Sheila said it felt like photos in the envelope. Maybe blackmail of some kind?"

He purses his lips. "Could be."

"Apparently, Asshole O'Connor is Anders Andersen's attorney. Sheila thought it was strange that he took the guy's civil case. I didn't press her on it because I feel weird asking questions about O'Connor."

"Oh, and I'm the one with hang-ups?" He squints, and I can almost hear the gears turning in his head.

"What'd you get?"

The elevator dings. As the door closes, he squints at the printout Sellers gave him. "She was here until ten p.m. on Saturday," he says. "Looks like she was the last one in. Cleaning crew got here at one a.m., left at three. No one else was here until Sunday, when an associate deactivated the alarm at eight."

"So the cleaning crew was in her office," I reply. "That explains how pristine it was. And the no-trash thing."

"They shred everything, anyway," he says. He tips his head at my messenger bag. "That computer might have something on it, though."

"Yeah, I'll get it to Sims. I'll have him and Roberts talk to the cleaners too."

He tries not to wince at Sims's name. I don't say anything. The elevator comes to a stop, and we get off, almost running into a woman in a power suit.

"Excuse us," I say.

She glowers at both of us and gets on.

"The Andersen thing sounds like a decent lead to me, maybe minus the O'Connor connection," Goran replies. "You want to run him tonight or wait till morning?" He looks at his watch. Tom is a family man—he has a wife and two daughters at home, so he hates thirty-six-hour shifts a lot more than I do.

"I'm on it. Go home."

He nods and pops a fresh piece of gum into his mouth before pushing into the revolving door.

"What I can't figure is why she'd tell me any of that in the bathroom instead of calling me later. She's concerned enough to lie about her boyfriend but otherwise seems free of suspicion—caution, even," I say once we're out on the sidewalk. "I only let her talk to me in there because I didn't want her to clam up if I asked her to call me later. It's as if it didn't even occur to her that that creep Sellers—not to mention O'Connor—is probably recording everything that happens in there. She's totally naïve."

He chuckles. "Not everyone is paranoid like you and me, partner. She probably figured it was better to say something now, rather than wait and have us find out about this Andersen guy later. Then we have to come back, ask more questions. It's just easier to be out with it."

"God, what an asshole Sellers is," I say as we approach the car.

"They all are," Goran replies. "Every last one of them. Don't think that Martin was innocent."

"That's not at all like you, Tom. Seriously, where is happy-go-lucky Goran? I miss him."

My phone buzzes in my pocket, and I pull it out. It's a text message from Cora, who wants to know what I'm up to and if I want to get a bite to eat.

Working, I reply. *Call you later.* It isn't easy with Cora. On one hand, I want to spend as much time with her as possible. On the other, I know it'll never be the same. We love each other, but I keep waiting for the other shoe to drop on this friends-with-benefits thing.

We pull into the Justice Center parking lot a little after five thirty. I park the car, and we both get out.

"Meet me back here early. Six thirty," I say.

We walk to his new Chrysler.

"Autopsy's in the morning. Don't be late. And it's your turn to buy breakfast."

"You want happy-go-lucky, check this out." He waves his hand under the door handle. The car beeps, and I hear the click of the locks opening. He grins.

I roll my eyes. "Goran, all new cars do that."

"Call her back," he says, pulling the door open. He's been happy that she speaks to me again because apparently, I'm easier to be around when she does.

"I will," I reply. "But first, I want to get a jump on this Andersen thing and keep digging into Martin. You know, look into her kids."

"Tomorrow, then." He closes the door and starts the car, making a show of pressing a button instead of using a key.

I flash him a peace sign as he pulls away. Then I head inside and up to the squad room on the sixth floor.

Fishner is alone in her office when I get there. I say hi to Roberts, swing my leather jacket over the back of my chair, and head her way, considering whether to ask my boss about her connection to Heather Martin.

She waves me in. "Anything?"

"We got her computer. Encrypted. Nothing other than that. You know how lawyers are. There's one lead that I'll run down tonight after I run back by Lake View. Guy named Anders Andersen." I don't tell her yet about the business card, the burner phone, or the O'Connor connection because I don't want Carrothers knowing more than he has to, given how far up our asses he is right now. It'll all go into the report, but another day won't hurt anyone.

She nods.

"Autopsy's in the morning."

She taps her pen on her desk blotter.

"Anything from Eric Martin?" I've been around this block too many times not to suspect the husband first, followed by the kids and other relatives. People love to kill their relatives. It's kind of messed up.

"He has an alibi," she replies. "It checks."

I raise my eyebrows and listen to the second hand ticking on my watch.

"He was having an affair," she says. She puts her pen down and steeples her fingers. "That's why he didn't report her missing right away—he was with the other woman. He only admitted it when Carrothers explained what this looks like."

"What does it look like?" I ask not because I don't know but because I need to get a read on how she and the captain see things.

"It looks like a rage killing followed by a bomb in an SUV that was designed to take out you, your partner, and anyone within ten feet of her vehicle."

We're lucky it was on a switch and not a timer. "Any sign that Eric Martin harbored that kind of rage?"

"No. I'd be very surprised if he had anything to do with this."

"Even from a distance? Maybe he hired someone. What about the kids?"

She nods slowly. "Possible but unlikely. I'll look more deeply into it tomorrow. He knows not to leave the city until we get this tied up. As for the kids, Elise lives in Columbus, and Julian is in Michigan, working for the state. You can check them out, but tread carefully."

God, I wish she would stop saying that. She has to know that it makes me want to do the opposite. "Who's the other woman? Want me to talk to her?"

She's affectless, and it weirds me out. "Her name is Abby Kasinowitz. She's a neurobiologist at the Clinic."

I take my notebook out and give her a spell-that-for-me face, and she does. I can ask my best friend, Josh, who also works at the Cleveland Clinic, if he knows her.

"He claims he met her online through one of those sex apps."

"What, Tinder?" I try to reason through why a big-wig-insurance-guy-slash-city-councilman would use Tinder in the first place.

"No, but something like that designed for the very wealthy. And no, I will talk to her. You focus on working to get info on Martin's actions leading up to her death."

"Yeah? I could make a couple phone calls, talk to Abby tonight, verify his alibi so we can keep this moving."

"I promised Eric that I'd look into it myself," she says with some finality. Again with the first name.

"Are you going to talk to her tonight?"

She sighs. "Yes, Boyle, I'll talk to her tonight."

Okay, then. I nod and turn to leave.

"That doesn't mean that I won't keep you posted," she calls. "Look into this Andersen guy and give me a report on his whereabouts and his possible connection to her after the autopsy."

She has to know how weird she sounds.

I let it go and head to my desk, where I text Josh about Kasinowitz then call the number from the business card. It leads me to some voice-verification service that says I should speak my name before it will connect me, so I hang up and turn to Roberts, who is doing something on his computer while eating peanut butter from the jar. "Did you get anything on Andersen?"

He gives me height, weight, DOB, and an address in Old Brooklyn, on the opposite side of the city from the Martins.

"Anything else?"

"Not yet. I've been busy tracking down the office cleaners. You want me to keep looking into him?"

"Nah, stay on the cleaners. Thanks. Where's your partner?"

"Still working on the phone, and then he was gonna head home. Girlfriend problems."

I nod and pull the burner phone out of my bag. "Will you get this to him and have him do a data dump?"

"Sure thing." He holds up his hands as if I'm going to toss it to him, and I do. He glances at it then starts making a phone call on his landline, and he arranges to meet with the cleaning people in an hour.

Back at my desk, the first thing I discover is that Andersen was indicted for involuntary manslaughter a couple of years ago. Evidently, he got sloppy with a restoration job and forgot to reconnect a guy's brake lines all the way. The guy ended up dying on the Ohio Turnpike when the car wouldn't stop. It looks like Andersen pleaded it down to misdemeanor negligence, paid some fines, and avoided serving any time, thanks to Jeff O'Connor. I'm a little surprised Andersen's still in business—and that anyone would take their car to him—but maybe it was an honest mistake.

The *Plain Dealer* tells me that Andersen was a big-deal military guy, an explosives expert who won a medal for something he did in Iraq. That detail gives me a surge of adrenaline. I run my own BMV check: his last known home address is in Old Brooklyn. He turned forty-one last month. He's six four, two ninety, so he's big enough to match the larger footprint at the scene and probably strong enough to have killed Martin without an accomplice.

I write it all down and click over to the *Plain Dealer* website. There he is, the object of a profile by Alexis Edwards, the best reporter the *PD* has. The piece ran just before the accident that killed one of his customers. In the photo, which is just over three years old, he has a shaved head and smiles with his mouth but not his eyes. He stands in front of a restored '72 Nova. It's a sweet car. All I really get from the piece is that he did two tours in Iraq and opened his own business when he got home. His passion for muscle cars and motorcycles came from his dad, who helped him restore his first car back in the day, or so he says.

There is no social media for Anders Andersen beyond a Facebook page for Andersen Restoration. It features photos of him standing next to various cars with happy-looking people behind the wheels. There's a whole photo album of work he's done on motorcycles too. I get a little adrenaline rush when I see a picture that he posted last week of him next to an old Ducati. He's wearing a black hoodie with a leather motorcycle jacket over it. I mean, a lot of people wear that kind of thing in Cleveland this time of year, but it matches what Martha Rodgers said the man near Martin's SUV looked like—the man who threw evidence into a storm drain.

It's not likely that we have his DNA from an involuntary manslaughter charge, but it's worth checking. He got out of the military before they started collecting DNA. Prints will be in AFIS, though, so that's something.

I send Jo Micalec a quick email asking her to let me know when she's processed any of the physical evidence from either scene.

A deeper public records search verifies that Jeff O'Connor represented Andersen in the criminal negligence civil case last year after he was acquitted on the manslaughter charge. Andersen won the civil trial.

I make a note of the plaintiff, anyway. His name is John Snyder, and he sued Andersen on behalf of his brother Mark's estate.

There's no direct link on paper, beyond the law firm, to Heather Martin, but I still decide to pursue Andersen. I run an internet search on "coolest muscle cars" then call Andersen Restoration. A guy answers in a deep baritone, and I ask in a cutesy voice if I can talk to Mr. Andersen.

"That's me," he says. "What can I do for you?"

I make up some story about how I just inherited a '64 GTO from my grandfather and say I'd like to bring it in to see what he can do to make it pretty again, something about how it runs but needs cosmetic work. I damn near gag over my own saccharine voice, but whatever. Sometimes nice—even fake nice—works.

He says he'd love to see the car, and we make an appointment for tomorrow after lunch. I tell him my name is Candy Cooper.

I wonder how surprised he'll be when he sees me get out of the police-issue unmarked Charger wearing my leather jacket, Glock, and shield, with my burly partner in tow. The Charger has a big V-8. Maybe that'll soften the blow.

CHAPTER 10

At about seven, as I'm typing my abridged reports for the day, my phone beeps with another message from Cora, which contains only two question marks and a grumpy-faced emoji.

Instead of replying, I call her back. As the phone is ringing, Fishner approaches on my right, looking like she has news.

"Way to get back to me," my ex says, but I can hear the smile in her voice.

"Hold on." I look at my boss and take note of her preoccupied expression. Fishner doesn't usually avoid eye contact.

"I don't have all night. I have TV to watch," Cora jokes as I pull the phone away from my ear and mute it.

"Kasinowitz verified Eric Martin's alibi," Fishner says. "He was at her place on Saturday evening, through Sunday morning. She says her security system has video of her exterior doors and that the video evidence will corroborate the alibi."

She reaches for a dry-erase marker and turns to the crime board, and I wince. *Please don't touch my crime board.*

"I'm sending Roberts to get the video first thing in the morning."

"I'll update the board."

She replaces the marker in the tray and steps back. "Agenda for tomorrow?"

"Andersen. I have an appointment with him. Sims is working on cell phone location data for the vic. We'll go from there."

She nods and pulls the belt on her coat tighter. "Good night, Boyle."

"'Night." I wait for Fishner to leave. "Sorry," I say to Cora. "You want to grab a bite to eat?" I roll my chair over to the board and cross off Eric Martin's name. Next to it, I write the word *alibi* and Abby Kasinowitz's name.

"I already had dinner. You missed your opportunity," she says in a joking tone.

"What are you doing later?" I wince. I didn't mean it that way. "I mean, I've still got a couple of things to do, but I could swing by and—"

She chuckles. "I'm binge-watching season eight of *ER* and going to bed early. I just texted you to be a pain in the ass."

I stand as I tell the computer to print the reports. "What, no yoga?" Cora got really into yoga after we broke up, and she's the reason I bought a yoga mat. I figured if it helps her manage the tragedy of the end of our official relationship, it might help me, too, and it sort of does.

"Already done."

"Overachiever."

She laughs. "Call me later this week?"

"Sure. Enjoy your trashy soap opera."

"You know it's great. You love it. We'll talk soon." She's quiet for a moment. "You holding up okay?"

Grimes. "Yeah, I'm doing all right, I guess. It isn't quite the big thing I expected it to be."

"I hope times are changing. I'm glad. Call me."

"Will do. See ya." I end the call and walk to the printer. Maybe one day I'll get used to being friends with her. I don't know. I guess I don't have to know.

I sign the reports then slide them into the letter tray on Fishner's door. On my way to my desk, I see Maliq Sims in the hallway. "Hey, Sims, you got a minute?" I ask him from across the squad room.

"Sure, what's up?" His voice is a deep baritone, which always throws me when we talk in person, because he can't be more than five nine. He heads my way, brushing something off the lapel of his well-tailored suit jacket.

"Anything on Martin's computer or the cell phones?" I lean against my desk.

"Still working it. She had security out the ass on the laptop, and we'll probably never get into that. Better than government security, if you ask me. As for her regular phone, I should have locations and call records by tomorrow morning. There's only one number in the burner, and from what I could get so far, she only made calls from that phone in or near her office building. I'm cross-checking the number."

I nod.

He makes a face like he knows there's more.

"What's up with the Lowell murder book?" I switch off my desk lamp.

He nods. "Yeah, I can tell Goran's pissed at me. Is that why?"

"Yup." I pull on my jacket.

Sims rubs his neck. "I was looking into another cold kid murder, doing a favor for a friend of mine. It was her son who got killed. Turned out there was some overlap with the Lowell dude, and I started thinking maybe he did the little boy too."

"What kind of overlap? What's the other case?" I try not to sound like I'm interrogating him. I cross to my locker in a nonchalant way.

"Lowell's mama used to babysit for the boy, who was friends with the vic, Martina. They were neighbors for a time. I thought it was strange, given the whole black-and-white thing. But I'm thinking he mighta had something to do with it. Kid died in the same way. Evidence of sexual abuse. That's all."

"You know it's Goran's hot-button case, yeah? He wasn't happy when he saw the murder book on your desk." I pull my gun out of my locker and shove it into its holster.

He shakes his head. "I had no clue, or I would have gone to him right away."

"You probably should have talked to one of us, anyway," I say.

"Yeah, I'm sorry." He winces and looks from me to the binders on his desk then back at me. "Look, I'm not second-guessing what y'all did. I'm the new dude. I'm not—"

"I'm not trying to give you a hard time, Maliq. We're just a closer-knit squad than what you're used to. We take shit like this personally. Goran is thinking all kinds of shit he shouldn't be, you know? Getting his panties all in a bunch over some kind of misunderstanding."

"Yeah, I'll talk to him." He purses his lips. "Thanks for the heads-up."

I nod and close my locker before changing the subject to the Heather Martin case, my way of letting him know that, as far as I'm concerned, it's water under the bridge.

THE FIRST TIME I EVER had an instinct to revisit a scene was during my second case as a detective, back when I was in Sex Crimes and was partnered with a good old boy named Jerry Goodlin. I'll never forget the look of pride on his face when I suggested it. At his retirement party, after he'd had a few, he told me that was the moment when he knew I'd be a good detective. It's all about going back once the dust has cleared and the techs are gone to get a better sense of the scene. The precise locations of things, yeah, those are all in the reports, on the map that I made. But even if a quieted-down crime scene doesn't hold any additional physical evidence, it might show me something that we've missed.

Seeing it after dark and with no police lights or crime scene techs might show me something too. I'll see it the way the killer saw it.

I enter through the back entrance off Mayfield, get out, lock the gate behind me, and pull into the service area, which is still surrounded by yellow tape. I take a deep breath and look around carefully, given that I'm here alone.

It's gonna get chilly tonight, and the wind rustles the remaining leaves in the trees as though rain might be on the way. I pull my jacket around me and traipse over to the edge of the woods where Tom found Heather Martin's purse. I stand there for a minute and drink in the scene from this angle. *The outbuildings. The shed. The place where she died. The place where Greenwade found the necklace and the fingernail. The footprints, the tire tracks.*

I've got to ask Jo about those tire tracks. I suspect the killer used her car then dumped it in front of Martha Rodgers's house. If he entered from the back, he could have pulled up by the shed and wrestled her out. But no footprints are there. Maybe he dragged her, and the weight of her body obscured his own prints. There are no drag marks in that direction. She was barefoot when we found her, and we didn't recover any shoes. It's possible that she walked into the shed. Not willingly, though—he had to have incapacitated her, at least temporarily. The signs of struggle in the shed tell me that she was conscious for at least some of the time they were here.

I wonder where her clothes are. We didn't recover any clothes from her SUV or from this crime scene, and Patrol and the techs were here until this morning finishing the canvass. He might have kept them as a trophy of some kind. I add *find her clothes* to my mental agenda.

The transponder we found in the storm drain is needling me, but there's not much I can do about it until Jo works her magic and tells us what it's for. It's not a garage door opener; I know that much. It's not an E-ZPass—it's too small for that. It's almost like one of those iClicker things that college kids use in big lecture classes to record attendance and take quizzes, but it's not that either.

The ground by the shed isn't soft. It's possible that he pulled his vehicle up next to it and pushed her in. The tire tracks would have come from him pulling away. It's also possible he waited, watched her leave the shed, then left the footprint as he watched her crawl to the embankment.

That would make him one sick dude.

The sun sets behind me, and I contemplate the mark that violence leaves, the palpable force of it, the way it penetrates a place, hours, days, years after it happens. Some cops swear they can smell the tang of it for decades, that they can walk into a house and know that someone died a violent death there.

I wouldn't go that far, but I have to agree that death changes the energy of a place. Even a cemetery.

I wander around for forty minutes before taking the main road to the front office. On the way out, I stop to introduce myself to Bobbie Butler and ask her a few questions about Anders Andersen, given that he's the only lead we have. I hold my badge in my left hand and knock three times. She unlocks the door and regards me with narrow-eyed suspicion when I introduce myself.

"When are you people going to be done with this?" she asks. "It's almost nine o'clock. You can't just come in here like this. How did you even get in here?"

"The Mayfield entrance was open."

She shakes her head. "Paul hasn't been right since he found that woman. I guess I'll have to go lock it myself. This is affecting everyone. How is anyone supposed to get work done when they can't even get to their tools?" Her voice has a shrill edge to it, and I hope she doesn't freak out.

"I locked it for you," I reply. "And we'll let you know when things can get back to normal." I jam my shield down onto my belt and follow her through the doorway. "Until then, keep it blocked off, okay?" I fix my gaze on the stack of forms in front of her, which appear to be billing statements. I don't see Andersen's name anywhere.

She eases into a chair. "Uh-huh. Please try to stay under the radar." She rolls her eyes and perches her reading glasses, which hang from a beaded chain around her thick neck, on her nose. "I just can't imagine why this has to go on forever." She shakes her head and turns to her forms then moves one to the end of the pile.

"Ms. Butler, this is a murder investigation." I square my shoulders and resist the urge to cross my arms.

She heaves herself out of her chair and waddles over to her filing cabinet with the forms. "I understand that." She shoots me the side-eye. "Really, I do. I deal with death all day long, every day."

I let it go. "What can you tell me about Anders Andersen?"

She sets the forms on top of the filing cabinet and plants her hands on her hips. "Mr. Andersen is a very nice man. I've known him for quite some time. He's always been pleasant. He brings fresh flowers for his parents at least once a month."

"Anything else?" I lean against the partition that separates the spot where I'm standing from her office area.

She yanks open the second drawer and begins filing, ignoring my question.

I watch her in profile and get the sense that wheels are turning in her brain. She's trying to decide whether to level with me—I can tell by the set of her mouth and the way she's avoiding eye contact.

I lean forward over the partition and fold my hands. "Look, Ms. Butler, I know this is inconvenient. And really, we'll get out of your hair just as soon as we get a better handle on what happened to the murder victim. So if there's anything you can tell me that I might want to know, even if you think it's silly or irrelevant, now would be a great time to do that. Let's start here." I pull my phone out and bring up a picture of Heather Martin. "Have you ever seen this woman before?"

She squints through her glasses. "Only from the news reports. The poor woman."

I swipe to the next picture, one of Eric Martin that ran in the *Plain Dealer* a few months back. "How about his man?"

She nods enthusiastically. "He's a councilman."

"Has he ever had any business here?"

"No. I would remember that."

"You're doing great. Thanks. Anything else you can think of? Anything about Mr. Andersen that I should know?"

She purses her lips and narrows her eyes. "Well, I'm not sure."

I search her face and wait for her eyes to meet mine.

Once they do, she decides to tell me. "Oh, okay. But only because you apologized for the inconvenience. Paul and Anders used to be friends. Oh my, I'd better sit down." She toddles over to her chair and throws herself into it with some effort. Her reading glasses fall against the top of her large bosom, riding along her polyester neckline, and she leaves them there. "Why don't you come over here and take a seat?"

I nod, thankful that she's not still planning to be a difficult pain in my ass. I make my way through the small wooden gate in the partition and slide into a brown vinyl chair across from her desk.

"Detective Doyle, is it?" she asks. She takes a sip from a McDonald's cup on her desk.

"Boyle." I smile to show her how nice I am and what a good idea it would be to keep talking to me.

"Sorry, right. Anyway. Paul, my brother—I think you spoke with him already. He said something about having to answer a tall woman cop's questions."

I nod. "Yes, I talked to Paul. Is he here now?" It would be good to talk to him again.

She shakes her head. "At his piano lesson, but he should be home by nine fifteen or so." She taps a finger on her desk. "Paul isn't normal. He isn't like you and me."

"One of the other detectives told me he has Asperger's."

She nods. "Right. Do you know much about Asperger's?"

"A little. I have a friend who works with kids at the Clinic." It's not a total lie. Josh is a pediatric oncologist. I vaguely remember him having a patient who had Asperger's about six months back.

She keeps nodding, her ample chins following her head. "Mm-hmm. Well, Paul is very high functioning. See, our parents died when he was fourteen. I was already twenty by then." She chuckles. "I'm not sure why they waited so long to have Paul, but you know how those things go."

I nod, hoping that this isn't going to take the rest of the evening and wondering what their parents' deaths have to do with Paul being high functioning.

"He and Anders were good friends when they were boys," she says. "They used to build things, study things together. I'll never forget Paul's elevator. He made it with an erector set and one of those big batteries. What are those called?" She holds her hands about four inches apart.

"Dry cell?"

She nods with enthusiasm and smiles for the first time since I've been here. "Yes, dry cell. It took him a month, but he built a working elevator. Anders was his assistant. At least that's what they used to say. It was incredible that Paul would talk to him, since Paul has always had a hard time talking to anyone, especially boys his own age. That hasn't changed."

It's not lost on me that she's talking about her fortysomething brother as if he's a child, and I remember my own instinct when I was questioning Greenwade.

"They made the elevator, built their own tree house, made all kinds of things. They can't have been more than eight or nine when they made that elevator. That was when we knew Paul was good with tools, good with his hands. He can fix anything. See this watch?" She points at an old-looking watch on her wrist.

I nod. *Good enough with his hands to make bombs?*

"He fixed it right up. I thought it was broken forever."

"Ms. Butler, I don't mean to rush you," I say in my witness voice, "but—"

"Oh, right. I know. I'm sorry. Once I get talking…" She takes another sip of her drink. "Anyway. I'm not sure why I'm telling you all of this. I guess I always hoped that Anders would ask Paul to come work with him, you know, at his business. Paul is so good with engines and things." She blinks her watery eyes at me as though she's deciding whether to continue.

I try to look sympathetic, and I guess it works.

"When they were fourteen, right before Mom and Dad died in the fire, Paul and Anders decided to make some bombs."

I raise my eyebrows and avoid making a show of the little swoosh of adrenaline that just hit me. *Yup. I thought so. Could the transponder be some kind of detonator? I have to talk to Paul again.*

She waves her hands in front of her face. "Not *bad* bombs. Just boys being boys. They got caught blowing up mailboxes, shoeboxes, someone's old doghouse, that kind of thing. They never *hurt* anyone. They were just experimenting."

Experimenting with bombs goes beyond kids playing together. "What happened with the bombs?" I ask. "How many bombs are we talking?"

She purses her lips. "Well, I can't say for sure. They got in trouble for the last five."

I slide my notebook and pen out of my jacket pocket. "What kind of trouble?"

She shakes her head, and her chins follow. "I'd just as soon not say. It was a difficult time."

I sit forward in my chair. "What kind of trouble?" Juvenile records are sealed, and it would make my life a lot easier if she'd just spill.

"They got in trouble with the police. And the FBI was involved, since mailboxes are federal."

"When was this, exactly?"

"Paul was fourteen." She closes her eyes and nods. "Yes, that's right. It was the year before I married Patrick." She gestures to a photo on her desk of a man with thick glasses and a graying red beard.

"What happened, exactly?" I ask, wondering how she could possibly not remember when her parents died.

She sighs. "It was a long time ago... But basically, they got caught blowing stuff up. It was the Cleveland Police who caught them. We were living on the West Side then, in Old Brooklyn." She looks at me and blinks fast, like I should be proud of CDP or something.

She continues. "Anders lived one street over. He and Paul used to play together all the time, from back when they were little boys. That summer was no different. In fact, our families were happy that they kept each other company. We had a shed out back that they called their 'workshop.'"

I write some of this down.

"It was late summer, maybe mid-August. Right before the boys were going back to school. All I remember was that I got home from work—I still lived at home then, cause it was before I married Patrick—and the police were there. They arrested Paul and Anders. There was a lot of hullabaloo. Mom was upset, and Dad was angry. Everyone kept trying to tell the police that Paul wasn't like you and me, but they took him in, anyway."

"What happened after that?"

"I don't know. Some FBI people came and scared Mom and Dad, saying that these were federal charges and they might charge the boys as adults. It was some kind of crackdown."

There's no way in hell anyone would charge a couple of fourteen-year-olds as adults for blowing up mailboxes unless the kids had priors. I make a note of this. "Do you remember if Paul served any time?"

She shakes her head. "I don't remember exactly what happened, but he was home the next day. Anders wasn't, though. He ended up having to do community service. That was when he and Paul grew apart." She shakes her head. "It was so sad. We only reconnected when his dad, and then his mom, died several years back. He brings them flowers every month," she reminds me.

But Andersen's once-a-month visit coincided with the murder of Heather Martin and the subsequent bomb in her vehicle. I'm a cop. Coincidence troubles me. "When was Andersen here last?" I already know the answer, but I want to see if she does too.

She narrows her eyes. "Come to think of it, he was here on Saturday afternoon."

Good thing I have that appointment with him tomorrow. "Are he and Paul friends now?" I ask, remembering that Greenwade called him "Mr. Andersen" at the crime scene.

"You'd have to ask Paul. I try not to micromanage."

"You said there was a fire that killed your parents. I'm sorry to ask, but can you tell me more about that?"

She looks surprised. "What would that possibly have to do with your murder investigation?" She takes a haughty breath. "I've already said too much."

"Can you tell me about the fire?" I repeat, following a hunch. "Look, I'll be honest. It's public record if there were fatalities. So you'd be saving me some time, but—"

"Oh, you police and your public records." For some reason, she makes air quotes around "public records." Then she apparently reconsiders as I open my mouth to thank her for her time. "There was a fire. Paul was at school, and I was at work. We never could figure out why they were at home during the day like that or why they didn't get out. That's all I know about that."

"Was Anders at school too?"

"I'm sure of it. Anders always did well in school." She says it as if it's enough to rule him out as an arsonist, bomber, or murderer.

"How did his parents die?"

"His mother died of cancer years ago, when he was still in the service. His father died in a hunting accident about five years later."

I thank her for her time, and she heaves herself out of her chair and back to the filing cabinet.

"Will you be here tomorrow in case I have more questions?"

She closes the filing cabinet drawer in what looks to be a deliberate show of patience. She takes a deep breath and puts her hands on her ample hips. She's done with me, and I can tell before she opens her mouth. "I've already answered questions." Again with the air quotes, but this time they correspond to "questions." "Questions from you people, questions from reporters. Questions from people whose loved ones are buried here. Questions from people who aren't sure they want to keep the plots they're paying for, given that someone was murdered here."

"I'll leave my card. My cell phone number is on the back. If you think of anything, call."

She titters, and I leave. I want to go talk to Greenwade now, but I know better—I need my partner with me.

In the car, I send Roberts an email asking him to find anything he can on the bombs when he gets in tomorrow.

Then I text Cora to see if she's still awake, but she doesn't reply, so I hit the gym for a quick run then head home, where I busy myself by learning all about the house fire that killed Jean and Henry Green-wade as I consume twice my bourbon ration for the day. Possible arson, the report says. The bodies were too burned to know if they were dead before someone started the fire. The newspaper article mentions that two juveniles were questioned in connection with the fire, but no charges were filed.

CHAPTER 11

Ibolt upright in bed, faintly aware of the sound of my own scream-ing. My hands are in fists, and every muscle in my body is so tense it aches. I shake my head and open my eyes. It's still dark. I grope around for my phone and look at the clock. Tuesday, October 28, 4:14 a.m. No messages or missed calls.

I'm supposed to get up and write it down the way Dr. Shue wants me to, the way I've been working on. Apparently, writing it down will help me to change the narrative or something.

After I shot Arsalan, I had a nightmare almost every time I slept, which wasn't often. It probably sounds promising that it's been a while, that the nightmares have tapered off, and that overall, they've become less about my tragic recent past and more about my tragic future.

This one wasn't about me killing another human being, and it wasn't the gallows dream. It was about my little sister's murder and my dad hanging himself, which he did when I was twelve, only I was the detective assigned to the investigation, and nothing made sense. I take a couple of deep breaths and try to push the image out of my head.

I email Shue and ask to schedule an appointment then get up, close the window so the rain doesn't come in, and trudge to the din-ing room to write in my stupid composition book.

Ivan skitters into the dining room ahead of me, so I feed him be-fore sitting down to record the dream. I sigh, wondering if I'll ever be right in the head or if this is going to go on until I die.

I close the notebook and slide it to the edge of the table before going back into the kitchen, where I make a pot of coffee and watch it drip into the carafe until there's enough to fill my mug. I step over to the window in the kitchen and gaze out over the parking lot. My car is in its regular spot, and I briefly consider getting a new one—the thing is over fifteen years old, and it's starting to look it.

I set down the coffee cup and stretch my shoulders, deciding what workout to do today. My yoga mat is in the corner—I don't hate yoga nearly as much as I thought I would. I drag the mat into the living room, do fifteen minutes of sun salutations while Ivan circles the mat and meows as though he's still starving, and try to make my mind as blank as possible.

Then I flip on the ridiculously loud stereo that I got myself for my birthday in August and set my phone to play a psychedelic rock song I've become obsessed with while I brush my teeth and get dressed. On my way to the gym, I contemplate the likelihood that Anders Andersen and Paul Greenwade were the two juveniles questioned in the deaths of Greenwade's parents. Greenwade certainly doesn't *seem* like someone who would kill his parents, but first impressions aren't always accurate. We'll need to talk to him again. His relationship with Andersen, combined with the fact that Andersen was an explosives expert, gives us some interesting circumstantial evidence.

I power through my workout, shower, dress for work, and text Goran: *Pick me up in the parking lot.*

"Morning, sunshine," I say as I get in. "I talked to Sims. There's an explanation for that murder book, so you can unbunch your undies."

I fill him in, and he seems relieved. I also tell him what I gleaned from my conversation with Bobbie Butler, and he agrees that we'll follow up with Paul Greenwade.

Fifteen minutes later, we're making small talk as we walk to the morgue, which is housed in the basement of the brand-spanking-new steel-and-glass county crime lab. We sign in with Security then wait in the airy lobby for ten minutes before an assistant comes to get us, and I wonder, not for the first time, why autopsies always happen in basements. I suppose it would freak people out to stumble upon a postmortem from outside, but that's why there are blinds and privacy glass, and here they even have the fancy shades that close automatically when the sun hits them, not that the sun shines all that often in this town.

It's cold in the autopsy suite, and I pull my jacket around me. Watson hits a button on a remote control, powering on the video and audio recording, then pulls a white sheet off the naked corpse. Heather Martin's body occupies one of three stainless-steel tables, each with its own floor drain beneath. I glance through the glass to the viewing area, but the lights are off—something about saving electricity—so I see all three of our reflections. Goran and I look tired.

At some point before Watson opens her up—external examinations are just as important as what he'll find inside—he rolls her over and points at the bruising on her back. "Looks like some sort of cylindrical object."

"What, like a baseball bat?" Goran asks.

"Or a chair leg?" I add.

Watson shakes his head. "I'm guessing something narrower. Maybe some sort of rebar or ground stake."

"What, like what you use to prop up a fence?" Goran asks.

"Yes, but smooth. Not notched like those are. And look at this." He gestures at striations on her wrists.

"What, handcuffs?" I ask.

He nods. "Not police-issue, though, I don't think."

Bondage tape at the scene. Black rope with complicated knots. Handcuffs that aren't police-issue. A black business card with only a phone number that requires voice verification to connect to anyone. This could be a bondage thing, some kind of S and M gone bad. But that would be atypical. I took a class in college about the sociology of sexuality and learned all about how BDSM is actually safe, based in consent, that kind of thing.

I need to talk to Jo again about that other evidence, anyway. "What about the chair leg?" I ask.

I cringe when Watson tells me.

The color drains from Goran's face too.

"My guess is that it caused a lot of internal damage. There would have been a lot of bleeding prior to the beating. It looks like she was conscious for most of it. He saved most of the head injuries for last, save for the one on the side of her head. My guess is that he knocked her out that way, but it didn't incapacitate her for long." He winces. "I'll do the rape kit first."

A vile metallic taste creeps up in the back of my throat, and I excuse myself for a minute. In the bathroom stall, I lower myself into a crouch and take several deep breaths before vomiting bile into the stainless-steel toilet. To think I thought that delaying breakfast would save us. I know better by now. I've been around this block before. I worked Sex Crimes for long enough to know that people will do all kinds of heinous things to each other and not think twice. I rinse my mouth several times then trudge down the hall.

When I get back, Goran is in the far corner of the room with his arms crossed over his chest. He's not usually squeamish—neither of us is—but seeing her battered body on the cold steel table and hearing Watson dictate what he's found... If it didn't affect us, we wouldn't be human anymore.

I clear my throat. "Anything under her nails?"

"Yeah, looks like dirt, wood fragments, grass, what could be black leather, carpet fibers. We'll get it processed today, maybe tomorrow." He leads us over to the body and lifts one arm after the other, gesturing at her forearms. "Defensive wounds. The right arm is broken in six places." He gestures at an X-ray displayed on a large TV mounted to the wall, next to another X-ray of her shattered skull.

He points at her neck, near her carotid artery. "Bruising here and on the other side. It looks like he deliberately collapsed the arteries from the exterior, likely with his thumbs. He has big hands." He shows us the marks. Sure enough, there's a thumb-shaped bruise on either side of her neck and finger-shaped bruises on the back, and it's not the kind of hold most people know about—the guy is likely military or law enforcement.

Once he pulls out the Stryker saw, it's time for us to move to the opposite side of the glass wall, where we'll have a two-way audio feed with the pathologist but will be spared the possibility of being splattered with gore.

"Black leather," Goran says.

"Motorcycle jacket," I reply. "So the killer might have been who Martha Rodgers saw." I roll my head, trying to get the tension out of the back of my neck. "Question is, how'd he disable Martin to get her to the cemetery?"

"You think she went willingly?"

"If all the injuries happened at the same time, she might have, which would mean she probably knew him." I ponder that for a few minutes and return to the major motivators for violent crime: money, sex, and secrets. "It's anybody's guess. I do wonder if we're gonna find out that she was abducted in her own vehicle."

The whole postmortem, all three and a half hours of it, is captured on video. At some point—I think as Watson weighs her liver—I look away to stare at the camera mounted above the steel table at the steady red LED that says it's recording. My gaze flicks from Heather Martin's remains to Goran's face to the bright light over Watson and back again.

"It's organized," I verbalize for the first time as Watson sews the Y-incision closed with thick brown thread. "He has to have done something like this before. Based on the crime scene, these injuries, the damage to the carotid, the systematic way he—" I stop myself there and let a slew of words run through my head: *premeditation, postmortem, people, paraphilia, pathology, putrid, pallid, purgatory.*

"I tend to agree with you," Watson replies as he ties the knot. He stands back and gazes at me through the glass. "He knew what kind of damage he was inflicting. I'll chart the pattern of injuries for you, but we're basically looking at a woman who withstood a great deal before the final blow to her head. That's what killed her, by the way. Blunt force trauma caused a massive cerebral hemorrhage." He matter-of-factly lists a bunch of other things that could have killed her if he hadn't smacked her in the head: lacerated liver, ruptured spleen, punctured lung, blood loss.

In other words, the killer bound her to that chair, raped her with the chair leg, then beat her to death.

"I'm thinking your murder weapon might be a police baton," he adds. "One of the newer ones."

"I don't know what's worse," Tom says, "chair leg or baton."

Watson shudders.

My mood darkens even more. I stand in the corner and glower. "Choke hold plus baton equals someone with law enforcement or military training."

Watson nods. "Or a solid command of YouTube."

Goran purses his lips. "There's no way Paul Greenwade has the strength to inflict these kinds of injuries."

"We still have to follow up with him today," I mumble. I check my watch. "Let's head up to see Jo. We have over an hour before we need to take the fake GTO to Andersen Restoration."

"Okay, Detectives," Watson says, "I've got to get to that backlog. Let me know if you have any questions. I'll have the report to you this afternoon."

Goran and I mumble our thanks then walk silently down the brightly lit hallway to the stairs. He yanks the heavy metal door open and gestures for me to go first.

"How do you want to handle it with Greenwade?" I ask on the landing.

"He could have been an accomplice. He could have made the bomb."

"Mm-hmm."

I push the door open at the top of the stairs and step into another hallway, this one lit by natural light pouring in through floor-to-ceiling windows on the opposite wall. "Let's hope Jo has something for us."

We turn left then right through the double doors of the crime lab. Jo's office is in the far corner, and the door is open. We walk gingerly through the space, where technicians with microscopes and computers examine evidence, and I pop my head through the door.

"Oh, hi," she says from behind three widescreen computer monitors. When she sees us, she gestures for us to come in. "I was just looking at the tire tracks. They're a match to Martin's vehicle. And the mud you recovered from her tire matches the mud at the cemetery. And before you ask, we don't have any DNA for your guy Anders Andersen." She stands and stretches forward, letting her wavy hair touch the floor. "It's hell to get old." She returns to her chair.

"Isn't that the truth?" Goran says.

I get no sense of vindication from the fact that the woman was abducted in her own vehicle. "Anything on the inside of the vehicle? And what about that transponder thing?"

"A couple of human hairs—they look like hers—in the far back, near where they recovered the bomb, along with urine and saliva. The transponder, I'm still working on, but I'm betting it's some kind of listening device."

"Listening device? Like spy shit?"

She chuckles. "We'll get it opened up and take a look. I'll let you know as soon as I do. So you can quit sending me messages about it." She winks at me.

"Her urine, her saliva?" Goran asks, even though he knows it's too early to make that call.

"Tox will take a while."

Goran and I both nod at her.

"How were the seats set?" I ask. "Was the driver's seat back far enough for a guy that's six two to drive it? And how about the passenger seat?" If Andersen and Greenwade were working together, that would explain the two footprints, the shed lock, and getting into the cemetery when it was locked. It might explain why Greenwade picked up evidence at the scene too—maybe he was trying to hide it, or maybe he screwed up.

"Yeah, my guess is that the seat was set for someone with longish legs. Someone your size or bigger," she says to me.

I squint. My own car seat is pretty far back.

"The passenger seat was closer to the dashboard." She looks at Tom. "Someone as tall as you would hit his knees on it." So Andersen could have been driving while Greenwade rode shotgun. The more I think about it, the more it makes sense that there could have been two perps. One would have had a hard time controlling her, especially given that she had police experience and would know self-defense.

"But there's no way of knowing when either seat was moved," Tom says.

"Right. How tall was your vic?"

"Five three. So she would have fit in the front. What about the bomb?" I ask. "You really think that thing"—I mean the transponder—"was to some kind of recording device, as opposed to being a detonator?"

She nods. "It's not a detonator, and so far, the bomb looks like a fairly typical homemade pipe bomb. I'll have more details tomorrow or the next day, probably around the same time I have tox."

"Anything on the necklace? The rope?" I ask.

"You'll love this—bondage rope. And I was correct at the scene about the tape."

Goran and I exchange glances. Mine is an I-was-right look, while his is one of confusion and maybe disgust.

"Fingerprint match on the necklace to Paul Greenwade. He retrieved it at the scene, right?"

"Yeah, but he said he picked it up with a handkerchief."

"I'll have DNA in a few days," she says, "assuming that Watson got anything from the rape kit."

"Not likely. Chair leg."

She grimaces.

"Thanks, Jo. Bye."

We walk to the car in relative silence and get in. I can tell that Goran is brooding.

"Stop thinking about Martina Lowell," I say.

"How'd you know I was thinking about that?"

"You're an open book. And we've worked together a long time. I told you, I talked to Sims. He's working a cold case as a favor to a friend of his. Just talk to him about it. If you need an excuse, he's supposed to have Martin's location data today."

He grunts. "Did you get sick back there?"

I pull out of the parking lot, deliberately expressionless.

"You haven't done that in a while."

"Yeah, the chair-leg thing got me." I accelerate onto Jennings Freeway.

He nods. "What about the bondage stuff? You think she was kinky?"

"Could have been." Something occurs to me. "Especially given that black business card. I called the number, and it went to some voice verification thing. We need to look into that later."

He shoves a stick of Doublemint into his mouth.

"Either way, she obviously had secrets."

"We all do," he replies.

We're quiet for the rest of the drive.

CHAPTER 12

Andersen Restoration is over on the West Side in Old Brooklyn, near where Bobbie Butler said they all used to live but in a run-down section that so far has escaped gentrification. To get there, we pass another place that used to be a different car repair shop, and a bell goes off in my brain. I think it's where Anna Mattioli, the wife of the famous cop-turned-memoirist, was killed back in the day. I slow the Charger and glance over my partner and at the building, which today is boarded up and covered in graffiti.

Fuck dyke, it says. It's actually nicely done, the kind of graffiti that some might call art. It's surrounded by other, less-artistic gang signs.

I ease to a stop at the curb by the old mechanic's shop and squint at *Fuck dyke.*

"What are we doing?" Goran asks.

I push my sunglasses up onto my head and try to remember what Joe Mattioli wrote in his book—that stupid bestseller that I couldn't even finish—about his wife's murder. "Similar," I mutter. My gaze flicks to the rotted-out carcass of a fifties pickup truck. "When did this place close?"

"Huh? This isn't Andersen Restoration. It's up there. Make a right on Brookpark." He points at the map on his phone. "You're talking in riddles. Don't we have an appointment with this guy?"

I glance at my watch. "We still have ten minutes before the appointment. When did it close?"

"Dunno. Why? You need more work done on that piece of crap VW of yours? You should get a new car." He chuckles. "You could upgrade to the Chrysler 300. It's fantastic. Best car I've ever had.

And it's all-wheel-drive, which is good for you and your stunt-driver stuff." He winks at me.

"Yeah, I've been thinking about a new V-dub." *But I'm trying to save money in case I have to retire early in disgrace.* "Anyway, you know Joe Mattioli wrote that book, right? I mean, you have to have seen it on the news or whatever."

He narrows his eyes. "You reading it or something? Why? Where are we going with this?"

"I started it. It's horrible. But I got through the chapter on how his wife died. Her name was Anna. She died here."

"Uh-huh, and? Liz, we—"

"Now that we're here and I'm thinking about it, she died in ways that are really similar to our vic, and we're looking at a very organized killer. Anna Mattioli was beaten and raped with an object at some point during the beating but prior to death. Tons of blood everywhere. Tied to a chair. It wasn't robbery. It's a lot like the way our vic died."

"How do you remember stuff like that from a little piece of a book you read?" He laughs.

I push my sunglasses back up my nose and tap on the side of my head. "My mind is a steel trap. You know that already." I attempt a smile. "You know what I'm getting at."

"Show me the evidence, partner. It would really surprise me if the Mattioli case had anything to do with this, and Andersen would have been, what, sixteen when Anna Mattioli died?"

"Did you know Mattioli? You were, what, a rookie back then?"

"Nah. I was out in the fourth back then. He was already downtown. He had a reputation, though. Him and his partner—"

"Ray Gibson. Mattioli paints Gibson as kind of a tool in the book." *A doofus, a dipshit, someone who was far below Mattioli's own intelligence and ability.*

"Yeah, Mattioli was always the smart one. They were part of a pretty bad time in the department. It's nothing we should be messing around with. No one thought he killed his wife, and there's no evidence to link—"

"Now you're the one talking in riddles. You sound like Fishner. 'Tread lightly.'" *We shouldn't be messing around with it, but that doesn't change history.* "You think she's gonna let us do our jobs? Why is she protecting Eric Martin?"

"It was bad," he repeats. "A lot of those guys... Well, we all heard that they did stuff to women. Other women, who were cops."

"Women such as Heather Martin?" I ask. "There's *another* connection that I don't like. Martin didn't last long on the job. Think she bailed because of something that happened to her? Maybe Mattioli did something to her and that's why she left for law school. If she was a rookie with you and Fishner, that would make him part of whatever it is you're not telling me, right?"

He rolls down the window. "It's gotta be coincidence."

"You don't believe in coincidence."

"I get what you're saying, but there's no way in hell Joe Mattioli has anything to do with this vic. He's too busy signing autographs and doing interviews, if his little appearance on Channel Eight is any indication." He chomps his gum. "Let's run down this lead and see what happens. Stick with the agenda, partner. Right now, it's all Andersen and Greenwade. We'll check in with Sims to see what our vic's movements were before she died and figure out what's on that recording device, assuming that's what it is. We gotta dot our i's and cross our t's on this one. You heard Fishner."

"Uh-huh." I guide the car away from the curb and head to keep our—my—appointment with Anders Andersen, sans cool muscle car.

Goran keeps raving about his new car. "It has heated seats."

"So does my Passat."

"It has Bluetooth and CarPlay, so I can connect my phone and listen to music." He's going for the jugular there—he knows how important music is to me.

"You have my attention now, but any new car is gonna have that."

"It's an American car. I'm surprised VDubs are still legal. Didn't that guy threaten to outlaw German cars?" He winks at me, knowing full well how I feel about politics.

"Don't go getting all patriotic on me, now, partner." I hit the left-turn signal when I see the sign for Andersen Restoration. "You know that most American cars are actually made overseas, right? And a lot of quote-unquote 'foreign' cars are made here." I pull in next to a big rig that's parked in the empty lot next to the house.

"I thought he owned a restoration business," he says, unbuckling his seat belt. "How are we gonna handle this guy?"

"He does. Look over there." I point at a three-car garage about a hundred yards away. Several older cars are parked next to and in front of it, including an old GTO. "See that? I'd drive that."

He guffaws. "You'd be terrifying in that."

I grin and push my door open. "Let's go talk to this guy. Plan is to throw him some softball questions then ask him where he was on Saturday night. We need to pin down his connection to Martin. Shit, watch out." I point at a big, growling dog who strains against his chain, which is wrapped around a tree to the left of the garage.

"Let's hope that chain holds him."

I lead the way to the garage, because I'm ostensibly the one with the appointment.

Goran looks over his shoulder at the dog. "I think he's okay. He's sitting now."

"I'm sure he's friendly. Why don't you go pet him and find out?"

"I'm not getting near that dog." He stops and reaches for my shoulder. "Listen. I'm gonna let it go after this, but I feel bad about stuff that happened a long time ago, and I'm worried about Sims and the Lowell case. I don't like any of it."

I make a conscious decision not to ask him about what happened a long time ago. The time isn't right. I squeeze my eyes shut then let them pop back open.

"You know how I feel about coincidences."

"Let it go, Goran. Seriously. Let me quote Fishner. 'Get your head in the game.'"

He nods.

"We have to believe Sims about Lowell. Let it go." I clap him on the shoulder. "I'm the one who's supposed to be all over the place. Remember?"

He forces a smile and nods.

Once we reach the side door, I yank it open, and we walk inside. Behind a small, dingy counter, a very large bald man stands with his back to us, doing something on a computer. "Mr. Andersen?" I say in my pretend-I'm-not-a-cop voice, hoping he won't do anything stupid like run.

"Just one sec," he replies. He closes a window on the computer screen and turns to face us. When he does, he fails to hide his surprise—his thick eyebrows come up briefly, and he flexes his massive jaw. "*You're* Candy Cooper?"

I guess I don't look like a Candy.

"Something like that." I pull my police ID out of my pocket and flip it open. "I'm actually Detective Boyle, Cleveland Special Homicide. This is my partner, Detective Goran. How'd you get that black eye?"

He looks back and forth between us for a few seconds, as if he's trying to make a decision. *He's going to run.* Goran must see it, too, because he hulks in the doorway. Another door, behind the counter and to his left, leads to what I presume is the garage work area. The garage doors are closed. I calculate that I could leap the counter and tackle him if need be, but he's easily got a hundred pounds on me. And we're only here to question him. We have no evidence to arrest him. He shifts from foot to foot and blinks fast a few times.

"Sir, we just have a couple of questions. Nothing to worry about," Goran says from behind me, but it doesn't have a visible effect on the other man.

I'm watching Andersen's hands to make sure he doesn't reach for a weapon or something. Whether he's guilty of killing Heather Martin or planting a bomb remains to be seen, but he's hiding something.

People act crazy when the police show up, whether they're innocent, guilty, or some combination. The innocent freak out because they've seen too many TV shows where people who haven't done anything end up convicted and on death row. The guilty get defensive because they think we're on to them, unless they're the kind who get off on watching police work. The not-quite-guilty-of-this-particular-crime are the worst, though, because they're convinced that we're going to bust them for their pot plants or stolen vehicle or fake ID or whatever the hell, so they get twitchy and start to entertain notions of running from us, even if all we want is information.

Honestly, at this phase of my career, I couldn't give two shits about their whatever the hell, unless it involves sex crimes, murder, or it would seem, police brutality. I sometimes wish I could come out and say that to guys like Andersen, just so they would calm down and give us the information we need.

"Sir?" Goran says. He moves closer to me.

Andersen takes a visibly deep breath and blinks some more. "You said you were with Special Homicide. I can tell you right now that I didn't kill anyone."

Interesting tack to take, especially given the lawsuit against him for forgetting to reconnect those brake lines.

"Okay, that's great," Goran says.

I guess I'm bad cop today, which is fine by me.

"Would you be willing to chat with us for a few minutes?"

The big man runs a hand over his bald head. "Yeah, I guess. Come on in this way. I have some chairs out in the garage."

Once in the garage, which smells like old oil and stale smoke, Andersen pops a cigarette into his mouth. A radio blares in the corner, reporting a bad car accident that occurred last week. He quickly shuts it off before lighting the cigarette, inhaling deeply, and blowing the smoke out of the side of his mouth. He gestures at three old metal chairs. "Have a seat."

I cross my arms over my chest. "I prefer to stand." I glance around the garage but don't see anything that sends up an immediate red flag. There's no obvious bomb-making gear or bondage equipment.

"Suit yourself." He hits his cigarette again, plops into a chair, and looks at Goran without hiding his trepidation especially well. "What's this about?"

Goran eases himself into the other chair. "We appreciate your time," he says in his good-cop voice. "Like I said, we just have a few questions." He squints at the tattoo on Andersen's right wrist. "Marines, huh?"

Andersen nods and glances at me.

Goran grins. "I was Navy."

The other man grunts, but I can see that he's warming to my partner. He glances at me again but looks away immediately.

"Where were you on Saturday night?" I ask.

He clears his throat. "Saturday, like this last Saturday?"

I nod.

"I don't really remember. We could ask Winona, though."

"Who is Winona?"

"My wife. She's in the house. Want me to get her?"

"That's okay," I reply. "We'll talk to her on our way out."

"I could text her." He puts out the cigarette and stands, pushing the chair back behind him. "Just let me go get my phone." He backs toward the door on his left, and I step forward.

He's gonna run.

Goran holds out a hand. "That's okay. Just—"

Andersen spins, and I jump forward, but he's big and strong and shoves me aside. I hit the doorframe hard, and it knocks the wind out of me. Goran goes after him, and as soon as I'm able, I jog out into the driveway, calling Dispatch for backup as I pick up speed, side-stepping the dog, who is barking its head off and straining against its chain.

Out of the corner of my eye, I catch movement by the house. A woman runs after me, screaming, "What the fuck? What is going on?" I don't slow down, because I see that Goran is losing steam as he chases Andersen through a large yard and toward the woods. Question is whether I'll be able to restrain the guy.

My legs churn through the fallen leaves, which are slick from this morning's rain—I'm closing in on him. "Stop!" I yell, but he keeps going. I pass Goran, and my lungs feel as if they're on fire, but I keep moving as quickly as I can. Once I'm close enough, I jump forward and tackle him. My weight pushes his torso forward, and he tries to shove me off, but I manage to knee him in the left kidney, which brings him to his knees.

"Slow down, fucker."

He continues to struggle. It takes all of the strength I have to wrench one of his arms behind him, and I can't help considering how effective a choke hold would be. *No,* I remind myself, straddling him and pinning his arm to the small of his back.

"I didn't kill anyone!" he yells.

I pin his other arm to the ground with my boot. "That's funny, because we didn't say anything about you killing anyone, now did we?"

"Fuck you!"

Goran jumps into the fray and yanks Andersen's hands together, allowing me to stand. He cuffs the man, and we wrench him to his feet. He falls forward onto his knees.

Is he crying? He's crying.

The woman comes up on the side, shrieking. "What is going on? What the fuck did you do, Anders?"

"I didn't do anything," he mumbles through his tears. He sputters and coughs.

"If you didn't do anything, why are you handcuffed in the woods? You're such a piece of shit loser!" she yells.

Well, this is interesting. She's about my height but twenty pounds lighter and is wearing a pair of striped pajama pants, a red Marines hoodie that must be his, based on how big it is on her, and a pair of cheap-looking gray slippers. She's younger than he is by a few years.

"Get up," Goran says, pulling on the man's arms. "You're coming with us. You shoved my partner back there, and I call that assaulting a police officer."

"What the fuck did you do, you piece of shit?" the woman asks, red-faced. She runs forward and kicks Andersen, who is still on his knees, in the chest. He falls forward onto his face, and she kicks him again.

"Jesus Christ, Winona, what the hell?" he sputters.

I move between Andersen and Winona. I hold out a hand, ready to restrain her if necessary. "Ma'am, please."

"I won't *please.* Is he fucking you too?" She takes a swing, but I duck, so she attempts to shove me backward. I'm ready for her, so I grab her arm, twist it around her, and cuff her. It's a pretty badass move, if I do say so myself.

"Assaulting a police officer is a really, really bad idea," I say. *This has turned into a complete disaster. Where the hell is our backup?* "Looks like you're coming with us too."

We lead them out of the woods. The whole time, they keep arguing with each other, until Goran tells them to shut up. "Seriously. Just stop it."

"You asked me how I got the black eye," Andersen yelps as we near the car. "It was this crazy bitch! She hit me in the face with a cooler!"

"Whatever, you shithead. You probably liked it," she says.

Holding Winona's arms behind her—she can't get far with the cuffs on, but I'm sick of running—I yank open the Charger's back door and nod at Goran. "In the car, fucko," I say to Andersen, who tries to put up a fight but has clearly run out of energy.

Goran helps him in, making sure he doesn't hit his head, then closes the door.

Winona tries to kick the car. "What a fucking asshole loser! I can't believe him! What the hell did he do *now*?"

I drag her away from the car and say a tiny, silent *thank you* when I see the patrol car turn onto the driveway. "Ma'am, please get control of yourself."

She flexes her jaw. "Why am I in handcuffs?"

"Breathe."

"I didn't do anything." She struggles against the cuffs.

"You assaulted my partner back there," Goran says, "and now you're coming with us. We have questions."

The patrol car pulls up, and we're greeted by Officers Robinson and Miller, neither of whom I know well. "Detectives," Robinson says, giving Goran a little salute but ignoring me. "What do we have here?"

"Take her downtown, sixth floor," Goran says. "We've got the other guy."

Miller shoves Winona into the back seat of the patrol car, careful not to whack her head. Once he closes the door, she starts kicking the safety cage.

"She's either nuts or on something," I mutter.

I catch Robinson looking at me out of the corner of his eye, but he turns away when I attempt eye contact.

"So we're just transporting her?" Miller asks.

"Ten-four. We'll meet you at Justice," Goran replies.

In the car, I feel my mood darken. *Why was that uniform staring at me like that? I suppose I have one guess: the Grimes bullshit. Whatever. I don't have time for that right now.*

"What the hell am I under arrest for?" Andersen bellows from the back seat.

"Did anyone say you were under arrest?" Goran asks. "I thought you were coming willingly to answer a few questions."

"It's better for you that way," I add. I send a quick text to Fishner, asking her to have someone follow up with Paul Greenwade. *Be careful with him. He's on the spectrum, and he'll clam up.*

Andersen huffs and goes silent, as he remains the rest of the way to the Justice Center.

CHAPTER 13

Goran pops a piece of Doublemint into his mouth, followed by a toothpick. "We can't really hold them on anything unless one of them confesses to something."

"Yeah, I know. Something is really off between the two of them."

He narrows his eyes. "Think he's good for it?"

"Your guess is as good as mine. It's still early. Let's go talk to him. What's your plan?"

"Softball questions to start, then we get into the good stuff. Come at him and make him think we know he did it. The usual."

"You gonna keep trying to bond with him over the service?"

"I might, yeah, if you want to put the pressure on him."

"Yeah, why don't you start the interview, and then I'll slam through the door at some point and try to scare him."

He nods. "What about his wife?"

"Let her sit on her hands for a while. Maybe she'll calm down."

Fishner appears at the end of the hallway and walks our way with her arms crossed. "Who's the woman?" she asks.

I fill her in as we slip into the observation room to watch Goran begin interviewing Anders Andersen.

"Wait—they *both* assaulted you?"

"In a manner of speaking. I'm fine, though. I figure we can keep them on it if we need to, but maybe we can get them to crack first. Something is definitely up with them."

She nods. "Do you want to book them on the assault? It might be good to send a message to the city at large."

I avoid rolling my eyes but only just. "What they did was hardly assault. I mean, he shoved me into a doorframe, and she took a couple of swings. Like I said, I'm fine. No visible bruises. It'd be hard to prove, and it's kind of the last thing I need right now."

She makes an unintelligible sound.

I watch Andersen through the glass. He's glancing around and fidgeting, but I can't get a read on what he's hiding. "I've got a magic trick up my sleeve," I say to Fishner. "He may have threatened our vic. I'm thinking blackmail."

"Do you have evidence?"

"Not yet, but an intern at the law firm said that Martin received an envelope from him and that he'd been calling her a lot in the weeks leading up to the homicide."

She narrows her eyes. "Is there another connection between Andersen and our vic?"

"Well, he was up on manslaughter charges, and—"

"I know that from the board and your reports. What's the connection?"

I blink slowly and take a deep breath to avoid asking her what the hell she's asking me that for—it feels obvious to me. "O'Connor was his lawyer. Beyond that, I don't know. We need to find the contents of that envelope. The intern said it felt like photographs, but we didn't find anything in Martin's office. Are you going to let us search her house?" *Why haven't we done that already?*

She sighs. "Eric Martin's alibi checks, Boyle. We've been through this."

Who are you protecting, and why? "It's not really about him. Those photographs could be helpful."

"I'll ask Eric to take a look around and report back to me."

"Lieutenant, with all due respect, I'm a little concerned that we're not following procedure here. This is a high-profile case, and my ass—and my partner's—is on the line at a time when

I—we—can't really afford to be screwing up. If we can just go take a quick look around, with his permission, of course—"

She chuckles. "Since when do you care about procedure?"

Her attempt at levity gets a smile from me, but I'm not feeling good about this. "How about you ask him to let us in and take a look at her stuff? She has to have a home office. We could keep it to that, if he's guarding national secrets or some shit. I'm not interested in anything beyond figuring out who killed our vic. You have to know that. I mean, we can 'tread carefully,' but—"

She starts to make her annoyed-with-Boyle face then relaxes it. "We're not intruding into his private life. He has an alibi, and he's been very clear that he does not want us snooping around his home."

Andersen starts waving his free arm around in the interview room, and Goran glances toward the glass.

"That's my cue," I say. I push off the wall and take two steps to the door. "I'm assuming that, since you didn't say no, that means that we can go talk to Eric Martin and take a look around."

"Better to beg forgiveness than to ask permission."

Who the hell are you, and what have you done with my L-T? I take a breath then shove open the door to the interview room, where Goran and Andersen sit on opposite sides of the table. Andersen jumps and glances at me, back at my partner, then at me again.

"Why'd you try to run?" I ask.

"Wouldn't you? Think about it. If you came to talk to me, you obviously know about what happened with that guy's brakes. I swear it was an accident, but that didn't seem to matter. And last time I was arrested, the cops weren't very gentle either. I ended up with a couple of broken fingers."

I make a mental note to verify whether that's the truth. "You're not under arrest yet. Tell me about your little blackmail attempt."

He glowers at me. "I don't know what you're talking about. If I'm not under arrest, what the hell am I doing here?"

"Yeah? You want us to book you on assaulting me back there, or do you want to cooperate? Tell me why you were sending photographs to Heather Martin. Cooperating with us is the right move."

"I didn't kill anyone, and I sure as shit didn't kill her."

"Prove it, Anders." I square my posture and cross my arms across my chest. "Photographs. What were they of? And why were you harassing her on the phone?"

Goran leans back in his chair, and Andersen flexes his jaw.

"Here's what I figure"—I walk toward the table then lean forward onto my hands—"you needed money to pay off your little settlement, so you got some dirt on her somehow. Then you sent the photos with a demand for money. When she didn't pay, you lost your shit and beat her to death. Question is, why use her vehicle to move her? And why leave her vehicle where you did? Why set up a bomb?"

He shakes his head. "What? I didn't make a bomb. I didn't kill anyone. I didn't take a car. I don't know what you're talking about. I think I need a lawyer. I want my phone call."

Fishner knocks on the glass three times, which means she wants us out. *Fuck.*

"Before we get a lawyer for you, why don't you tell us where you were on Saturday night? You can make this easy for yourself. As I keep saying, cooperating with us is the best thing to do. We can get you a lawyer, but do you really want lawyers involved in this if they don't have to be?" I'm on a tightrope, but at least I know it.

He sighs. "I told you, *I don't remember.*" He squints. "I was at home with my fucking crazy wife, warding off blows. Yeah. I remember now."

"This went on all night? Can anyone else corroborate that?" Goran asks.

"Probably the neighbors. That was the worst night last week, and there have been a lot of bad nights. She's psychotic."

I nod. "Psychotic enough to kill someone?"

He laughs. "Hell yeah. She's tried to kill me four times this month."

"Is she homicidal in general? What does she know about Heather Martin?"

He squeezes the bridge of his nose. "She's psychotic, I told you. I don't know what she knows about Heather Martin. Good luck getting her to make sense."

Goran and I exchange glances. "Tell me about the photographs and why you were making so many phone calls."

"Not without my lawyer."

"Tell me about Paul Greenwade, then."

Andersen tries to conceal his surprise but fails. "What about him? We were friends a long time ago. He works at the cemetery where my parents are buried. I haven't hung out with him in a long time. We sort of went our separate ways."

I decide not to bring up the fire that killed Paul Greenwade's parents until Roberts gets me the information I need. "Did you kill Heather Martin? You know, make good on your threats when she didn't come through with the money?"

"Fuck. I'm as stupid as she thinks I am," he mutters at the table. He looks at Goran then at me, and I could swear he's going to cry again. "No. I said I was going to kill her, but I didn't. Some asshole beat me to it."

"So you *would* have, but you didn't have the opportunity? That sounds weird to me," Goran says. "Why were you blackmailing her? What'd you have on her?"

"Lawyer," he replies.

"Okay, Anders. We'll get you your phone call." I'm hoping Fishner will let us keep him in the room and stewing until he decides to dish on the blackmail attempt—assuming that the intern was correct and telling the truth. He looks and sounds like he's telling the truth, and I'm pretty sure he's not smart enough to lie that well to us, but one never knows.

Goran gets up and opens the door for me. "Sit tight," he says to Andersen. He pulls the door closed behind us.

Fishner looks back and forth between us and finally lands on my partner. "What's your read on this?"

"We verify his alibi with the neighbors, and we've got nothing," Goran says. He turns to me. "So we need to find those photographs."

"Get on the neighbors," Fishner says.

I nod. "Roberts is working an angle about a federal explosives charge when he was a juvenile. I'll check in and see what he's gotten so far."

"Do that. Then talk to the wife," Fishner says, "and give me a report before doing anything else."

"Ten-four, Lieutenant," he replies.

Once the door closes behind her, I tell Goran about the weird conversation I had with her earlier about Eric Martin. "She basically told me to defy her orders. It's strange."

"This is a weird one," he replies. "Let's see what Winona has to say for herself."

"I'll take her. You watch. Come in on my signal."

"Ten-four."

I GRAB A DIET COKE from the vending machine then enter the interview room. I hold the can out in a peace offering to the obviously agitated woman across from me, taking her in now that she seems to be getting under control. "Brought you a drink." I open the can and slide it to her before taking the seat opposite hers.

She's in her late thirties but seems as though she's lived a hard life. She's gaunt in the way some drug addicts are, and I briefly consider that she might be on drugs. Opiates, maybe, given the epidemic around here. Could be meth. Or maybe she's just skinny. Her face doesn't say addict—she just looks exhausted. Her brown hair, which was perhaps once cut and styled but has grown out, hangs in front of her face, and her roots are graying at the temples. She slouches over the table and extends a hand to grab the drink. Her nails are painted light pink, but the paint is chipped. Overall, she looks as though she used to care about her appearance but stopped relatively recently. "Thanks," she mumbles before taking a sip.

"What was that about back there?"

"What was *what* about?" she asks in a tired voice. She slumps back in her chair and rolls her eyes.

"Why'd you lose your shit?"

"Is he fucking *you* too? Just tell me. I won't be mad." Anders said she was off her meds, but the vibe I'm getting is more resigned than crazy.

"No. But that makes me wonder who he *is* fucking. Tell me the story."

She sips her Diet Coke. "What story?"

"How long have you been married?"

"Too long. I should have left his cheating ass years ago, but here we are."

"How long is that, exactly?"

She squints at me and flips her hair out of her face. "Shit, we're coming up on twenty-five years. Why am I here? If it's because of Anders's black eye, I can explain. That asshole has been cheating on me for too long, and I'm sick of it." She looks as if she's trying to come up with a more compelling reason. "That and he... uh... he *does stuff* that doesn't sit right with me."

"What does that mean?" If we need to hold her, we could probably book her on domestic abuse, but her husband doesn't seem like the type to cooperate with us long enough to get a warrant for her.

She sighs as if I'm the stupidest person in the world. "His weird kinky shit. I mean, I knew about it before, but he acted like it was no big deal. At first, I was cool with it—I mean, back when he was faithful to me—but then it got out of hand. What's the word? It escalated."

I haven't forgotten the black business card that I found in Heather Martin's office or the bondage tape, and kinky shit makes for good blackmail material. I stay quiet to leave room for her to talk.

"Look, I know this looks bad. I shouldn't have hit him in the face. But after I saw the emails, I just lost it." She sips her Diet Coke as though it's no big deal that she clocked her husband in the face with a cooler, and she seems to have forgotten that she punched me a couple of times earlier today too.

I briefly wonder if it was a full-sized cooler or a smaller one. "How long have you known?" I'm shooting in the dark. I still don't know exactly what we're talking about, but she seems like she needs room.

"Can you take this stupid handcuff off of me?" She gestures with her eyes to her left hand, which is cuffed to a ring on the table.

I stand and slide my keys out of my pocket. "Sure." I chuckle, but it's an act. "That can't be very comfortable."

After I uncuff her, she rubs her wrist. "Thanks." She flexes her fingers, makes a fist, then stretches her hand. "Listen, I don't want to press charges or anything. I mean, I'm willing to answer your questions, but all of this is some kind of misunderstanding."

I sit down again, wondering what the hell she would press charges for. "What is a misunderstanding?"

"The whole thing. Why you came to talk to him. Why we're here right now. He didn't mean for that guy to die. He's just a stupid fuck."

"Winona, I'm confused about what we're talking about here. Are we talking about you assaulting your husband, you assaulting me,

Anders cheating on you, or what you may have done to a woman he was sleeping with?"

"Wait—what? I didn't do anything to any woman. It's not her fault he's how he is. If she gets into that stuff, that's up to her."

"How is he, exactly? Say more about that. If you can show me that what you did was self-defense, we should be able to get this cleared up pretty quickly," I lie.

She sighs again, and the exhale sounds almost like a growl. "I can't believe he called the police for something that happened *three days* ago."

I don't tell her that he didn't call the police or point out that it would be very strange indeed for him to do so only to run from us.

"Anyway, I found the emails. He and some rich bitch were screwing. He said in the emails that he had pictures and was going to share them with her husband or some shit. He was arranging meeting times. And it wouldn't be the first time. He promised after last time that he was done going to that club, done cheating on me. We were trying to get pregnant—in fact, I might be pregnant right now. I don't know. I'm probably too old by now."

I don't fill the ensuing silence. I watch her, trying to gauge whether she's going to dish or if she's another dead end.

"Okay, here's the deal." She sits up straighter. "We've been together a long time. Since his senior year of high school. It wasn't supposed to end up this way. I ended up getting fired from my job because of that stupid lawsuit. And I feel bad for that guy's family, I really do. But Anders didn't do it intentionally. He just sucks. That's it. He sucks."

"What club?" I ask.

"There've been a couple. I don't even know."

I nod. *A secret club?* "Do you remember the names of the clubs?"

"No. I never knew them." She twirls her hair. "Wait. I do remember one thing. I found a weird black business card once. It only had a phone number on it."

I nod and glance at the mirror. "Tell me more about the emails. Who was he corresponding with?"

"Some woman named Heather. He's into bondage and shit, but I'm not, so he has to get his kicks elsewhere. He used to belong to some other gross club, but he told me he was done with that. We were going to try to have a baby and start over. I was so stupid to believe him." She runs a hand through her lank hair.

"I used to have a really good job. I was a physician's assistant at MetroHealth. But then I got fired. HR said it was for being late too many times, but I *know* it was because of the lawsuit. So now we're just fucked, because who wants to have their car restored by a guy who doesn't reconnect the goddamn brake lines? No one, that's who. We lost our medical benefits, everything. I have no idea what I'm gonna do."

She looks completely dejected, and I almost feel bad for her. "Do you remember anything about the meeting times or what the emails said?"

"I have a few saved on my phone. I'll show them to you if you get it for me."

"Okay, let's see what we can do about that. Does he ever hurt you?"

"Physically? No. After the last time, I told him I was done with that shit."

"Do you mean bondage, that kind of thing?"

"Yeah. He's into that stuff. He gets his kicks from tying women up and making them beg."

"But he doesn't hit you?"

"No."

"Does he ever have sex with you without your consent?"

"No. He just sticks his dick in other women, and I get angry. It hasn't been easy, you know. The whole thing is just stupid. I don't know why I haven't divorced him yet."

I'm starting to get a clearer picture of their relationship and the kind of man Anders Andersen is. "What else can you tell me about the emails? Do you have any sense of who Heather is?"

"Some rich bitch. I know he was trying to blackmail her, but it was probably just one of his stupid sex games. My guess is that he got photos of her somehow and was trying to get money from her to pay off the lawsuit. As it is, he's gonna have to sell the business, and then what? Shit. I need to get a new job."

"Do you have the emails anywhere other than your phone? Maybe printed out or saved on a computer?"

"They're all on his laptop in the shop. Like I said, I took a couple of screen shots and saved them on my phone."

I glance at the mirror and assume that Goran will get her phone—and a search warrant for Andersen Restoration.

She sips her Diet Coke. "Look, I know what this looks like, and I'm sorry I swung at you back there. It's embarrassing how mad he makes me. Then he tries to make me think I'm crazy. But I'm not crazy. I'm just more pissed off than anyone should ever be for reasons that go way beyond my stupid husband."

I nod. "I get that. We just have to see if he wants to press charges because of the black eye. He says you hit him with a cooler."

She laughs. "Are you kidding? He wouldn't dare. I know too much about him. He's in deep shit."

"What kind of deep shit?"

"You know, this and that."

"No, I don't know. What kind of deep shit, exactly?"

She sighs dramatically. "Like with the lawsuit, no business, hanging out with lowlifes, and trying to get money any way he can. I'm pretty sure he lost our last five hundred bucks gambling on—get this—the fucking *Browns*."

"Ouch. Can you verify your whereabouts on Saturday night, into Sunday morning?"

"What, just this past weekend? Yeah, I was at an early Halloween party at my sister's. Her number is in my phone. I ended up just staying at her house because I couldn't stand the sight of that fucker—and because he was supposed to pick me up but never showed. It was the day after I found the emails."

So he doesn't have an alibi after all. "You found the emails last Friday, then?"

"Yup. I was in the shop doing the books when a notification came up from her. It said that he was messing with the wrong person and to leave her alone or she would have Mistress Natalia take care of him."

"What did you do then?"

"I marked it as unread so he wouldn't know I saw it. I wanted to see what he would do if I called him out. I confronted him that night. The answer? He lied. Like usual."

"What did he say?"

"That it was someone with the wrong email address and he was just fucking around by replying."

"How did he respond?"

"He made up some story about Mistress Natalia not wanting to be involved in it, this and that. I don't remember, exactly."

"Is that the kind of thing he would do? Mess with someone who sent a message to the wrong email address?"

She shakes her head. "Not really. I mean, I've never seen him do anything like that."

"How did he act when you confronted him about the emails?"

"He told me to mind my own business and said that what I don't know won't hurt me. I got, like, really, really angry… That's when I hit him with the cooler."

"Okay. Can you confirm for me that you were not with your husband on Saturday night or Sunday morning?"

"No, I just told you. I was at Tiffany's—she's my sister—Halloween party. We were with, like, twenty other people. They can tell you. Is that when that woman died? Oh my God—did he kill her? He said he was going to hang out with Derek." She rolls her eyes. "But I wouldn't be surprised if he did something really fucking stupid, especially since he never showed to pick me up and didn't answer his phone the thirty times I called. I assumed he was fucking around on me, but if he was killing someone, that's a *whole* different story."

"We're still investigating," I reply. "What do you know about your husband's past?"

"Uh… He was in the Marines." She smiles. "He was an explosives expert. I've always thought that was cool. His parents died. He has a younger sister who lives in Colorado, but she quit talking to us a while ago." She squeezes the bridge of her nose and inhales. "We graduated from Rhodes—go Rams—three years apart. He joined the service, and I hung out here. When he got out, we got married. He opened the business, and the rest is history." She frowns again. "That fucking asshole. This isn't how things were supposed to go."

"Did you know him when he was younger? Say, thirteen or fourteen?"

She shakes her head. "We moved here right before my freshman year. I met him when he was seventeen and I was fifteen."

I push my chair back and stand. "Can I get you anything else? Do you mind sitting tight for a few minutes?"

"I'm good, but thanks. Can someone bring me my phone?"

I smile. "Sure. Thanks, Winona. I'll be back in a few. Oh, one more thing. Who's Derek?"

"Derek Struthers." She knits her eyebrows together. "Is Anders in, like, real trouble? I mean, I hate all of them, but I don't want to see them get in trouble."

"What else can you tell me about Derek?"

"He's in construction. He's a dick."

I let the door close then lean against the wall.

"What the fuck?" I ask Goran. "Wow."

"Her phone is locked, but I say you take it in and have her show you the emails and the map of where the club is." He grins. "We might just have the asshole cornered."

CHAPTER 14

Fishner comes tapping down the hallway, and I know before she opens her mouth that she wants to detain Anders Andersen until we can get more evidence to book him for the murder. She looks me up and down, probably worried that I'm going to come unglued or something, even though I haven't done that in a while. "Good news for your pal Paul Greenwade. The cemetery has cameras on the offices and living quarters, and we've got him entering his place at ten p.m. and staying there until the next morning."

Relief hits hard enough to surprise me. "Who talked to him?" I can't help hoping they didn't scare him. There's no way in hell he was involved in this.

"Roberts."

I roll my eyes.

"We're going to hold Andersen on assaulting you," Fishner says, "so I need to take your statement."

"But—"

"Becker is on her way. If we need to indict him, we will. We need to send a message."

"At least let me verify Winona's alibi so that we can cut her loose." She doesn't strike me as being anything but sad and dejected, and she can do that at home.

"I'm on it," Goran says. "Tiffany, right?"

I grit my teeth. "Okay, then I need to take her phone in to her so that we can get these emails. If we're detaining Andersen, you obviously want us to gather evidence on our vic and her associations with him. Am I right?"

"Boyle."

"Hear me out." I look at my watch. "We can only hold him for a few more hours. That gives us enough time for Goran and me to run down a couple of leads, look into the black business card, track down Derek Struthers, and—"

"We can't hold him that long without charging him with something. Not given what's happening with the police and his allegations that one of ours broke his fingers."

"I'll ask Winona about that when I go back in."

She hands me the cell phone. "Fine. But I'm getting your statement when Becker gets here. And we have to let him call his attorney."

Fucking Jeff O'Connor. "Let's hope whatever is on here is enough for a search warrant for the house and garage," I mutter as I push past her.

As I enter the interview room, Winona twists the tab off her Diet Coke, drops it in the can, and rattles it around.

"I got your phone," I say as I take my seat. "Will you show me the emails?"

She holds out her hand. "Yeah, sure. Whatever. Can I go soon?"

"We just need to verify your alibi with Tiffany, and you'll be out of here. Will you say her number out loud, please?" I pull out my notebook and pen.

She recites the number then taps around on her phone. "Here. They're all in the photos, because I took screen shots, like I said."

I take the phone from her. The emails, a back-and-forth between Andersen and Martin, confirm my suspicion that he was attempting to blackmail her. One is especially compelling: *Give me what I want, or I release the photos of you and E.M. to your whole law firm. Think Sellers will like that? I doubt it. You'll be giving up your corner office. Or you can do what I say.* It makes me wonder if her husband is involved with the bondage scene, too, which could be damaging to his burgeoning political career.

Another email contains photos of someone who looks very much like Heather Martin, but she's naked and in a compromising position, bound to some kind of table. A man built like Andersen and wearing a black latex suit stands over her, holding a cat-o'-nine-tails. It says the same thing, that Andersen is going to share the photo if Martin doesn't cough up some cash. He reminds her that he's "only asking for fifty thousand."

"Winona, I need your permission to copy these photos."

"That's fine. Whatever. Just get me the hell out of here soon."

Fishner opens the door and hands me a consent form. In a whisper, she requests my presence in the hallway once I have Winona's signed permission to copy the contents of her phone.

I slide the form across the table and hand her a pen. She scrawls a signature at the bottom without reading the form. "Is that it? Can I go now?" She shoves everything my way.

"Be right back. I do need to take this with me, though," I say of the phone.

She nods. "Can I get another Diet Coke, then?"

"Sure." I smile as I pull the door open. "One more question," I say from the doorway. "Did Anders ever have broken fingers?"

She laughs. "Yeah, that dumb shit. He dropped a car onto 'em."

"He dropped a car onto them?"

"Yeah, like with a jack. He knows he should use the lift, but he was under a car, using just a fucking tire jack. He's lucky he didn't get killed."

"When was this?"

She squints. "Whenever the fuck that lawsuit was. Why?"

"Were you there when it happened?"

She nods.

"So cops didn't break his fingers?"

"No, why?"

"Just curious. Thanks." *This guy's blackmail plans never seem to work out.* I let the door close behind me then join Goran in the hallway. "Where's Fishner?"

He nods at the observation room.

"Oh, good. Maybe I won't have to give her a statement." I roll my eyes.

He chuckles. "The wife's alibi checks, but boss wants us to keep her occupied long enough to get the search warrant. Doesn't want her there when we are." He narrows his eyes. "Think he did it?"

"Looks that way. Question is why." I turn to walk down the hallway, looking for Sims, who can copy phone data more quickly than I can.

I find him in the mail room, fiddling with the copier. He gives me a little salute when I walk in holding Winona's phone in an evidence bag. "Got something for you."

He kicks the copier.

"Problems?"

"Something like that." He removes his original, which is held in a manila folder with a metal clip, and holds it behind his back.

I blink at him and extend Winona's phone. "This phone contains screenshots of emails sent between Anders Andersen and Heather Martin. Winona claims to have had the originals at one time, but her husband deleted them. Can you get me the originals?"

He takes the bag with one hand, keeping the folder in the other with its tab facing his leg. "I can't figure out why anyone uses these shit phones. You can get a better one for even cheaper."

Why is he hiding that folder? It had better not be more Martina Lowell info. "Can you get me the emails or not? And can you do it quickly? Because I've got to cut her loose soon."

He nods. "I can definitely try. I'll need her to unlock it first. And if she gave me her email password, it would be even easier."

"Great. She's in interview two." I move behind him and pretend to check my mailbox, but really, I'm attempting to see the folder. No such luck. I'll have to snoop later.

"All right, Boyle, I'll get on this right now," he says as he leaves the room.

WE GET THE SEARCH WARRANT quickly, and after I talk Fishner out of taking a statement about Andersen shoving me—and after eating lunch—Goran and I head to Andersen Restoration with a forensic team and two uniforms.

"I'm starting with the rig," I shout over the dog's loud barking, pointing at the trailerless semi parked in the grass.

"Makes no sense," Goran replies. "If it's him, it's not his rig. Let's start in the garage and make our way inside from there."

I sigh.

"You know I'm right."

"Fine." I gesture for a forensic tech as we zip ourselves into Tyvek suits.

"I'm not a fan of these suits," Goran grumbles.

"But you look so good in Tyvek."

He grunts. After we slip on the booties, we enter Andersen's workspace, which is exactly how we left it hours earlier, complete with the overturned chair in the garage. I direct the tech to bag some of the cigarette butts in the hopes that we'll recover his DNA and get a hit on the evidence from the crime scene. We're looking for a black motorcycle jacket, a black hoodie, bomb-making equipment, and anything else that will show that Andersen murdered Heather Martin.

"Here's something," Goran calls from the office as I'm poking through cans of paint and myriad tools in the garage. "This is good. Come check this out."

I peek around the doorway to find my partner spreading photos onto the counter in the office. "Are those pictures of naked women?"

"Ten-four, partner. And one looks a lot like our vic."

I walk over to look at the photos. "That one"—I point at it—"looks almost identical to one that Winona had saved on her phone. The one he sent to Martin with the threat." I squint at the other photos and slide a different one my way with a gloved hand. "This one looks like it could be her too." I don't see anyone who looks like Eric Martin.

"This is some weird shit."

"Yeah, well... Winona said he's into kinky stuff. It looks to me like we have near confirmation that he was involved with Martin, though, which could give us even more motive. Let's keep looking. Bag those. I'm going back into the garage."

Nothing in the garage is remotely interesting, but everything changes when we get inside the house.

"This place is disgusting." Goran gestures around with an empty evidence bag. "Don't people clean up after themselves?"

"How long have you been doing this? You know as well as I do that people in general are disgusting."

"But seriously. Look at that." He points at a coffee table, next to a recliner, that contains about thirty takeout containers. "How hard is it to throw your trash away?"

"Think of it as more possible DNA, partner. Check this out." I hold out a burner phone, and he slides it into an evidence bag. "Oh, shit, Goran, we just hit the motherlode. Look at this." I slide a bunch of magazines and newspapers to the floor and open the trunk. "What do you think is in here? Is it ever this easy?" I pull the lid open.

On top is what appears to be a locking chastity belt for a man. "Bag," I say. Underneath is a variety of sex toys and leather harnesses, neatly arranged by size. We bag those too. The next layer contains black bondage rope, bondage tape that looks similar to the tape at the crime scene, a weird assortment of metal instruments, and a laptop.

"How much you wanna bet there are more pictures on there?" he asks. "This is some creepy shit. I mean—"

"Let's find out." I open the computer to find that it's unlocked. On the desktop is a single folder, which contains thousands of photos, organized by name. There's an entire file for Heather Martin. In a subfolder marked "D.," there are photos of a smaller man with a plethora of other women. "Could be Derek Struthers. Could be his accomplice," I mutter. "We need to follow up on this Derek dude."

In the bedroom, we find a black hoodie in Andersen's size and a black motorcycle jacket that looks as though it would fit him.

"How stupid is this prick?" Goran mutters, still visibly uncomfortable.

"He's either guilty and stupid as shit, or he's not guilty and we're heading down a rabbit hole. Pick your poison."

"I'm going with guilty and stupid as shit."

"My money is on rabbit hole. This would be way too easy, and Winona said he isn't into hitting people—all his kinky shit is consensual—and none of the photos depict anything beyond regular S and M shit. I suppose we'll find out. Let's get all of this into evidence, and we'll go from there."

At the forensics van a couple of hours later, we take stock of what we've found. "Bondage equipment, dirt, wood, grass, motorcycle jacket, carpet fibers, packets of manila envelopes," I say, shining my flashlight into the back of the van with relief tempered with cynicism. A text comes through from Sims: *Got the original emails. It's not just our vic he was trying to blackmail.* I show the message to Goran.

"Hot damn. And don't forget the laptop with the photos," he adds.

"Check and check. Looks like we can keep him for a while. Even if he didn't kill her, he's obviously guilty of something."

"No murder weapon, though, and no signs of bomb-making supplies."

"Yeah, but this is good circumstantial evidence. We need to talk to Fishner and Becker. We'll check in with Sims first, though. Maybe there's something in those emails that will lead us to a witness."

"This Derek dude, maybe?"

I close the back door to the van. "Olivet," I call to the tech, "can you get all of this to Micalec ASAP? We're taking the laptop for our tech guy." I wait for Goran to say something rude about Sims, but he doesn't, and I don't tell him about the folder Sims was hiding from me.

He removes his Tyvek suit and shoves it into a bag. "Sure thing, Boyle."

As Goran and I walk to the car, I send Micalec a quick text: *More evidence on its way.*

On it in the morning, she replies.

FISHNER CALLS A BRIEFING when we return, so we gather in the conference room. It's past dinnertime, and my stomach grumbles.

"Okay," she says. "What did you find at the Andersen property?"

"Solid circumstantial evidence," I reply, taking them through the photos. "If any of this comes back a match to what we found at the crime scene, we have our guy. Micalec is on it starting tomorrow morning."

Roberts chuckles when he sees the bondage equipment and turns to Sims as if to make a joke, but the other man appears more focused on preparing his part of the briefing. *Maybe the folder was nothing.*

Fishner narrows her eyes. "What about the knots?"

"Well, there's that, and there's also the black business card we found in her office."

Sims stands. "I think I know what that's about." He turns to me and gestures at the iPad. "May I?"

"Sure." I sit.

He pulls up my photo of the business card. Next to it, he pulls up a screenshot of an email, which contains the same phone number. "I did a reverse search for the number. It goes to an internet phone service that allows users to require a voice verification to connect, so I had to get creative."

He swipes to a photo of an old brick building with a sign outside that reads Leather & Lace.

Roberts guffaws again, and Fishner shoots him a look.

Sims clears his throat.

"A little internet digging tells me that it's not just a dive bar." He advances to a photo of the inside, which does indeed look a lot like a shitty old dive bar. "This is the main room. Looks like a regular bar, right?"

I make note of a cigarette machine, which looks like it belongs in the Smithsonian, in the corner. "Where is this place?"

"Just outside of Chardon."

"*Chardon?*" Goran asks. "Chardon has a population of, like, five thousand people. That's impossible."

I elbow him. "BDSM isn't limited to big cities."

Everyone looks at me.

"I mean, it's not." I don't want to remind them that I learned most of what I know about kink from a sociology-of-sex class that I took in college. They still harass me about having a college education.

"Anyway," Sims continues, "this is where the phone number leads." He looks vaguely proud of himself. "And that number was in one of Andersen's emails. I should add that it looks as though he was attempting to blackmail several other high-profile people in Cleveland." He swipes to a collage of photos with a name and a title below each one.

We collectively gasp when we see the county safety and protection chief, a high-ranking official who oversees the sheriff's department and the medical examiner's office. There are also photos of three Cleveland City Council members.

"Thing is," Sims says, "he's a dumbass. He didn't try to hide any of this on his computer."

Fishner uncrosses her arms and pinches the bridge of her nose. "Combined with the circumstantial evidence from the Andersen property, I think we have enough to book him."

I lean forward onto my elbows. "What about the city council connection?" This could turn into a horrible scandal, which would be both good and bad for the city. If the media seizes on the city council, the police can keep doing whatever they—we—want.

Fishner glares at me.

"Okay, then. Sims, have you found a money trail? Has this guy actually gotten anything from these people?"

"I don't know yet, but that's not all." He swipes to another photo, a BMV shot of a scrawny-looking man in his early forties. "This man, Derek Struthers, appears to be Andersen's accomplice of sorts. I was able to hack into Andersen's email account directly, which is how I got all of this."

No one asks him how he did any of it.

"Derek Struthers might be in some of the photos we recovered at Andersen's property," I add.

"Good work, Sims," Fishner says. She turns to Roberts. "Anything on your end?"

He rolls his massive shoulders back and looks impressed with himself. "Well, I was able to get bits and pieces of Andersen's juvie record. Looks like the info Boyle got from the woman at the ceme-tery—"

"Bobbie Butler," I add.

"Was good. He never served any time. Community service, promises not to do anything like that again. That led me to his ser-vice record, and he was in fact an explosives expert in the Marines, but he's been mostly clean since then. Basically, there's nothing there that connects with this."

Fishner nods then turns to me, looking expectant. "Tomorrow, first thing, you and Goran follow the Derek Struthers lead. Sims and Roberts will visit Leather & Lace. I want a full report at the end of the day tomorrow. We'll have another briefing at five o'clock."

We all nod.

"What are we doing with Andersen?" Goran asks.

"The four of you will stay as late as you need to tonight to com-pile evidence. It looks like we have evidence of attempted extortion at minimum. Coupled with the assault on Boyle earlier, we can ar-rest him for *something* while we track down more evidence for the Martin homicide. Becker couldn't make this briefing, but she's on her way."

I make a face. Julia and I might be sort of friends these days, but it's still too early to get her involved. "Winona mentioned a different club too. I'll try to track it down."

It strikes me that Fishner is covering her own ass, and I don't like it.

"FOOD," ROBERTS SAYS as soon as the lieutenant leaves. He runs his hand across his high-and-tight haircut. "We need food if we're re-ally gonna be here all night."

My stomach grumbles again. "We won't be here all night, but I agree that we need food. Here or elsewhere?"

Goran stands in the corner with his arms crossed, glaring at Sims, who doesn't seem to notice. I shoot him a glance, and he fakes a smile.

Becker knocks then enters. "Hey. What do you have for me?"

I roll my eyes. "Sorry. That wasn't directed at you. It's because you're here way too early on this one, and we're all famished. We're supposed to be assembling evidence to give to you on Anders Andersen. Here's what we have so far." I take her through the list but allow Sims to give his updates. It can be easy for me to talk over guys I outrank, but Sims is a good detective, and what he's gotten could break this case wide open.

Becker pushes a wayward copper-colored hair out of her face. "Have we gotten complaints from any of Andersen's other potential victims?"

Goran steps forward, obviously wanting to take control of the conversation. "Not as of now, no."

She leans a hip against the wall. "If we don't have a victim, we don't have a crime. And I'm not seeing a lot to take to a judge for the homicide."

Sims takes a step back, shaking his head. "Seriously? We have a direct link to Heather Martin and a phone number that Andersen used in his blackmail messages. There are multiple crimes here." He gestures at the screen, still displaying the BMV photo of Derek Struthers.

"Could be unrelated," she replies. "I can't get you a warrant until we know for sure that these crimes are connected. Even then, we need forensic evidence. We have absolutely nothing on Struthers other than a file folder labeled with an initial. That doesn't quite cut it."

Fishner isn't gonna like this.

"She's right," Goran says to Sims.

I have rarely known my partner to agree with the assistant prosecutor, and my gut says he's doing it just to egg Sims on.

"Hey, man, I just busted my ass to get all this. Now you're gonna tell me it's for nothin'?" He steps toward my partner, who puffs out his chest.

"It's just ones and zeroes on a server somewhere, buddy." He points at Becker. "She's saying we need real evidence. Evidence that comes from real work, not playing on the internet all day."

Sims takes a deep breath and makes a fist.

I get to my feet and step between them. "Stop it." I put a hand on Goran's shoulder. "Cut it out. Listen to what she's saying. We obviously have evidence of some kind of wrongdoing, but it may not be our squad that investigates it. We're investigating the death of Heather Martin, not whether Andersen attempted extortion on half of the county. Remember?" I feel his shoulder relax, but his nostrils are still flaring.

Julia smiles at me as the men stare each other down.

"Goran, I need to see you in the hall," I say.

He doesn't look away from Sims.

"Now." I step back and hope he'll follow me.

"Whoa," Roberts says. "This is getting intense. How about everybody just chills out for a minute? I'm sure we can figure something out. Right, guys?"

I clench my jaw and stare at my partner. "Goran."

He finally stomps out of the conference room. I turn to Julia, and we exchange a glance before I follow him.

He's down the hall by the vending machines already, pacing.

"What the hell was that about? What is going on with you? It is really not cool for *me*, of all the people in this whole world, to be the one trying to calm *you* down."

"I'm sorry, Boyle. I just think that guy is up to something."

I catch Fishner out of the corner of my eye, striding out of her office and heading in our direction, so I turn away from her and speak in a low volume. "Without him, we would have no evidence whatsoever that gets us anywhere."

"That's not true. We would have a lot of things."

I squeeze my eyes closed and let them pop back open. "Tom. Listen. You have to stop this. He's a good detective, and he just uncovered a whole lotta bad shit on Andersen—"

He crosses his arms in front of his chest.

"Don't do that."

"I will. I don't like any of this high-tech stuff. What happened to good, old-fashioned police work?"

I pat his shoulder. "It's okay, old man. You and I can focus on the good, old-fashioned police work and leave the newfangled Google nonsense to the whippersnappers."

He chuckles and drops his arms.

We head back down the hallway. "Are you all right? Can you behave nicely in the conference room with the others?"

"You've gone from calling me an old man to talking to me like a child. Pick one or the other." He seems both amused and annoyed.

"I just want you to chill out, partner. We've got good evidence so far. Tomorrow, we talk to Derek Struthers—assuming we can find him. And we go from there. Just let Sims do his job, okay? He's good at it."

He nods and opens the door, and I lead the way into the conference room, where Sims is leaning back in his chair, trying to look relaxed. The twitch in his jaw gives him away.

"Get me the evidence, and I'll get you your warrant," Becker says.

"In the meantime, we're holding him on assaulting Boyle," Fishner adds. "You have seventy-two hours to get enough evidence to book him on Heather Martin. We cut Winona Andersen loose, and I've asked Patrol to keep an eye on her."

I unplug my iPad from the projector and flip its cover closed. "Ask at the bar if there's a Mistress Natalia there," I tell Sims and Roberts. "Winona mentioned something about her."

"Ten-four," Roberts replies.

Goran turns to leave, and Sims gets up and follows him. Behind Goran's back, I hold out a hand and mouth, "Let me talk to him first," at the younger man, who nods.

I hit the bathroom and meet Goran at our desks. He's on his phone, so I quietly slide my stuff into my messenger bag. He wraps up the call by saying "I love you too," so it has to be Vera.

"How's she doing these days?" I shut off my lamp.

"She's good. The girls are good. I don't know why I'm so angry."

"It happens, partner. It happens to the best of us. Wanna grab a bite?"

He stands and shoves his laptop into his bag. "Nah. Thanks, though. I gotta get home."

"Just chill. It'll be fine. Let the new guy do his new-guy things. Okay?" I pull my jacket on.

He nods, and his face is less red than before. "What time tomorrow?"

"Meet you here at nine. Then it's all Derek Struthers."

"You got it." As he leaves, he glances over his shoulder at me. "Good night, Boyle."

Never in a million years did I think I would be talking that man off a ledge. It's always been his job to calm me down when I lose my shit.

I guess being the calm one feels okay, but it makes me anxious. I'm too used to Tom being slow and methodical. Maybe I take it for granted.

I swing by Cora's on the way home, but she isn't there, so I shoot her a text, stop at Chipotle for a burrito and the liquor store for beer, then return to my cat. I change into sweats and listen to The

Clash while I comb the databases and social media sites for Derek Struthers. I don't find much, but at least we have an address. He lives over on the West Side, close to Edgewater.

CHAPTER 15

Wednesday morning, Goran and I meet next to the Charger and decide to grab a quick bite at Shackley's Diner, one of our go-to greasy spoons, before we head out.

"You seem like you're in a better mood today," I say between bites of my breakfast sandwich.

He jabs his omelet with his fork. "Something like that." His eyes twinkle. "I think I'm gonna talk to Boss Lady about Sims."

I almost choke on my food. "No. You have to stop this right now."

"I can't deal with it. You know how it is. Imagine if he was looking into, I don't know, any one of ten cases that stick in your craw."

I narrow my eyes, imagining those ten cases. "I would talk to him directly. I wouldn't involve Fishner. We *need* him on this, and you know it." I stare at him. "Is this some kind of fragile-male-ego thing?"

He sighs. "Honestly? It might be." A fly swoops in, but he shoos it away before it lands on his plate.

I take another bite of sandwich. "Let it go, Tom. Please. Get over it. Let the young guy do his thing, and let him be good at it. What if he solves the Lowell case? What if it turns out that the asshole who did that stuff to her has been out there for all these years, maybe doing stuff to other little kids? Then what?"

He knits his eyebrows together and sits back in the booth. "You have a point."

"Uh-huh." I finish my sandwich and sip my coffee, watching him carefully. "I need you to promise me that you will not pursue this, at least not until we wrap this up with Heather Martin."

He scrapes a piece of omelet through his hash browns and nods. "Fine. I won't talk to her until we wrap up Heather Martin."

That's not good enough. But why am I trying to protect Sims? What if Sims really is up to no good? What was in that folder he seemed to be hiding? No, Boyle. Don't let Tom's paranoia infect you. Sims is just doing his job. He wasn't hiding the folder. He was just making copies. "Let's go find Derek Struthers."

He takes a last bite then stands before throwing a twenty on the table. "You've got lunch," he says, pointing at me.

"Uh-huh." I pull my jacket on and grab my messenger bag. "I'm driving."

We're silent on the way to the car and for most of the drive to Edgewater. It's unusual, but I try not to think too much about it. Goran and I have had plenty of disagreements over the years, but they're usually short-lived. I hope the Sims thing isn't going to be a problem. Underneath it all, I hope that he's not misdirecting his feelings about my testifying against Grimes onto Sims. Everyone seems to be ignoring the Grimes case, and it's weirding me out a little.

I slow the car on West Eighty-Fifth and creep up to the address. It's an older, well-kept two-story house on a street with many of the same. At the end of the street is an elementary school and a park—all in all, it's a nice neighborhood.

Goran unlatches his seat belt. "What's the plan?"

"We see if he's home and pretend we're investigating the extortion. We ask him a few questions and gauge his response. If he seems hinky, we go from there."

He nods and pushes his door open. I follow suit then round the back of the car to meet him, and we walk up to the front door together. He knocks three times on the door then rings the doorbell. I glance around, taking note of the Halloween decorations, the fall flowers, and the fact that someone takes good care of the place. On the mailbox is a placard that reads Derek Struthers & Janelle McArdle.

There's movement behind the door, and we both take a step back.

A thirty-something blonde answers, holding a toddler on her hip. "Well, this can't be good," she says with a bright smile. "What can I do for you?" Her hair is in a messy bun, and she's wearing yoga attire.

The toddler squirms, and she sets him down but grabs his hand to stop him from running out the door.

"We're here from CDP." Goran holds out his ID. "I'm Detective Goran, and this is Detective Boyle. We're looking for Derek Struthers. Is he available?"

Her smile falls. "Um, no, he's not here. He's at work. What is this about?"

"We just have a few questions," Goran says. "It shouldn't take long. Mind telling us where he works?"

She pulls her phone out of a pocket with her free hand, and I notice a substantial diamond on her ring finger. "Let me get him on the phone. I can't imagine what would happen if you showed up at his work."

Why would a guy with money hang out with Anders Andersen? It has to be related to the bondage clubs.

"Why would that be a problem?" Goran asks.

The toddler squirms and finally bites her. "Jimmy! Stop it right now." She turns to us. "Hold on. I need to put him in his swing. I'll be right back."

"Can we come in?" Goran asks.

She picks Jimmy up and hesitates—only briefly, but it's definitely a hesitation—before allowing us inside. "Stay there," she says. She disappears down the hall with the child, giving us time to look around.

The house appears to have been renovated recently. Everything is nicely painted and well-kept. To our right, Jimmy's toys are scattered on a blanket in the living room, which is filled with light and tasteful midcentury furniture. Above the mantel is a clock that reads 10:10 a.m., and in the fireplace is an ornamental candle arrangement that probably cost a fortune at Pottery Barn. To my left, there's a door that must go to the garage. I step into the entryway to the living room and catch a glimpse of the woman placing the toddler in a swing that hangs between the living room and dining room. From here, I can see that the dining room is tastefully decorated too. She catches my eye, and I smile then move back into the hallway.

The kitchen must be down the hall to the left, across from another entrance to the dining room, and there's probably a three-season room out back. Between here and there is a door that likely goes to the basement. At the end of the hall, a door is ajar, and I catch a glimpse of a pedestal sink. Must be a bathroom.

Jimmy emits a happy squeal, and the blonde traipses back into the hallway to talk to us. "What is this about?" she asks again.

I notice the phone in the pocket of her leggings. I know as sure as I'm alive that she texted Struthers to give him the heads-up, but I need to figure out what to do with that—she could be involved.

Goran adopts his good-cop voice. "We just have a couple of questions. It's completely routine."

"Where does he work?" I ask.

"He's a contractor—we own McArdle and Sons. Right now, he's working on building a house in Richfield."

I pull out my notebook. "Derek Struthers is your husband? And Jimmy is your son?"

She nods and looks away.

"Why would it be a problem for us to ask him a couple of questions?" Goran asks, still in his good-cop voice.

I'm going for neutral today—at least so far.

She crosses her arms over her chest. "He's meeting with the homeowners, and things haven't exactly gone very well."

"In what way?"

She sighs. "You'd better come in. I need to keep an eye on Jimmy, and we might as well just sit down and talk."

Because Derek Struthers is on his way, because you texted him, I don't say. It strikes me that Derek is the one meeting the homeowners, even though Janelle's name is on the business. *Where are the "sons"? I bet she can't wait to hand the reins to little Jimmy one day.*

She leads us to the dining room and fusses with Jimmy for a minute before gesturing for us to sit down. *I would bet money that he told her to keep us occupied until he gets here.*

Goran makes a face at the toddler, who smiles. "How old is Jimmy?"

"Eighteen months yesterday," she replies. She undoes her hair then puts it back into a messy bun. "Why do you need to talk to Derek?"

Goran and I exchange a glance, and I try to communicate my inkling that she could be involved in the extortion—maybe the murder. "We're investigating a homicide, and we hope that he can give us some information about a person of interest," I reply.

She leans back in her chair. "So he's *not* a person of interest?"

"Not at this time, no." I hear Julia's voice in my head, reminding me that all we have is a computer folder with an initial.

"Who is the person of interest?"

Jimmy shrieks, and she turns to him, smiles, and waves.

"We can't really say."

It goes on like this for several more minutes, and we don't get anywhere. Suddenly, a loud knock on the back door makes all of us jump. "Who could that be?" Janelle muses. "I'll be right back."

Why would he knock on his own door? And how did he get here from Richfield so quickly?

I hear a woman's distinctive voice. "Where the fuck is he?"

"Shit, Goran, it's Winona," I whisper as I get to my feet.

"Holy hell." He moves past me and into the kitchen.

I feel strange leaving Jimmy alone, so I stay with him. "Hey, buddy. What's going on?" I've never been especially gifted at talking to babies.

He coos and holds his hands out as if he's asking me to pick him up.

"Better just stay there, little guy."

There's a loud crash in the kitchen. "Boyle, get in here!" Goran shouts.

"Be right back, Jimmy." I slide into the kitchen to see Goran between Janelle and Winona with his arms extended, holding them away from one another.

"Winona, what a pleasant surprise," I say. "How about you chill out for a minute so we can avoid having to take you back downtown? No repeats of yesterday, okay?"

"Fuck this bitch," she says in a low growl.

"No, fuck you!" Janelle shouts. She struggles against Goran's hand, but he has her backed into the refrigerator.

"Let's everybody just calm down, okay?" I move toward Winona. "Let's all just calm down, and we can have a little chat." *What the hell is going on here?*

Winona takes a breath and backsteps through the outside door. "This was a mistake. I'm sorry. I'll leave."

"Yeah, you can get your trashy ass the fuck off my property." Janelle tries to get by Goran, but she doesn't have a chance.

"Ma'am, please," he says.

I follow Winona through the back door, leaving my partner to deal with the high-strung yoga mom.

"Shit." She turns away, shaking her head. "Goddamn it."

I guide her down the stairs of a wooden deck and over to a patio set that sits on a stone patio next to a swing set in the backyard. "C'mon. Tell me what's going on here."

She bows her head, and the unmistakable rise and fall of her shoulders tells me that she's crying.

"Winona, let's have a seat."

She takes a seat facing the back fence, and I angle a chair next to her so that I can see the back door of the house. I catch Goran giving me a thumbs-up through the glass and relax a little.

"I never should have come here." She sobs.

I awkwardly pat her on the shoulder. "How do you know these people? What are you doing here?"

She sputters and sighs then wipes her eyes with a sleeve. "She's my other sister."

"So all of that before about not knowing much about Derek Stru—"

"Yeah, of course I know him. I didn't tell you before because talking about that asshole makes me physically ill. He took the fucking company from us. It's McArdle *and Sons*, right? Well, our peach of a dad never had a son, so he left it to that asshole when he died."

Jesus, that sucks.

"She was always his favorite, with her perfect fucking little Barbie self and life." She gestures around. "Look at this place. I would love a place like this. But it's not like fucking *Anders* would ever have been in the will. Derek did what he had to do, the fucker."

"What does that mean?"

"It means that he married a much younger woman and angled for the company, which he got. They're loaded. Do they help us? No. And that's exactly why Anders was trying to blackmail those other people. We don't even have enough to pay utilities, and here they are. I came here to demand what's rightfully mine. We need fifty thousand to pay off our debts, and then we can get the fuck out of this fucking city for good."

I'm no family counselor, but this sounds like a shit show. "Let me get this straight. Janelle is your sister, and Derek is your brother-in-law. They own the business and don't give you a cut, so you came here today to demand money?"

She nods. "If you knew anything about our shitty family, you'd get it. I was supposed to be the one to go to college, but no. Of course Janelle goes to college. I was supposed to be the one to have a baby. Nope. Not me. It's all her. I was supposed to be the one to inherit the business. Nope, nope, nopety—Dad gave it to them because he liked Derek better than Anders." She shakes, and her face gets red. She's making fists.

"That really, really sucks, Winona."

"You have no idea how much. Yesterday just about pushed me over the edge."

"But Derek and Anders hang out? They're still friends?"

She nods. "Anders is a fucking bastard. They all are. I'm gonna get out of here for good, start a new life somewhere. I just need the money to do it."

The mass of men lead lives of quiet desperation, my dad used to say, quoting Thoreau.

"Why doesn't an internet search of Derek lead to McArdle and Sons?" It's not the most sensitive thing to ask, but it's been needling at me.

"Because the whole thing is in her stupid fucking name. Keep it in the family and all. Technically, she owns it, but the whole idea was that Derek would run it. Now, I guess it'll go to Jimmy one day." She softens. "I do like that kid." I follow her glance to the back door, but it's quiet inside the house.

My phone buzzes in my pocket, but I ignore it.

"Look, I lied. Anders was with me on Saturday night. We got in a huge fight, and I threatened to leave, but I just went and sat in the shop. Anders hung out inside, doing God knows what. I didn't see him leave at all. And I wasn't at a Halloween party." She gives me a sheepish glance. "I told Tiffany—who hates this bitch as much as I do—to lie for me. I really wanted to see that fucker go down. But not like this."

So Andersen is basically cleared. Back to the beginning. Shit.

A neighbor's dog starts to bark as a large black pickup truck pulls into the driveway. It stops in front of the garage, and I see McArdle and Sons emblazoned across the side in silver letters. A man kills the engine and pushes the door open. *Derek Struthers.* He's heavier than his BMV photo suggests—too heavy to be the other man in the sex photos, assuming they're recent.

His gaze is trained on his phone, so doesn't see us as he stomps to the back door.

Winona makes a move next to me, but I gently put a hand on her shoulder. "Let's not make this any worse than it is, okay?"

She nods.

"I'm gonna need to you come downtown and make a statement about your husband being at home the other night, okay? And other detectives are gonna want to talk to you about your husband's blackmail attempts."

She nods again.

There's a loud bang inside the house, and I'm terrified that someone has been shot. "Winona, come with me." I grab her and lead her to the driveway, where I point at the Charger. "Go sit in that car. Please don't go anywhere. Please." This is completely against protocol, but I can't leave Goran inside alone, and I don't trust Winona not to freak out again if I take her back inside.

"What? Am I in trouble?"

"No. Sit in the passenger seat if you want. Just please don't go anywhere."

She searches my face. "Okay."

There's another bang as I approach the door, so I draw my weapon. "Goran," I call through the screen.

"In here, Boyle."

Exhaling hard with relief, I push through the screen door and into the kitchen. Goran sits at the dining room table with Janelle and Derek Struthers, looking as though they're having a nice little chat.

I reholster the Glock. "What was that noise?"

Derek makes a goofy face at Jimmy. "Oh, sometimes the wind blows the doors shut upstairs. I always tell her to keep the windows closed, but—"

"I just love this weather," Janelle finishes.

What the fuck is this? How is she so calm after what just happened with Winona? I lean against the doorway.

"Did you get rid of Psycho Bitch?" Janelle asks.

I nod. "What was that about?"

"She's nuts. And her dirtbag husband is even more nuts. I don't want them around Jimmy." She turns to her husband. "I wish you would stop talking to them."

He shrugs.

"So you maintain that you were *not* with Anders Andersen on Saturday night?" Goran asks Derek.

"No, I wasn't. We hang out sometimes, but I've been trying to put some distance there. The guy's a weird one."

"What do you mean, 'weird'?" Goran asks.

Derek blinks rapidly. "He's into some kooky stuff is all. And he was trying to get money from a bunch of people around town."

My phone buzzes again, so I excuse myself and step into the kitchen to check it. I have two text messages from Roberts. *Leather*

& Lace isn't the right bondage club. Heading back to the squad. and *What's happening on your end?*

I tap out a reply. *Winona Andersen alibied her husband. Tell Fishner. Kicking the extortion to the districts.*

I glance at their refrigerator and notice all of the happy-looking family photos, pictures of Jimmy at various stages, and magnets advertising McArdle and Sons. Then I stand in the doorway.

"'Get money' how?" Goran asks.

Good to get as many on the witness list as we can before we send Andersen's case to district detectives.

Derek looks from Goran to Janelle, who nods slowly, and back to Goran. "He cooked up this whole scheme. Winona could be involved too. So could that oddball guy he hangs out with. What's that guy's name, honey?"

"Paul something or other."

The hairs on the back of my neck come to attention. *Greenwade?* Goran glances at me.

"Can you tell us what you know about the scheme?" I ask. This has gone from verifying an alibi to something entirely different.

The man looks at his son then at his wife. "Honey, will you take Jimmy upstairs?"

I can't tell if he's trying to protect the woman or the kid. I take a step back into the kitchen to text my friend Leah Ramos, who investigates financial crimes. *Got a good one for you, complete with two, maybe three witnesses.*

Janelle nods, stands, pulls Jimmy out of his swing, and leaves the room.

"He's into kinky stuff. He's a member at sex clubs. I have no idea how Winona doesn't know—maybe she does. I don't know." Derek looks embarrassed. "I only know because I was watching their dog back in February and opened a trunk in their house, looking for a blanket—they never turn the furnace on. I know I shouldn't have, but I looked at the computer, and... Well, I found things that made me uncomfortable. Which is why we don't hang out much anymore."

"And you aren't involved in any sex clubs?" I ask from the kitchen.

His jaw drops. "No! Of course not!"

"What about the 'scheme,' as you called it?" Goran asks.

My phone buzzes with a text from Ramos. *Send me the deets.*

I do. Then I step forward into the dining room. "Mr. Struthers, let's cut to the chase. Can you verify your whereabouts on the evening of Saturday the twenty-fifth?"

Goran glares at me, but Andersen's attempted blackmail isn't our crime to solve, nor is the McArdle family drama. Time is moving quickly, and our chance of finding Heather Martin's killer is dropping by the hour. Something is needling me about Greenwade—sometimes the least likely suspect is actually a homicidal maniac.

Struthers blinks at me. "I was home with Janelle and Jimmy. We watched *Frozen* and fell asleep early."

"And you didn't leave the house at any time?"

He shakes his head. "Not till the next morning, when I got up to go to the gym."

"Can anyone other than your wife verify that you were home?"

He squints as if he's thinking. "The security system will show that no one left. I can get those records for you if you want. What is this about? I thought you were investigating Anders's blackmail ideas."

"We are. Another detective will be by shortly to follow up. Her name is Leah Ramos. Thanks for your time, sir. We'll be going now."

Goran stands and obviously tries not to glower at me.

Derek stands and gestures for us to follow him to the front door. "Let me know if I can help with anything," he says as he pulls the door open.

"Thank you," I reply. I pull a business card from my wallet and write Ramos's number on the back. "Give her a call to set a time."

"Okay." He looks concerned.

"Thanks again for your time," Goran says.

We turn to leave, and I hear Jimmy squeal upstairs before Derek Struthers closes the door behind us.

"What was that about?" Goran grumbles on the way to the car.

"That was about not wasting time on people who didn't kill Heather Martin."

"You don't know that."

"Goran, they all have alibis. We need to kick Andersen to Ramos and start over." I flex my jaw and feel tension creeping up the back of my skull.

He checks his phone. "Fishner moved the briefing to one o'clock."

I nod at the car. Winona sits quietly in the back. "Then we should figure out what to do with her."

"She's not under arrest, and you just said you don't want to investigate this case."

"I said I don't want to investigate a *blackmail* case. I have every intention of investigating the homicide."

"I say we kick her loose and let Ramos follow up with her."

I narrow my eyes then walk to the car. I open the passenger door and let Winona out. "Winona, I need you to drive to this address"—I scrawl the address of the third-district station on the back of a card—"and ask for Detective Ramos."

She takes the card. "Yeah, maybe."

I put my hands on my hips. "Just do it. Let him take the fall for what he did, and get the hell out of Cleveland."

She nods and looks as though she might cry. "Thank you," she whispers.

"You're welcome. Take care of yourself," I call after her.

Goran gets in the car and slams the door. I watch Winona walk to her car, open the door, get in, and drive away, then I join him in the Charger.

"What the hell, Liz?"

"What are you so pissed off about?" I put on my sunglasses and start the car. "They didn't have shit to tell us about our case. Ramos will take it from here. I'm saving time so we can get back to our actual jobs." I ease away from the curb.

I feel him staring.

"What?" I ask as I hit the blinker to turn left on Detroit Avenue.

He sighs. "I hate it that you're right. I hate that this guy isn't who Sims said he was and that it's a dead end. I hate everything about this case. I hate what's going on with you and the whole department. I just hate it. I need to take some vacation days. It's getting to me."

I make the turn then swing into a driveway, push my sunglasses up onto my head, and turn to face him. "Goran, relax. Whatever happens with Grimes has nothing to do with this. Let's get back to the squad and do paperwork on all of this until it's time for the briefing. It's all good, partner. Okay?"

He nods, and I back out of the driveway.

"I still don't like it," he says under his breath. "It reminds me of the bad old days. And you owe me lunch."

CHAPTER 16

We get back to the squad in time for Fishner's one o'clock briefing. Tom and I are last into the squad room—Fishner stands at the head of the table next to Jo Micalec, with Sims and Roberts on either side. Becker is there too. I smile at her and take the seat next to Sims.

"What happened with Derek Struthers?" Fishner asks.

"His alibi is clear. Unfortunately, so are Andersen's and Greenwade's," I reply.

Becker stands and grabs her briefcase. "That's my cue. Let me know when you have evidence to indict. Liz, will you give me a call when you have a chance?"

I nod, and she exits the room. Goran glares at Sims, so I shoot my partner a look. He scrubs a hand across his face.

"Okay," Fishner says. She turns to Jo. "Where are we on physical evidence?"

"Well, the device"—she puts a photograph of the transponder on the screen—"isn't a recording device, so there's that." She chuckles. "I'm not usually wrong, but I was dead wrong on this one." She advances to a photograph of the inside of the thing. "It's actually an RFID chip, which I imagine opens or closes some kind of door."

"I knew it," I mutter. The question is what kind of door.

"There's good news too," Jo says. "We got DNA off of one of her fingernails. It'll be a couple of days, but if he's in the system, we'll get him that way."

"Great work," Fishner says.

"That's all I've got," Jo says. She looks at her watch. "I've got to get back, but I was around and figured you could hear it directly from me."

"Thanks, Jo," we all say.

She says goodbye, and Fishner turns to me. "What is happening with Andersen?" She puts his picture on the screen.

I give the download on Andersen and Struthers and almost scream when Goran makes a snide remark about the fallibility of technology. Sims rolls his eyes.

"All three of these guys are moving lower down the list of persons of interest," I say, leaning back in my chair. "Their alibis are relatively solid."

Fishner nods.

"I did let Leah Ramos know about Andersen. She should be following up with Struthers on the blackmail allegations later today. I'm expecting to hear from her soon about how she wants to handle the arrest, assuming there is one."

Fishner sits heavily in her seat. "Roberts and Sims, what did you get at Leather & Lace?"

Roberts expels a breath. "Nothing. It's not the right club. The owner gave me a membership list, and no one involved with this case, at least so far, is on the list."

So we have no suspects. Great.

Sims chimes in. "The club owner was surprisingly forthcoming. He said that Andersen used to frequent the place but hasn't been there in at least three years. And there's no Mistress Natalia there. Never has been. I asked whether they knew of a Mistress Natalia anywhere in the area, but they said no."

"So there's that," Fishner says. She squeezes the bridge of her nose then leans back in her chair, obviously frustrated.

"You want the good news?" Sims asks.

We all nod.

"I got the dump on her regular phone, which gives us a lot of information."

I narrow my eyes. "What about the sex app that Eric Martin used? Was that on her phone?"

Sims shakes his head. "Looks like it was mostly a business phone. My guess is that she used the burner for everything else."

"Think we need to look and see whether Andersen and Martin connected on the app at all?" I ask.

"Good call," Fishner says. "Sims, get on that this afternoon."

Goran, whose silence is becoming awkward, chomps his gum loudly.

"What's the plan for the rest of the day?" Fishner asks.

"I'm on the sex app," Sims says.

"I'm following up with Andersen's neighbors, just to make sure he's clear," Roberts replies.

"Boyle? Goran?"

"Paperwork and trying to figure out what club Andersen was affiliated with," I reply.

"I'm with her," Goran mutters.

My phone buzzes in my pocket. It's a text from Leah Ramos, which I read aloud: "*Keep him there. I'll arrest him this afternoon. Thanks for the tip. Your guy Struthers has good info.*"

"Roberts, act fast with those neighbors," Fishner says. "All right. Get to work. Keep me posted. The captain wants a full report tomorrow morning."

"Ten-four, L-T," Sims says, standing.

We file out of the room and back to our desks. Per her request, I call Julia Becker, but it goes to voicemail.

A COUPLE OF HOURS LATER, I've finished working on the Struthers report and am thumbing through our vic's text messages when Julian Martin, her son, returns my call. He leaves me a message while I'm in the bathroom. "Detective Boyle, this is Julian Martin. I can't believe what's happened. I'm trying to get time off work to come back to Cleveland, but maybe you could come to me or talk on the phone. Oh my God. Anyway, call me back when it's convenient. Thanks."

For some reason, I was expecting the opposite, given their mother's phone records—it seems like she was a lot closer to Elise. But text messages tell us only so much. Most of what Elise sent are updates about school, various things about a guy named Sam, worries about one of her sorority sisters smoking too much pot. Martin's replies, written using correct grammar and punctuation, seem supportive enough. There's a lot of "You can do it!" and "I want to meet this Sam" and "Katie has problems, and they aren't your problems." An occasional smiley-face emoji. Lots of xoxo, that kind of thing.

I guess it looks typical, but then again, I'm not sure what typical mother-daughter relationships look like. I just gave my mom my cell phone number, like, six months ago, she recently learned how to text, and I sure as shit don't text her about my life. I briefly consider what I'm going to do about my brother, Christopher, but there isn't time for that right now.

Anyway, I call Julian back from the landline, so that "Cleveland Division of Police" will show up on his caller ID. He answers on the second ring, and I introduce myself.

"Detective," he says. "Oh my God."

"I'm very sorry for your loss, Mr. Martin," I reply. "Thanks for calling back."

"Please call me Julian," he says, almost in a whisper. "I'm so sorry I didn't call right away. This has been a lot to process."

"Julian, I'm sorry to have to do this, but I do have some questions. First, though, can you tell me where you were on Saturday night, into Sunday morning?" The questions I have would be much better asked in person. It's hard to gauge someone's reaction—whether he's telling the truth or lying or some combination—over the phone. It also surprises me that he's willing to talk to me, given that he hasn't seen my credentials.

I hear him take one of those shuddering breaths that mean he's trying not to cry. "I was with someone," he whispers. "I'm sorry. Can you hold on?" He doesn't wait for me to answer before I can tell that he's walking somewhere, likely with his phone at his side.

I sit back in my chair and glance around the squad room at my fellow detectives, who appear to be engrossed in work.

"Okay, I'm sorry," he says. "I'm not out at work, so I came outside. I was with my boyfriend on Saturday night. We went to a club here—I live in Lansing, Michigan—and then back to his house."

I ask for the boyfriend's name and phone number, and Julian gives it to me.

"Are you going to call him?" he asks.

"It's a formality," I say. Then I verify that he's a civil engineer for the state of Michigan, that he's lived in Michigan since he enrolled at the University of Michigan—his mother's alma mater, and it's not lost on me that Elise attends Ohio State and they're huge rivals—six years ago. It's best to ask people easy questions and get them feeling comfortable before moving into harder ones. "What can you tell me about your mom?" I ask. "Any hobbies, friends other than your parents' mutual friends, places she liked to go, that sort of thing?"

Goran stands and hands me a Post-it: *Going down to the records office.*

I give him a two-fingered salute.

"She was married to her job. She was just absolutely committed to it. That's part of why this is so fucking hard for me—we didn't talk enough. All I know about any of this is what my sister told me, which she heard from my dad, who I guess talked to some police captain or something."

I squeeze my eyes closed and rake my free hand through my hair, feeling my frustration grow by the minute and wondering why I'm not angrier.

"She's always been a huge mystery to me," he adds. "Even growing up. It was like this strange woman was there in my house. I mean, she's my mom and I look like her and all that, but she never let anyone get close. It wasn't like other people's relationships with their moms. When I got older, we became friends, but she still kept everyone at a distance. Even Elise—they texted all the time, but Mom never shared anything with anyone. It was all one-sided."

Fishner walks over to the crime board and puts a check mark after Anders Andersen's name, meaning that he's no longer a suspect. Roberts must have gotten ahold of the neighbors. Then she steps back to survey the board for a minute.

"Hello?" Julian Martin asks.

I swivel in my chair so that I can better watch what Fishner is doing. "Do you talk to your sister much?"

"Maybe once every couple of weeks," he replies. "And if you want to know if I talk to my dad, the answer is no. He can't deal with the fact that I'm gay. I'm, quote, not his son anymore."

Answering the unasked question. Interesting. This guy must really need to talk if he's doing all this sharing with a faceless, at least to him, Cleveland detective.

Sounds like it's gonna be a fun funeral. "When was the last time you spoke with your mother?" I ask.

A car door slams. "About two weeks ago," he replies. "She called and said she and my dad were getting divorced, that she was filing soon but he didn't know yet. Fucking philandering asshole. She just wanted me and Elise to know first, I guess."

I sit forward in my chair and ask him a few more questions, but he doesn't know anything else. When I lean back, Fishner is in her office with the door closed.

"There's something I want you to know, though," he adds as we're wrapping up. "She was a really good person. I mean, we might not have talked all the time or been what some would call a normal family, but my mom was a good person. I have the letters to prove it. When my dad disowned me, she wrote to me all the time." He chuckles sadly. "I never could figure out why she wrote me letters instead of emails or texts, but it always meant something to me. And now I never get to tell her that. At least I still have the letters, I guess."

I wonder what was in those letters. "Can I see them?"

"Um... I'd rather you not, unless you really need to."

I don't really need to.

"She was a police officer a long time ago. You know that, right?"

I nod even though he can't see me. "Yes... Uh, yes."

"Well, she left the department after she was sexually assaulted—gang-raped—by a bunch of other cops. She'd always wanted to go to law school, and she figured that was her opportunity."

Goddamn it. Sexual assault by a bunch of other cops is not what I want to be investigating. And why is he telling me this? Maybe he needs to get it off his chest.

"Anyway, she worked at the prosecutor's office—I'm sure you know all of this, so I'll skip ahead. When she and Max Sellers started their defense practice, she did it for noble reasons. It wasn't to make money. But when she ended up being really good at it—so good that Elise and I barely saw her—she made a lot of money, which my asshole father spent most of. My mom lived surprisingly frugally, at least she did when I last saw her."

I let him keep talking, hoping he gives me something to go on and simultaneously wondering why it is that he's telling all of this to a stranger.

"It always upset her, at least according to the letters, and I should reiterate that all of what I'm telling you came from the letters, that Sellers turned into such a slimeball. Honestly, he's the reason why I didn't go to law school—I didn't want to become a greedy bastard like he did. They ended up bringing other slimeballs into the practice, and it always upset her because she really cared about doing the right thing. That was one thing I learned from her: just do the right thing, no matter the cost."

I shiver a little and expel a breath. *I could get a warrant for the letters, but maybe we don't need them. Still. They're there if we do.*

I tell him to call me if he thinks of anything and thank him again for getting back to me.

Regardless of Fishner's insistence that we leave him alone, or her weird riddles from before, it's time to go talk to Eric Martin. I hope he's still at work. That way, we aren't being directly insubordinate—we won't be "bothering him at home." *Does Fishner know about the divorce?*

When I stand and swing on my jacket, I notice that my boss is on the phone with her office door closed, so I grab my gun from my locker and head out. I text Goran and tell him to meet me at the car.

My phone starts to blow up as soon as I slide behind the wheel. Julia Becker, Fishner, Goran. They're all calling at the same time. Cora sends me a text message telling me to call when I have a minute. *What the fuck?*

I answer Goran. "Get down here," I say. "We need to go talk to Eric Martin. Now. I just found out from the son that our vic was filing for divorce."

"You haven't heard." There's something in his voice that I don't recognize.

The call goes dead as he opens the passenger door. His face is tense and worried. My phone keeps vibrating in my lap.

"What?" I ask. "Grimes?"

He pulls the door closed behind him. "Acquitted."

"Ah, shit. Okay." My stomach turns into a cold lead ball. I close my eyes and take a deep breath before starting the car. "Think it's ever gonna stop raining?" I ask as I turn right on Euclid. I feel him watching my profile, but I don't turn to make eye contact with him.

"Liz."

He's hoping that I don't lose my shit like I used to have a tendency to do. I won't. Not anymore.

"Julian Martin says his mom was planning to divorce Eric Martin. We need to ask some questions about that, given the goddamn fucking dead-end shit show that this case is turning out to be."

"Grimes won't be reinstated," Goran replies. "The department is going to make an example of him. Especially with the DOJ stuff."

Shit, right. I forgot I'm supposed to talk to that guy tomorrow. I brake behind an old woman in an old Honda. "There are gonna be riots," I say. I finally look at him, and whatever he sees must upset him, because he reacts as though I've said something truly screwed up. "What?"

"You don't have to pretend to be okay. We've been through this before. You can just cut it out, all right?"

I turn back to the road. "Fine. I'm not okay. I'm not okay for a lot of reasons. But I'm also not going to worry about being gang-raped, if we want to return to his little threat, and I'm not going to obsess over this. He's a dick. He lost his job. The end." I accelerate into the left lane to pass the old woman. *Heather Martin was gang-raped by other cops, or so she told her son.*

"Are you surprised?" he asks.

"Surprised by what? Surprised by the acquittal? Fuck no. People never convict cops." I slap the steering wheel. "But the fact that most of the department seems to have my back, that no one has—at least yet—acted like an asshole? That, I'm surprised about." *Heather Martin became a prosecutor because she couldn't be a cop anymore afterward.*

He stays quiet.

"You know I wouldn't have testified, right? I never would have said anything." I guess maybe we should have talked about this before now. *Heather Martin became a defense attorney because she believed in doing the right thing.*

He takes a breath. "It's not like it used to be," he says in a soft voice. "Twenty years ago? This never would have happened, because we weren't that kind of department then."

"Oh, come on, Tom. We both know we've always been that kind of department. It just used to be hush-hush. What about all that shit that happened in the nineties with the female cops?" These days, especially with the MeToo stuff, it would be all over the media, in the same way the Grimes case has been. Hashtag rapegate or something. I don't know a lot about it, but I do know that there was a band of older, male cops who used their rank to intimidate, harass, and sometimes assault female ones. No one ever came forward—it's just department lore. *Heather Martin never came forward about the assault.*

He cracks his window in spite of the rain. "Yeah, okay. I guess you're right."

"What's different is that people are done putting up with that shit," I say. "We're under a microscope, and problem is? We deserve to be."

"Ah, c'mon. Let's not go that far. You know how much more paperwork we're gonna have to do now, just if somebody thinks we looked at 'em cross-eyed?"

I nod. "Yeah, and it's too bad for cops like us, and I'm sure as I'm alive that I'll bitch my ass off about it when it happens. But maybe it'll get us to think twice, you know?" I stop at a traffic light and turn to look at him. *Just do the right thing, no matter the cost.*

He doesn't look like he wants to have to think twice. He chomps his gum then rolls it through his mouth to the other side then back again.

"You know what I'm saying, right? This isn't some kind of trea-son thing. I'm a fan of the blue wall of silence or whatever it's called these days. But guys like that have to be stopped." I roll my shoulders back against the seat and notice how tense they are.

"What's the deal with Eric Martin? Did you tell Fishner what we're doing?"

I fill him in, complete with the "No, I didn't tell Fishner any-thing" part of the answer. She can be pissed about it later.

I glance at the dash clock. It's 4:25, and I vaguely wonder whether Eric Martin will still be at work. My phone doesn't stop buzzing the entire way to his office in Mayfield Heights.

CHAPTER 17

Arbor Health is housed in a nondescript concrete-and-glass building off Mayfield Road. I pull into the parking lot and immediately notice two things: one, almost all of the spaces closest to the door are marked as reserved, and two, no one has done landscaping here in a long time. "This place is a dump," I mutter.

Goran keeps looking at me as if he wants to say something. I swing the Charger into a reserved space near the door and kill the engine. I grab my phone from the console but don't look at it. I shut it off.

He reaches for my arm. "Boyle."

I make eye contact. "Don't look at me like that. Please don't look at me like that. We have a job to do here. Our only agenda is to talk to Eric Martin and figure out whether he killed his wife—or had her killed. This isn't about me, and it isn't about you. C'mon, Tom. I really need you in the game here. You've been a shit for a week now. Enough's enough."

He blinks, and I swear I see tears, but he wills them away. He removes his hand from my arm. "Okay. Back in the game. Sorry about all of that. You know how it is. I mean, it's Lowell. It's Sims. It's the whole thing." He looks at his own phone. "We have Martin's credit card records," he says.

I unbuckle my seat belt and shove my door open, and he follows suit. He stares at me across the top of the car. "Please stop looking at me like that. I'm not gonna ask you again."

He blinks, and we round the front of the car and walk to a side entrance. "What's the plan?" he asks.

"Follow my lead."

In the generic lobby, I locate the directory. Arbor Health is listed as occupying the top two floors of the five-story building, with the main office on the fourth floor.

Goran hits the button for the elevator. When it arrives, several suits get out and push past us, and when we get in, I'm hit by the smell of strong perfume. "You'd think it would wear off during the workday," I mutter.

"Huh?"

"The perfume. Do you smell it? It's atrocious. It's giving me a headache." I squeeze the back of my neck then roll my head from side to side. As the elevator doors slide closed, I catch a distorted glimpse of myself in the shiny metal and realize my shoulders have risen about two inches. I take a deep breath and roll them back and down before turning to my partner. "Julian Martin said, not in so many words, that his dad is a complete asshole. Serial philanderer, homophobe, general stupid rich white dude. Our vic filed for divorce two weeks before she was killed."

"He wasn't on the list of Andersen's blackmail victims."

"No, but she was. Maybe she was cheating too."

The elevator dings, and the doors open to reveal a hallway with two glassed-in suites at either end. The one to the left is in frosted glass, and the one to the right is in clear glass, which reveals what looks to be a reception desk behind the double doors. I head right with Goran at my side.

Once in the lobby of Arbor Health, I put on my best friendly-cop act for the young woman and man behind the desk. "Hi there," I say in my Candy Cooper voice.

"Hi, how can we help you?" the man asks.

The woman presses a button on her phone headset and turns away.

"We're here for an appointment with Eric Martin. Is he in?" I don't stop smiling.

"Huh," the guy replies. "It's just about time for him to leave. Let me see." He taps a button on his phone headset. "Mr. Martin, your appointment is here. Oh, I see. Okay. I'll find out." He turns to me and pushes up his rimless glasses. "What is your name?"

"I'm Detective Elizabeth Boyle, CDP. But I'm here because I just got an inheritance and am interested in investing in Arbor Health. My boss, Lieutenant Jane Fishner, suggested that I talk to Mr. Martin directly." *Shit, now she's gonna be really mad.*

He repeats the information, waits for a beat, and stands. He points down the hall and at the corner office. "Mr. Martin is right in there. You and your husband go ahead and help yourself to a bottled water on the way."

Goran is my husband. What a riot. "Thanks so much. I didn't catch your name?"

"Adam," he replies.

"Thanks, Adam," I say in a singsong voice as we head down the hall.

Once we're out of earshot, Goran actually chuckles. "What's for dinner tonight, wifey?"

"You *wish* we were married."

He shudders. "Not really."

We both laugh, and I'm grateful for the moment.

Martin's office door is ajar, but I knock, anyway, to keep up my act.

"Mr. Martin, hi!" I extend a hand to the tall, slim man. "I'm Liz. My boss, Lieutenant Fishner, suggested that we talk to you."

He shakes my hand, and I notice his watch again. It looks heavy, and I wonder whether it's uncomfortable to wear. He isn't wearing a wedding ring and doesn't appear to be particularly distraught. "You want to invest?" All business. What a surprise.

"Do you mind if I close the door?" Goran asks.

"Sure, go ahead. Have a seat." Martin crosses from behind his desk and gestures at a small table with four chairs around it. "Can I get you anything to drink?"

Such hospitality. The office is completely void of family photos. "I'm fine."

"I'm good too," Goran says.

"I'm so happy that Jane sent you my way," Martin says as he sits. He carefully crosses his legs in his chair.

"Oh, me too," I reply. "This seems like such a good opportunity." *He doesn't recognize us from the squad room the other day because he doesn't pay attention to people who can't do something for him.*

"Well, it is. Let me tell you a little about our company." He prattles on for about five minutes, talking up what a great firm his is, and we should really work with him because they're based in Cleveland, and this and that.

I make interested noises throughout.

"I've also got some connections on city council—I was elected last year."

"Oh, congratulations." I have to force myself to say it.

"So how much are you looking to invest?"

"Why didn't you report your wife missing?" I ask.

Goran takes a breath.

"What?"

"When did you notice she was gone?"

His eyes go wide, then he blinks. He starts to cross his arms then apparently thinks better of it. "Wait—what?"

I have to admit that watching his indignant surprise is satisfying in some sick way. "And why haven't you talked to your son? He seems awfully distraught, which is kind of what I would expect, given the circumstances of your wife's death."

His face reddens, and he stands. "What is this?" He gives in, crosses his arms, then uncrosses them immediately. "I will not answer any questions about my late wife without my lawyer present. This is preposterous."

"Listen, Mr. Martin," Goran says. "This is completely routine. We just have a couple of follow-up questions from the other day."

"If it's completely routine, explain why I feel so attacked. And why did you lie to me when you came in?"

"I'm sorry, sir," I say in my witness voice. "I got carried away." I stop myself from laughing, and it occurs to me that I'm being mean to this guy not because I think he killed his wife but because he oozes privilege, and I'm taking sick pleasure in watching him squirm.

"I am under advice from counsel not to speak to the police."

"Who's your attorney?" Goran asks.

"Martin Sellers, of course. We all go way back. Now, if you'll excuse me, I have work to do. I will add that my alibi has checked and that I'm completely innocent. I have done nothing wrong, and I'm sure that your lieutenant didn't send you here for this. What is this?" He looks as if he might cry. "She won't like it when I tell her what you've done."

I stand. "We're just trying to piece together what happened to Heather."

He squeezes the bridge of his nose. "Aren't we all," he mutters.

I glance at his desk, and behind his briefcase sits a transponder that looks a lot like the one we recovered from Martin's SUV. "What's that for?"

He follows my gesture then looks stricken. "Uh, it's... Uh... I really need to talk to my attorney."

A bell rings in the back of my head, and I kick myself when I realize it should have gone off a long time ago. I know what our next move is.

"Thanks for your time, Mr. Martin. Sorry to bother you." It wasn't exactly the outcome I'd been hoping for, but then again, I'm not sure what I was hoping for.

He makes a couple of noises but doesn't say anything.

"Sir?"

"Wait," he finally says. "Look, I really do want you to find her killer, so I'll say this. Sellers will kill me, but I'll say it, anyway. She was more distant even than usual. It started about a year ago. She was always distant—I never knew where I stood with her—but it really ramped up. She was barely ever home. She worked constantly, or that's what she told me. I was convinced she was hiding things from me—she even installed FireVault on her laptop—so I did what any man would do."

"You mean you began having an affair?"

He scrubs a hand across his face. "I had more than one affair. I mean that I began a real relationship with Abby."

"Abby Kasinowitz?" She's his alibi, at least according to Fishner.

He nods. "I thought Heather was having her secretary lie to me. She can't possibly have been working twenty hours a day."

"Is there anything else you can think of that might help the investigation?"

He shakes his head. "I'm just sorry," he says.

"Sir, have you looked around in her home office?" I'm softening but only because I want him to give me information.

He nods then squeezes the bridge of his nose.

"Did you find anything unusual?"

"Like what? What would I have found? She kept everything locked up at work, in her laptop, that kind of thing. She didn't share much with me. She never really did, but over the past couple of years... You could drive a truck through the gap between us. I don't remember the last time we had a real conversation, let alone made love."

"Any photographs, that sort of thing?"

He shakes his head, and I glance at Goran, hoping that Good Cop will ask if we can look in her office ourselves.

"Thanks again for your time," my partner says.

I hand Martin a business card. "Please call if you think of anything."

He takes the card and nods.

Goran pushes through the door, and I follow, leaving the almost-bereaved husband standing in the middle of his office and likely wondering what just happened.

We thank the two at the front on our way out.

"What the hell was that all about?" Goran asks as we head to the elevator.

"I'm not sure, but I know what that stupid transponder is for."

He hits the button and gives me a questioning look.

"If memory serves, it allows the Rec Room—an S and M club on the West Side that I investigated when I was in Sex Crimes—to track who enters and exits the dungeon."

The elevator opens, and we step on. "The *dungeon*?"

I roll my eyes. "Goran, you act like you don't know anything about kink."

"I don't." He hits the ground floor button.

"In that case, the dungeon is where folks can indulge their wildest bondage fantasies. They're common in those kinds of clubs. And since Sims and Roberts got nothing from Leather & Lace—they probably don't have that kind of tracking system, anyway—my guess is that the Rec Room is a safe bet for our next set of questions."

He knits his eyebrows together. "Do you have any idea how much shit we're gonna get from the L-T for being here like this today?"

"Not if it leads somewhere. Seriously. Trust me."

"I was wondering when you were gonna go rogue," he mutters as the elevator doors open. "I had a feeling it would correspond with the verdict, and here we are."

We exit the elevator, and I stop in the lobby. "I am not 'going rogue,' and this has absolutely nothing to do with the verdict."

"Uh-huh, okay. Let's get back and explain ourselves before he has too much time to talk to her."

"You think he's calling her?"

"Of course. You saw the guy. We just ruined his whole day."

"You'd think his day would already be pretty shitty, given that his wife was brutally murdered in a cemetery."

"Yeah, you'd think."

WE HAVE TO PUSH THROUGH a gaggle of reporters to get inside. "Detective Boyle," Alexis Edwards from the *Plain Dealer* calls over the din, "do you have any comment about today's verdict?"

I resist the urge to flick them off. Goran holds out an arm and leads me to the steps.

"Fuck this," I mutter in the elevator.

"Yeah, that sounds about right," Goran replies, staring straight ahead.

Once we're back in the squad, Fishner summons us immediately. When we enter her office, she looks less red-faced than I'd expected.

"Sit down," she says. "Update me on this case. How does it stand with Eric Martin, whom I told you not to interview without me?"

I stop myself from wincing. "Look, we had to. It would have been egregious not to."

She balances her pen between her thumb and index finger, and Goran and I exchange the glance that means we're not quite sure what's coming.

"We did get out of him that Martin had been more distant than usual, starting just over a year ago. He said she's always been private—to the point where he said it seemed secretive, like she was hiding something. But he said she really pulled away last year. Claims that's when he started having the affair, though their son says he's been a philanderer for a long time."

"'Pulled away' in what way?"

I fill her in.

She sighs and gives me the tell-me-more look. Goran shifts next to me.

"We've got a lead to run down. There's a club over on the West Side. I think she was a member. I need to look into it. It's touchy and something we probably don't want the media to get wind of."

"Touchy how?" she asks.

I don't want to get into this right now. I hate explaining my instincts to her because then they stop making sense to me. "Look, it's probably nothing. I'm just checking it out as a formality. I'll keep you posted. But Eric Martin is cleared, at least in my mind. His security system backs him up, Kasinowitz backs him up, and his behavior today, although weird, seems consistent with who he is."

"Are you still operating under the premise that he might have had her killed?"

"It's not my gut," I reply. "I see no reason why he would do it, given that he's the one who was having the affair and the kids are grown."

"There's something else," she says.

I raise my eyebrows, more from the way the energy shifts in the room than anything she's saying to me. It goes from all business to something that I can't quite put my finger on.

Fishner sets her pen on her desk. "Heather Martin's credit card data shows that her Visa was used to pay for a room at the Renaissance on the night of her homicide."

"And?"

"I have Sims and Roberts investigating that lead."

"And?"

"Detectives, I am concerned about the publicity our squad is receiving, especially given today's verdict. You noticed the reporters outside, correct?" She doesn't wait for us to answer. "I will remind you to tread very carefully, given everything that's happening with this case, with Captain Carrothers, and with your Department of Justice inquiry. I hope that you will have your attorney present tomorrow for your questioning."

Carrothers should just let us do our jobs. She's talking like a politician again. I cross my arms in front of my chest and stare her down as the thin line of anger travels from my head to my chest. *Breathe, Boyle. Don't go back to your old ways. This is your boss.* I blink at her until she gives in.

"The captain—all of the brass, really—are worried. This case may go to Homicide. Wrap it up quickly if you want to clear it." She tosses the pen onto her desk.

"*What?* No—we're closing this one. What the hell is happening with Carrothers?" I ask. Before she can answer, I turn to Goran. "Will you back me up here?"

He looks incredulous. "I'm worried, too, Boyle. Grimes is out on the streets, and he made those threats, and the repor—"

I swear my face is going to explode. "Since when do we 'tread lightly' just because some asshole makes threats or reporters want to talk to us?"

Fishner appears to be working to conceal a strange look on her face.

"Are you going to let us do our fucking job or not?" As soon as it's out of my mouth, I regret it.

"The captain is concerned about this squad for reasons I'm sure I don't have to review with you right now, and I know you have a lot invested here. I can't imagine you in a regular homicide job, can you? So tell me what's happening with Maliq Sims and the Martina Lowell case."

I could be put on desk duty indefinitely, "for my own protection." They could kick us all to the districts. They could decimate the squad just for optics. He's been threatening it for a while now, ever since I pulled the trigger on that pedophile.

"What?" Goran asks tightly.

"He didn't do anything wrong," I say. "I talked to him about it. He was looking into Lowell because he thought he saw a pattern with her case and a cold one he's working as a favor to a friend."

Her face is stone.

"He should have made me aware of the cold case. Which he did not. You and I both know that sometimes my detectives need to be reminded of what authority looks like. There are consequences."

I stare at her for a beat. She's unwavering, and it freaks me out.

"Look, it was all a misunderstanding," Goran says. "I got upset, but then I realized he's just investigating it as a favor to a friend. It's water under the bridge. I'll talk to him."

She nods. "Don't be late for your appointment with the DOJ," she says to me. She puts her reading glasses on and picks up her pen. "Go home, Detectives."

I'm pretty much over it with all of these people.

Back at our desks, Goran tries to talk to me as the landline trills away. "I can't believe you narced on him, Tom. This is straight-up bullshit."

"I didn't."

"Then how does she know about the Lowell case?"

"I have no idea. Maybe she saw the murder book on his desk too."

"Uh-huh." I shut my lamp off and jam my iPad into my bag, resisting the urge to shove everything off my desk. "Well, if you get an idea, let me know. I'm leaving. See you tomorrow."

"I guess I'll do the report on the Martin interview."

"Yeah, I guess so." I turn to leave.

"Boyle, please be careful."

"I'm always careful, Goran. You know that. I'll see you tomorrow."

IN THE PASSAT, I SWITCH my phone back on. I have eight voicemails, but I skip through the messages from Cora, Josh, my mom, Fishner, and Alexis Edwards. I listen to Becker's message first, since she's the one with the legal expertise. "Liz, it's Julia. First off, please be careful. Don't do anything stupid. And just be honest with Briscoe. Marutiak"—my lawyer—"will have your back. Just don't say anything other than simple answers to his questions, and it'll be all right."

I tap on the next voicemail, which is from a number I don't recognize. Turns out, it's from Sheila, the intern at the law firm. She sounds scared. "D-D-Detective, I just want to let you know that I got a threatening text message. It said that if I talked to you again, what happened to Heather would happen to me too."

I call her back right away. "Hi, Sheila."

"Hold on," she replies.

I hear her walk down a hallway. "Did you recognize the number?"

"No, it was private."

"Did you recognize the voice?"

"No. It was a man's voice. He sounded drunk or like something was wrong with him. Do you think it was a real threat?"

"You never know. Do you have someone you can stay with? Family?"

"I can stay with my boyfriend, I guess."

"Do that. And let me know if you get any more threats."

"Okay. Thanks. I have to go."

Three beeps tell me that she's ended the call.

"Fuck it all," I mutter. Before I pull away, I text everyone else to tell them that I'm fine and not to worry. Then I call Jason Marutiak, my lawyer, to be sure that we're still on for tomorrow. We are.

CHAPTER 18

About forty minutes later, I pull up next to a nondescript brick building and kill the VW engine but not the stereo. I brought my own car because I'll probably follow orders and go home after this. I let the song finish then yank the key from the ignition.

The Rec Room is relatively deserted this early in the evening, at least upstairs. Back when I worked sex crimes, I ended up in the dungeon a couple of times for investigations, and I'm fairly certain that folks are down there at all hours of the day. Unless Martin was down there before she died, I don't care what people do behind closed doors.

I take a seat at the bar, which functions as sort of a gatekeeping lobby, if I'm remembering correctly, and scan my surroundings. It's dark but looks redecorated, maybe within the last couple of years. There's a dance area in the back, with colored lights in the floor, and a DJ booth. Tables sit in front of the staircase leading down, and on the other side of the room is a staircase that goes up. Everything is red and black—it's a stereotype, I guess—even the plush velvet sofas in the corner. It looks dark but otherwise normal to anyone who's never been here before.

A woman approaches from behind a door in the far corner. She looks like she means business in a Morticia Addams kind of way, and I don't recognize her from when I was here all those years ago. She's a little taller than I am, with a strong build and wearing a black wig and a lot of makeup, which doesn't really match her benign black jeans and blouse.

"You are police?" she asks in a voice that's surprisingly high-pitched for her stature. She has some kind of Eastern European accent that sounds artificial and practiced.

I give her a close-lipped smile. "I'm not Vice."

She squints at me. "We don't do anything here that would interest Vice, anyway." Something changes in her face and becomes more guarded.

I give her a real smile. "I know. I'm not trying to cause problems for you or for the club—"

She interrupts me with an arched eyebrow and a grin. "Oh, you want to join, then? Welcome." Her mouth slides into a grin. "I am Mistress Natalia."

A surge of adrenaline hits me.

"Let me get you an application. Dom or sub?" She's more young Angelica Huston than Carolyn Jones, if we're still on the Morticia Addams thing.

I chuckle. "No, no, neither. I'm here investigating a homicide." I pull out my badge wallet and slide it to her, trying to avoid the gaze of the couple in the corner, the only other people here this early.

"I see," she says, not looking at my ID. "Well, in that case, come with me."

My phone buzzes in my pocket.

"No phones here," she says. "You will take that outside."

I look at it, anyway—it's a private caller. "I'm sorry," I say to the dark woman. "I have to take this." I slide off my barstool and make my way to the door as she sidles away.

"I'm watching you," a man's voice says. The call ends.

I resist the urge to bounce my phone off the sidewalk.

I stand there for a minute, gazing around to see if anyone is watching from nearby, before I face the front door of the Rec Room. I mentally map the three floors of space, all safely hidden behind the blacked-out windows of the former warehouse.

When I go back in, Mistress Natalia waits on the stool that I vacated. When she sees me, she stands and leads me to a small office in the corner, where she gestures for me to sit on a rickety wooden chair that's shoved between a filing cabinet and a cash safe. When she closes the door, I see a black latex Catwoman suit hanging on the back of it. She leans on the edge of the desk. I would just as soon have reversed the seating arrangement so that I can tower over her, but there's not much I can do about it now.

In regular light, she looks about forty, give or take five years. "Sorry about the phone policy," she says. "We must be careful." She flicks an eyebrow at me. "So tell me how to help you," she says, batting her false eyelashes.

"Are you in charge here?"

She gives me a throaty laugh. "In many more ways than one."

I don't respond.

"Yes, I am the owner and the woman in charge." Something underneath that fake accent says Chicago to me. She reaches over to the desk, grabs a shiny black business card, and hands it to me. Mistress Natalia, it says in silver cursive. Then it gives the address of the club and a phone number. The phone number doesn't match the one on Martin's card, but the aesthetic sure as hell does.

"Last name?" I remove my notebook from my pocket.

"My given name is Cathy Smith, which is far too boring for me." She drops the act but not by much.

"How long have you owned the bar?" I don't look away from her.

She goes behind the desk and sits in another creaky chair. "About two years," she replies in her regular voice. "When my dad passed, I inherited some money. I bought this place." She gestures around it with fingernails that are close to two inches long. When I don't respond right away, she keeps going. "I know about the *club's* reputation from a few years back," she says, emphasizing "club" to correct me, "but I've done my best to clean it up, so to speak."

"In what ways?"

She sighs, but her eyes gleam. "Made it absolutely exclusive in most regards. No sex is allowed anymore, at all. No electronic devices other than our issued key cards. No blood outside of the designated area. House safe words, dungeon masters. A list of rules that, if members violate them, will get them kicked out for good. I'm very serious about all of this. It needs to be safe." She taps a finger against a palm and smiles. "Some members quit because of the new rules. We allow beginners now. We have a class once a month, a sort of bondage 101. I've tried to make it more of a community and less of a cult."

"It was a cult before?" Images of what I saw those years ago in that dungeon flash in my brain. There was lots of black latex and ball gags.

She laughs. "No, I was exaggerating. But I know what used to go on here, and I made it my mission to change it. The BDSM community isn't what everyone thinks it is. People's proclivities. That's all they are. Proclivities. It's all just play."

I blink at her, hoping that she's not going to give me some kind of preachy lecture.

She doesn't.

I pull out my phone, and she makes a face. "I just want to show you a picture. A few, actually." I pull up the picture of Heather Martin. "Have you seen this woman in here before?"

She blinks. Recognition flashes in her eyes but only for a split second. She looks at me, and her eyes grow darker. "We have a very strict privacy policy," she replies.

"This is a homicide investigation. You can tell me now, or I can subpoena you." I'm lying, but she might not know that.

"You'll need the subpoena," she replies.

"Any of these guys?" I show her photos of Eric Martin, Anders Andersen, and Derek Struthers.

"I said we have a confidentiality policy."

"Okay, then, how about this?" I swipe through the photos until I get to the transponder.

Her eyes open wide before she can stop herself, but she doesn't say anything.

"Listen, I'll say again that I'm not here to make trouble for you. I'm trying to find out what happened to a woman who was very badly beaten."

She nods and pushes a strand of wig hair off her face. "It opens the dungeon door," she replies. "Only our dungeon masters have them."

"Names?"

"Are you kidding me?" She chuckles. "Absolutely not, not without a warrant. Confidentiality is an issue here, as I'm sure you can imagine." She folds her hands on the desk.

It's time to take a different approach. "Mistress Natalia, I really appreciate your time. I'd be grateful for a couple more minutes of it, and for any cooperation you can give me now, without getting the court system involved."

She smiles at my use of her professional name and sits back in her chair.

"Do you have any surveillance cameras, anything like that?"

She laughs. "Not a chance. It's in the membership contract that we don't—and won't."

"Is there a way to tell when a transponder was used to unlock the door?"

She shakes her head. "It's a simple system."

"Were you here on Saturday night?"

"I'm here every night."

"Anything strange about that night that you can recall?"

"Not a thing," she replies. "Regular Saturday night."

"Any way of keeping track of who's here at any given time?"

She raises an eyebrow and looks back and forth between my eyes. "No." She settles on my left eye and blinks. She's a good liar.

"Can I look at your member list?" Might as well just go for it.

"Absolutely not."

"I won't share the details with anyone," I reply, my voice even. "I am simply investigating a homicide."

Her eyes get bigger for a moment. Her face returns to normal, then I watch her slide all the way back into character. "Tell me more, then."

I cock my head to the side.

"About you not sharing details." She stands.

I have about six seconds to weigh my options. Play the game, get the information. Don't play, maybe get it with a warrant. But then I hear Julia Becker in my head, telling me that we don't even know if Heather Martin was a member of this club, so there's not enough evidence for a warrant. And she would be correct. "I will not share the details of the member list unless and until I have to," I reply. "And I would be grateful to know who was here on Saturday night and whether you recognize the woman from the picture."

"'Mistress Natalia.'" She runs a fingernail across her desk, her eyes narrowed in my direction.

"Mistress Natalia," I repeat.

She stares me down, her eyes dark. Yeah, that doesn't really do it for me, but I need this information, like, right now.

"'And, Mistress Natalia, I will be forever in your debt for whatever information you have to give, and I will not harass any of your members,'" she says.

I repeat her without rolling my eyes.

After about ten more minutes of this kind of crap, which I admit gets stranger by the second, she confirms that Heather Martin was here on Saturday night and that both she and Eric are dungeon masters. She also gives me two lists, one of all two hundred eighty-four members and one of the sixty-two members—several with a name-less plus-one—who were here the night Martin died. Just in case I change my mind, she also gives me a copy of the rules and the membership application. She pats my cheek as I leave the office.

I look around again for the mystery caller, but I don't see anything suspicious. In the car, I contemplate that Heather Martin was here right before she—or someone—used her credit card to get a room at the Renaissance, and we have sixty-two potential witnesses. I type a text to Goran, then it occurs to me that he'll be pissed that I flew solo to the Rec Room, so I erase it.

I hope Sims and Roberts got something from the hotel. Maybe someone saw something. Maybe the killer was there and got caught on video carrying bondage equipment and bomb-making supplies.

Roberts answers on the fourth ring, just as I'm about to hang up. "Boyle, what's up?"

"Anything from the hotel?"

"Yeah, we're talking to one of the managers, a Veronica Keaton, right now. We're trying to get surveillance footage, but she's giving us the song and dance. My next call is to Becker for a warrant. A credit card hit seems like solid evidence to me. Anything on your end?"

"This and that. I have a line on a club where Martin was a member. I'll have more details at the morning briefing."

"Ten-four. Hey, you doing okay?"

"Yeah, I'm fine. Thanks for asking. Listen, I'll see you tomorrow, okay? I'm getting another call." I tap to take the other call—Goran—before Roberts says goodbye.

"What, you're gonna start sending me a message and then erase it?"

"What the hell, Goran? Were you just sitting there looking at your phone and waiting for three dots telling you that I was typing a message?"

"No, I was sending you a message. Look, I don't like what happened today. I need to know a couple of things. Do you have a few minutes? I'm still downtown. Maybe we could grab a drink."

This is thoroughly unlike him. He's such a family man that he's usually at home long before I leave for the day. I check my watch, and it's only quarter after seven, so I don't bother arguing. "I'm out in your neck of the woods. Want to meet near your house?"

"I'll see you at Shorty's in twenty minutes. I won't even ask why you're on the West Side."

I hang up before he can say goodbye, and try to process what the hell is happening with the case, with my partner, with the verdict. Then I fire up the VW and pull away from the curb.

Shorty's is a dive bar that Goran and I have visited a couple of times. It's far enough from downtown that few public servants frequent it, which is fine with me—I'd just as soon not talk to anyone right now. It takes me only three minutes to get there from the Rec Room.

As the bartender slides me my bourbon and my beer, it hits me: *Grimes was acquitted. Someone called and said he was watching me. I'm not stupid enough to think those things are unrelated—it could have been him or one of his cronies.* I take my drinks to a corner booth and drop into a seat facing the door. I try to zone out on the basketball game on the big screen—LeBron is playing but not for Cleveland—but my mind keeps looping back to that moment in the courtroom when O'Connor called me a murderer.

On a smaller screen in the opposite corner, Joe Mattioli is talking about his cop book on some news show. The captions are on, and I follow along as I wait for my partner. *It just had to be written. The whole thing is all about my own experiences. Police work was a lot different then. It was more a gut-instinct thing. Nowadays, detectives have all kinds of technology at their disposal. I guess it's become more a science and less an art.*

He has big lips and a bulbous nose, and that shirt is too tight to wear on television. I roll my eyes. The host, a blond woman who appears to be in her early twenties and who is trying much too hard, asks a question about his wife's death.

Yeah, that hit me hard, the caption says. *Gibbie and me were both devastated. He was my partner, you know? And we were all close. Anna's death is a big part of why I wrote the book. I wanted her story to be told. Last I checked, it was still an open homicide, and there is no statute of limitations on first-degree murder.*

The host asks how long Mattioli will be in Cleveland and what his plans are. Something that brutal had to be premeditated. The question is about whether there's a connection between Anna Mattioli's death and Heather Martin's.

I'm back in my old stomping grounds! I'm catching up with the boys from the old days but mostly just visiting family. I brought my son, Giacomo, with me, and I'm showing him around.

The camera cuts back to the host. *One last question, Detective. What do you think about recent events in Cleveland involving the police? I could cite the Department of Justice inquiry, the acquittal of Officer Grimes*—it cuts to a photo of that smug asshole, smiling with a bunch of kids at some bike safety event—*or the increasing pressure to eliminate the excessive use of force that some officers employ. Do you have any thoughts?*

He looks straight at the camera with his beady brown eyes. *Force is sometimes needed. You can read about that in my book. As for the DOJ, well... I suppose it's just smoke and mirrors. I can't imagine this Justice Department doing much about whatever Grimes or anyone else was accused of. And as for Grimes, well, I think he was just doing his job. I'm not sexist, but all of the witnesses against him were lady cops, right? I think that says something. I think it was a setup. Guys can't even compliment a woman anymore without getting accused of something, you know?*

I want to slap the shit out of him. The host thanks him for his time and plugs his book. Apparently he's doing a reading at a local bookstore this weekend. Maybe I'll go just to mess with him.

I toss back the rest of my bourbon and move to the beer. *Fuck.* My phone buzzes against the wooden table.

It's Cora. "Hey. You okay?"

"Yeah."

"Do you happen to be watching television right now?"

"Surprisingly, yeah. I saw it."

"And you're okay."

"Yeah."

She sighs. "We need to talk."

"I don't like where this is going."

She laughs. "It hasn't even started. We just need to talk. Can you swing by?"

"I'm about to have a burger with Goran, but I'll come by when we're done. I'll text you." I hang up and set my phone on the table then lift my beer. The bartender catches my eye, but I look away, knowing full well that I don't need another bourbon. *Could Mattioli be staying at the Renaissance?* I shoot Roberts a text. He replies seconds later: *First thing tomorrow. I just signed out.*

Goran arrives, orders a Budweiser, and slides into the booth, across from me. "Before you say anything," he begins in a soft, firm voice, "I just want to set the record completely straight." He calmly puts both hands on the table in front of him, but he doesn't fool me. "I did not say anything to Fishner about Sims. I need you to believe that. I also need you to know that the whole Grimes case has really gotten to me."

"I—"

"Let me finish."

I sip my beer.

"Back in the day, I was around when some really bad shit went down, partner, and Grimes... Martin... All of it brings it all back. And I feel terrible about the things I said about her way back when. I feel terrible about playing softball with that guy. I feel terrible that you stuck your neck out like that, and I feel terrible that he got off. I feel terrible that I don't know what to do—the blue wall of silence is real, but you're my partner, and you did the right thing." He scrubs a hand across his face.

The bartender returns with Goran's beer. "Thanks," he says to the other man. We order a couple of burgers.

"So you feel terrible?" My attempt at humor falls flat.

He nods.

"Then I guess I shouldn't tell you that Joe Mattioli was just on television, denouncing 'lady cops' who testify against model citizens and upholders of the law whose names are Grimes?"

"No, you shouldn't tell me that."

I shift in my seat. "Goran, look. I believe you when you say that you didn't say anything about Sims, but then the question becomes how Fishner knows about it, since I'm sure as I'm alive that Sims didn't tell her himself, and Roberts probably has no clue. I believe all of what you just said. I'm sorry you feel terrible. I pretty much feel terrible too. Thing is, we don't have time for that. We have a case to work. You heard Fishner. If we don't close it soon, Carrothers is kicking it to Homicide, and we know it'll go on the shelf if it ends up there. They just don't care."

He clenches his jaw. "Yeah, that guy was part of the bad old days too. I'm just saying, Liz..." He sips his beer. "It all stinks. All of it."

"This might be a good time to tell you that I think I broke the case wide open." I give him the download about the Rec Room.

"That's freakin' weird." He laughs. "She thought you wanted to join the club?"

"Stop being such a prude. What matters is that I have a list of names. Remember that necklace we found at the scene?"

"Vaguely, yeah."

"It had the initials E.M. on it. We've basically cleared Eric Martin. So I figure we go through that list first thing tomorrow, find anyone with those initials, and start there."

He holds his beer up, and we clink glasses.

I fill him in about what Roberts and Sims are up to.

"Mattioli is a creep, but I'd be real surprised if he had anything to do with this. Why wreck his fame and fortune to kill a woman he knew thirty years ago?"

I'm not convinced. If Mattioli was part of the bad old days... Well, given how his wife died, it makes me wonder. I mean, beatings like that aren't exactly common. I fully plan on running my own investigation, whether it's on or off the books, on that guy.

"Let's hope we can get surveillance," he mutters. "You cool with the DOJ tomorrow?"

I nod. "I have an attorney. He's supposed to be there. I've never met him before, but Becker recommended him."

"Think we're ever gonna live it down? That night in the alley?"

I shake my head. "Your guess is as good as mine, partner."

Our burgers arrive, and we talk about LeBron James while we eat. Goran pays the tab, and we walk out together. I don't tell him about the threatening phone call—I don't want him to get his undies in a bunch and insist that I stay with him or something. "Thanks for dinner, partner," I say as I unlock the Passat. "See you in the morning."

He gives me a little salute then gets into his new car.

CHAPTER 19

On my way to Cora's, it starts to rain again. "We need to talk" is never a good thing. We used to joke that it's the worst sentence one can say to someone they love. She didn't sound like she was kidding. On the phone, she had the deep, serious voice that she uses when she's talking philosophy or books or art or murder or "we need to talk."

I should have called her back right away. All four times.

I pull up in front of her house, which is pretty close to my apartment, at 9:02. Her cat, Meowmix, sits in the window, and the blue glow of her TV shines through the blinds. *Shit, I forgot to text her.* I pull out my phone. *Here.*

I see the TV shut off and a lamp come on, followed by the porch light. She opens the door as I'm getting out of the car.

"Hey," she says. She's wearing joggers and a sleeveless T-shirt, and she looks amazing.

"Hi," I reply. Once inside, I remove my gross cop boots and Garrison belt, which I leave on the floor next to the boots, complete with my Glock.

"Beer?" she asks. She's oddly calm.

"Sure." I follow her into the kitchen and take a seat at the island. I find myself tracing her tattoos with my eyes. The botanical designs go across her back, down both arms, and back again.

She slides me a beer and arches an eyebrow.

I take a sip and arch the other eyebrow.

"What happened the other night. What's been happening for months."

"You mean trying to get back together, so to speak?" I wince as I say it. It sounds so corny and inadequate. That's not it at all. Not to mention that saying it makes me feel stark naked and totally exposed, which is becoming a real theme these days. I sip my beer again.

She smiles in a sort-of-sad way.

Neither Cora nor I is really a friends-with-benefits person, but we've been doing this since last Christmas. Until the Grimes thing and then the city coming apart and Heather Martin dying the next day, we'd been spending a lot of time together. Enjoying each other. Falling into a rhythm.

"You've been really involved in this case." She leans against the counter and crosses her arms. "And I know it's a big deal for you to try to right the world's wrongs. But it brings shit back, Liz. In a big way. As if you didn't have five minutes to call me back. What if it was important? What if I needed something? Needed you? What if I've been *worried* about you? What then?"

I know where this is going, and something tightens behind my sternum, but I simultaneously relax my shoulders. "It's not like it was before," I almost whisper.

"And the whole thing with the Grimes testimony. Why not just *talk* about it? I—we, as in, the people in your life—shouldn't have to read about this crap in the newspaper."

I don't say anything.

"We've been down this road before." She crosses her arms. "The drinking."

Whatever. You were drunk last week too, I don't say. I sip my beer again, and the irony isn't lost on me. I'm pretty sure she wasn't drunk for the fourth night that week.

"We need a break." Cora closes her eyes. "I need to sort this out for myself. I'm feeling things that scare me when it comes to you."

I broke her heart once. That's what she means. I can imagine her, leaning there against that counter where we made Thanksgiving dinner for her dad and best friend and her husband and their little kid and my brother almost three years ago. It'd felt almost like having a family.

I guess it is sort of weird that we're still doing whatever this is. Most people just break up then move on. Sometimes, if they're lucky, they stay friends. They don't usually stop seeing other people and start sleeping together again, though, especially not after all the time that's passed. I guess I've never really done relationships in the way most people do. Neither has she.

She keeps going. "I don't want you to think I'm holding a grudge about anything from before. It's not a grudge. That's not me. And I'm sorry. I just wonder if we need to be done with all of this, or if what we have going is working, or what. You know? I need a minute to let myself feel it before I can say much more. This is harder than it should be for me."

I hold my beer a little tighter. "What do you mean by 'this'?"

"I can't lead you on. I also can't commit to you again, not right now. Not while you're like this, so immersed in work and incommunicado. And I'm not okay with being so, I don't know, nonchalant about everything. It's not like me. I need to know where I stand. I need to be a priority."

"A couple of missed phone calls led to this?" I still can't look at her. It's too much. Something hot uncoils in my chest and moves into my stomach.

She sighs. "It's not just that. It's the past *three years*. It's all of it. I'm forty years old. I can't do this anymore. I need stability. I want to know whoever I'm with is there all the time. I want to live with my partner and make a life together. I want a lot of things that I'm just not sure you can give me. And I don't mean this in some kind of fucked-up, needy way either. I'm just being honest with you."

"Okay. I'm sorry." I take a big gulp of beer.

"Liz, I love you, and I always will. I just don't know if I can be with you. I need space and time." She takes a deep breath.

I blink back hot tears. "You can have space. I'm sorry." I finish the beer and slide it to the edge of the island.

"For God's sake, stop apologizing for who you are. You have to stop doing that."

"Okay. I'm not sorry, then. But you can have space, and I will always love you too."

She sniffs like maybe she's going to cry, and it pushes harder against the inside of my chest too. "Take time away from me. Go on dates," she says. "See other people. Hang out with Josh. Work twenty-four hours a day. Do whatever you do when you're not with me, whatever you did before me."

My eyes won't stop burning, so I squeeze them closed and shift around in my seat. "That's it, then?" It doesn't make sense, but it also does, and maybe she's right. Maybe it's not working. People love each other but can't be together all of the time.

"I don't know." She's definitely crying but trying to hide it. She glances at my beer. "One more?"

I nod. *I need to cut back.*

At some point, I end up in the bathroom again. It's where I always go when I'm about to lose my grip. Shue made me talk about it once. Her take on it was that I need to feel safe, that kind of thing.

Whatever. I can punch tile walls without damaging property. That's kind of how I look at it. Only now, I can also name my feelings.

So I run the water, splash it on my face, and name them. I surprise myself when "relief" appears on the list. Cora is, and always will be, out of my league. Cora deserves someone who works regular hours and doesn't immerse herself in shitty murder cases. Cora deserves a normal person, not some traumatized and emotionally numb shell of a woman.

My phone buzzes in my pocket. I think about the photos on my iPad. I'm surrounded by devices instead of people.

Is this where we live now, in some kind of digital space, mediated by phones and iPads and computers?

I sound like an old person. I sound like Tom.

Cora is right. I already know all of it. I watched my mom disintegrate for twentysomething years from alcohol and pills and whatever drove her to those things. Numbing agents, I guess. She just couldn't do it without them. She couldn't numb the pain—she couldn't face the pain in the first place. And she destroyed a lot. She damn near broke me, and she made my brother into a sniveling little boy of a man.

I think back to Christopher at the football stadium the other day. Maybe he'll be okay. I hope he's okay because of more than her sobriety. He's always taken it personally, I think, when she gets sober and then falls off the wagon again. He holds on to hope. I should call him.

My phone buzzes again, and I silence it.

I learned a long time ago not to take it—my mom—too seriously. She could come undone, go off the rails at any time. Could call me while slobbering all over herself at some police station after she gets busted for DUI, asking me to help her get out of this little jam. Or maybe someone could call me, tell me I need to get to the hospital because she's on life support after wrapping her car around a tree or taking three too many pills.

At this point, that Vicodin-and-vodka combo of hers could kill her.

I should probably feel guilty that it might be a relief if it did. That if she just disappeared, I would be okay. We would bury her. We would say some kind of prayer. We would be sad for a minute. We would reminisce as much as children of addicts can. And then we would move on.

I'm such an asshole for thinking about any of this right now. I stare myself down in the mirror and prepare to reenter the kitchen, where I will face the loss of one of a handful of people I've ever loved.

Heather Martin's mangled body. The blood in the shed. The chair leg. The police baton that we still haven't found. Anders Andersen, Winona Conway. This possible new lead with some unknown person with the initials E. M. The corruption. The misogyny.

The only thing I'm good at is solving murders.

I threw it all into the fire, way back when, when Cora asked me to move in with her. I'd been working a case involving a prostitute and her toddler daughter, and it pushed me over the edge. I shut myself down. I just couldn't feel anything at all.

What a pathetic excuse. I chose this as my job. I mean, sure, it called to me. But no one made me do it. No one but me made me an emotional cripple. I could have gotten therapy a long time ago, and I didn't until the department forced me to.

I don't want to be a statistic, the lone wolf cop, nursing her pain with a bottle and a case. At one point, I might have been okay with it. Not anymore.

I push open the bathroom door.

At some point, as I'm sharing my damn feelings in the kitchen where we've had so many conversations, I'm gripped by the need to touch her, to hold her. I say as much, and she asks whether I'm drunk.

"No. Not drunk. I had two drinks, plus the two here."

"You gotta watch it, Liz."

"Yeah, I know," I reply. "Four is supposed to be my limit."

Then she asks what I'm waiting for. So I take her in my arms and let it all go, crying and sputtering and slobbering into her hair, the whole deal.

She responds by pulling me closer. Meowmix rubs on our ankles. It goes on for at least fifteen minutes.

I've never come unglued in front of anyone before. I've never felt more vulnerable in my life. I tell her as much.

"That you're here instead of crying in your bathroom at home means something."

I try to smile, but I'm too exhausted. I'm not used to this. I have to ask, though. "Look, I know. I know all of it. I hear you."

"What tea do you want?" She starts the kettle.

I want a big glass of bourbon. "Something relaxing."

She makes our tea then slides my cup across her kitchen island.

I blow on my mug and tell her that I don't want to see other people.

She nods and levels her gaze at me. "It's what I need right now."

I take a deep breath. "Okay." I can't tell if she wants me to fight for her, but part of me knows that it's over regardless of what I do. "I respect it. You. I respect you."

She nods and blinks the tears out of her eyes. "Tell me about this case you're working, then." She wiggles her eyebrows. "I'm a detective, too, you know. Maybe smarter than your average bear."

I shove my feelings into a box then give her the download. I tell her all about everything that's happened, the dead ends, the leather club, and my weird, nagging, and probably unfounded suspicion about Mattioli.

I've never talked to her about work before. I always thought I was protecting her by leaving it out. But maybe that was stupid. Maybe I didn't trust her. She's the smartest person I know, and I mean that in every possible way—she should have my job, and I should have hers. But whatever, that's not how the math worked out.

"Look deeper into Mattioli," she says. She yawns. "He probably didn't kill your vic, but I bet he did something."

"Yeah, he probably did. Let's go to bed." I pause as I gauge her reaction.

Her shoulders tense.

"I don't mean it like that. I mean sleep. Tomorrow, we move on and see other people or whatever. I hope we can be friends. Real ones."

She smiles. "Let's."

I'VE ALWAYS BEEN A morning person, and I awake before dawn. I make Cora a fresh pot of coffee and write a note that reiterates everything I said last night: I understand, I respect you, do what you need to do, call me if you want to, and don't if you don't.

I draw a picture of a pumpkin and a ghost at the bottom and write "Happy Halloween" next to them—I'm kind of a sucker for Halloween. Then I pull on my boots and leave.

CHAPTER 20

Once home, I feed Ivan then put on a newish doom-metal album that I've been obsessing about. I take my time getting ready then head to work to keep my appointment with DOJ Investigator Chris Briscoe. It seems like more of a pain in the ass than anything, but I'm still nervous enough to need deep breaths.

I'm supposed to meet with my attorney thirty minutes before we talk to Briscoe together. All of my communication with him has been via text message and voicemail, so I half expect that he won't show at all, but when I get to work, he's sitting in my visitors' chair.

Goran arches an eyebrow, and I shrug.

The lawyer, who looks like a lawyer, stands and extends a hand. "Jason Marutiak."

I shake his hand. "Elizabeth Boyle. Let's head down this way to talk in private." I shed my jacket, toss my bag on my desk, make a face at Goran, then lead my attorney down the hall.

Marutiak is everything I envisioned: average height and average build, with the right amount of stubble, a good haircut, a loud shirt, and a bow tie. *Damn, I'm good.* We stop by the vending machines.

"Thanks for coming," I say somewhat stupidly.

"I don't think you have much to worry about," he replies. "The DOJ isn't going after cops anymore—it's not like it was during the last administration. I've reviewed your case. Just tell the truth, and you'll be fine."

I nod.

Behind him, Roberts comes down the hall in vampire teeth. "Happy Halloween," he says in a Dracula voice. He goes into the men's room.

Briscoe enters the room, and he doesn't live up to the hype. He's probably a couple of years older than I am, and although I'd pictured one of those super-ripped government types with a high-and-tight haircut and a blue suit, he's wearing gray pants, a boring gray-patterned tie, and a white shirt. His build is average, and he has a decent haircut.

"Detective Boyle." He holds out a hand. "It's nice to meet you." He ignores Marutiak.

I mutter something about how it's nice to meet him, too, and extend my hand. His handshake isn't nearly as clammy as I'd expected.

He smiles and gestures at the chair across from him at the table. "Have a seat, please, both of you."

I almost laugh, given that I've said the same thing to countless suspects over the years. I vaguely wonder whether he always sits there, facing away from the mirror, and then I wonder who else is behind that mirror—*Fishner? Carrothers?* I take a seat.

"Detective, Counselor, as you know, this is just an informational interview. We're not looking at you for anything criminal." He takes the seat across from us. He taps his fingers on a manila folder that has my name written on the tab.

I try to look relaxed, but I catch a glance of myself in the mirror, and I look like a pissant. Marutiak looks bored. I try harder to soften my face and jaw.

"We're just collecting information, Detective Boyle. May I call you Elizabeth?"

"Liz. You may call me Liz." I make note of the pitcher of ice water and three cups on the table but resist pouring a glass and chugging it, lest I come off as nervous or guilty.

He grins. "Liz. I just have a few questions, and then I'll get out of your hair. Do you have anything to say off the record before we begin video and audio recording?"

"No."

"In that case"—he hits a button on a machine near him, and a red light on the camera to my upper left comes on—"interview of Detective Elizabeth Boyle, Cleveland Department of Police, Special Homicide, badge number one-seven-six-one. The date is October twenty-ninth, and the time is eight hundred hours. Present are Detective Boyle, her attorney, Jason Marutiak, and myself, Special Agent Chris Briscoe. We are here today to discuss the officer-involved shooting of one George Arsalan, whom Detective Boyle shot and killed on—"

My mind goes blank. Marutiak shuffles in his chair. I zone out but consciously remind myself to return to the present.

"Detective Boyle—"

All I hear is "How does it feel to be a murderer?" But that isn't what he asked. "I'm sorry, can you repeat that?"

Marutiak moves his pen from his notepad to the table.

Briscoe grins. "Sure. I asked how you're doing today."

"I'm doing great, thanks." I clear my throat. "How are you?"

"I'm doing great too. Can you tell me about George Arsalan?"

"About the guy or about the case?"

"Both would be great." His grin is getting annoying.

"My partner and I were assigned a homicide of a fourteen-year-old girl. We caught it on the late shift." *Unnecessary information, Boyle.* "Our investigation led us to a man named William Coby, whom we—meaning our entire squad, which included several detectives focused on things such as IP addresses—found to be operating a large-scale child-pornography ring out of Muncie, Indiana. We traveled to Muncie, tracked down Coby, and brought him in.

"We questioned him for approximately nineteen hours, at which point he told us that the man we were looking for was right here."

"Here meaning Cleveland?"

"Yes." I gesture around. "Coby claimed that he had no idea what was on the servers, claiming to be 'just the tech guy.' We booked him, anyway, for the child pornography."

"Who is 'we'?" Briscoe asks.

"Well, the prosecutor, my partner, my lieutenant, and myself."

"And what are their names?"

I watch myself flinch in the mirror, not wanting to implicate anyone. *You're not pointing fingers. Answer the question.* "Detective Tomas Goran, Lieutenant Jane Fishner, and myself. Also present was Assistant Prosecutor Julia Becker."

"Continue."

"At some point, right around the twenty-four-hour mark and under a bit of pressure, Coby gave us an address. We—"

"What kind of pressure?"

"That's irrelevant," Marutiak says.

"Is it? I mean, we're discussing excessive use of force here." He's not grinning anymore.

"It's fine," I say. "The kind of pressure we put on people. We threw his finances at him, his priors. That kind of thing."

Briscoe sits back in his chair, and my leg starts to jiggle beneath the table. I will it to stop.

"The address he gave was for an apartment on the West Side. My lieutenant told my partner and me to go get him. Our goal was to bring him in for questioning and nothing more. We had other members of our squad confirm that a man named George Arsalan did indeed reside at that address." My mouth goes dry, but I avoid pouring any water. Julia's advice echoes in my head. *Just answer the questions.*

"Would you like some water?" Briscoe asks.

"I'm fine, thanks. Goran, my partner, and I arrived near the address at approximately twenty-three hundred hours, accompanied by two zone cars—cruisers. We noticed that there was an alley in the back with a fire escape leading to what we assumed was his apartment."

"What caused you to make such an assumption?"

"The address that Coby gave us included an apartment number, 4B, so our assumption was that he lived on the fourth floor, the top one."

"Continue."

"There appeared to be three entrances to the building. My first inclination was to have the zone cars cover the front and the side, leaving Goran and me on the fire escape."

"What caused that inclination?"

"It would have been obvious for him to go out the front or the side. The fire escape would have been risky, but we're trained to predict the unpredictable."

He nods.

"So that's what we did. While I parked the car, my partner went back into the alley to cover the fire escape, with the uniforms on the two main egresses.

"I got out of the car and started into the alley to meet my partner, at which time I witnessed a man fire three shots at my partner from the fire escape. Fortunately, Goran rolled behind several trash cans and wasn't hit. Two bullets hit the trash cans, and one hit a brick wall behind him."

"He was not injured, correct?"

"Correct."

"What happened after that?"

It all happened so fast. "I shot and killed George Arsalan."

"Where was he standing when this occurred?"

"He was on the first landing from the ground."

"How many shots did you fire?"

"You can't possibly expect her to remember that," Marutiak says.

"It's fine. I fired three shots, and all of them hit him in the chest. He dropped then fell to the ground from the landing."

"Before you shot, did you say anything to him?"

"No, sir, I only had time to react."

"You did not confirm his identity?"

"No, sir, I only had time to react. He was shooting at my partner." I don't regret it. He would have killed Goran.

"And later, when his identity was confirmed, were you relieved?"

"Is this on the record?" Marutiak asks.

Briscoe rolls his eyes but shuts off the recording device. "Off the record."

"Of course I was relieved. He matched the description of the man we were looking for, and he exited through a window onto a fire escape."

"How did you know that, given that you were parking the car?"

"I trust my partner."

"Did your partner vocalize at any time that he knew the man was Arsalan?"

"No. Look, it was one of those scenarios that we talk about in training but hope never happens. I walked into an alleyway and saw a guy shooting a big gun at my partner. I did what I had to do."

He turns the recording back on. "Were there any civilians present?"

I take a breath. "Yes. Behind me as I entered the alley, there was a woman with a child."

"And this witness has been identified and questioned, correct?"

"I believe so, but you'd have to check with Internal Affairs."

He nods. "Do you, Detective Boyle, believe that you acted fairly?"

"I do." Not always but usually.

He shuts the recorder off again. "That's all I've got. Thanks for your time." He stands and reaches for my hand again.

Marutiak stands, and I follow. I take Briscoe's hand and shake it, and he wishes me well on his way out the door.

That was the weirdest six minutes of my life, and I feel numb.

Marutiak shoves his notepad and pen back into his bag. "That went well."

"Uh-huh. Thanks."

"I didn't do much, but the bill is in the mail." He grins.

"How do you know Julia?" I ask as we head out the door.

He winks—*winks*—at me. "We have mutual friends. I have to run, but be in touch if you need anything. Okay?"

I nod, and we part near the elevator. Briscoe gets on, and I head to my desk.

Goran raises his eyebrows as I flip on my lamp. He moves his laptop to the side. "How'd it go?"

"Fine." I flounce into my chair and stare at the crime board. "What are you working on?"

"This list you got from the Rec Room—where you should not have gone alone." He gives me his dad look.

"Don't look at me like that. We had this conversation already." I don't mention the threatening phone call because I can't deal with him being worried about me. If it's important to the case, I'll figure it out.

He nods. "There are two people out of sixty-two with the initials E. M. on the member list."

"There are also the nameless plus-ones."

"Yeah, but we gotta start somewhere."

Roberts walks over, still in his Dracula teeth.

"It's gotta be hard to eat all day with those in," Goran quips.

"It's hard to talk too." He spits the teeth into his hand. "Joe Mattioli is indeed staying at the Renaissance. He has the presidential suite. My guess is that's why Veronica Keaton is being a pain in the ass about the surveillance. We're working on a warrant now."

"Once you get that, check to see if anyone is staying there with the initials E. M."

He nods and shoves the teeth back into his mouth.

"You talk to Fishner today?" Goran asks.

"No." I look over at her office. The door is closed, and the light is off. "Where is she?"

"She had a top-secret meeting with Carrothers." He leans forward and lowers his voice. "This all stinks. It's bad."

"We'd better solve this case, then. Tell me about E. M."

He slides his laptop in front of him and squints at the screen. "Well, there's one guy, Eddie Montague, who lives on the East Side. Looks like he matches our suspect's description—he's a good-sized guy and has a motorcycle registered in his name." Goran turns the laptop around and shows me Montague's picture.

I shake my head. "He's African-American. Our guy is white and probably working alone."

He nods. "Yeah, and his record is clean. The other guy's name is Elias Maxwell. Based on his social media, he's a personal trainer at BodMachine. Similar build but no motorcycle. He drives a brand-new Camaro. Orange."

"Oh, so he's *that* kind of douchebag."

He laughs. "He has a couple of priors. No felonies, but it looks like he pleaded to misdemeanor assault last year. Hold on." He clicks a couple of times then looks excited. "He was charged with unlawful sexual conduct with a minor. I guess he had sex with a sixteen-year-old... And he's thirty-two."

I make a face.

"He pleaded it down to a misdemeanor-one."

"I wonder how he pulled that off. Huh."

"Judges are busy?"

I smell Julia Becker's good perfume and hear the clacking of her heels before I see her. She sidles up to Goran's desk, carrying her briefcase. She's wearing a well-tailored gray suit and a light-pink shirt today. "Hey," she says in that deep alto of hers.

Goran flicks his chin at her. "What's up? Where's your Halloween costume?"

She chuckles. "Where's yours? I'm here to get paperwork from Roberts on the Renaissance warrant." She pushes a lock of copper-blond hair out of her face.

I glance across the squad, where Roberts and Sims are huddled around Roberts's computer.

Becker looks at Goran then at me, and I watch something like sympathy come up behind her eyes. "Do you have a minute?"

I stand and stretch. "Sure."

She leaves her briefcase in my chair, and we walk down the hall toward the vending machines. "Thanks for the tip on Marutiak," I say. "He didn't do shit, but it was nice to have someone on my side in there."

"He's an asshole, but he's a decent attorney. I'm glad it worked out for you." She bats her eyes at me.

I lean against the wall. "How do you know him?"

"He relentlessly asked me out for about two years when I got the job in the prosecutor's office." She gives me a sly grin. "At some point, I indulged him, and we went on a date, at which point we both realized he wasn't my type. He is fundamentally uninteresting, which I suspected and confirmed."

I raise an eyebrow.

She maintains eye contact. "I've got to get to work on this warrant, but I wonder if you might swing by my office later. I have a couple of things to discuss with you."

"Well, I'm kind of in the middle—"

"Liz, I'm only going to say this once. Watch your back."

I make a face. "Why?"

"I'll tell you more later, but the scuttlebutt is that Grimes is recruiting a posse."

I try not to laugh. "Did you just say 'scuttlebutt' in a sentence?"

She rolls her eyes. "Just be careful, okay? No shenanigans. Keep Goran with you when you're on the clock, and watch your back when you aren't."

"Yeah, you said that on the voicemail."

"He threatened you."

"I know." I push off the wall, stubbornly avoiding telling her about the phone call, and we head down the hallway side by side. She gives me a little smile then walks past my desk and over to Roberts and Sims. "Give me the download," she says to the two men.

I turn off my lamp and grab my bag. "Let's go talk to Elias Maxwell."

Goran follows suit. "Let's."

Fishner catches us in the hallway and asks for an update. She looks tired, almost haggard.

"Are you okay?" I ask before I can stop myself.

She blinks at me. "I'm fine. Tell me what's happening."

Goran clears his throat. "We have a lead on an Elias Maxwell. He's a trainer at BodMachine—"

I can't stop myself from chuckling. They both stare at me.

"We're going to try to talk to him now," he says.

She nods. "Keep me posted. Regular briefing at three."

"Ask Roberts and Sims about the Renaissance angle," I say. "I think Becker is getting them a warrant for the surveillance footage."

She nods then walks away.

We take the stairs all the way down to the basement, where the car is parked. Goran shoves the door open and gestures for me to go first. "I'm driving today."

I toss him the keys. "What's up with her?"

We walk to the Charger.

"No clue, other than she had to talk to that jerk Carrothers again today."

We get in.

"Are you ever going to tell me the deal with him? What do you know that you're holding out on?"

He adjusts the mirrors. "He's a dick. He's a horrible, horrible dick." He shoves the car into Drive. "He was part of the whole boys' club way back when, and I heard him say things I would never repeat to you or to anyone. He's why I don't play softball anymore. Once I got partnered with you, my tolerance for that crap went out the window."

"What does that mean?"

"It means that it's easy to act like a sexist jerk when you're surrounded by other sexist jerks. Best thing that ever happened to me was getting you as a partner and Fishner as a boss. You make me look at stuff differently. It makes me a better cop and a better dad."

"I'm flattered." *So Carrothers is just like a lot of cops.* I almost feel bad for Goran. He could have ridden that privilege a long way, and instead he's stuck with me. "You going trick-or-treating later with the girls?"

He pulls out onto Ontario. "Yeah, if I can get out of here on time. Their costumes are adorable—Vera made them. Hannah is a purple princess, and Lily is a green dragon."

"Dragon costumes can't be easy to make."

"Vera is a wizard with the sewing machine. She's been working on that dragon costume for, like, a month." He turns right onto Lakeside.

"Well, let's get this in the bag today, and you can go trick-or-treating."

He laughs. "I always steal all of their Almond Joy bars."

I make a face. "No kid likes Almond Joy. You're following the script perfectly."

He makes a right into McDonald's. "I'm gonna need coffee. You?"

"Always."

I search for BodMachine in my phone's map app while we're waiting. "Think this is our guy?"

"Could be. At this rate, probably not. But he could be."

"We need to find out if Heather Martin was a member of Bod-Machine."

"Should be easy enough to do."

The drive doesn't take long—it's only three minutes from the Justice Center. Goran and I continue to make small talk about Halloween, and for a moment, everything feels almost normal. As long as we aren't talking about the boys' club, Carrothers, Sims, Martina Lowell, Grimes, or weird phone calls, maybe everything *is* normal.

CHAPTER 21

BodMachine is next to the Hilton, in a newly renovated redbrick building that also contains an advertising agency, a jewelry store, a stationery store, a vegan restaurant, and an upscale cocktail bar. The city has been trying to class up downtown, which I guess is fine, although there's been a lot of gentrification and displacement. This place used to be a hotel, and I wonder whether it's haunted.

I look down the block. "Walking distance to the Renaissance."

Goran nods and parks illegally on the street—one benefit of driving a police car—and we get out and meet on my side.

He squints at the sky, which has darkened all of a sudden. "It's gonna rain," he says.

I pull my blazer around me. "Or snow. It's not Cleveland unless you're trick-or-treating with your costume over your poofy coat."

He chuckles. "Too true. What's the plan with this guy?"

I move closer to the door, trying to get out of the wind. "Same script as Andersen. We start with basic questions and wait to reveal that we know about the Rec Room. If we start with Saturday night, we're good."

A short bodybuilder type pushes through the door and almost runs into me as he jams a protein bar into his mouth. He doesn't excuse himself. I roll my eyes.

Goran lets me go through the door first. The interior is designed in the latest style, all industrial brick, exposed ducts, recessed lighting, poured concrete, and fake succulents in mason jars. A flat-screen TV with the building directory hangs on the wall across from the elevator. Beckoning to us at the end of the lobby is a set of frosted-glass-and-brushed-nickel doors with *BodMachine* and the gym's logo, a machine icon behind the silhouette of male and female torsos flexing.

People are lined up to get into the vegan restaurant. *Maybe Cora would like it here. She's been vegan for, what, six years now?* I stop myself. "Think that place is any good?"

"Is there steak? Pulled pork? Wings?"

I laugh. "No."

"Then no, it's not good."

We walk together, and I yank open the door to BodMachine.

"Jeez," Goran mutters as we enter. "Who thought to do everything in orange and red?"

"They're probably going for eighties retro," I whisper out of the corner of my mouth. I glance at a banner hanging on the front desk. *Power Up! First month free! Free juice bar! Start today!* Loud dance music blares from speakers in the fitness room, which is behind a short glass block wall.

A young man and a young woman are perched on high stools at the desk. The woman wears gray leggings and an orange shirt emblazoned with the logo and the word "trainer," and the man, who is Asian, is all in black and gray.

When they see us, the man stands and smiles. "Power up!" he says, flexing to match the logo. "Are you here for a membership?"

I approach the counter. Goran stands behind me and looks around.

"Not so much," I reply. "We're looking for Elias Maxwell. Is he here?"

"He can't train you unless you have a membership. We have a special right now. The first month is free!" He glances at the badge on my hip. "And if you work for the city, we waive the membership fee. That's a savings of two hundred dollars." His name tag, which is brushed nickel to match the rest of the accents in this place, tells me his name is Adam.

I look back into the workout area, where a large man appears to struggle under the weight of a barbell. Next to him is a hugely muscular dude in an orange shirt. The woman smiles then leaves the area behind the desk. Goran makes an indiscernible sound.

I put on my best fake grin. "That's great, Adam, but we're here to talk to Elias about another matter."

"Is that him back there?" Goran asks.

Adam shrugs. "Eli called off again today, which sucked, because I had to call all of his clients again. Once people get started at Bod-Machine, they don't want to take days off, and most of them haven't worked out *all week*. I would die. You gotta power up!" His phone makes a whistling sound on the desk, and he grabs it and looks at it. He laughs then types something, completely ignoring us for a moment.

Goran and I exchange a glance. "Can people come and work out without a trainer?" I ask when he's done.

He shakes his head. "That's not how it works here. This is a unique fitness experience."

I glance at a sweaty older woman who is moving at hyper speed on an elliptical machine. The woman in the orange shirt stands next to her, looking at her phone. "What did Eli say was wrong?"

Adam looks confused. "Huh?"

"When he called off. What reason did he give?"

"Oh. Uh, I'm not sure."

I pull a picture of Heather Martin up on my phone and hold it out to him. "Have you seen this woman before?"

He smiles. "Yeah, that's Heather. Man, she goes *hard*. She's shredded."

"How long has she worked out here?"

"You know what's weird? She hasn't been here all week, and she's a five-a-week client." He looks puzzled.

"Who's her trainer?"

"Eli."

The blood rushes to my head.

"They're great together. He really helps her get her aggression out. Wait." It looks as though something clicks in his brain, and he drops the salesman act. "I haven't been able to get ahold of her to tell her not to come in, but she hasn't been here. Weird. I should probably get the manager."

"Yeah, that would be great." It's becoming more difficult for me to restrain my sarcasm.

"I'll be right back." He steps away from the desk, and I turn to Goran, who is squinting around the space.

"This place is awful," he says.

I mentally compare it to my own dingy gym, which has everything I need and none of the bullshit. I nod. "Pretty much. Question is, where is Elias Maxwell?"

"Yeah, and did he kill her? If he did, *why*? It makes no sense. It must be connected to the sex thing."

"Not necessarily. In fact, I'd be surprised. Most BDSM is completely consensual and not at all likely to lead to homicide."

He gives me a look as though he's grossed out.

"Don't look at me like that, and quit thinking in stereotypes. Don't be that cop."

He nods. "You have a point."

An African-American woman enters behind us. She sees the badge on my hip, makes a face, and visibly avoids us. She scans her card, mutters something, and continues down the hallway. She disappears through a brushed-nickel door that I assume is the locker room.

Adam returns with a fortysomething man who is also clad in black and gray. "This is Jon. He's the manager."

"What's this about?" Jon asks Goran.

I take a step back, since it's clear that Jon regards me as the sidekick.

"We're looking for Eli," my partner replies. "We just have a couple of questions for him. It's totally routine."

Not so much, especially given that they're connected both here and at the Rec Room, but good lie, partner. We lie to stop people from freaking out.

Jon crosses his arms across his sizable pecs. "Eli isn't here today."

"Yeah, Adam said he called off. Any idea why?"

Jon frowns, and his posture goes rigid. "It's none of my business. I don't ask what Eli does when he isn't here."

Goran leans forward onto the counter, trying to cultivate a buddy-buddy feel. "Hey, man, I promise this is routine and has nothing to do with this place. When was Eli here last?"

Jon's jaw flexes, and he looks at me then back at Goran. I manage a smile when we make eye contact. "He hasn't been here all week. Something about having to go out of town, his sister is sick. You know the drill. It's probably bullshit."

Adam's phone whistles again, and he snatches it up from the counter. He laughs then goes into the fitness room with it. The African-American woman emerges from the locker room and meets him near a squat rack. He slides his phone into his pocket and high-fives her.

"Where's his sister live?" Goran asks.

"Columbus, I think. But like I said. It's probably bullshit. The guy's a good trainer, but he's on the bubble. In fact, I just decided that he's fired."

I arch an eyebrow.

Goran stops leaning, reaches into his pocket, then palms a business card. "You have a home address for him?"

"Probably. But can't you get that from public records? I really don't have time for this." He uncrosses and recrosses his arms, and I start to wonder what his deal is.

"Sure, we can. But why not make it easy for us?"

"I'm not in the business of making things easy for people. If you have a warrant or a membership, you can come in. Other than that? Have a good day."

Run-of-the-mill asshole. I turn to leave.

"Here's my card," Goran says as I push through the door and enter the lobby. I make it to the front doors by the time he's out of the club.

We walk through the cold rain and to the car together in silence.

Once in and belted, I type Elias Maxwell's home address into my phone. "Looks like we're going to Ohio City." I sip my coffee, which is cold.

"If he's been calling off all week, then—"

"Then we need to find him and question his ass."

It starts to rain harder, so Goran turns the wipers and headlights on before pulling away from the curb.

ELIAS MAXWELL'S ADDRESS turns out to be a tattoo shop nestled among restaurants and boutiques with what looks to be a small apartment above it. We park then exit the vehicle. "Damn, this is the kind of rain that *hurts*," I mutter.

Goran pops a toothpick into his mouth. "How do you think we get up there?"

"Maybe around back?" We walk down an alley and behind the building.

"Bingo." I point at an orange Camaro that's parked next to a plain brown back door in a small alcove. "And there's a mailbox."

"Think there's another way in and out?"

"Probably, if it's a rental."

"How 'bout I block him in with the car and we go from there?"

"Works for me. I'll go talk to the tattoo people once you're back here. We can ambush him."

He nods and trudges to the car.

I walk to the door in hopes that the alcove will block the rain. *I wonder if Cora has gotten tattooed here.* I stop myself again and survey the area. The gravel parking lot is occupied by Maxwell's car, a dumpster, and what appears to be a smoking area for the tattoo shop.

Goran rumbles to a stop, wedging the Camaro into its spot. I give him a little wave then walk around the building to the front door. A big gust of wind blows rain against my back, and I wonder why the hell I didn't wear a raincoat today.

An electronic bell goes off when I enter. A hand-painted sign is mounted in the middle of the wall between the flash art. Artistic Renderings, it says in old-school script. The buzzing sound of a tattoo machine echoes down the hallway even over the black metal that plays on the stereo.

"Be right there!" a guy calls from behind a partition.

I step over to a podium that holds a phone and an appointment book.

The buzzing sound stops. He peeks out from behind the partition. "You want to make an appointment?"

"I'm actually looking for the guy who lives upstairs. You seen him lately?"

The man steps into the hallway, removes a pair of disposable gloves from his hands, throws them into a trash can, and comes my way. He's tall, skinny, bearded, and covered in tattoos. "Yeah, I think he's here. His car's out back. He doesn't really talk to us."

I extend a hand. "I'm Detective Boyle. CPD."

He shakes my hand. "I'm Lee."

"Are you here every day?"

"Yup. This is my shop." He gives me a proud smile. "That guy do something?"

"We just have a couple of questions for him. Are there other artists here?"

He nods. "Yeah, but they won't be in till later. I usually work solo until two or so."

"Is there another way into his place, other than that door out back?"

"Just a fire escape, but the ladder's broken. The guy who owns this building sort of sucks."

"What do you know about the guy who lives upstairs?"

"Who, Maxwell? He's a complete douche. He drives a Camaro with an automatic transmission. I was out smoking about a week ago, and he was standing back there with some woman, telling her all about how he got a system installed just so he can roll through residential neighborhoods and blast the bass late at night." He chuckles. "So he's *that* kind of idiot."

"Anything you remember about the woman?"

"Older than him. She looked fit, like, gym-fit. Longish blond hair, nice clothes. I only saw her for a minute or so before I left."

"Were they arguing?"

He shakes his head. "They looked pretty buddy-buddy to me. I figured they were dating or something."

"Any idea what day that was?"

He squints at the ceiling. "Friday, maybe? No. Hold on." He flips a page in the appointment book then nods. "Saturday."

"You're sure it was Saturday?"

He nods more vigorously. "Absolutely. I had a regular client right before I saw him out there, and I remember the tattoo."

"What time was this?"

"Just before it got dark. Six thirty, maybe?"

I slide my phone out of my pocket and bring up the picture of Heather Martin.

"Yeah, that's definitely her. She was wearing that same necklace," he says, pointing at the phone. "I only remember because she was wearing all black clothes, so the necklace stood out. And my girl-friend loves jewelry, so I'm always scoping it on other people."

This guy has a hell of an eye for detail. I guess that's what you want in a tattoo artist.

"Did you catch what they were talking about or whether she had a vehicle? Anything at all?"

"Nah. I try to avoid that guy. They were just smiling and laughing next to his stupid Camaro. I don't remember seeing another car."

"Can you give me the landlord's info?"

He laughs. "Actually, no. He sends someone by on the first and collects the rent in cash." He looks sheepish. "It's not real above-board."

I nod. "Thanks so much for your time, Lee. I really appreciate it." I remove a business card from my wallet. "If you hear anything weird upstairs, will you give me a call?"

"Absolutely." He takes the card and puts it in his pocket before gesturing at the partition. "I gotta get back to this client, unless there's anything else?" He raises his eyebrows to show that he wants to be helpful. And he already has been.

"Would you be willing to head downtown whenever you have a few minutes to give a formal statement?"

"Sure. I'm off tomorrow. Will that work?"

"Perfect. Thanks again."

He smiles. "Have a good day, Detective. Stay dry out there."

I return the smile then exit the shop. The rain is turning to sleet, and I pull my blazer around me, cursing myself again for not wearing a heavier jacket or bringing an umbrella.

I take the other way around the building to the alley so that I can scope out the fire escape. Sure enough, the ladder, which should be attached, is lying on the ground next to several paint cans.

As I'm walking to the car, I'm hit with the image of George Arsalan on the fire escape. *I fire three shots, and he's down.*

I shake my head, yank open the car door, and drop in next to Goran. "It's him. Excellent witness—the guy who owns the shop. Says he was here on Saturday evening with Heather Martin."

"No way."

"Way. Let's see if he's home. Fire escape on the side is disabled." I lean forward and shake some of the water out of my hair.

We open our doors at the same time, and I round the back of the car to meet Goran near Maxwell's back door. We huddle under the awning, and my partner rings the bell. "This door probably just leads to a stairway," I muse.

He begins pounding on the door, but no one answers.

I open the mailbox to find a lot of mail. "He isn't home. Tons of mail."

"But his car's here."

"If he thinks we're looking for him, not driving an orange Camaro is probably smart."

He nods and pulls out his phone. "I'll get an unmarked to sit on this place." He requests an unmarked car to this location for surveillance and for all units to be on the lookout for Maxwell.

I tap his shoulder and mouth "Rec Room."

He requests that another car sit on the club.

"Let's go talk to the Renaissance people," I say once he ends the call.

"I thought Roberts and Sims were on that."

"Yeah, and all of this is taking too long. It can't hurt. I'll tell Roberts what we're doing." I tap out a quick text message, and he replies almost instantly: *We got the warrant for surveillance footage and the room charged to Martin's card. Sims and I are heading there now. Meet us there?*

I hold out the phone, and Goran squints at it.

"Let's go," he says.

Thunder rumbles overhead as I type a reply: *Be there in fifteen minutes. Meet you out front.*

CHAPTER 22

The rain intensifies as we drive, and at one point, Goran has to brake hard behind a pizza-delivery driver. I avoid making a smart-ass comment and instead focus on what we know so far.

It feels too easy. There has to be a layer we're missing. Even if Maxwell is our guy—and it looks as though chances are good that he is, given the Rec Room and BodMachine connections and the witness's statement about seeing him with Martin on the night of her murder—we have to find him, question him, and either collect more physical evidence or link him to what we already have. A preliminary search says he doesn't even have a sister, so he lied to his boss.

I check my watch, see that it's two forty-five, then text Fishner that all four of us are going to miss the three o'clock briefing.

As usual, she calls instead of replying. "Get surveillance if you can. Do you have any updates?"

Sometimes, I wonder if she calls me just because she loves the melodious sound of my voice. I give her the download on Elias Maxwell.

"Interesting. Okay. I'm off to my lieutenants' meeting. Keep me informed."

I continue to silently speculate about what the hell is going on with her. "Ten-four."

Suddenly, the rain stops, and the sun peeks out from behind dark clouds. Goran chomps his gum with gusto.

"Maybe the girls are in luck for tonight."

"Yeah, but it sure as hell doesn't look like I'll be joining them." He flexes his jaw.

"We can do our best."

We pull up in front of the Renaissance, and Goran parks the car behind Roberts and Sims. The four of us open our doors almost simultaneously, get out, then meet to the left of the front door.

The man behind the valet desk comes running over. "You can't really park here," he says. "This is for valet guests only."

Roberts badges him. "This is police business."

The man looks affronted but returns to his podium when Roberts puffs out his enormous chest.

Goran makes a big show of saying hello to Sims, and Sims rolls with it. "I'm hoping to get done in time to take my son trick-or-treating," the younger man says. "You got Halloween plans?"

"Yeah, if we can get this guy. I figure we can let him sit on his hands till tomorrow."

At least they're playing nice today. I give them the brief version of the day's events.

Sims nods then turns to Roberts. "Warrant?"

He taps his suit jacket over the inside pocket. "It's for surveillance footage and the room charged to Martin's credit card. I've been in touch with the security manager, Veronica Keaton, and she's waiting for us. She says the room has been cleaned since Martin's stay—assuming that she stayed here—but that it's vacant right now."

The four of us head toward the front door. "This is your party," I say.

The three men shoot me their respective versions of a questioning look.

I nod, and we proceed. I smile in spite of myself as we take turns through the revolving door.

The Renaissance looks like it always does, all gold and marble and money. Goran and I stay back and lean against a pillar as Roberts and Sims approach the counter, ostensibly to ask for Veronica Keaton.

Goran elbows me in the side and gestures to a group of people in costume who are entering the bar.

"What? It's Halloween."

"When did Halloween turn into this? What happened to ghosts and goblins?"

I narrow my eyes. "If memory serves, at some point in the eighties."

"But a sexy handmaid? That's an insult to the show."

"Not to mention the book."

He pops a toothpick.

"You've read it, right? The show is great, but the book is a classic."

"You and your degrees."

"Don't start that with me. I'm simply recommending a book based on a TV show that you obviously watch."

He looks at the front door then faces the pillar. "Don't look now, but that's Joe Mattioli."

I turn and pretend to be talking to Goran, but really, I'm watching Mattioli walk across the lobby. In the flesh, he looks less bloated than he did on TV. He's about five ten, two forty, and most but not all of it is muscle. He's traveling with a guy who looks like a younger version of himself, two attractive women, and—

"Goran, it's Maxwell. He's here. He's with Mattioli."

"Shit."

"We don't have an arrest warrant."

"At least we know where he is."

"Let's go to the bar and talk about this."

"We can't let him leave our sight."

"Too late. He's by the elevator."

Goran scans the elevator area. "You go. I can't. Mattioli will recognize me."

"Are you—"

"Just go!" he whisper-yells.

I jog to the elevator and get on with Mattioli's entourage. I step on just as the doors are closing, slip my badge from its belt clip to my pocket, and pretend to be enchanted with my phone. I make sure to stand right by the door, facing forward so that none of them can see my face. Given what Mattioli had to say about female cops, it wouldn't surprise me if he knows exactly who I am.

The elevator goes all the way to the top floor, so I have to pretend to be a dumbass. "Wait, what? I thought we were going down." I put on my Candy Cooper voice, but I'm pretty sure no one buys it. What matters is that they all exit on the top floor. Mattioli leads with Maxwell and the women close behind, and I know they're headed to the presidential suite. I worked a sexual assault case here years ago, and in spite of the remodeling, the floor plan has to be the same.

The good news is that not a single person pays attention to me. I ride the elevator to the ground floor, where Goran is waiting.

"Presidential suite," I say. "Confirmed."

"We have a problem," he replies. "Robertsims—that name is never going to leave them—are up against a brick wall. Keaton says something happened with the Saturday footage and it got erased."

"Shit. At least we have Maxwell here, right now. Think we can get a warrant?"

"Not until we do the dirty work," he replies. "She says we can have a go at the trash. We gotta go talk to the housekeeping people."

"I just found Maxwell, and I get to go through trash?" I shake my head. "Nope. I'll wait down here and make sure they don't leave."

"*We* found Maxwell, and *we* get to go through trash. We can't do anything more till we get the green light from Fishner. And something tells me we need more evidence for that."

"Isn't there some kind of backup for the surveillance?"

"Who knows? Your guy Sims is on it, though. Let's go see what they've got."

I make a face.

"They went that way." He gestures through a door marked Employees Only.

I follow him down the hallway and through the door, hoping with everything I've got that I don't have to dig through hotel trash. Used condoms, needles, booze bottles, bloody Kleenex, poopy diapers... Who the hell knows what's in there?

We end up in a very metal-and-white space. A small Hispanic man greets us and leads us over to where Sims and Roberts stand next to a pile of laundry. "Laundry done every day," the man says. "Laundry no good to you. Trash another story."

I shake my head. "You guys, we need to get Patrol out here."

Roberts tosses me a pair of gloves. "Or we could do it ourselves and save the time and bullshit."

Sims tips his head at his partner and attempts a smile.

I make a face. "Or we could follow procedure and get Patrol to do it." I tap my phone and call for four patrol officers.

About two hours later, after we've watched four disgruntled uniforms comb through reams of disgusting detritus and find nothing of interest, my phone rings with an unknown number. I hesitate before answering but only just. "Detective Boyle." I glance at the clock—it's after five already.

"Hi, Detective. This is Lee from the tattoo shop? You were here earlier. I just wanted to let you know that I heard noises upstairs. I think our douchebag is home. Sounds like he's moving furniture around."

Jesus, enough time has passed that he's home? "Thanks. Someone will be by soon."

"Boyle!" Goran calls. "Patrol got a hit! Maxwell is home. We gotta go get him. See? I told you I should have stayed in the lobby."

I look sympathetically at Sims and Roberts.

"What's this?" a uniform asks, pulling something from the trash.

"That looks like the tape Micalec found at the scene," Roberts replies from across the room.

I slip my gloves off, and Goran does the same. "Bag it. Bag the whole section. We're going to pick him up," I say, "but keep going here. Get everything you can."

They both nod at me, and Goran and I take off for the car. "It's all circumstantial," I say. "And I'm driving. Keys. You call Fishner."

"Yeah, until Jo gets us a DNA hit. Have faith, Boyle." He tosses me the keys, and I catch them. He fumbles with his phone but eventually holds it up to his ear.

We sprint to the car and get in, and I pull away as fast as I can.

"We've got a hit on Maxwell," he says into his phone as I drive. "Right. I know it's circumstantial, but both Patrol and the witness put him back at his apartment."

I gun it through a yellow light.

"He was at the Renaissance. We witnessed him get onto an elevator with Joe Mattioli, a younger man, and two women." Another pause. "We have enough," he says. "We're bringing him in for questioning."

I make the ten-minute drive in half that and slam the Charger into Park behind the orange Camaro. Operating purely on instinct, I get out of the car, make sure Goran is behind me, and move toward the door with my hand on my weapon.

Goran rings the bell then pounds on the door. Behind it, there's the sound of someone coming down the stairs, then it opens.

Elias Maxwell greets us with a grin. "Oh, hi. Come on in."

I keep my hand on my Glock and follow him up the narrow stairs, half expecting an ambush.

"Let's not mess around," Goran says from behind me. "Are you Elias Maxwell?"

He faces us once he reaches the landing. "Indeed I am." He holds his arms out and flexes, just like the silhouette on the BodMachine logo. "And I'll save you a whole bunch of time. I killed Heather Martin. She deserved it. What's next?"

CHAPTER 23

I'm trying to figure out if Elias Maxwell is on something or otherwise compromised. Most people don't confess to murder as soon as they see a pair of detectives.

Goran approaches from behind me with his handcuffs in his hand. "Yeah? You killed her? What happened?"

Maxwell faces the wall as if he does this every day. "She just couldn't shut the fuck up. All she had to do was shut the fuck up, but she couldn't."

Goran cuffs him then pats him down. "Were you dating or something?"

Maxwell laughs in a cheerless way that freaks me out. "Not at all. I was her trainer at the gym, and I maybe knew her from somewhere else too."

Goran flips him around. "Sit." He points at the top step. "Don't try to run. You'll just fall down the stairs."

We take a quick look around, knowing full well that we don't have a search warrant, though the confession is probable cause.

I open a drawer in his dresser and find a coil of rope that looks a whole lot like what we found at the murder scene. "Goran!" I call. I take a photo of the evidence in situ.

"We've gotta get him to Justice," my partner says. "We'll come back with a search warrant and the whole crew. We've got the dirtbag."

We get him into the car with little fanfare, other than the fact that he doesn't shut up. They usually go silent or speak purely in obscenities, but this guy is off his leash, going on and on about whatever pops into his head. He's either on drugs or insane.

At some point, he kicks the metal grate behind my head. "I recognize you, Lady Cop."

"Oh, yeah? That's great," I mutter as I hit the turn signal.

"Yeah. I was at my friend's trial. He got off. I'm kind of surprised you're still out and about, given all that uncomfortable stuff that happened."

My blood runs cold.

"Shut up, asshole," Goran says, "unless you want to tell us more about what you did to Heather Martin."

I glance at Maxwell in the mirror. He's grinning. "I beat the shit out of her. She deserved it. She was bad news going back, like, twenty years. And she just couldn't shut up—the whole time I trained her, she kept saying shit like, 'I'm punching this heavy bag and imagining Joe Mattioli's face. I'm doing this dead lift and thinking about kicking the shit out of Jeff O'Connor.' She couldn't help herself. She needed to be taken out. Those guys are like family to me."

I blink fast and grip the steering wheel hard. I feel Goran looking at me. I slide my phone out of my pocket and start recording what this guy is saying.

"You probably deserve it, too, Lady Cop. I mean, you broke the rules, you know? That wasn't cool."

I focus on how my hands feel on the wheel.

"That other lady cop too. What was her name? Black chick."

Neither Goran nor I respond.

"Hey. I'm talking to you. What was her name? Oh, I remember. DuBois. She'd better watch her back. Both of you. You're too angry. All of you. Best to step out of the way and let men do a man's work."

I make a mental note to warn DuBois.

"How do you know Joe Mattioli?" Goran asks.

"Wouldn't you like to know?" Maxwell chuckles.

I glance at him in the mirror again, and he seems to be having a grand old time, a much better one than I would be having if I was going to be arrested for capital murder.

"Yeah, we would," my partner replies.

"Well, *off the record*, I was best friends with Giacomo. I'm sure you know that's Joe's son, right? Now he's a cop in Chicago. But whatever. I practically grew up in that house."

"So you were around when Anna Mattioli was killed?" I ask.

He laughs, and it's so sinister that I get a chill. "Maybe I was, and maybe I wasn't. Hey, bucko," he says to Goran. "What's it like working with a chick like this? You must get it somewhere else. I don't really see the two of you doing the nasty."

"Why'd you do it, man?" Goran asks, and I hear the tension in his voice. "And why make it so easy for us to find you?"

"I'd do anything for my family. Anything. And that bitch had it coming. Like I said. She kept talking shit about Joe, and I couldn't have that. Joe is like a dad to me. She was gonna go public with a bunch of shit she claims happened back in the day—we all knew it—and I couldn't let that happen. I figure life in prison is a small price to pay for doing the right thing."

I raise my eyebrows and blow out a breath. A small price to pay, indeed.

"But while we're on the subject, I'm not saying anything on the record without my attorney present. You know, I might just get away with it, especially with that bimbo prosecutor of yours."

"Fat chance," Goran mutters.

"I can't believe you got in that elevator, Lady Cop. Did you really think we wouldn't make you? I guess you're not as smart as you think you are."

Hardly anyone is.

WHEN WE REACH THE JUSTICE Center, we all see that a crowd has gathered. "Oh, what's that?" Maxwell asks from the back seat. "Looks like you guys fucked up again." He laughs. "Joe's right. This city is on its way down. It all started with electing a black guy as mayor. What a bunch of bullshit. And that kid deserved it. They all deserve it. We need to clean this city up."

The crowd, which is made up mostly of brown people, appears to be nonviolent. Several people hold up Black Lives Matter signs, and a woman with a megaphone leads them in prayer.

"Ha—prayer isn't gonna help you now, sweetheart," Maxwell says.

I guide the car into the underground parking area, find a spot, and slam it into Park. "Dude, has it ever occurred to you to shut the fuck up?" I can't help myself.

Maxwell just grins like an idiot.

Goran opens his door, and I follow suit. We exchange a glance before he lets Maxwell out of the car.

"See? That's what I mean." He looks at Goran as though he's holding the Holy Grail. "I'm saying, man, I don't know how you deal with such a mouthy bitch."

Goran yanks Maxwell's arms up behind him to a point that looks uncomfortable.

"You're on the wrong side of it," Maxwell says, wincing. "You're protecting her, but really you should be demanding that she be fired. After all that shit with my boy Grimes, I'd think you'd know. I guess I should tell Joe about you too."

"What does that mean?" Goran growls. He shoves Maxwell forward, and we all walk to the elevator.

"It means that, now we're here, I think you should call my lawyer. Jeff O'Connor. I'm sure you know him." He leers at me.

"What about the bomb? Why do that?"

He laughs again. "My plan was to take all of you the fuck out, along with whatever shithead thug was walking by. Bad neighborhood. Needs to be cleaned up."

I resist the urge to trip him and watch him fall onto his face, and I can't help wondering about the Mattioli connection. Surely, this prick didn't act alone.

WE GET HIM INTO THE interview room, where he takes a couple more cheap shots at me then demands his attorney a few more times. Goran shoves him into a chair and cuffs him to the table. "You piece of shit."

I stand in the corner, silently seething.

"Jeff O'Connor. Call him. And anything I said back there? Good luck proving it."

I recorded it, you stupid motherfucker. It feels as if all the blood in my body just caught on fire.

"Call him now, please." Maxwell winks at me.

Goran watches me carefully, knowing that the recording will never be admissible in court and that I can be volatile.

But not here. Not with this guy, who is just waiting for me to make a wrong step. I blink twice at Maxwell then leave the room with Goran right behind me.

Feeling as though I might puke, I head directly to the bathroom, ignoring my partner. I lock myself in the corner stall and lean against the wall. *You know how to do this. Breathe. Just breathe.* I obey my own commands for a couple of minutes, but when I'm done, I'm just closer to tears. I leave the stall, wash my hands, and splash cold water on my face. After drying with a paper towel, I exit the bathroom.

Fishner is waiting for me next to the vending machines. "My office."

"I have to call his attorney."

"No. Goran is handling that. First, you and I are going to have a conversation in my office." She has her scary-calm voice.

"What the hell did I do now?"

She doesn't answer. She walks past me and down the hallway, clearly expecting me to follow, which I do.

"Of fucking *course* Jeff O'Connor is his attorney," I mutter as we enter her office. "It just figures. He fucking says he did it, and now that's all we have. That and a necklace with his initials on it and a stupid piece of tape."

"Boyle, don't take it personally." Fishner closes her office door and shuts the blinds on the windows facing the squad room. "You didn't do anything. But you also can't be involved in an interrogation with O'Connor present. Not yet. Not given what's happening outside."

I walk to the window and look at the street below. More people are arriving at the demonstration, and I hope to everything holy that the cops behave and it stays nonviolent. "He set a trap for us. He tried to kill us with that stupid bomb. And now we can't do anything about it, and I'm sure as I'm alive that someone put him up to this." *I want to nail him to the wall, and now I can't.* "He confessed. I have the whole thing recorded on my phone. He thinks he did the right thing. He's *proud* of it."

"You have to trust your partner."

I take a deep breath and let it out slowly, feeling my heart rate drop a tiny bit. I roll my shoulders back and down then face her. "I do trust my partner."

"Then—"

Suddenly, the rage I've been trying to control since that day on the witness stand—maybe for my entire career—comes up from behind my sternum, and I can't stop myself. I square my stance, crossing my arms across my chest to stop my hands from shaking. "What I don't trust is this entire culture of bullshit. Misogyny. Racism. Rampant stereotyping. Like, everyone thinks it's"—I wave a hand toward the door—"because of the Rec Room—and please, unlike everyone else, believe me when I say I'm *not* a member of a club like that—but it isn't."

She starts to speak.

"No. I'm not done. At this point, I've got nothing to lose with you, Carrothers, Goran, this whole job... I've got nothing to lose. So I'll say it. All of this is because of stupid little men and their rage at women in power. That guy hates women like me. He hates women like you, like Becker, like Heather Martin. And that fucker O'Connor just enables him and all of the assholes who are just like him." My eyes feel hot, as if they're about to pop out of my head, and I'm waving my arms around without really noticing.

"I don't trust that anyone but me gives two shits about who brutalized Heather Martin like that, and I don't trust that anything we do will make a difference, beyond placating the brass and keeping the media happy. Maybe we should call the reporters and have them watch the fucking sausagefest that's about to occur in there. Oh, but wait. They're too busy covering the demonstration outside, which is peaceful but is sure to include a bunch of cops in riot gear. It's not a good look. All of this is bullshit." A little shot of adrenaline hits me when I realize that I'm talking to my boss this way. *Whatever. It's too late now. I'll be suspended. Maybe I'll go on vacation.*

She takes a breath as if to speak but stops, looking slightly surprised.

"I used to think justice and the law were at least related. If I hadn't? I would *never* have testified against Grimes. You know it. You know me. I would have lied. I would have done anything to get out of taking the stand. I would have told Becker to fuck herself. I wouldn't have done it if I hadn't genuinely thought he would go to jail for what he did to that guy."

She eyes me carefully.

I squeeze my eyes shut for a moment then open them and blink a couple of times. Everything has that weird sharpness, just like it did that day on the witness stand. "And I don't like it, but what can I say? It's all bullshit. You know it—I *know* you know it, and that's why you've been holding back, having secret meetings, tiptoeing around, trying to keep Carrothers happy. I'm sorry, but that's just how it is. Take a stand, Fishner. Quit playing politician and stand up for something for once." I'm suddenly exhausted, so I drop into one of her visitors' chairs and lean forward, my elbows on my knees. *I will not cry in front of her.*

But it's too late. The tears come hot and fast, and I wipe them away with a hand.

She stands in front of me then leans against her desk. "I can't argue with you."

"See? I knew you—wait. What?"

"You're right, and I can't argue with you. What we need to do is make absolutely certain that all of the evidence aligns against this guy. If someone else was involved, we'll figure it out. Then we move forward."

I sit back in my chair. "What does that mean, 'We move forward'?"

She sighs. "We get an indictment against Elias Maxwell. We try to put our squad back together. Maybe we bring in some kind of group coach or—"

I shake my head. "You aren't getting it. I'm talking about a much larger problem than this case. I'm talking about what I saw Joe Mattioli say on TV last night. I'm talking about the threats Grimes made against me. I'm talking about threatening phone calls, which I've received since the verdict. I'm talking about—"

"Boyle, I get it." She sits in the chair next to me, and it's weird. She's never done that before. She turns to me. "I get it all too well, for reasons I'm not prepared to explain to you right now." She sighs.

"I hear you. And I won't ask why you didn't say anything about the threatening phone calls." She knows me too well.

I blink fast a few times and feel my blood pressure drop. I run a hand through my hair. "What do we do now?"

She gives me a sad smile. "We go watch Goran and Roberts interrogate this guy. We'll take note of all of it. We'll use the circumstantial evidence to get concrete evidence, and then we'll call Becker. We'll indict him. And then we'll move on. The only way to change the culture is from inside it. So don't throw it all away just yet." She stands. "Okay?"

I stretch my neck.

"I overheard you say a while back that you've been reading Joe Mattioli's book," she says, rounding her desk to her regular chair as if none of what just happened actually occurred.

"Yeah, on and off. It's not very good."

"If what Maxwell said to you in the car is true, we should take a look at him. But we have to be very careful. Don't roll your eyes."

"I wasn't."

She picks up a pen and balances it between her thumb and forefinger. "If we go down this road, there will be no turning back."

"Will you quit talking in riddles and just tell me what I am or am not allowed to do?"

She looks very sad and very tired. "Way back when, Mattioli was involved in a group of men who committed acts of violence against women. Heather Martin was one of those women." She gulps and sets the pen down. "If Maxwell stayed in that house for any length of time, this doesn't surprise me. None of what's happening surprises me. I wish it did."

"Then, what, the fact that Martin and Maxwell are both members of the Rec Room and BodMachine is just coincidence?"

She narrows her eyes. "Probably. It's a big city, but it's also a small town. Let me hear the recording."

I play all twelve minutes of it for her, and she winces twice.

"Seems likely that he met her at one of the two places, developed a relationship with her, realized who she was, and put two and two together."

"So he genuinely believes that killing her was an ethical act? If Mattioli was like a dad to him, I guess it makes sense. It's just totally convoluted."

She nods. "I want you to let Goran and Roberts question him. I will watch. I'll put Sims on triangulating Maxwell's location data, and we'll see if it matches."

"It will."

"Well, we have seventy-two hours after we arrest him formally to find out."

I nod.

"After the questioning, we'll book him on whatever we can cobble together. I'll call Becker. I'll get someone out to search his apartment. Maybe some kind of physical evidence will turn up there."

"If it does, it's open-and-shut. Especially if we can get him to confess on the record." I stand, feeling invigorated enough to work all night and liking her plan. "What do you want me to do about Mattioli?"

"What I don't know won't hurt me. Stay under the radar." She picks up the phone receiver. "I've got to call Becker. Go get some fresh air, and I'll meet you in the observation room."

I nod.

I just went off on my boss.

The only way to change the culture is from inside it.

CHAPTER 24

I do as I'm told and go outside for some air. The rain has stopped, replaced with bright sun, puffy clouds, and blue sky. I stand in the sun and wish, not for the first time, that I smoked. It would get me outside more.

Wondering what's happening with the demonstration, I decide to walk over to Public Square for a minute. They're still working on major renovations over here, but it's always been one of my favorite parts of the city.

I perch on the edge of the outdoor amphitheater and watch a small gaggle of remaining protesters head down Ontario. I glance at my watch. It's already six thirty, so there's no way that Goran and Sims are going to be able to take their kids trick-or-treating. It sucks. Then again, it's an occupational hazard. It occurs to me, also not for the first time, that in some ways, I'm an ideal cop. I don't have a family. I don't have a relationship anymore. I'm closer to my partner and boss than I am to almost anybody else. It's too bad I didn't perjure myself on the stand. It would have meant I could stay an ideal cop.

A group of high schoolers make their way through the square in their Halloween costumes. When they reach the amphitheater, they line up, and someone takes their picture.

I take a deep breath and let it out slowly, trying to remember my last Halloween costume. I squint at the yellow leaves on the trees and recall my dad dressing us as the Three Stooges—it must have been the year before my sister died. I chuckle when I imagine Christopher dressed as Curly, my little sister as Moe, and me as Larry.

To stop myself from getting lost in reverie, I push off the concrete ledge. My phone buzzes in my pocket. *We're ready,* Fishner says. She actually sent me a text message.

As I walk to the Justice Center, I try to get my head around the meaning of "What I don't know won't hurt me." It's not like her—she's usually a micromanager, and she's never told me to violate policy and procedure before.

Then again, that's not exactly what she meant. She said to "stay under the radar." I wonder whether that means I'm to fly solo on my off-the-books investigation of Joe Mattioli. I guess the first thing I should do is finish his book—it might lead me toward asking the right questions. As it stands, the only things I have to go on are Fishner's allegations, which are off the record, a suspect's illegally recorded rant, which is off the record, and an alleged connection between that suspect and the retired detective.

I won't be able to talk to Mattioli directly, at least not at first. I'm too much of a liability to be tasked with questioning a misogynist like him. But I also can't ask any of the guys in my squad to do it, not if I'm staying under the radar. Fishner must not think he's involved in the homicide. The alternative makes no sense.

A kid on a motorized scooter almost knocks me over as I stride down Ontario. At least he apologizes.

I push through the side door of the Justice Center then end up on the elevator with a couple of uniforms who look at me but don't say anything. It's unclear whether they're deliberately giving me the cold shoulder. They get off on the floor below mine.

When I step off the elevator, the first thing I see is Fishner, who stands near my desk with Captain Carrothers and Julia Becker. *Oh, so it's gonna be that kind of party.* I sigh and head down the hallway to the vending machine, where I buy a can of sparkling water.

Fishner catches my eye as I approach my desk. She gives me the look that means "I hope you're going to behave yourself in front of the captain." Becker gives me a wan smile and a little wave.

Carrothers just glares at me. "Detective Boyle, nice of you to join us." He obviously stifles a sneer.

What the hell did I do to deserve this? There's no point in wondering. The proof is in the pudding. In the interest of professional decorum, I give him a little salute then turn to Fishner. "Where's Goran?"

"In the conference room with Roberts and Sims, filling Roberts in on the information you gleaned in the car while Sims gets location data."

"Are we getting an arrest warrant?" I ask Becker.

She nods. "But we're going to need more than the evidence collected so far to indict him."

"Maybe he'll confess again."

Carrothers crosses his arms. "What, exactly, did he say in the car?"

At this point, I have nothing to lose. I pull my phone out of my pocket, open the voice-recording app, and play the recording for him.

About six minutes in, right as Maxwell starts to talk about Joe Mattioli, Carrothers waves a hand. "That's all I need to hear." He squeezes the bridge of his nose then shakes his head.

I feel you, buddy. "Is O'Connor here?"

Becker nods. "He's meeting with his client now."

I sip my water and wait for someone to announce what's happening next.

Carrothers glares at me again. "It's damned unfortunate that you have such a problem with Jeff O'Connor, given that you're exactly the right person to interrogate this suspect."

I shrug. "No disrespect, sir, but it's not entirely my fault that I have a problem with Jeff O'Connor."

Fishner changes her face into the "Don't fuck this up" look.

He nods. "Well, it's unfortunate. That's all I'm saying." He faces Fishner. "I'm sticking around for this. We need to vindicate Mattioli before the press gets wind of their connection."

I stop myself from wincing. The observation room is small, and one of the last people I want to be in there with is Carrothers, who is not setting a good example of how to run an investigation. We can never set out to vindicate this person or that person—we have to follow the evidence. Full stop.

Sims comes barreling out of the conference room, looking as though he has news. "Location data matches."

"That was fast," I reply.

"I have my ways. He was at home when the tattoo witness saw him, at the Rec Room that evening, and at the Renaissance until—"

"That dumb fuck. Did he *want* to get caught?"

"If he thinks he's avenging the men of the world, yes," Becker says.

Carrothers raises an eyebrow and makes a strange sound.

"More specifically, he thinks he's avenging Joe Mattioli," Fishner says.

"I do not want Mattioli involved in any of this," Carrothers says firmly. "This is not an investigation of him or his family." He points down the hall, where Maxwell and O'Connor sit in a room. "Your job is to put that guy where he belongs." He turns to Becker. "And *your* job is to keep Mattioli's name out of the record."

She looks affronted. "With all due respect, Captain, I do not work for the Division of Police, which means that you do not hold rank over me. I work for the prosecutor, and I have an ethical and legal obligation to include on the record anything that might be necessary to this case."

I want to hug her.

The look on his face says it all. He puffs out his chest and turns to Fishner. "As I said. Put Maxwell where he belongs, and keep Mattioli out of it. I'll call the prosecutor's office and see if we can work out a deal." He walks down the hall.

"Yes, sir," she replies softly. She and I exchange a glance, and I give her a tight nod.

"Like hell you'll work out a deal," Becker mutters under her breath. She's red-faced and tense—I'm not sure I've ever seen her so angry.

"Uh, guys? Do you want to know more about the location data before we question the guy?"

Carrothers turns around. "Yes, Detective."

Sims steps over to us with a map printout and two highlighters, and I gesture for him to use my desk. We circle around. "He was at home at seven o'clock." He puts a green dot on the map. "Heather Martin's phone was there too." He puts a yellow dot on the map. "He was at the Rec Room at least between eight thirty and eleven—he received several text messages during that time." He puts a green dot on the map. "Heather Martin's phone was also there during that time." Yellow dot.

"Where it gets interesting is when he gets to the hotel." Green dot. "She was also there, but her phone goes dead at midnight." Yellow dot. "His does not. At approximately two twenty a.m., he gets a text message triangulated to a tower at East 105th and Superior." He puts a green dot there. "He must have shut his phone off after that. It goes quiet until late the next day, when he's back at home."

"Look at where Lake View Cemetery is," I whisper, pointing at a spot close to East 105th and Superior. "That's exactly the route I would take to go from the hotel to that cemetery."

Becker nods. "It's still circumstantial, but it adds a lot. I can go to a judge with this."

"That's not all," Sims says, looking giddy. "On Sunday, the day we found her car? Location data puts him in that area too." He puts a green dot on the map next to Fairfax Park. "Then it goes quiet again until Monday, when he's back at home."

"Let's keep adding charges," Becker says. "Nice work, Detective." Sims grins. "Thanks."

"Have you found any other numbers repeating the same pattern?" I ask.

He purses his lips. "Not yet, but I'll get on it. It could take a while. It's a lot of data."

"It's time to question him," Fishner says. "Sims, will you please get Goran and Roberts? Tell them we'll be in the observation room, ready when they are. You work on getting all of this into a report."

"Yes, ma'am," he replies. He goes back into the conference room.

Carrothers heads down the hall, and Fishner faces me. "Boyle, you and Sims see if you can get any video evidence from the Renaissance's backup server, and then talk to the witnesses and see if they have anything on Maxwell." She looks at the crime board. "Martha Rodgers, Mistress Natalia. Anything you can."

So she's playing the Maxwell-is-guilty angle. But what about Mattioli? "Ten-four, boss." I don't really want to stand in a room with Carrothers, anyway.

She nods and follows the captain down the hallway. I flounce into my chair and pick up our Nerf football.

"Liz, do you have a minute?" Becker asks, barely above a whisper. "Just quickly."

"What's up?"

"I need to talk to you about a few things." She looks worried.

"Is everything okay? Are you okay?" I set the football on my desk and sit up.

She smiles, but it's forced. "I'm fine. I just need to talk to you about a couple of things. Are you free later?"

I run a hand through my hair. "It kind of depends on what happens here. I think so?" I force a laugh. "I mean, I don't really have any social plans, if that's what you're asking."

She looks back and forth. "It's kind of important, but we can't talk here, and I have to run to catch Judge Cole before he leaves for the day if we're going to get this warrant."

"Yeah, just let me know when and where."

She nods. "Okay. Thanks."

"Are you sure you're okay?"

"Fairly sure." She picks her briefcase up from my visitors' chair. "Gotta run. You'll hear from me later." She turns to leave.

"Okay." *This job gets weirder and weirder every day.*

CHAPTER 25

Sims and I haven't worked this closely together before, so it's interesting to see how he operates. We sit at opposite ends of the table in the conference room. He's busy digitizing his map—it'll look better on the record that way—while I make a series of phone calls. From time to time, he squints at his screen and either smiles or grunts.

The first call is to Veronica Keaton at the Renaissance. Even though Jo Micalec is likely to get some physical evidence from the trash, it would be good to have surveillance footage, too, especially if Mattioli or one of his other cronies was involved. She doesn't answer, and I don't leave a message.

The second is to Mistress Natalia, who I guess has allowed my phone number through the voice-verification service. "Detective, how are things? Have you considered my offer?"

"I'm actually calling to ask you to come in at some point tonight or tomorrow. We need to get a statement from you on the record."

"You have found the killer?"

I want to tell her to knock off the fake accent, but whatever. "We have a suspect in custody, and we need your statement as part of gathering evidence for the case."

"I cannot do that." I can almost hear her lean back in her chair. "It is too risky for my business."

"Cathy"—I hope that using her daytime name will get her to cooperate with me—"this is a big deal. It's a murder investigation, and the murder itself was one of the most brutal things I've seen in my career. How would your club's members like it if they knew a dead

"

woman was a dungeon master?" I would never alert the media, but she doesn't know that.

"What if it goes to trial? Then I will have to testify, no?"

I squeeze my eyes shut. "It isn't likely to go to trial. Over eighty-eight percent of cases in Cuyahoga County end in plea deals."

She's silent for a minute. "I have a Halloween party to host tonight," she says in her Cathy voice. "I can come in tomorrow. Will you be there?"

I hadn't planned to be here tomorrow, but I guess I can talk to you. "I can be. What time works for you?"

"One o'clock."

I tell her where to park and what elevator to take then thank her for her time, half wondering if she's really going to show. All we need from her is confirmation that Elias Maxwell and Heather Martin were involved in a BDSM relationship at the Rec Room—should the case go to trial, that will be enough for a jury. Most people make judgments. It's just how the world works.

The third call is to Lee at Artistic Renderings. He doesn't answer, so I leave a message: "Lee, this is Detective Boyle. We spoke earlier. I'm calling to thank you again"—I mean, the guy identified the necklace and tipped us off when Maxwell got home earlier—"and ask that you give me a call back at your earliest convenience. I'd like to get your statement on the record. I know we made arrangements for tomorrow, and I'd like to confirm a time. Thanks."

My fourth call is to Martha Rodgers, the primary witness from the bomb scene, but a disembodied voice tells me that her number is no longer in service. *I'll have to go see her.*

Just as I toss my phone onto the table, Sims gives a little cheer and pumps his fist in the air. "Shit, Boyle, I just nailed this guy's coffin shut."

I raise an eyebrow, and he turns the laptop to face me.

"He posted a photo on Instagram of one of those creepy statues at Lake View—early on Sunday morning."

"It's as if he wanted us to catch him," I mutter. *Which probably means he's covering for someone else.* "Good work, Sims." I eye him for a minute.

"I never thought it would be so easy. Man, when I got this assignment, I was sure it would be like the other cases y'all have had in the past. Y'know, convoluted shit."

"It's never that easy. It is never easy. Just because we have our guy... Think of it this way: if he didn't *want* to be caught? We wouldn't have caught him. A woman is dead." *And the entire city is crumbling.* I tap my pen on the table until I realize it's a Fishner mannerism. "If you want my opinion, it's *more* convoluted this way. They never confess."

"Yeah, I hear you. I didn't mean it that way. I just got excited about the digital stuff. I mean, it's my whole game, you know? And this dumbass—I mean, he posted on Instagram."

"He might not confess on the record." *And it isn't a game, but I know what you mean.*

He nods. "I know." He takes a breath as if to speak, but his phone rings. "Sims. Uh-huh? That's great, Ms. Keaton. Can you send it to me? Yes, that's my email. I'll wait." About thirty seconds later, his computer dings. "Okay, just let me check it—thanks for sending a zip file." He clicks around then grins. "Okay, this is perfect," he says. "I'll be by later to get the server itself, but this will work in the meantime. Thanks."

I stretch my shoulders. "Anything good?"

He grins. "We'll see. Looks like I'm lookin' at this all night."

I stand. "Don't forget about the other phone triangulations. I have to run out to see a witness. I'll be back"—I glance at my watch—"in about an hour. Will you tell Goran and Boss Lady I'll be back no later than eight?"

"Sure thing," he replies, focusing on the screen.

I leave the conference room, walk to my desk, grab my coat and bag, and head down the stairs to the car. If we can connect Maxwell to the bomb in Martin's SUV, he'll go away for a very long time.

I have to bypass Public Square because of the Halloween celebration there—it's nice that the rain seems to be holding off, and I suppose it's good that the protest appears to have ended. It takes me about eight minutes to get to Fairfax Park, using my lights to fly through red lights.

I pull up in front of Martha Rodgers's house and kill the lights. The neighborhood is deserted. I shove the door open, and a strong gust of cold wind blows down off the lake.

Her porch light is on, as are several lights inside, but no one answers the door when I knock. BooBoo, her dog, barks behind it, and I move to the left to look in the window. It looks like a nice, well-kept house, but there's no Martha Rodgers.

Out of the corner of my eye, I catch a zone car creeping around the corner, probably just doing a regular patrol. It slows to a stop behind the Charger and idles—it looks as though the guy behind the wheel is running a check on his computer, which is odd as hell, given that the Charger is a police vehicle.

Something in my gut tells me to stay exactly where I am instead of approaching the car, and I don't like it. Becker's words echo in my head, telling me to be careful. I shouldn't be here alone. I should have gone on the record about the threatening phone calls. I'm no superhero.

Two male officers exit the vehicle. My hand automatically moves to my Glock, but I put on a big grin and wave them over, wishing that Goran was here with me.

"Evening, Detective," the older and bigger one says. I recognize him from somewhere and watch him shut off his body camera. "Looking for someone?"

I squint at his name badge: Householder. "Just trying to get a last-minute witness statement." My voice shakes, and I hope they didn't hear it.

"Yeah? From who, the person who lives here?"

I nod. As he approaches, the dog goes bonkers behind the door. His partner stays back, which I find odd. Householder climbs the stairs, and I instinctively turn so that I have room to run if I need to.

He gets a little too close to my face, but I refuse to step backward even though he has six inches and about eighty pounds on me. "And who might that be?" he asks with a sneer.

"Look, Householder, I really don't have time for—"

He jams a finger into my sternum, and it hurts. "You have time for what I say you have time for, rat."

"Seriously? You're doing this on a witness's porch?" I fumble in my pocket for my phone.

"Don't bother calling anyone," he says.

He leers at me, and I place his face. He was at the Grimes trial. *Shit.* I resist the urge to run—his partner appears to be waiting for me to do just that. He stands about fifteen feet from the porch with his hand on his weapon.

He reaches to grab my shoulder, and the door opens. BooBoo runs out, barking and growling at Householder but ignoring me. The big man takes a step away from the dog but keeps his eyes on me.

"Now, BooBoo," Martha Rodgers says, "be nice to the man." She eyes him with suspicion. "Detective, how are you?"

"I'm fine." I thank everything holy that I'm telling the truth. "I just have a couple of follow-up questions for you. Do you have a few minutes?"

She watches BooBoo do his business in the yard then whistles for him. He comes running up the stairs and growls when Householder moves away from me.

"Come on in," she says, holding the door ajar.

"Thanks, Householder. I'll see you around," I say to the man.

He gives me a menacing grin. "Yeah. You will. Until then, Boyle." He smiles at Martha. "Ma'am."

I follow the older woman into her home. As she stands at the door and watches them leave, BooBoo takes a flying leap at a recliner in the corner then curls into a ball. "Sorry it took me so long." She faces me. "I was in the bath. Can I get you anything to drink?"

Why are you being nice to me? "I'm fine, but thanks. Do you mind if I sit down?" My heart is beating too fast, and I don't feel very well.

"Of course." She extends a hand, indicating for me to sit on the couch. "Do you mind if I ask what was going on out there just now? You sure you don't want some water? You look a little pale."

Why was my instinct to run from him instead of fight him? "A glass of water would be great. Thank you."

She nods, clearly concerned about me. While she's in the kitchen, I put my head between my legs and take several deep breaths, hoping the color returns to my face. *You've never been scared like this before, Boyle. Get it together. Get it together.*

"It looked to me like he was bothering you," she says as she hands me the glass of water.

I take several sips then set the glass on a nearby coaster. She sits in another chair across from me.

This is so amazingly unprofessional that I don't even know what to say. "He was bothering me. Thank you for opening the door when you did."

"Yup. I knew it. I can recognize an angry white man from ten miles away." She nods slowly.

I clear my throat and attempt a smile. "We're making an arrest, and I wonder whether you would be willing to look at some photos. Maybe you would recognize the man who set up the bomb?"

She nods. I pull my iPad from my bag, set Maxwell's photograph into a six-pack with five other men's BMV shots, and hold it up for her. She takes a pair of reading glasses out of her robe pocket and perches them on her nose before taking the device from me. She looks at each face in succession before her eyes move back to the upper right—Maxwell. "That's him," she says. "I mean, I think that's him." She hands the iPad to me.

"Are you certain?"

"As certain as I can be. I only caught a glimpse of his face, but single ladies like me need to pay attention." She removes her glasses. "You know what I mean?"

I nod and create another six-pack that includes Mattioli's photo. "Recognize anyone here?"

She points at the retired detective. "Him, but only from TV, up on talk shows talkin' about how his shit don't stink."

I chuckle. "Just to be sure, can you confirm the number of men you saw outside the other night?"

"Just the one."

Shit, it won't be easy. "Would you be willing to give an official statement? Not tonight but in the next couple of days?"

"Of course. Girl, you still don't look right. Is it about that policeman who got away with beating up the black man? Oh, wait. You was the cop who testified against him." She smiles.

She must watch Channel Three. "Something like that."

She nods wisely. "I thought so. That motherfucker should have gone down. Whole city is gearing up for demonstrations. Good for you, girl. Good for you."

I'm a little surprised by her use of the f-bomb, but I let it go. I give her a wan smile. "Yeah, he should have." I stand. "Thanks for your time, Mrs. Rodgers. And for the water."

"You tell me where to go and when, and I'll give you that statement." She follows me to the door. BooBoo looks up but doesn't move from the recliner.

I take out my wallet and remove a business card.

"I already got your card," she says. "Justice Center. What floor? And when?"

"Tomorrow at twelve thirty work for you?"

She nods. "I'll see you then. And I'll wait for you to get in your car and pull away before closing this door."

This is a brave woman. "Thanks. I appreciate it."

I step onto the porch and make sure Householder is gone then pull my phone from my pocket and call Fishner. She doesn't answer, but I pretend as though I'm talking to her as I walk to the car, just in case. Once I'm in and unscathed, I lock the doors, start the engine, and pull away from the curb. I should tell Goran what happened. I should tell Fishner. I should tell someone, but I can't—I'm not a snitch.

As I'm driving, I can't help it—I start to cry. It's not bathroom-meltdown level, but there are definitely tears. I think about the "tools I can use," as Dr. Shue would put it, and try to place the emotion. She would be so proud.

It's fear, sure. But mostly, I'm crying out of relief that they didn't hurt me, and gratitude for Martha Rodgers, who probably never in a million years expected to be helping a Cleveland Special Homicide detective hold her shit together.

My phone buzzes as I'm pulling onto Ontario. It's Goran. "What's up?" I ask.

"Hello to you too. We got him. Becker got the warrant, and we're sending him to booking. She's gonna go for the indictment tomorrow."

"On a Saturday?"

He chomps his gum. "High-profile case. What's happening on your end? Where are you?"

"Just got a positive ID from the Fairfax Park witness. She can place him at the bomb scene."

"Yes! Hell yes, Boyle!"

"Mm-hmm."

"Where are you now?"

"Pulling into the parking garage."

"We're all going for drinks. Meet you downstairs?"

"What about reports?" I ease the Charger down the ramp and into its spot.

"We can do those in the morning. C'mon, Boyle. Why aren't you happy about this? Fishner's gonna buy rounds. Becker's even coming. It's a good night."

"I am happy about this. Sure. Meet me down here." I'm not really in the mood to celebrate, but it's tradition, and I would just as soon not go home alone.

I have a brief back-and-forth in my head about whether or not to tell him what happened, ultimately deciding on not. He'll just worry. "See you in two minutes."

I end the call and trudge to the Passat, unlock it, get inside, and start the engine. I let my head fall back against the headrest. Goran's new Chrysler is parked on my left, and I gaze at its shiny splendor as I wait for him.

He knocks on my window, and I force a big grin. I roll the window down and give him a half-assed high five.

"Good work, partner," he says.

I mumble the same.

"Meet you at Smitty's. The guys are following. I think Carrothers is even coming."

Oh, great. "Sure. Meet you there. I'll follow you." If I follow him, he'll get out first and wait for me. It makes me sick that I feel like I need him—or someone—to protect me. I shake my head. Once he pulls away, I do the same.

It takes only a couple of minutes to get to Smitty's, where we're obviously going to crash a Halloween party. It's a cop-and-firefighter bar, and I try to shove paranoid thoughts out of my head. *What if*

Householder is here? I stare at myself in the rearview mirror. *No. Don't do that. That's what they want. Go inside and have a good time.*

I kill the engine. Goran waits for me behind my car, looking positively giddy. "So you're back to your regular jovial self?" I ask as I approach him.

"Hey, I was worried. Arresting this scumbag is the best thing I've done all week." We start walking to the door. "It sucks I missed trick-or-treat, but Vera sent me pictures. Look." He shoves his phone in front of my face, looking like the proud papa that he is. "Wait. Look." He zooms in on his daughter Lily's face. "Isn't she adorable? We're taking them to Boo at the Zoo tomorrow afternoon."

I chuckle in spite of myself. "Why is Boo at the Zoo on November first?"

He slides his phone back into his pocket and holds the heavy wooden door open for me. "Tomorrow's the last day. I figure we'll actually get time off after we knock out those reports."

"Famous last words," I mutter.

"I'm taking vacation after tomorrow. I put in for it earlier. I need a few days to catch my breath. Don't be mad."

"I'm not mad."

The bar is filled with people in Halloween costumes—clowns, princesses, furry animals, sexy handmaids, sexy cops, and the like. A few are out of costume, but they'll probably say they're dressed as law enforcement. I guess it sort of is a costume.

"Hell, where are we gonna sit?" Goran gestures at the bartender and grins.

"There's a table in the corner. I'll meet you over there." I push past the people in costume, hoping that none of them want to assault or kill me, and make my way to the corner, where I position myself with my back against the wall, facing the door. Householder and his partner are probably on until midnight, which gives me a couple of hours to pretend to enjoy myself.

I play with my phone. I just want to tell someone what happened, but I don't want to be a buzzkill at this party. Goran returns minutes later with two pitchers, Fishner, Roberts, Sims, and Becker. They all file in around the table, and Goran pours a beer for each of us.

"What is this pissy light beer?" I ask in a poor attempt at humor.

"It's better for you than that sludge you drink." He winks at me.

Fishner stands and holds up her glass. "To the amazing detectives in this squad. You worked well as a team, and I'm proud of all of you." She catches my eye. "Good work. Cheers."

We clink glasses and drink our swill. "Did he confess?" I ask Goran at some point a couple of rounds in.

"As good as. O'Connor is worried—this is a losing case, for sure. They're gonna have to take a plea. With all of what you and Sims got? He's cooked. What an idiot. Patrol is searching his house now, and I guarantee they come up with tons of evidence. That rope. What an idiot."

"Most criminals are, lest we forget."

"True that." He turns and talks to Sims, and I'm relieved that they appear to be getting along. I still can't figure out who reported the new guy looking into the old case to the boss.

Becker slides her chair over my way. "Do you have a few minutes after this?" she asks. She seems less nervous than she was earlier, but she's a hell of a good actress.

I nod, drain my third beer, pour another half, and toss it back. Fishner apparently notices the empty pitcher and gets up to have it refilled. "How about now?" I ask.

"Now could work, but this isn't the place."

I glance around at the partygoers, who seem less like they're staring at me the more I have to drink. I check my watch—it's only eight thirty. "Want to go get some food?" I ask.

She nods, and we both stand. I lean down to Goran. "I'm starving. Julia and I are going to grab a bite. Call me in the morning?"

He wiggles his eyebrows, and I smack his shoulder. "It's not like that. You know this."

Thankfully, she is focused on a conversation she's having with Fishner.

I don't give a shit anymore what they think. Let them say I'm sleeping with her. I just don't care. I'm too tired to care. I say good night to the guys, but Fishner stops me as Julia walks to the door. "Good work, Boyle. Remember what I said. Please be careful."

I nod. "Good night, boss." Then I follow Becker to the exit.

The cool, almost cold, autumn air is a relief when it hits my face, even if the rain has started again. "Where to?" I ask.

She pulls her coat more tightly around her. "I'm fine with whatever, as long as it's on our side of town." She means the East Side. I live in Cleveland Heights, and she has a condo in neighboring Shaker Heights.

"How about The Pub? It just opened not long ago. I've been there once. It's decent."

A man in a Jason mask exits the bar and looks at us. I look from him back to Julia, but she seems unconcerned. He turns away from us, pushes up his mask, and lights a cigarette.

She nods. "I'll meet you there."

ONCE WE'RE SEATED IN a cozy booth at the pub, I order a real beer. Julia orders a glass of Sauvignon Blanc. "Are we really having food or just a conversation?" I ask.

She takes a sip of water. "I'm just going to come out with it, and then we can decide. I strongly suspect jury tampering in the Grimes case, and I'm concerned that the same thing will happen with O'Connor as Elias Maxwell's attorney."

The server returns with our drinks. I take three large swigs of my beer. "No shit? Who's O'Connor working with? The bailiff?"

"That's my guess. I just have to prove it."

"And what then?"

"Well, we would go to trial ag—"

"No. I won't do that again."

"Liz, just listen. We would go to trial again, and he would likely be convicted. If we can prove jury tampering, O'Connor will be disbarred."

"I won't do it again."

"Even though you did the right thing?"

I bark out a bitter laugh. "I may have done the right thing, but now Fishner is asking me to work off the books, and that's not even to mention a uniform threatening me in front of a witness tonight or the threatening phone call I got yesterday. I'm not doing it again. It will get me killed. These people are for real, Julia." *Yes, you will do it again. You can only change it from inside, and Grimes deserves prison.*

"Wait, what? Start with the threat tonight." She looks genuinely concerned.

I tell her what happened earlier.

"I told you not to fly solo. That is exactly why."

"Is anyone even investigating Grimes's threats against me, what he said in court? And what about the rookie, DuBois?" The back of my neck gets hot and tense, but none of it is her fault.

"Yes, there is an internal investigation occurring into the possible jury tampering."

I roll my eyes. "Great. Those are always so fruitful."

She chuckles.

"What, you think this is funny?"

"No, I just wonder how you always end up in these situations."

"Your guess is as good as mine."

She spends a few minutes trying to talk me into helping her, but I stand firm in my no. If I can just ride this out, eventually everyone will forget that I ever testified.

I watch her switch gears, feigning nonchalance. I know full well that she's not done.

"What does Fishner have you doing off the books?"

The server comes over and asks if we want to order any food. We decide to split an order of nachos.

I sip my beer and gauge how much to tell her. At this point, I should be able to tell her all of it. My shrink would agree.

"What does Fishner have you doing off the books?" she repeats.

I lean forward slightly. "Mattioli."

She shakes her head. "Don't do it. Stay far away from him."

I arch an eyebrow.

"He's protected through and through. You think it's bad with Grimes? Step on Mattioli's toes, and we'll all see what 'bad' really is."

"Yeah, but I think he's behind Elias Maxwell. I think he's behind the murder."

She takes a deep breath and another sip of wine.

"Why else would he be running with Mattioli? Why did we find them together at the Renaissance? Why is Sims going to find them on video together on more occasions?"

"Wasn't Maxwell good friends with Mattioli's son? It seems believable that he would hang out with a father figure while Mattioli is in town."

I roll my eyes. "Occam's razor be damned."

She chuckles. "Go on, then."

"Why did Maxwell basically admit that he killed her to avenge Mattioli? The way I see it, Maxwell is guilty of killing her. But Mattioli is guilty of putting him up to it. It's all so much like that stupid book too—"

"What's like the book?"

"In the book, he describes how his wife died. And it's just as horrible as what happened to our vic. There are a lot of similarities."

"It's possible that Maxwell read the book and tried to copy—"

"That's too coincidental. I don't buy it. And there's something else."

She cocks her head to the side.

"Fishner and Goran have both basically said two things that bother me. One, Mattioli was involved with some kind of systematic hazing of female cops back in the day, which may or may not have involved both Fishner and Heather Martin."

She nods.

"Two, the whole thing with Fishner basically telling me to investigate him without telling me to investigate him... She's never done that before. It's beyond strange."

"You can't fly solo on this. Not if Grimes and his boys are after you."

I nod. "I know. Therein lies the problem, if you know what I mean. If I can figure all of this out, they'll all go down. But figuring it out means that the goons can kill me—or worse."

"Easy solution is to let me handle this through the prosecutor's office. If I initiate an investigation into O'Connor, a lot will come out."

"O'Connor has nothing to do with it. He's just an asshole. He isn't connected to Mattioli, unless you know something I don't."

She shakes her head.

The server brings our nachos, and I order another round. Screw my four-drink max. "I think you should do your thing through the prosecutor's office, and I'll look into Mattioli. I don't expect it to be dangerous. As far as anyone knows, I'm off for, like, three days after I get a couple of witness statements tomorrow and do the reports. I'll check in with, um, people who care about me."

She does her little hair-toss thing. "I'm planning to get an indictment against Maxwell tomorrow. That will buy us some time. How long is Mattioli in town?"

Something occurs to me. "It's too much of a coincidence that he's here while Heather Martin is murdered. I'm telling you, Julia, he's connected to all of this somehow."

"Are you at least telling Goran what your plan is?"

"I don't even know what my plan is, beyond going home and finishing his book. But no, I'm not telling Goran. He's been volatile, and he's planning to spend tomorrow with his family. He needs the time. He's actually taking vacation days. He's elated that we have Maxwell in custody, and I want him to have that feeling."

She sits back and crosses her arms. "So you're doing exactly what you shouldn't."

"That didn't sound like a question."

"It isn't a question. We've been working together for a while now. I know exactly what you're going to do, and I just hope it doesn't get you killed."

I laugh. "I don't plan to do anything that will get me killed. Daylight hours only. I dead bolt my door. And I have an attack cat." My attempt at levity feels forced and stupid.

She picks at the nachos. "Will you at least do me a favor and keep me in the loop?"

"What, like check in with you? It's nice that you're worried about me." I feel myself blush a little.

She smiles. "Yes, like check in with me. I like you, Liz, and I'd be sad if you died."

I laugh, and it's real this time. "That's the nicest thing anyone has said to me in a long time." *Does she get the tension too? Does she enjoy our weird flirting the way I do?*

"I'm serious! And this is on me," she says when the server brings the check. She hands him her credit card without looking at the total. "Thanks for listening. And I know what you're going to say, but if I get good evidence, will you at least consider going to trial again?"

"Get good enough evidence, and you won't have to go to trial again, because Grimes won't have an attorney or any way out other than a plea bargain."

She applauds. "Very well done."

The server returns, and Julia leaves a big tip before signing the check. I'm a big believer that how people treat restaurant workers says a lot about who they are, and all of the evidence suggests to me that Julia Becker is a quality person.

We walk out together. "Oh, that's just great," she says sardonically when the sleet hits us.

"Well, it's almost November," I reply, pulling my jacket around me.

We walk to our cars, and I briefly wonder if I'm too drunk to drive. It's only a few blocks. I'll be fine—I'm barely buzzed.

"Watch out for the captain," she says nonchalantly.

"Who, Carrothers? I already know that. The guy's a snake."

She nods. "I am going to follow you to your apartment and watch you go inside. Turn a light on when you get in, and then I'll leave."

I laugh. "Are you serious?"

"Yes, I'm serious."

"Fine." I unlock my car but continue facing her. "Let me know what happens at the indictment tomorrow, okay? I'm working on getting you even more evidence. You'll have the reports tomorrow afternoon."

She kisses me on the cheek, and I damn near fall over.

"Be careful," she whispers.

"I will."

I watch her back away from me and unlock her Lexus. We get in our respective vehicles, and she follows me home. I walk to the door with my hand on my gun and my eyes all over the place as though it's a crime scene. There's a brick that someone always uses to prop the door open, and I take it upstairs with me. There will be no door propping just now. When I enter my apartment, I slide the dead bolt then turn a light on. I walk to the window in time to see her pull away.

"That was interesting," I mutter to Ivan as I put on my favorite Fugazi album. I walk into the bedroom and change clothes, but I don't put my gun in the safe. It comes with me to the dining room table—I set it next to *(Un)Solved*, Joe Mattioli's shitty cop memoir.

I grab a beer from the fridge then drop into a dining room chair. Ivan weaves between my legs, but I can see his bowl from here, and it's full, so I give him a scratch. Before I can get the book open, he jumps into my lap and begins to purr.

"Ivan, you've never been a lap cat." I rub his ears, and the purr gets louder. "What gives?"

We go on like this for a while, and I wonder if even the cat has noticed that I'm trying—and sometimes failing—to be nicer these days. I slide the book closer—it's a hardcover, so I can prop it open on the table with one hand—and turn to where I left off. I have to flip back a few pages to remember what's happening in the narrative, but after I scan for a few seconds, it comes back. Mattioli and his partner, Ray Gibson, have just come from their captain's office. Mattioli claims that Gibson gave incriminating information about another detective to the brass, and he has strong feelings about it.

That day, Gibson showed me his true colors. I'd always thought we'd be partners forever, but in the captain's office that November morning, he revealed that he didn't have it in him. He was beneath me, beneath all of us. "Give me the car keys, Ray," I said, and he handed them over because he knew he was done leading our partnership, and that meant I would drive from then on.

I couldn't even look at him in the car. Out of the corner of my eye, I caught him staring out the window, totally silent—he couldn't even explain himself to me. I couldn't believe that he'd ratted out one of his own, with me right there in the room. I started to worry that the other guys would think I was complicit, that I'd given information too. More than that, though, I started to worry that he was a dirty, stinking rat through and through, and that he'd get some wild hair up his ass and decide to talk about our antics together too. We never did anything illegal, but we didn't always follow the rules.

Poor Gibson. He was probably just trying to do the right thing. I take a big swig of beer, and Ivan jumps off my lap and skitters away.

Gibson was always such a pussy, and I don't feel bad using that word. One of the worst things that's happened to the police in this country is how effeminate everyone has gotten. We used to be tough, masculine, and ready to lay our balls on the line to get the job done. Now, the whole department has gone soft. I'm not trying to be sexist, and although I was called a chauvinist pig more than once in my career, I really do believe in old-school chivalry and would only treat a woman in the nicest way I could. I'm just realistic. I genuinely believe that there are some jobs more fit for men and some more fit for women. Say what you will. I'm old-school, and I instilled that in my boys too.

I roll my eyes then remember that his kid is a cop in Chicago and briefly wonder whether, like Grimes, he uses illegal choke holds.

About a year before Anna died in the most tragic way I can imagine, I realized that I had to be hard on my boys. When Giacomo, whom Anna and I named after my Sicilian grandfather, was seven, he came home from school one day, crying. Anna, bless her heart, had tried to console him but to no avail. He'd been bullied at school by an older boy, one who had been causing problems in the neighborhood for at least three years and who was fully on my radar as a potential criminal. I remember getting home from work that day to find my wife with Giovanni in his high chair, screaming his little head off, and Giacomo crying on the kitchen floor.

"Get up," I said to my older son, but he just kept crying. "Get up," I repeated. "Be a man."

He slowly stood but looked down at the floor.

"Look at me, son," I said. "Look me right in the eyes."

He blinked, his lower lip still quivering as though he might keep crying, but looked at me.

The moment I saw his soft brown eyes on mine, I knew it was time. "Put 'em up," I said, raising my fists.

I remember Anna telling me to stop and me telling her to mind her own business. I feel a little bit bad about how I used to talk to her, especially since she was the mother of my children.

"Giacomo, raise your fists," I said. When he didn't, I slapped him across the face.

That was the day I taught my son to be a man.

It's more of the same for a couple of chapters, almost to the point that I can barely keep reading. Then I get to some good parts, including a chapter about Elias Maxwell joining the family most Sundays for dinner, how Mattioli encouraged Maxwell to join the service when he graduated from high school—he joined the Navy, which takes me back to the knots at the crime scene—and the description of how his wife was bound and beaten in their basement. Now that I'm reading it again, I guess it's not as much like Heather Martin's homicide as I originally thought, and Maxwell was stationed overseas when Anna Mattioli was killed, which is as good an alibi as any.

I read the police reports and saw the pictures. She'd been bound to the sewer pipe and beaten with a nightstick in the basement of that garage in Old Brooklyn. I'll never forget those pictures—they're burned into my brain.

I skip forward, since I already read that part, until I get to a piece about Gibson.

When Anna was killed, a light went out inside me. I was no longer the man I thought I was. It devastated me. Still, I managed not to cry at her funeral and to hold it together for the boys.

By that time, Gibson and I were back on speaking terms. A few months before Anna died, he'd tried to explain why he did what he did. He said he was taking one for the team, because he really thought Navaros was dirty. He claimed that Navaros had been accepting money from some local drug guy in exchange for looking the other way on all kinds of crimes.

Dirty cops are everywhere, but I'm not sure I would blow the whistle on drug money. There's a fine line—a thin blue one, actually.

I remember slapping him on the shoulder and telling him it was water under the bridge. And he came to Anna's funeral and bought me a few rounds at the bar afterward. All in all, he wasn't so bad, even if he broke the blue code of silence. He knew better, but I guess he figured it was worth it.

Navaros did turn out to be dirtier than a pig in shit, and I remember thinking that maybe Gibson wasn't as stupid as I thought he was.

I'm gonna have to talk to Ray Gibson about his old partner. Maybe he can give me information that will connect him to Heather Martin. Question is, who is going with me? Because I'm sure as shit not going alone.

I take the book to bed and finish it. My gun stays on the night-stand.

CHAPTER 26

The weather is gorgeous on Saturday morning—it's one of those crisp fall days with a slight breeze and promises at sunrise of a bright-blue sky. Soon, and especially if it keeps raining, all of the trees will lose their leaves, then the snow will start. Until then, and in spite of it all, I'm in a decent mood. *I'm sleeping again,* I think as I eat a bowl of oatmeal at the dining room table. *I'm not shoveling peanut butter into my mouth over the sink.* I laugh, and the cat looks at me as though I've lost my mind. I guess it's just become harder to sustain a bad mood.

I see Dr. Shue on Monday. It'll be good to tell her that—she'll be proud of me.

I get to the squad early to get a jump on the reports. Even though I hate it, I'm better at paperwork than Goran is, and I want him to have enough time to take his girls to the zoo.

It's hard to keep my brain working on Elias Maxwell, at least now that I think I know that there's so much more behind it all. But I do, and I'm almost done by the time Goran arrives. "Morning, sunshine," I say as he flips his lamp on. I hand him a stack of papers. "These need your signature."

"You're on fire."

I finish typing a sentence about my visit to Martha Rodgers's house, not including my little run-in with Householder, then turn to him and remember what Fishner told me last night. "Vacation days, huh? When does that start?"

He gives me a bashful smile. "Tomorrow, assuming you keep going with the reports so fast."

"You've never taken vacation days before."

"Don't look at me like that."

I narrow my eyes. "I'm proud of you, Goran. You were turning into a cranky bastard. Enjoy your time. How long will you be out?"

"I'll be back a week from Monday."

I nod and turn back to my computer. "Good riddance." I glance at him to make sure he knows I'm kidding.

It goes on like this for a while. We finish the reports quickly.

"Want to come to Boo at the Zoo with us?" he asks, standing and shutting off his lamp.

"I'm waiting for a couple of witnesses to come in and give statements. So I'd love to, but I can't. I want to wrap this up today." *So that I can investigate what's really going on,* I don't add.

He nods.

"It's gonna be weird without you next week, Goran. I hope you get some rest." I mean it—they're not just words.

He smiles and switches out pieces of Doublemint. "I'll miss you too."

"Have fun with the fam."

"Yeah, I think we're gonna go see the football hall of fame tomorrow."

I roll my eyes. I'm not really sure how to end the conversation, knowing full well that the investigation isn't over. To him, it is, though, and that counts for something in my book.

It's the first time I'll truly be alone in my police work. He'll be royally pissed when he finds out that I worked alone on something potentially dangerous, but he'll get over it.

He stands there awkwardly.

"Leave, Goran. Go home. We're done here." I drive a staple into the last of the reports. "I'll keep you posted. Becker'll get the indictment today. It's all good."

"Yeah, but you'll be bored." He knows I won't catch a new one without him, and he's right to worry about what happens when I'm bored.

"I've got odds and ends to do. I'm sure Fishner will put me back on that floater and maybe assign a case from the shelf. It's all good. Go to the zoo. Send me pictures." I hope the boss doesn't do any of that. I need time to burn Mattioli's empire to the ground first.

"Will do. Thanks, Liz."

"No problem." I stand and stretch before taking the last of the reports to Fishner's mailbox. When I get back, Goran is gone.

LEE FROM THE TATTOO parlor calls at about eleven thirty to confirm a time. I tell him to come in anytime, and he's here within fifteen minutes. He's still a nice, helpful guy, and his statement hasn't changed.

Neither has Mistress Natalia's, although she puts on a big show for me in the interview room. At one point, and only because she's on my turf, I get slightly irritated, but she still gives me a statement and signs it.

Same with Martha Rodgers.

The case against Elias Maxwell is basically a lock. It feels too easy, and I wonder what the hell we've missed.

BECKER CALLS A LITTLE after four to tell me that Maxwell has been indicted on one count of capital murder, one count of kidnapping, one count of felony explosives, and four counts of attempted assault. I grunt and nod and say all the things I'm supposed to say, but it feels forced. I've been waiting for the indictment to proceed—even I'm not so stupid as to go out into the city alone until the main bad guy is in lockup—by deep cleaning my apartment all afternoon, and I'm slightly annoyed that I have to stop.

"Are you all right?" she asks.

"For the most part, yeah. This all just seems like too much of a lock. Is he gonna take a plea?"

"It looks that way. My boss is willing to let him plead to murder two, felony explosives, and one count of attempted assault, which will put him away for thirty years."

That isn't enough time, but he'll never go to trial for any of this. "Parole?"

"Not a chance in hell. I'm meeting with O'Connor and the judge later today. I'll make that absolutely clear."

"Well, at least another dirtbag will be off the street."

"Have you watched the news at all? There's a huge demonstration on Public Square this afternoon. Are you still downtown?"

I shake my head then realize she can't see me. "No, I left hours ago. Have you heard from Fishner today?"

"No. I gotta run. Keep me in the loop, okay?"

I chuckle. "Sure." She's replaced the flirting with her usual curt tone, and I don't know if I'm relieved or disappointed.

In spite of the morning's bright-blue sky, it starts to rain as I'm taking out the trash, and it shows no signs of stopping. It's just a typical November day in Cleveland. I hear Dr. Shue's voice in my head, rambling about self-care or some shit, and decide I need to recharge the old batteries before hitting the pavement again. I spend the rest of the day inside my pristine apartment with my cat and my guitar.

SUNDAY MORNING, I WAKE up early and without my alarm then trudge downstairs for the *Plain Dealer*. I put on a pot of coffee, feed Ivan, and look out at the rain, which has pulled down most of the golden leaves on the trees behind my building.

I run to the gym for a quick workout. Once home, I flip on the Channel Three morning news program, but it's filled with a bunch of garbage about needles in Halloween candy—hint: that never happened—so I shut it off. I turn to the newspaper instead. There's the usual crap about the president and Congress doing this, that, and the other thing, so I toss the front page to the side instead of allowing myself to be consumed with rage. The local section is all about the local election coming up on Tuesday, and I make a mental note to vote.

Too much sitting and not enough moving always gets me. The grim weight of the world threatens to hold me down, so I call Josh to see what he's up to. He doesn't answer, so I leave a voicemail.

I haven't talked to my brother in over a week, so I call him too. No answer. He's probably still pissed about the football game last week.

That's about the extent of my list.

I run out to grab some beer and snacks for this week's game and return just in time for kickoff. I grab the Arts & Leisure section of the paper and take it to the couch with a bowl of popcorn and a beer.

The first thing that catches me is the photograph of a thirtysomething woman in front of a backdrop of books. I read closer: *Meet Gillian Swift, Case Western's literary superstar.* That kind of thing isn't really my bag, but something in the look in her eye makes me keep reading.

And it turns out that she's studying police memoirs and documentaries. The article tells me that she hasn't been in Cleveland long but that she's published a book about authenticity in memoir and autobiography. At some point, the reporter describes her interest in Joe Mattioli's book—and conveniently plugs his reading tonight at Blue Owl Books.

I glance at the TV. The Ravens have already scored a touchdown on the Browns, and there are still thirteen minutes left in the first quarter, so I dig my laptop out of my bag and run a search on Gillian Swift.

I end up with a number for her office at Case Western Reserve University. I call and leave a message.

I MUST HAVE DRIFTED off at some point, because I wake up with the weird feeling I always have after naps, as if I've lost time and ended up with a jigsaw puzzle that's missing pieces. I push myself off the couch and notice that it's dark. *Jesus, six hours is a long nap.* I make my way into the bathroom, where it occurs to me that now would be as good a time as any to get my head back in the game and go talk to Ray Gibson.

Back on the couch, I run a quick search. Turns out Mattioli's old partner lives about an hour from here, so I decide to take the trip out to Lake County to put a face with a name and get the rundown on what really happened back in the day. If it goes well, I might ask him about the possible connection to Heather Martin, but that could get hinky. I'll play it by ear.

I shower, brush my teeth, change into my cop clothes, and get ready to go, but then it strikes me that I need to be careful. I'm not so stupid that I think I should go alone. I run through the list of possible people. I need someone who will stay in the car just in case I need help, not someone who will want to be involved with the questioning. I need someone who isn't part of my squad, because I'm not supposed to be doing any of this, at least not visibly. I also need someone who knows how to handle herself in a potentially dangerous situation and who will have my back if I need her to.

The list is pretty short, and with Goran on vacation, all roads lead to Cora Bosch.

I can hear Becker in my head, telling me to be careful, but that doesn't stop me. I grab my phone from the coffee table and call my ex to ask for one last favor. *I'm such an asshole,* I think as the phone rings. *I should hang up.*

"What's up?" she asks on the fourth ring.

"Hey. You busy?"

She doesn't speak right away.

"This is a work thing, not a relationship thing. And I hate myself for even calling you, but I can't think of anyone else to ask."

"Okay..."

I briefly fill her in.

She sighs. "Seriously?"

"I'm sorry. And thank you for even considering it."

"What will Fishner say?"

"I'm not worried about that right now."

"Jesus Christ, Liz. Seriously?"

I wince, regretting calling her. I'll just go alone. It'll be fine.

"Fine. I'll help you."

"Thanks, anywa—what?"

"Pick me up at work. Text me when you get here."

Why is she working on a Sunday night? I don't ask. Instead, I head to the Justice Center to grab the Charger. *Mattioli did something. The question is what—and whether he put Elias Maxwell up to the homicide.*

My focus sharpens on my way to pick up Cora—whom I'm thinking of as Detective Bosch in this particular moment—and I consider my options. I could have her come in with me, but he'll know right away, given that our badges are different, that something is off. I could ask her to stay in the car. *Yeah, I'll do that.*

About twenty minutes later, I pull up in front of the Cleveland Heights Police Department in Severance Circle. I shoot Cora a quick text, and she's outside within three minutes. She opens the door and climbs in silently. She puts her seat belt on.

I don't say anything. I just put the car into Drive and pull away. We're through Cleveland Heights and into Euclid before one of us speaks.

"Thank you for doing this. I appreciate it."

"You didn't give me much choice." She keeps her gaze focused outside her window.

"Well, I still appreciate it."

"If it's between participating in your crazy stunts and having you get killed, I choose participation." She turns to face me. "But I'm not very happy about it."

I glance at her. She looks both irritated and resigned. "I don't really need you to do much. Maybe just stay in the car."

"I shouldn't be doing this at all. This is exactly something you would do. This"—she gestures around the car—"is so completely you that I don't even know what to say."

I guide the car onto Lakeland Freeway.

"Is there anything else I need to know beyond what you said on the phone?"

"Not really. I'm just looking into Mattioli—which you suggested I do—and it's led me to this guy." I give her a few more details about Gibson, based on what I read in the book.

She nods. We're quiet for the rest of the way there.

Gibson's house is in the middle of nowhere. At one point as the rain starts again, the GPS freaks out and leads us along a weird dirt road that runs parallel to some railroad tracks. An old deciduous forest is on my left—*a park, maybe?* No, we're too far out for a park. Then I see a house, with a light in a single window, just ahead, across the tracks.

"This is fucking creepy, Liz," Cora mutters.

"The plan is for you to stay in the car. If I'm not out in forty-five minutes, come in with your weapon drawn."

She sighs. "Fine."

I guide the Charger across the tracks, maneuver around a couple of strut-shattering potholes, and park behind an old windowless van. When I step out of the car, a bright outside flood lamp, like something from a grocery store parking lot, flips on and blinds me, and my right hand moves to the Glock out of instinct. A figure moves behind the curtains, backlit by the yellow light of a lamp, then the front door creaks open. A big dog barks from somewhere behind the house. Out of the corner of my eye, I catch Cora surveying the scene.

"Who's there?" I hear the voice before I can make out the face.

"Ray Gibson?" I call as I squint into the rain.

"Who wants to know?" he asks.

The dog keeps barking. "Hazel, shut the fuck up!" he bellows, and the dog stops.

I don't like making decisions when I'm blinking into a bright light in the rain and can't read the person I'm talking to, but I have no choice. My eyes adjust. A good-sized man stands in the doorway, peering my way. I decide not to get back into the car and drive away.

"My name's Boyle. I'm Cleveland Police. I just have a couple of questions," I respond, still next to the car, feeling the rain change to mist and back again that quickly as the wind whips through the trees behind me.

"Well, come in, then," he replies after a short pause. His voice is hoarse. I watch him flick a lit cigarette to the side of his concrete steps.

I move forward. There's a small porch on the right side of the house, but it looks as though it would crumble under the weight of an adult. I can't see the dog, but she's panting under the rhythm of the rain, and I hear her chain rubbing against concrete. There she is, on the side of the house, bolted to a ramshackle garage. Behind her is a big old Chevy truck that looks like it's from the seventies. Two of the tires are flat, so my gaze moves to the van in front of my car, which must be his daily driver. The dog looks to be a German shepherd, straining against her chain. I can't tell if she wants to say hi or if she wants to rip my throat open. Either way, I'll leave her alone.

Next to her is another concrete staircase leading down to the outside door of a basement that I imagine to be very, very wet and musty.

I raise my hand to shield my eyes from the light. "Gibson?" I ask as I approach the man.

"Yeah, you found me," he replies.

As I get closer, I make out the blue glow of a television through the front window—it looks like the local news is on, spouting info about our arrest of Elias Maxwell and the indictment yesterday.

"It's late," he says right after I catch a glimpse of Jeff O'Connor walking alongside his client on the TV screen. "What do you want?" He scratches the three-day stubble on his chin and looks down at his ratty white T-shirt, embarrassed. "Lemme get a shirt on. I didn't expect visitors, especially not a woman detective." He chuckles and gestures for me to come inside.

I shouldn't be in here alone. I shouldn't have brought Cora here. I should be here with CDP backup. In an ideal world, Goran would be here with me.

"You're a detective, right?" He doesn't wait for me to answer. "Wait there."

I do as I'm told. He moves down his wood-paneled hallway and up the staircase at the end of it, leaving me with a collection of old, muddy shoes and a coatrack that looks like it's seen better days. A dirty old Carhartt and a Browns hoodie that looks like it needs to be laundered hang from it.

To my left is a closed door that doesn't look original. If this is an old farmhouse—and it has to be, given its location and architecture—the door should be hardwood, not this light copy. The hallway is dark and bare of pictures or artwork, save for a still life of a fruit bowl about halfway down the hall. At the far end of the hall is another door, also on the left. Based on its location, it must lead to the basement. Another staircase leads up. On my immediate right is a big room that contains less furniture than it should: a recliner, a couch, a coffee table, a lamp, and the TV sit clustered together in the expansive space. *This place was nice once,* I think as I gaze at the high ceilings and crown molding.

On the side table next to the recliner is a collection of remotes, a half-empty bottle of Canadian Mist bourbon, a red coffee mug, a pack of Merit cigarettes, a Zippo lighter, and an ashtray. The ceiling fan is on, swirling the blue smoke around the room. Its light fixture is missing two of the four bulbs, so it casts an eerie light across the room. A fireplace glows, and a stack of wood stands next to it. The only thing on the mantel is an old police badge case that, from here, looks like it contains a gold shield.

He'd have kept it if he retired in good standing, so he must have.

No artwork, no photographs.

A large archway separates the living room from what must be the dining room and kitchen, but no lights are on, so I can't make out what's back there.

He coughs as he descends the stairs. "Sorry about that," he says as he moves toward me down the hallway. He has a blue shirt on, tucked into his jeans. Smells like he's applied cologne. Mouthwash doesn't cover the whiskey breath as much as he hopes it will.

He looks a lot like his old police ID, even though he's been retired for over fifteen years. He's got cop written all over him. Maybe it's the boozy doe eyes, maybe it's the set of his shoulders. Maybe the haircut, which he probably gives himself every couple of weeks with a pair of clippers in his bathroom. Maybe it's something else, but I could read him from a football field away even if I didn't know he'd been CDP, which is oddly reassuring.

I nod. "Do you have a few minutes?" I'm being nice—it's obvious that he has a few minutes, or he wouldn't have spruced himself up.

"Sure. Want a drink?" He gestures at the living room. "Come on in. I have a fire going. Chilly out there tonight, huh? Have a seat." He watches me move into the living space. He watches me look into the dining room and chuckles. "You're Homicide, aren't you?"

There's no point in lying. "I am. Special Homicide." A gust of wind rattles the front window, but I can't see the car or my backup through the thick film of old smoke.

He nods. "I know exactly who you are, Boyle," he says as he eases down into the recliner and scans my face. He bites a cigarette out of the pack and reaches for the lighter. "Seen you on the news," he says, the cigarette bobbing between his lips. He flicks the lighter open and lights it in one motion. "Have a seat," he repeats.

I choose the edge of the lopsided green couch, which sits next to a battered old dog bed, not sure how to interpret his tone.

"Most of the time, detectives work in pairs. At least they did back in my day." He exhales a cloud of smoke up into the ceiling fan and stifles a cough. "Drink?" he asks as he refills his coffee mug with Canadian Mist.

"No, thanks," I reply, even though bad bourbon would be a great accompaniment to this weird and probably misguided scene. The dog barks outside, and I stop myself from reacting.

"Hazel barks at everything," he says. "Don't take it personal."

"Listen, Gibson—"

"Call me Ray."

"Ray." I lean back against the couch cushion.

He hits his cigarette and appraises me. "I seen you on the news," he repeats. "You finally looking into Mattioli? What'd you do, decide to go through our old murder books after you brought in Eli? I woulda told 'em. I would have. Shit, I tried to. I always knew that motherfucker was up to no good. He never was any good. Him and Eli are both bad seeds."

I'm silent, deliberately so, hoping that he'll keep talking, wondering what caused the palpable animosity for his old partner and contemplating why he would make the logical leap to his old murder books. I cross an ankle over a knee, making a mental note to look into them, and wonder how drunk he is right now, on a scale of one to ten. My guess is five and a half.

"Heather Martin. That's why you're here, isn't it? She's proof." He shuts off the TV and leans forward, elbows on his knees. The light of the fire in the fireplace illuminates his face, and I can see that he was handsome once, before booze and depression and nicotine stripped his looks away. "He never was any good. She's proof," he repeats. He squeezes his forehead with the hand that holds the cigarette, and ash falls on the floor.

"Proof of what?" I ask.

He chuckles. "Look, I might be a drunk has-been, but I still know to ask you for your ID, even if you been all over TV lately. If it checks out? I might tell you what I know about good old Joe. It'll all make sense to you. You can finally put that asshole away, assuming you're smart enough."

I never assume I'm smart enough, but the comment vindicates my instinct that Mattioli is bad news. I slide my wallet out of my pocket and reach across the coffee table to hand it to him.

He closes one eye to read it then hands it back. "How long you been in Homicide?"

"A little under five years," I reply.

"You were on that big-deal kid case last year," he says as I slide the wallet back to where it belongs. "*Plain Dealer* did that big profile. Tryin' to make cops look like human beings. That stuff with your brother."

I nod, surprised that he remembers anything about that case.

"And now you're on this one. What, you got an in with the media or something? Or are you somebody's pet? Sleepin' with somebody you shouldn't be, maybe."

I bark out a laugh before I can get offended. "Not by half," I reply.

He narrows his eyes. "So you're a good cop, then, huh? Follow the rules?"

I chuckle, remembering the way Mattioli described his partner's detailed, neatly written notes in the murder books, the commendation in his jacket, the early retirement brought on by too much whisky and too many accusations. He might have been a good cop, too, once. "I guess you could say that," I reply, not mentioning the fact that I'm violating policy six different ways in being here right now. "Look, Ray, I—"

"Nah, there's more to it. You work for Fishner," he says.

It's not like Fishner hasn't done a couple of press conferences, but it still surprises me. I hide it well.

"Yeah? You work for good ol' Jane Fishner, don'tcha?" He doesn't break eye contact as he sips from his coffee mug.

"Yes, Lieutenant Fishner is my supervisor," I reply in an even tone.

He laughs, and I can't for the life of me figure out what's funny. "I remember her. From way back when she was a rookie. Good lookin' back then. She still good lookin'?"

I'm just not sure what to say to that.

"Anyway, what do you want to know?" he asks. He's struggling not to slur his words. "You think good old Joe killed Heather Martin?" He hits his cigarette one last time before lighting another one with it. "He always had a hard-on for her. Thought she was responsible for Anna dyin' like she did. Maybe he put Eli up to it."

"Ray, with all due respect, in what way would Heather Martin be responsible for Anna Mattioli's death?"

"Well, what would you be here for unless it was about Heather Martin and Joe Mattioli? You're the detective. You tell me." He blinks hard when smoke goes in his eye.

"This is totally routine," I reply. "I just have some questions about you and your partner's relationship, allegations of sexual misconduct against him, that sort of thing. You know I can't tell you if he's a suspect or not."

He laughs, a big belly-chuckle that reverberates through the room. "Yeah, right. Totally routine that a Special Homicide dick is clear the fuck out here, by herself, talking to me at nine at night. You can't bullshit a bullshitter, Good Cop. I may be old and drunk and retired, but I know how this works."

I nod. I'm starting to like this guy, in spite of his crass undertone and the thick cloud of sadness that encircles him.

"So, here's my guess. You think Superstar Joe put the kid up to doing Heather Martin. Or better yet, you can't eliminate him, but you can't prove anything either. You've run down a few leads that went nowhere, so you brought Eli in, and he confessed. You've got your own suspicions but no evidence, just your gut. So you're out here talking to me, without your partner and probably without Jane Fishner knowing about it, because there's nothing left to do but throw the murder book onto the shelf and call it a day. And something in you says you can't do that, cause you got something to prove, 'specially given all that shit you just said at Grimes's trial. Am I right, or am I right?"

I give him my blank face.

"Either that, or the brass is up your ass to pin this on Mattioli, what with all the 'brutality' going on lately." He makes air quotes around "brutality." He hits his cigarette then puts it out. "But nah, they wouldn't want you looking into Superstar Joe. Not now. So you're here on your own."

"What can you tell me about Joe Mattioli?" I ask. "Did you ever see him behave violently toward women?"

"All the time, of course," Gibson replies.

"Was any of this documented?"

"Hell no," he replies.

"What was his relationship with Heather Martin like?" I ask.

"Heather and his wife were best friends," he says. "Hey, toss me that carton of smokes over there, would you?"

On the floor in front of me is a half-empty carton of Merits that I hand him.

"Thanks." He peels the cellophane off a new pack, pulls out yet another cigarette, and lights it. "Anyway, Heather and Anna were best friends. Best fucking friends. Until one day they weren't."

This is new information. "Did they have a falling out?"

"Somethin' like that. You ask me, Joe threatened her. Heather, I mean. Word on the street was she caught him cheating on Anna, Heather told Anna, Anna went fucking ballistic, threatened to cut his balls off, all that kind of thing. I stayed the hell out of it."

"When was this?" I ask.

"Oh, hell. Lemme think. She died twenty-five years ago, so what would it be? Five years before that, maybe?"

"So you were all pretty young."

"Anna and Heather and Jane were young. You've seen my file. I'm sure you know I'm not that young."

Anna and Heather and Jane. *Fishner?* I nod.

"Listen, I shouldn't be telling you any of this. I know about what you did to that other cop. I've always said there's nothing worse than a snitch," he says. "That asshole made me out to be one in his book. Desecrated my good name."

"I'm not here to talk about that, Ray," I reply. *And you were a snitch, too, Ray.*

"Nah, I figured it out. You're here because you think Mattioli did it, and you hope that pinning this shitty case on him will, how do I put this? That you can atone for something. 'Cept that ain't how it works. Cause you'd just be tarnishing another guy. You know what I mean?"

"This is a homicide investigation." My neck gets prickly. "This isn't personal at all."

He laughs and sputters into a coughing fit violent enough that he drops his lit cigarette on the floor. "I'm just fucking with you. Calm down," he says. He picks up the cigarette and hits it. "Listen, you want the truth, Heather knew shit about Joe—shit about both of us—that he wouldn't want anybody to know. And that means I'm not gonna tell you. But I also doubt that Superstar would do something this dumb. If anything, he hired somebody to do it. Not Eli. Joe wouldn't do anything to that kid."

He's moving up to about an eight on the drink scale and making less sense by the second. It's time for me to go. "You're telling me that he had motive."

"A lot of people had motive against that bitch," he replies.

"Why do you call him Superstar Joe?" I ask on my way to the door.

"Cause he's fucking Teflon," Gibson replies, heaving himself out of the chair to follow me to the door. "I got bumped back to Property Crimes after some bullshit accusations, and Joe got promoted. That's how it always went." He opens the door for me. "Look, I'm sorry for giving you shit. But you gotta know that testifying against that other cop, that was fucked up."

"Thanks for your time, Ray." I hand him a business card. "If you think of anything, let me know."

"Yeah, I will. In the meantime, maybe you should ask your boss what she knows about all that shit that happened way back when. She might be more willing than I am to reopen old wounds."

So "Jane" really is Jane Fishner. Well, shit.

Back in the car, I don't say anything at first. Neither does Cora. It almost feels as if we're having some sort of silence contest. As I pull back onto the main road, I thank her again for coming with me.

"Just don't get yourself killed, Liz. That's all I ask."

I nod. "I won't."

I drop her off next to her car, and we say good night.

CHAPTER 27

Monday morning, I'm setting down my second cup of coffee and listening to Fishner tell me to look into a case from last year that I would just as soon forget—unfortunately, no one cares about dead sex workers, so running down witnesses will be impossible—when the landline on my desk trills away. It came through the operator downstairs, so I give the full greeting: "Cleveland Special Homicide, this is Detective Boyle."

"Hi, this is Gillian Swift from Case Western, returning your call?" Her voice is a soft, pleasant alto that's deeper than I expected. Her outgoing voicemail message is one of those robot voices. Honestly, I didn't expect her to call back in the first place.

"Hi. Thanks for calling. Can you hold on for a minute?"

"Sure."

I give Fishner the thumbs-up on the case I would rather not revisit, and she goes to her office.

I look around to make sure no one is listening. I'm not supposed to be spending any time on the clock investigating any other cops. Fishner was clear that this has to be stealth. Sims is doing some glassy-eyed thing on his computer, and Roberts is down the hall at the vending machine. I hit the hold button. "I don't have a lot of time right now," I lie—all I have today is time—"but I wonder if you'd be willing to meet with me about the book I mentioned in the message."

"Really?" she asks. "I sort of thought your call was a prank. But sure. I've never been interrogated by the police. It could be interesting, maybe even fun. I'll earn street cred with my students too."

She sounds like she's smiling, but I can't tell if she's kidding. "Well, it wouldn't really be an interrogation. I just have a couple of questions. Won't take long, I don't think." I glance down at Mattioli's book, which is exposed in my messenger bag, so I flip the bag's flap over to conceal it.

She chuckles. "I was joking. I'm happy to help. I have some free time this afternoon at about three o'clock. Does that work?"

That gives me four hours to finish the paperwork, dig up the murder book on Fishner's latest order, try to track down the books I can find on Mattioli and Gibson's old cases, come up with something to tell everyone in the squad, including my boss, and drive over to the fancy private university. "Yeah, that's perfect."

"I'm in the Guilford House. It's just off Bellflower. Good luck finding a parking spot unless you have a placard."

I assume she means a handicapped sticker. "I have a police placard," I say.

She chuckles again and says she'll see me later.

THAT AFTERNOON, I HEAD over to Case to keep my off-the-books appointment with Dr. Gillian Swift, Important Literary and Media Scholar. Her name reminds me of someone you'd see on an infomercial, some overly lipsticked gal trying to sell me something I don't need or want and encouraging me to call today so I can get two of the thing I don't need or want for the price of one. I didn't tell anyone but Becker I was leaving. Best to let them wonder.

Her office is in one of the old yellow-brick buildings. I think I heard that the university had cut its English department in half a few years back, so I'm surprised they hired this new hotshot. I'm sort of surprised that I know she's a hotshot too. Maybe it was that *Plain Dealer* thing, the way the article made a big deal out of a literary critic who also writes books a bunch of other eggheads care about and interesting articles about internet culture and, on occasion, best-selling fiction.

I park the Charger in a tow zone. The walk to the Guilford building is nice enough; the blue sky and yellow trees and big puffy clouds almost mask the fact that it's getting chilly enough for me to wear a sweater under my leather jacket.

Her office is on the third floor. The elevator looks sketchy enough that I take the stairs. I walk past a bathroom that's labeled "Faculty Women" and, before pushing through the heavy door, wonder if I'm allowed to use it. I make sure I look presentable before tossing my paper towel in the trash and exiting.

I find her office in the hallway then knock three times on her door, which is ajar. She has a variety of things taped to it, including a flyer for some lecture series on campus, a cartoon about proof-reading, a color copy of her latest book cover, a rainbow-flag sticker, and a picture of Oprah Winfrey giving people car keys. I hear her voice—she must be on the phone—and it's even richer in person than it was when I talked to her earlier. She gives a warm laugh to whomever she's talking to, says that she'll call back, then tells me to come in.

The space is nothing like I'd imagined. Back when I was in college, all the profs had walls of dusty bookshelves, bad fluorescent lighting, weird knickknacks, piles of papers on their desks, and typical store-bought artwork when they had artwork at all. Gillian Swift has the requisite bookshelves, but on one of them is a small stereo that plays a song I've heard before, and the large window behind her is propped open with a broken umbrella. Complementing the sunlight, which streams in and hits her red hair in a pleasing way, is soft illumination from a pair of floor lamps in two corners. I glance around and notice some plants, a couple of Stieglitz prints that remind me of the ones I have in my bedroom, and an appealing red-and-tan area rug under the two visitors' chairs.

"Come in," she repeats. She gestures for me to enter and closes her laptop, the only thing on her large wooden desk other than a small plant and a framed picture of two black-and-white cats. She stands and extends her hand. I take it and thank her for her time after introducing myself. I'm surprised four times over by her physical presence: her grip is strong, and she's younger than I expected—can't be more than thirty, thirty-one. She's almost as tall as I am, and I never had a prof who wore jeans, even nice ones like those. I'm a little surprised by how stunning she is; she's got the bone structure and facial symmetry that make a lot of people jealous, and she carries that little bit of extra weight well.

She holds my gaze for a second longer than most people would as the old radiator clangs and hisses in the corner. "That's why I have the window open," she says, flicking her eyes at the radiator. "They turn the heat on at the beginning of October—it'd be three thousand degrees in here without that umbrella. Do you want to talk here?" Her green cable-knit cardigan brings out both her hazel eyes and her fair coloring.

"Sure, yeah, here's fine with me," I reply. "Nice office." I wonder if I come off as raggedy and unpolished as I think I do.

"Then let's head down the hall for a cup of coffee first." She grabs a wooden cane from against the bookshelf then steps out from behind her desk. "You should see the other guy," she jokes, waving the cane back and forth a few inches off the ground.

I smile and raise an eyebrow.

"I'm the resident gimp." She laughs at the floor. "That's probably why they hired me. Call it 'diversity.' I'm surprised there aren't two of you—don't cops usually work in pairs?"

"Yeah but not today," I reply.

I let her lead me down the hall, past other offices and into a kitchen of sorts that doubles as a mail and copy room. Her limp is pronounced in the left leg, but it's clear that she knows how to use the cane. A balding middle-aged guy curses at the copier, and she walks over and tells the machine to behave before opening it up, deftly removing a crumpled piece of paper, resetting it, and making some joke about being the copier tech. She closes the lid, and it works again, and he thanks her. He doesn't seem to notice me.

I stand in the doorway, wondering who in the hell this woman is.

"Cream, sugar?" she asks as she pours coffee into two mugs.

"Cream, thanks," I reply, and she dumps a good amount into both mugs and stirs it in before holding the red mug out to me.

I take it and mumble my thanks.

"So what can I do for you?" she asks as she adjusts her weight against the cane, her coffee mug still on the counter.

"Can I get that?" I ask before I think.

She levels an even stare at me as the color rises in her cheeks. I watch her consider my question. She's probably used to people offering to help, and I wonder if it pisses her off the way it would me. She blinks and smiles. "Thanks," she says, nodding.

I grab her mug in the other hand and follow her to her office.

Instead of taking the seat behind the desk, she slides down into the chair next to mine and hangs the cane handle on the edge of the windowsill. "What can I do for you, Detective?" she repeats. Something twinkles in her eyes. Or maybe I'm imagining things.

"Like I said in the emails, I'm interested in your take on Mattioli's book and on anything you got from interviewing him that maybe I should know." I hand her coffee to her and set my own on the floor next to my chair.

She uses her free hand to pull her bad leg over the good one.

"The *Plain Dealer* ran the story. I read it, and I thought you could help," I add.

She sips her coffee. "What do you want to know?"

I shift in my chair and stop fiddling with the clasp on my watch by taking out my notebook. "I'm most interested in whether or not there's a way to know if he's telling the truth," I reply. "Especially about his wife and Heather Martin, the lawyer."

She gives me a slow nod. "Heather Martin, the woman who died. Well," she begins, "that's a loaded question. The truth question, I mean. We could sit here all day and talk about what truth is, not to mention the little problem of memory and what happens when it's mediated by language."

I chuckle. "Right, I know. I get that, and I'd discuss all those things with you if I wasn't chin deep in a murder investigation that's losing steam by the minute." I guess I said that out loud. "What I'm trying to figure out is if we—okay, you, since you're the literary guru—can tell what's true or not in the book, you know, by reading it and finding patterns or whatever, or if there are ways we—okay, I, since I'm the cop—might ask the right questions when I talk to him again." The cop and the literary guru. What an unlikely scenario this is.

"There are a few ways into it," she replies. "Honestly, he's been really consistent with the story—you've seen his talk show appearances?"

I nod. "A couple."

"He's been so consistent that it's hard to poke holes in the narrative. Do you think he had something to do with Heather Martin's murder?"

"What about the weird way he describes what happened to her?" I ask, ignoring her question. I lean forward. "I mean—and forgive me, because I'm not exactly a scholar—he puts himself there, right? In the scene in that basement. He describes her murder like he was there, in more detail than he uses in the rest of the book."

She leans forward and raises an eyebrow.

"And then the whole thing about Martin and her misconduct or whatever he called it. He basically blamed her for never prosecuting anyone, even though—off the record—the case was cold almost right from the beginning." I watch her purse her lips. "I mean, why go into such detail? Is it some sort of therapy thing, you know, 'writing through what hurts'?"

She sits back, nods, and gives me a knowing smile that unnerves me. "That raises a big question I'm asking as I write the article," she replies. "I asked him the same thing, but he wouldn't answer. He also wouldn't tell me why he didn't see the police reports when she was killed and what it would mean if he had. It would throw half the book under scrutiny, expose it as a bunch of lies, maybe a hoax. There's a lot going on in that book." She gauges my reaction. "And if he lied, we have to wonder why. I'm also interested in how thoroughly he describes what *might* have happened leading up to the beating, and whether it echoes what really happened to his wife. And whether she and Heather Martin were as close as he seems to think they were. You think he killed her, don't you? Even though that other guy was indicted?"

"Close how?" I ask. "Is this coming from the interview? There wasn't a whole lot in the book about their relationship."

She nods. "He didn't want to talk much about it," she says. "He seemed really uncomfortable. There's definitely something there that he's hiding."

"Everybody's hiding something," I reply without thinking.

"Yeah, I suppose you're right." She sips her coffee. "Would he have had access to those reports? Either as he was writing the book or, more interestingly, back when it happened?"

"Of course," I reply. "Don't quote me on this, okay? I can't be named in your article."

She nods. "No one will read it, anyway, but you have my word."

"Knowing Mattioli's reputation, I'd bet he was in on the investigation, even if he claims he wasn't. Reports are public record. You just have to know where to look. And he would have known where to look. So why he's hiding his knowledge becomes significant. Makes me wonder what else he's hiding, especially with regard to Heather Martin."

She narrows her eyes. "So you *are* investigating him."

"Not officially."

"I'll tell you this much. He creeped me out." She leans over to the bookshelf and pulls *(Un)Solved* off the shelf.

"Creeped you out how?"

She shudders. "It's hard to explain. He was adamant that we meet here. This was months ago, when the publisher sent me the advance copy and asked me to review the book. Right before I took the job here, so... February?"

I catch myself watching the way her mouth moves when she talks.

"Something just seemed off about him. Like he was there in the room, but he wasn't really. He kept staring right through me. Does that make sense?"

I nod. Suspects do that all the time. Especially the psychopaths.

"He said a couple of fucked-up things too. He struck me as a racist homophobe." She laughs. "Then again, a lot of people strike me that way these days." She opens the book. "I'm thinking about the weird voice shift in chapter twelve," she says. "Listen." She reads a passage that I remember about what happened when Mattioli got home and found his wife's body in the basement. "Hear all those adverbs?"

I make a face.

"Please don't think this is about grammar. That's not what I do. It's significant, at least as it relates to how readers process it."

I ask her what she means, and she says that, one, she's surprised his editor didn't make him take them out—something about the adverb paving the road to hell. Whatever, okay. Two, she tells me that if we read that section out loud, "the voice doesn't match the rest."

She flips back to an earlier chapter and reads a passage about Mattioli watching his first autopsy.

His response to that postmortem, at least as he's written it, is still strange to me too—I don't know anyone who wasn't shaken to the core by watching a Stryker saw do its work the first time. He almost sounds like he enjoyed it.

Then she moves back to what Mattioli claims happened to Anna and reads a couple more paragraphs. "See how it sounds different? He just sounds different there," she says, closing the book. "More excited here, more distant there. It's totally inconsistent. He sounds weird, too, whenever he's talking about his partner. Raymond Gibson."

"Uh-huh," I reply, making some notes in my notebook. "Did you ask him about any of this when you interviewed him?"

"Yeah, but that's what I mean. It was like he didn't hear any of my questions. He just wanted to talk all about how he wrote the book on yellow legal pads then paid his son to type it out for him. I'm not sure what any of it means yet."

"Yeah, me neither," I reply. It probably doesn't mean anything, but I'll have to ask him if and when I can. This might be a phenomenal waste of time, and I'm supposed to be working on a cold case, not drinking coffee with professors.

"Thanks for your take on this," I say as I stand to leave. "Let me know if you think of anything else."

She smiles and stands, too, then her leg buckles, and she stumbles forward into me. When I catch her, she looks away. The blush is back too. She pushes off me and leans against the edge of her desk.

"Sorry," she says. "Sitting for a long time messes my leg up."

I'm not sure what to say. *Act interested if you are,* Dr. Shue would say. "It's okay." I slide my notebook back into my jacket pocket. "How is it teaching? Do you stand the whole time?"

She looks surprised. "I typically lean on the desk, like this," she says. "But I'm pretty animated in the classroom. I hobble around, wave my cane." She grins. "I do okay."

"How do you like Cleveland so far?" I ask. "You came from, where, California?"

"I *came* from Pittsburgh," she replies, "with a detour through Eugene, Oregon, and then Sacramento." No Pittsburgh accent. I wonder if she ever had one.

"Please tell me you're not a Steelers fan," I say.

She laughs and shakes her head. "No, the NFL is misogynistic, theatrical bullshit. I only watch college football," she replies. "I was brainwashed at Oregon. Go Ducks." She pumps her fist in a half-assed way, and it makes me laugh.

"You have a great laugh," she says. "Cleveland is fine. I haven't met many people outside my department yet, but the ones I have met seem good so far." She flicks an eyebrow at me. "I've been going to Pittsburgh every other weekend or so, anyway."

I don't ask why. She probably has a lover there or something. A woman like this—smart, gorgeous, seemingly put-together—can't be single.

"I still have family there," she adds. "My dad's a cop. He thinks I walk on water because I got a PhD." She laughs at whatever mental image she has. "Do you have family here?"

"Yeah, my mom and brother live here," I reply.

She nods, and we stand together in silence until I decide it's time to go.

"I appreciate your time," I say. "Let me know if there's anything I can do. You know, to help with your article." *Stop talking, Liz. Get out of here. Get back to work.*

"Well, I'd be interested in your take on those reports," she says. "And maybe you could find out for sure whether or not he saw them. He'd have to sign them out, right? If he wasn't investigating?"

"Not really," I reply. "Like I said, they're public record. And all of the unsolved homicides are digitized these days. He probably still knows people too. There's no way to know."

My phone buzzes in my pocket. I wish to hell Fishner had never learned how to text. She wants to know where I am, what I'm doing, and when I'll be back. I grimace at it then put it back where it was.

"Would you be interested in continuing this conversation?" Gillian asks as I turn to leave. She clears her throat. "Maybe over drinks or dinner?" She meets my eyes and doesn't look away.

"Sure," I say, ignoring the little jump in my stomach.

"Want to give me your direct number? I'll call you." She limps around the desk and pulls her phone out of a brown leather messenger bag. She looks at me like she already knows the answer is yes.

I give her my number. "I'll send you a message now so that you have mine," she says. She types something then grins at me. "I have to get to class. Today, we're talking about the authenticity of sexuality in a handful of LGBTQ memoirs." She still doesn't look away.

Did Gillian Swift just ask me on a date? "Sounds interesting," I reply. I keep my face cop-blank, but I'm not sure why. Gillian and I walk along the hallway together, and I head down the stairs as she enters her classroom.

I don't look at my phone until I'm in the car. I have a message from Gillian that says: *You intrigue me. Drinks soon?*

Drinks soon, I reply. I don't tell her that she intrigues me too.

I check my watch. It's almost time for my appointment with Dr. Shue.

As I'm starting the car, I get a message from Fishner: *Grimes was here looking for you with a guy named Householder. We arrested both of them. IAU wants to talk to you first thing in the morning. Call me ASAP.*

I call her back.

"Boyle, this is not good. What are you doing? Get here now. Talk to Internal Affairs now. This is not good."

"Whoa, whoa. What's happening?"

"Grimes just showed up looking for you. He was violent and unhinged. He smashed a bunch of things on your desk and one of my office windows before Roberts could restrain him."

"What? Are you serious?"

"I'm absolutely serious." Her voice sounds weird.

"Is everyone okay?"

"Everyone is fine. But I need you to... Never mind. You can talk to them tomorrow."

"Boss, what's going on? You don't sound like you." I start the car.

I hear her sniffle as though she's crying. "It's fine, Boyle. Go do your thing."

"Are you sure? What happened, exactly?" I put the phone on Speaker and pull away from Guilford House. The clock on the dashboard tells me I have a little bit of time. "Look, I'm on my way back. Will you be there?"

"I'll be here."

We end the call, and I hightail it to the Justice Center.

MAINTENANCE IS BOARDING up one of Fishner's windows when I enter the squad room. I glance at my desk and find that everything that was on it is on the floor. Roberts and Sims are at their desks, looking worried.

"Go talk to her," Roberts says in a low voice. "She's freaking out. She won't let us leave, but we were supposed to sign out an hour ago."

"Just go," I reply. "I'll cover you with her." I gently knock on Fishner's office door.

She doesn't answer, so I enter to find her slumped over her desk. I rush over to her to make sure she's okay, but she pushes me away.

"Jesus Christ, Boyle," she says through tears.

"Are you all right? What's going on?"

She scrubs her face with a hand then stands. "Grimes and some uniform named Householder came in here today looking for you. I'm not going to ask where you were. When Roberts said he hadn't seen you, they went ballistic. Grimes put a chair through my window. Roberts finally restrained him, but—" She starts to cry again.

"Sit down. Just sit," I say in my witness voice. *This is so weird that I don't even know how to behave.* I guide her into her chair and lean against her desk. "What's really going on, Boss?"

"This whole thing is a mess." She blinks several times then starts laughing. "I'm so sorry. I can't believe I'm losing it like this in front of you."

I give her a warm smile. "Hey, it's okay. How many times have you seen me lose my shit? Call it karma."

She laughs. "Seriously, though. He was after you. He came here to kill you. It's a wonder he didn't kill someone else. Thank God Goran is on vacation. Thank God Roberts and Sims were down the hall."

"And Grimes and Householder are both in custody now, right?" She nods.

"Then there's nothing to worry about. I'm fine. You're fine. We're all okay. We'll put them all away, boss. Don't worry." I resist the urge to pat her shoulder, because it would be as strange as my current level of calm.

"I know. Okay." She pulls it together and stands. "Thanks."

"What aren't you telling me?"

"What do you mean?"

"I think you know what I mean."

She shakes her head. "Be careful, Boyle. This is deep and sinister. You're dodging bullets. Just be careful. Forget everything I said before. Just drop it. Get back to that case I gave you earlier... Just forget it."

I narrow my eyes.

"Detective Boyle, that is an order. Your shift is over. Go home. Be back here tomorrow, ready to talk to IAU. We need to get control of this. Of all of it—these guys who think they're above the law. IAU needs to know what you've uncovered."

I raise my eyebrows. "Boss, with all due respect, it's either that I'm dropping it or that I'm talking to IAU but not both. Which do you prefer?"

She sighs. "At this point, I don't really care. Let me know what you decide, and we'll figure it out in the morning. Go home. I'm going home. Everyone can go home and relax and leave all of this here."

I nod.

"What are you waiting for?" she snaps, suddenly angry. "Go. Now."

She doesn't stop me from leaving.

WHEN I GET TO DR. SHUE'S office, I can't decide where to start. I'm freaked out that I was the collected one back there and that Fishner seems so close to coming completely unhinged—it's like some sort of weird role-reversal thing. I'm not nearly as freaked out as I should be by the whole thing, but I didn't witness a couple of cops trashing our squad room.

Shue leads me into her office and gestures for me to have a seat in my normal spot, so I flounce down and lean forward, my elbows on my knees. "I have had a really strange fucking week." I blow out a sharp breath then chuckle in spite of myself.

She slowly lowers herself into her chair then crosses one knee over the other. She looks at me through her chic rimless glasses, and something is off in her warm brown eyes.

"Are you all right?" I ask.

She nods. "My back has been bothering me." I must be making a face, because she smiles softly. "Please don't worry. It's nice that you'd worry, but I'll be fine."

"I don't believe you, but I'll let it go."

Something tells me I'm right not to believe her, but she grins. "Tell me about your strange week."

I fill her in, and she asks the right questions, and I answer them in ways that seem to make both of us happy.

"I think I'm getting better," I say after we discuss the investigation and what happened today in the squad. "I really think all of this"—I gesture around the room—"has helped. I'm sleeping. I'm eating. I'm taking time for myself. Cora dumped me, but we all saw that coming, so life goes on. I think it's all gonna be okay, assuming that I don't get killed by some asshole cop with a vengeance."

She smiles. "I'm really happy for you, Liz."

I grin. "So I'm all good now?"

She shakes her head. "I still think you would benefit from additional sessions. But this might be a good time for me to tell you that I'll be out of the office for a while after next week. I have a colleague who—"

"No, I won't talk to anyone else." I blurt it out before I can stop myself, but then I realize that it isn't very nice. I shake my head. "I mean, I just don't want to talk to anyone else. It's okay—I'll just wait until you get back. You're who I trust. How long will you be out? Are you sure you're all right?"

She furrows her brow and removes her glasses, which I've never seen her do in the two years I've been coming here. Something changes in the air between us, and I sit forward on my chair.

"It's inappropriate for me to divulge details about my personal life." She puts her glasses back on and adjusts her hips in her chair. She winces but tries to conceal it.

"It might be inappropriate as shit, but something is obviously wrong. Please tell me that you're going to be okay, whatever it is."

She frowns but nods. "I'm taking a leave of absence to attend to a medical issue. I plan to be back in about six months."

Medical issue? Fuck. No. Back surgery? Hip replacement? That wouldn't take six months. She's too young for—

She squeezes her eyes shut and pops them open again. "I have breast cancer, Liz, and it's spread to the bones in my back. I have to have chemotherapy and probably radiation."

Suddenly the air gets stuffy and hard to breathe, and I slump back into my chair. "Holy shit. No. Are you sure? I'm sorry. That's a stupid question. Will you be okay? I'm sorry. That's stupid too. Is there anything I can do?"

"Not really, no." She chuckles. "There's really nothing anyone can do. I guess I just hope for the best and try to stay sane, myself, through treatment."

"I don't know what to say. I'm so sorry." Tears prickle against the backs of my eyelids, so I blink fast several times.

"Let's set a goal to have next week be our goodbye." Her eyes search mine. "It's a temporary goodbye. I have every intention of being back to work in the spring. You've done such great work, Liz, and I'm proud of you. I'll give you the name of my colleague in case you need her, but I'm confident that you'll be okay."

I feel like a baby bird getting ready to leave the nest. I barely hear the words coming out of her mouth. All of a sudden, I have an image of her in a hospital bed, small and scared, and it occurs to me that I don't know anything about this woman who knows everything about me. It becomes harder to stop the tears, so I rake my hand across my face. "Do you have someone to help you? Josh is an oncologist. Pediatric, but he knows his shit. Do you want me to give you his—"

She shakes her head. "It's not your job to fix this. You have to know that by now. It's up to me to handle what's happening in my life. I have an excellent support system and an excellent team of doctors and the ability to take the time off to recover. It could be much worse. Please don't worry."

"Right. Like I'm not gonna worry."

"Well, try not to worry too much." She chuckles. "That's our time for today." She pulls a business card off the table next to her chair and starts writing on the back of it. "Here's my colleague's name and number. Her name is Jacqueline Rhodes, and I think you'll like her very much. She's in the office downstairs."

I don't want to talk to Jacqueline. I want to talk to you. I stand.

She hands me the card, and I stuff it into my jacket pocket.

"I'll see you next week," she says.

"Okay." I smile and slide through the door.

In the car, I remove the card from my pocket and turn it over and over in my hand before shoving it back inside.

It startles me when Gillian Swift calls me just as I'm leaving the parking lot.

<h1 style="text-align:center">CHAPTER 28</h1>

"Hi, Detective Boyle," Gillian says in a sultry tone.

"Call me Liz."

"Okay, Liz, what are you doing tonight? Want to get that drink with me? I have something interesting to tell you. I went back through those chapters and found something that might help. And you didn't tell me you were a local celebrity," she adds. "Guess I'm not the only one in the paper, huh? I Googled you." She laughs.

I ignore that last bit and ease the Passat onto the Shoreway. *What am I doing tonight? I have no plans, beyond watching the corruption surrounding me grow deeper and deeper and worrying about my boss and my therapist.*

I could use a break. Maybe I'll have some epiphany while I'm out drinking with the English professor. "Yeah, tonight works. Where?"

"You're the native," she replies. I can hear the smile in her voice.

I think about it for a minute. "Where do you live?"

She laughs. "That's bold."

"I didn't mean—I just—"

"I know." She chuckles again. "I live in University Heights. Don't all the professors live there?"

"Only the arrogant ones," I reply, letting a smile creep into my voice too. *Holy hell, I'm flirting on the phone.*

"Well, I'm not arrogant enough to suggest that I know a good bar yet that doesn't charge a million dollars for a beer. Give me time," she replies.

"Do you want to grab a bite too? Or just drink dinner?" I ask.

The sound of her laugh makes me happy. "Food would be good, though after the week I've had, I care more about the beer."

Yeah, me too. I ask her if she knows where the Cedar Lee theater is, and she does—she's been there before. I tell her to meet me at the tavern next door at eight thirty, but then it strikes me that I should offer to pick her up.

"I'll see you then," she says before I get the chance. "Gotta run. Bye."

The line goes dead before I can reply or even think about what I'm doing.

I decide to walk to the tavern from my apartment. I live only fifteen minutes away on foot, and it's turned into a gorgeous fall evening, complete with light clouds against a dark, ominous, moon-lit sky. This isn't a big deal. It's just two people meeting to have beers and dinner and talk about some jerk's book some more. Maybe whatever she has to tell me will break the corruption case wide open.

This is what I'm telling myself when I see her, leaning against the brick wall outside the bar, with her weight on her good leg and her cane to the side and her head back and a totally contented smile on her face. This is what I tell myself as I walk up to her and notice the light in her eyes change—it darkens, it focuses—when she sees me. This is what I tell myself when she leans in and kisses me lightly on the cheek to greet me. And when she tells me that I smell good, and when I notice that she does, too, and when I open the door for her, and when I let her walk in front of me as we move to our table, and when I notice how good she looks in those jeans and that sweater.

"What'd you figure out?" I ask after we order our first round. She has good taste in beer too. I will myself to pay attention. I'm here for a work thing, even if I'm off the clock.

"Let's get right to work, huh?" she asks, a sardonic tone to her voice. "Are you one of those workaholic, can't-ever-unwind kind of cops?"

"Yeah, maybe." I feel myself blush. "Tell me why your week calls for booze, then," I say, not adding that my weeks usually do just that or that I'm determined not to become a drunk asshole like my mom was for twenty-five years.

She smiles. "Other than that meeting with you, which was splendid, it was a complete cluster fuck." The waiter brings our beers, and she has hers in her hand almost before he walks away. She takes a sip of the porter and groans. "The Midwest does beer better than anywhere," she muses.

"Tell me more," I reply then take a sip of my own pale ale. *Splendid.* Only an English PhD uses words like that in normal conversation. *Splendid.* I think about the word until it has no meaning anymore.

"About beer? Okay," she says, interrupting my train of thought. "I'm a beer snob. And I mean it. The best microbreweries in the country are here. Well, here and in Michigan. That's not what you were asking, is it?"

Her eyes twinkle, and I look back and forth between them before I catch myself and gaze at her lips instead. I know exactly where this could go, and I'm not stopping it. *"Let yourself be vulnerable,"* *Shue would say.*

"Have you been to the brewery?" I ask.

"It's pretty pathetic to go to a brew pub alone," she replies over the top of her glass.

I'm tempted to ask her to go, but I don't. Cora flashes in front of me. This is not Cora. This is someone else, someone new. Someone who doesn't know me yet, doesn't know the kind of crap I'm capable of and how much she'll regret it if she spends too much time with me. I feel guilty for things that haven't even happened yet but not guilty enough to kill it before it materializes.

She catches my hesitation. "So my week. Yeah, it sucked," she says. A piece of hair falls in front of her face, and I resist the urge to tuck it behind her ear for her. She tells me about some weird situation with the head of her department, a student crying in her office, and a rejection she received for an article that's close to her heart.

"Yeah, mine sucked too," I reply. Callous. I lack empathy.

"I would bet that, on a scale of things, your weeks usually suck a lot more than mine," she says. Kind, genuine.

She must catch my surprise. "Remember my dad's a cop," she adds. "The workaholic kind."

I make appropriate noises and ask appropriate questions, and we're talking about her family all of a sudden. Then she asks about mine, and I don't know what to say, other than an abridged version of the truth. I end with Christopher's anger last week at the football game, since that was the last time I talked to either of my two living relatives.

"See? The NFL," she replies. "I'm telling you, it's no good," she says after we order burgers and more beer.

We talk about that for a while. She has compelling arguments for why I should just stop caring about the Browns. Then we talk about what she calls "blind regionalism" when it comes to sports. "Think about it," she says. "How many people do you know who call themselves Ohio State fans? And what, beyond geographical proximity, makes that happen? I mean, did they all *go* to Ohio State?"

We banter back and forth about it. She's right, but I don't tell her that. "Explain the Oregon thing, then. 'Go Ducks.' Is that 'blind regionalism'?"

"Yes and no," she says. "Yes, in the sense that I never would have become a fan if I hadn't gone there. No, in the sense that I think attending a place like that really brings out the fanatic in anyone."

"That's a cop-out," I reply.

"Yeah, I guess it is. Where'd you go to school?"

"What makes you think I did?" I ask.

"Because you're sharp and you don't hide it very well, even though you think you do."

"I went to CSU," I reply after a beat. "I got two degrees there. Criminal sociology and the one I don't tell anyone about—art history."

She nods. "Yeah, I thought I was getting an artsy vibe. I would have guessed music, though."

I laugh. "I'm a musician too."

"Interesting combo. Why be a cop?" she asks. "Why not be a starving artist? That always seemed romantic to me. Or grad school and an illustrious academic career?"

"Why *not* be a cop?" I reply. "What's the difference? You and I both solve mysteries. I just get a gun and OT and better retirement."

"Good point," she says, "and I like that analogy." She holds up her glass. "Here's to a smart cop and a dumb academic having beers and dinner together."

We clink glasses and order another couple of rounds, and I'm surprised that it takes us so long to talk about Mattioli's book. Turns out a couple of the anecdotes in the book are inconsistent with newspaper reports from the time in which he was quoted, but I could chalk that up to bad reporting. Either way, I make a mental note of the cases and of how impressed I am that she did a bunch of research for me.

"There's more, though," she says. "I went back to my interview transcript with him and noticed that the way he describes his partner—"

"Ray Gibson?"

"Yeah. The way he describes him in the book isn't anything like how he described him in person. In our interview, he made it sound like Gibson was the greatest cop in the world, so I don't get why he wrote about him how he did."

Why talk shit about a guy you actually like? The plot thickens. I squint at the table. "From where I sit, that matters." *How much can I tell her? Maybe just a little.* "I talked to Gibson, and he didn't seem very fond of Mattioli. He admitted they did a bunch of bad shit back in the day, but that's all I got from him." *Why change the story? Why tell the truth—or another lie—to Gillian? It doesn't add up. I definitely need to talk to Mattioli tomorrow, but how am I going to get him to—*

"I have to admit, though, Liz, that while everything with the case is fascinating, I really just wanted to ask you out and couldn't figure out how, so I used my oversized research brain to lure you."

I laugh, and it feels oddly natural. "I suspected as much. I'm flattered." I feel myself blush.

"Are you seeing anyone?"

I tell her it's complicated, and she lets it go. At least I don't lie.

Then she tells me about her accident. She'd been riding her bike to class in Sacramento traffic when a drunk asshole in a BMW hit her, going close to sixty. Life flight, the whole deal. "I don't remember much. I was in a coma for a week," she says. "Fractured skull, about sixteen other broken bones, various other fucked-up things. They didn't think I'd be anything but a vegetable. Guess I proved them wrong."

"What about the leg?" I ask, not wondering out loud if it's why she's so high achieving.

"A vestige of what once was." She taps her left thigh. "I used to be a triathlete. Can you believe it?" She sips her beer. "I had fourteen surgeries in six years. They did their best. I ended up at Stanford Medical, of all places. They did their best," she repeats, as if that matters. She makes intense eye contact with me. "But hey, Liz? If that's the worst thing that ever happens to me? I'm still lucky. At least they didn't amputate it, right? At least I didn't die." She smiles a knowing smile at me.

I don't tell her that I want to see, to touch her scars. That her visible ones remind me of my secret ones, the ones I hide.

"Don't feel sorry for me," she says.

"I don't," I reply, and I'm being honest. "I respect it, what happened to you."

She nods and grins, and it's genuine.

After the waiter clears the glasses and I pay the bill against her protests, we head outside, and I walk her to her car. "I missed this weather," she muses, and I think about kissing her but reconsider. She reads it perfectly. "At some point," she says, "maybe you can fill me in on what 'it's complicated' means." Her eyes stay glued to mine—they don't shift back and forth like most people's. "In the meantime, I had a great time, and I'd love to hang out again."

We say our goodbyes, and I walk home quickly, briefly allowing myself to enjoy the fact that I think I just went on a first date with someone interesting, someone who isn't Cora, and for a fleeting moment, I regret saying "it's complicated." It's not, really. I push that away, though, and swing my attention back to Mattioli—I've got to talk to him in the next couple of days.

Once inside my apartment, I switch lights on, top off Ivan's food, then grab my Garrison belt, gun, and badge without pausing. I go outside and get into my car. *Maybe she's a possibility.*

My intention was to go to the Renaissance to talk to Mattioli, but I'm not doing that alone—I'll just need to figure out who I can get to go with me—maybe Fishner. I end up in front of a familiar house, trying to figure out what I'm doing here. I pull out my phone to send a message but end up tossing it on the passenger seat—it's late, and even if we're friends, it's too soon for me to pull this kind of late-night I-need-to-bounce-ideas-off-you shit, especially given that whole scene at Gibson's last night.

I watch her go by her front window and pray she doesn't see my car, but she does. My phone buzzes.

"What are you doing out there?" Cora asks.

"Sitting in my car," I reply. "I'm sorry. I shouldn't be doing this. I should go home and go to bed."

She opens the front door. "Come inside before the rain starts again," she says. And then, as if she can read my face from here: "It's fine. Hurry up. I'm bored and can't sleep, anyway."

I hang up and get out of the car.

"You want a beer?" she says as I remove my jacket and hang it on her coatrack.

I follow her down the hallway. "I'd love a beer. Thanks."

After she grabs two beers from the fridge, opens them, and slides one across the kitchen island to me, we make small talk for a few minutes. Then I tell her what happened. All of it, all of what's been happening. The Shue stuff, the Mattioli connection, Mistress Natalia, indicting a guy I think was put up to it, the corruption, the weirdness between Mattioli and Gibson. Briscoe and the DOJ investigation. What Gibson said about Fishner. Fishner losing her shit in her office. I say nothing about Gillian.

"Wait a minute," she says. "You were propositioned by a dominatrix?" She laughs, and the sound of it soothes me.

"In essence," I reply. "I felt like more of a private eye than a cop, if you want to know the truth. You know, using my wit and charm to outsmart the femme fatale who had info for me."

"But it was a dead end with the guy."

I nod. "And with every other guy. This stinks like shit."

"Yeah, sounds like it. What happened with Grimes?"

"He showed up in my fucking squad room."

"Oh, it's *your* squad room?" She arches an eyebrow and leans a hip against the counter.

I grin. "You're damn right it is."

I drain my beer, and without me asking, she opens the refrigerator and hands me another one.

"I thought you were worried about my drinking," I say.

"You're going to do it whether I like it or not, so you might as well do it here," she replies. "I'm more concerned about you flying solo and interviewing shady characters by yourself out in the middle of nowhere." She glances at my sidearm. "You should probably lock your gun up, though."

"I'm okay. I won't stay long," I say. Tomorrow, I need to figure out a way to get Fishner to help me interview Mattioli and maybe Gibson again. I can hear her voice in my head: *We aren't Internal Affairs, and they're retired.* But then I hear new-Fishner's voice telling me God knows what.

I swear Cora looks disappointed, but I let it go.

"So you moving on Mattioli?" she asks after a long pause.

"No, not now," I reply. "I've got nothing on him. And all Gibson really said was, one, I'm a traitor to my department, and two, Heather Martin pissed a lot of people off. Nothing I didn't already know. His place was creepy, though. Poor guy."

Cora appraises me with her soft brown eyes. "Why'd you come here? I'm not being an asshole. I just genuinely want to know."

I shrug. "Habit. You're good to talk to. You know the job. We're friends."

She nods with a sort of skeptical, curious look. "There's something you're not telling me, isn't there?"

"What do you mean?" I do deflection pretty well with everyone but her.

"This is gonna sound woo-woo yoga, but your energy is different. I can't tell if you're resigned or vulnerable or confident or all three or what." She's been into yoga since the first time we broke up. She seems more serene that way, so I guess it's good for her.

"In spite of the chaos, you're okay, aren't you?" she asks. "Like really okay."

"Yeah, I am," I reply. "I feel bad about my therapist being sick, but I'm okay."

"People get sick, Liz. She has access to a world-class hospital."

I nod. "Everything about this case is a cluster fuck shit show, but it almost doesn't matter. You know? I feel... just better. I just feel better. Like, personally speaking, I mean." I don't tell her that the enormous weight of us feels like it's lifted. I don't tell her that it's a relief to be here talking to her and not pining for something I know I can't ever have with her.

She smiles, nods, and pushes behind her ear a piece of hair that's fallen out of her messy bun. "You've always stalled out and then moved quickly," she says with a combination of amusement and sadness.

I'm not really sure what to say. That's kind of an understatement, all things considered. "I guess so. How are you? Anything exciting happen in the Heights in the past week, beyond accompanying a crazy Cleveland detective to the boonies?"

"Actually, yeah. I was gonna call you, but I didn't know if that was a good idea." She takes a sip of her beer, sets it down on the island, and leans forward with some ceremony. "I'm getting promoted. You can call me Sergeant Bosch from now on."

I tell her that's great, grin at her, laugh when she paints imaginary stripes on her arm, and ask her when it's happening.

"Next week," she says.

I tell her I'll be there. "You getting ink to celebrate?" Cora loves tattoos, and she loves being good at what she does. She's been angling for the sergeant job for two years now.

"Hell no, I'm not getting anything related to law enforcement on me, ever," she says. "I'm pretty stoked, though. It'll be regular hours, more money."

Her dream is to quit her job and become a full-time artist—she got into the whole cop game only because she was a sketch artist for the county and thought it would be "interesting"—her word—to be a detective. Honestly, I could see that dream of hers happening. I might live to work, but Cora works to live.

"More time on your ass pushing paper around too."

"That too. I'll have to up the work at the gym." She flexes her arm. "Start doing hot yoga or something."

"Nah, you're good the way you are," I say, and it feels normal and not strange.

"You gonna take the test?" she asks. Fishner has been on me for a while now to take the sergeant's exam. Josh and Cora, who are both smarter about things like retirement funds and paying attention to the physical limitations that come with middle age, have both expressed their support for my boss's wish. It's too much desk work for me, though. I would go insane.

"Rate things are going now, I'm stuck at D1 till I retire," I reply. Other cops might seem supportive, but Grimes has been working his behind-the-scenes campaign to tarnish my name since he was acquitted, and if I blow the lid off the corruption, I might end up in an unfortunate position. Fishner could make the promotion happen regardless, but there's no point in being a Detective Sergeant no one will listen to. I tell her as much.

"Fuck him," she says. "Even guys in my department know his name and not in a good way. Just watch your back." She's talking about the threats.

I pat the Glock. "He's in jail right now, and that's why it's not in a safe," I say. "He doesn't have it in him, anyway. He's a coward. We all know that."

She asks me how Josh and Jacob are, and I say that I don't know, that trying to adopt a kid is taking all of their time. Last we spoke was when we all saw each other at the bar, two weeks ago now.

It feels like it was a year ago, that night with them. With Cora. It seems like it's been a lot longer than it has. I used to lose track of time in a bad way. This feels different.

"What are you thinking?" she asks. "You have that look. What is it, the investigation?"

I smile. "No, it's a different look. It's not the investigation—it's not a kid case. Officially, the investigation is over, and the other side of it will be there until I solve it, even if I don't." I pause. "I'm glad that you and I decided to be friends," I say. "I could get used to this. To sitting here with you and not feeling all fucked up and tortured."

"But would you still be Liz if you did that?"

We both laugh.

"Yeah, I think I would be."

"What's the look, then?" she asks. "I'm not trying to prod. I'm just curious."

"Enough with the disclaimers. I get it."

"You're going to make me play detective, aren't you? Well, you already told me what's making you sad, so the look isn't that you're hiding your feelings. You said your brother is good and your mom is still sober. You didn't get promoted, and you don't seem especially upset that your department is riddled with corruption. You got an indictment. Which leaves one thing." She gazes at me, and it looks like a light comes on in her brain. "I knew it!" She points at me. "I meant it when I said you move quickly. Who is it, the prosecutor?"

I almost choke on my beer. "What, Julia Becker? Hell no. Have you been talking to Josh?" Josh has been after me for months to hook up with Becker, but I'm still not sure she bats for my team, and it's best not to mix business with pleasure.

She asks me a couple of questions, and I answer them.

Then she disappears down the hall without saying anything. After a few minutes, I hear the toilet flush and the water running in the bathroom and wonder with some trepidation whether I've hurt her. Historically, I'm good at that.

When she comes back, she sits on the stool next to mine at the island. "I'm happy for you," she says. She covers her hand with mine, and I look for the tingle, but it doesn't come. "I'm jealous as hell, but I'll get over it. I'm happy for you. Good for you, Liz."

I search her kind eyes for any hint of something she's not saying, but it's not there. With her free hand, she reaches across the island for her beer and raises it. "Here's to finally—fucking *finally*—figuring this shit out."

We clink bottles.

She hugs me before I leave.

When I get back to my car, I feel lighter, somehow. Almost free.

CHAPTER 29

I get home a little before midnight and sit in my car for a few minutes, feeling oddly upbeat again, a little buzzed, and confident that I'll connect the dots and that Fishner will do the right thing—it's just who she is.

That's why I don't notice him as I step out of the car. He must have been hiding next to the dumpster. It doesn't matter where he was, because this is how it's going to end, by getting hit with a Taser and a thick forearm choking me out. I gurgle some strained vibration from below the place where he's stopped my breath, and I kick. Both of my legs push us off the car, but he's too strong. We don't fall. He holds me in the air by my neck.

I try to claw his arm, bite him, anything. A familiar smell surrounds me: cologne and stale cigarettes and cheap whiskey. I can't get him off me. He's all in leather.

He reaches around with his left hand and wraps it around my neck so tightly that I barely register the Taser burns.

My brain slows down, and I crumple forward and hit the open car door. My arms don't extend like they should. There's a crack and a slap, then I'm on the wet pavement.

Something skitters across the asphalt. *My phone. Phone. Phone home.*

There's sharp pressure on—in—the left side of my head, then the blood comes. It runs down my face like melted wax, into my eye and into my mouth. The taste of it is sharp and metallic.

I'm facedown. The blood drips. *Struggle. Remember to struggle.*

Shit, my gun. He's got my gun. He's laughing and saying I should have locked it up somewhere. More pain. The back of my head sears.

There's my phone, under the car. I reach for it.

But he twists my hands behind me and tells me I'm getting what I deserve, that cops never rat on other cops, that I'm a fucking snitch, and this is what happens to bitches like me.

His boot comes down against the back of my neck, followed by the sharp click and skitch of handcuffs around my wrists. *My own cuffs on my own wrists.*

Try to scream. Just scream.

My head explodes in white heat, then there's cold, black silence.

WHEN I COME TO, THERE'S a sound. *Clink-clank. Clink-clank.* It's rhythmic and regular.

I'm not dead if there's a sound. *Clink-clank.* Metal on metal. Flagpole.

Breathe. Yes. Fuck, ouch, but okay. Breathing. Try not to move too fast. He might be watching. I pretend to be dead. But I'm not dead. There's no way death hurts this much.

Air. In and out. I slow it down. There's a smell. *Diesel? No. Melting plastic. Burning oil. Flesh, blood. Kerosene.*

I can only open one eye. The left one is sealed shut. I try to wipe it—*no.* My hands are locked in place. I blink my right eye. Everything is dark, dim, dusky.

I can't stand. I'm bound to something. *Clink-clank, scratch, scratch. Metal on metal.*

Damn it. Shit, I need to wake up.

Razorlike pain shoots through my head, sharp like a hot probe. I can't check my chest, but there's stinging and the sharp throbbing of broken ribs. I cough. *Fuck, no, I have to stop sputtering, or he'll hear me.* I cough again, and the taste of blood comes back with a vengeance. This is not good. It's probably a punctured lung. My left eye, left lung, left hand—only one of each is left. I'm half intact. It has to be good enough. I have to make it out of here.

Damn it. Shit, get it together.

But I'm so tired.

I WAKE UP AGAIN AND remember more. He beat me with a police baton after pushing me down some stairs. I know that much. I remember the glint of black metal as it came down on me again and again.

It's still too dark to see, but I don't sense anyone in the room with me. I'm tied to a metal pipe, and it's cool against the back of my head. If I move my arms, two things happen. One, a searing pain shoots through my left shoulder and down into my ribs. *Why just beat me up on one side?* I will myself not to laugh. He'll hear me, and I might drown in my own blood. Two, I can slide up and down this metal pipe, or I could if my leg wasn't stuck. The pipe is big—six, maybe seven or eight inches in diameter. A sewer pipe.

My left leg is connected to my wrists somehow. *Feel it, feel it, yes.* My right hand explores. I come across a plastic zip tie then my handcuffs. My synapses fire. Everything throbs except my right hand. Both of my hands are half numb. The cuffs are too tight.

Bind the chain. It hits me like a sledgehammer—a coherent thought. *Yes, the cuffs are weak in the middle. The chain will snap if I can summon the strength to twist them.*

No, I need to find something. A paperclip, a nail, a bobby pin. Unlocking them will be so much better than binding the chain that will cut my wrists and make me bleed out on this concrete floor.

Concrete floor.

Basement.

I need to open my other eye.

I shrug my left shoulder up and against the side of my face, but the pipe is in the way.

From somewhere outside: *Clink-clank, clink-clank, clink-clank.*

I time my own sounds to match. *Fuck-you, fuck-you, fuck-you.*

I get my shoulder up and against my face again. If I can just get enough friction on the cuffs... Almost, but I can't reach.

All right, eye. Stay shut, then. The right one is working okay now, anyway, at least enough to confirm that I'm alone. At least he didn't cover my head. I almost chuckle, but the pain in my left side is too much. I will myself not to pass out again.

After I struggle for several minutes, my blood coats the cuffs and lubricates the chain. It won't catch. *Fuck. No, I have to keep working. Twist it around. Ignore the pain. Don't give up. Blink the tears away. Maybe they'll wash the blood out of my eye. I can't pick the lock. There's nothing to pick it with. I'll breathe through it. Twist it until it catches.*

I keep going.

More time passes, then it happens. The chain breaks, and I fall over onto my bad side. My leg is still tied to my wrist, and the pain paralyzes me again. I move my right hand out and in front of my face, and there's blood—a lot but not too much. I peel my left eye open before feeling along my ankle for the zip tie, sharp plastic around the metal bracelet. He was stupid. He should have zip-tied my hands too. I can scrape it. I can grind it between the floor and the steel cuff until it snaps.

But shit, what is that sound? Above me. Footsteps.

I have to find a way out.

A train horn sounds in the distance. The train rumbles, getting louder. *Scrape the tie. Do it now.*

I'm frantic. Skitchskitchskitch against the concrete. I hammer it into the floor, pull it, kick my leg as hard as I can.

It snaps, and I splay. I lie there and listen to my heartbeat, trying not to breathe, trying not to cough, covered in viscous fluids in various stages of drying. *Wounds, heal yourselves. Body, please give me just enough.*

My shirt and jacket are open, my bra cut in the middle. I feel a long wound running between my breasts. The skin has already started to knit itself back together. My pants are undone and sliding down, and my underwear gone, the belt buckle clinking against itself and against the floor. I will myself not to think about it, not to worry about what he did to me. I need to find a way out. I just have to pull myself together long enough to get the hell out of here.

A window. If it's a basement, there must be a window, maybe a door. I stand and try to ignore the pain in my thigh. *Holy hell, did he stab me?* I pull up my pants, close them, and try not to think about the fact that they were down. The footsteps above stop.

My left hand feels broken. My left thigh is mangled. Not broken but torn. An eight-inch vertical rip in my pants, right over the quadriceps, matches the eight-inch vertical rip in the skin between my breasts. My pants and chest are soaked with dark and sticky blood that's clotting by now. I'll be fine if I just get out. It's not so deep that I'm dead. It's a flesh wound. *Don't look at it.*

I grope along the perimeter of the space. It's about twenty feet by eighteen. I find the steps but ignore them, because I can't go up there. There has to be another way out. Shelves line the walls. I try not to knock anything off, willing myself to be quiet, stealthy. *Hurry.*

I hear footsteps upstairs again, followed by a loud thump and the sound of an electric saw. I freeze in place until I hear laughter and the footsteps moving in the opposite direction. *What is he laughing at? I don't care. Just get out of here.* A dog barks twice outside. It sounds big.

I feel along the wall, and my right hand finds a doorknob. *A door. A door.* I stop myself from crying, because I don't have time for relief—I have to run. The door is locked, but I can get out if I find something to pick the lock with. It doesn't feel like a dead bolt, just a cheap old metal doorknob. I feel for the hinges. It opens in, so I can't kick through it.

I hobble around, trying to find something, anything—*yes, this will work. This brick will work.*

I time it with the sound of the flagpole. Clink-clank. Clink-clank. Clink-clank. Chunk. The doorknob rolls across the floor. I yank the door open and force myself to run.

I'm outside. *Holy shit. I need to get up these stairs. Quickly. No looking back.*

I fall only twice on my way out of the basement, once when my foot catches on some kind of vine and again when my mangled leg gives out. A bright-yellow parking-lot light burns above me. I'm at Ray Gibson's house out in the country, somewhere far away from anywhere I want to be. *Just run over there, across those railroad tracks, into those woods, and maybe Gibson won't get you.*

I take off in a slow sprint, ignoring the searing pain from the wounds.

I fall several times in the woods. I'm sure he's after me. He has to know I'm gone. *If he lets Hazel loose, what then?*

I can't keep going. It's too dark and too hard. It's too hard.

Keep going. Keep going.

So much blood.

Keep going. He's after you.

I can't breathe. Too weak.

Keep going. Keep going.

No, I'm down.

Get up, Liz. You can't lie here like this. Get up and keep going, or you're dead.

Somehow, I keep going.

Running along the opposite edge of the woods is a two-lane road. I can't tell where I am. I'm so confused. *Blink. Keep going.* It's familiar. I can get out of here.

There's rustling in the woods. *No. Run.* I have to find a phone or a gun. I have to find anything but him.

A gas station. *Right, there's a gas station up there.* Fresh Bait, the sign says. *Just get there. Don't think about the fact that all the lights are off. Button your shirt. Okay. Get there.*

Somehow, I make it to the door, but it's locked. *Screw this. Set off the alarm. Do something, anything.*

I'm so tired and so weak, and so much blood is gone.

Who is that? A monster in the glass. I'm hallucinating. I need to find something, anything to break the window with. There has to be a phone inside. *Over there. Rocks.* I get one and throw it.

It shatters the glass and my own grotesque reflection.

Everything goes black again.

<hr>

NONONONONO. WAKE UP. Wake up. You can't lie here and die. Get in there and find a phone. I prop myself up on my forearms. *Now. Pull yourself through the door.* I crawl inside. *Ignore the glass in your leg wound. Find the phone.* My fingers close around it. *Call 911.*

"Nine-one-one, what's your emergency?"

"I'm dead. I'm dead. Police. Police."

"Ma'am, are you all right?"

"No, I'm dead. Police. He's coming."

"Ma'am, please stay on the line."

"Please help me. He's coming. Get him."

"Ma'am, are you with me?"

Get him. Raymond Gibson. Please. Please.

"Ma'am, stay with me."

No, I can't. I can't.

ALL THAT STUFF PEOPLE say about their lives flashing before them isn't true. There is no return of those indelible moments I thought I would always remember, the ones I hoped would play like old super-eight movies in my brain. Me with my brother and sister when I was little, running along the lakeshore, happy. Me having a barbecue with my friends at a Fourth of July party. Playing my first gig. My professional triumphs. Personal ones. Falling in love for the first time, the second, the last. There is no final glow as I take my last breath, no warm white light, no omnipotent God waiting there for me. There is no swirl of rainbows. There is no one there to record my last words, my profession of undying love for someone who couldn't make it to my end. There are no dead loved ones there on a warm sandy beach, extending their arms as I run toward them, telling me that everything is okay now. There is no total comprehension of the answers to all of my existential questions.

There is only me, breathing one minute and not the next.

My heart beats until it stops.

It just goes black, and that's the end.

AND THEN, WHAT A CLICHÉ: voices. Men talk. A woman hovers over me with a penlight, saying something about a pulse, a weak pulse.

My pulse? She rolls me over, and the pain reminds me: *Yes, I'm alive. Alive. Not dead yet. Breathing, heart beating, a weak pulse.*

Someone puts a plastic mask over my face. A voice tells me to breathe, that it's oxygen, that I'll be okay now, help is here. They cover me with a blanket. "Get her on the board," someone says, and someone else stabilizes my neck with a hard plastic brace.

I blink and try to talk.

"Don't talk," someone says. "Don't try to talk. Just breathe."

But I have to tell them. Ray Gibson. Get him, please.

"Pupils responsive," the woman says.

"We got him," a man says. He wears a black shirt and a gold star—a sheriff's uniform.

Right. I'm out here in Geauga County, in the middle of nowhere.

"He's in custody," the man says. "We apprehended him as he approached this location. You called just in time, and good job. You got out. I think he would have killed you."

"It's Gibson. Ray Gibson. Gibson." I struggle with the mask. He can't hear me through it.

He holds the mask in place. "Shhh, you'll be okay."

"It's Gibson. Tell Fishner."

"Don't talk, just breathe. You're going to the hospital."

"I'm a cop. CPD."

"Don't talk."

"Do a rape kit," I whisper.

"Shhh, just breathe."

I black out again in the ambulance. I'm pretty sure they have to shock me back to life once, maybe twice, maybe more. At some point, I hear a siren coming from above me.

Please, just let me die.

Please, don't let me die.

CHAPTER 30

The verdict at the hospital is that I have a punctured lung, along with lacerations to my left leg, chest, wrists, face, and scalp. Major blood loss, contusions of various sizes and shapes, burns from the Taser, and a bruised kidney. Seven broken ribs, two broken fingers, a sprained wrist, and a severe concussion. I'm lucky that my major organs are intact and lucky not to have shattered vertebrae, not to be in a wheelchair.

Lucky.

I have minor surgery on the leg because they have to sew the muscle as well as the skin. The smashed bones in my left middle and ring fingers, they pinned and screwed and tethered with some kind of overly complicated splint to the good fingers on either side. I guess they couldn't wait for me to wake up, or I might have lost the fingers. Screws stick out. I can't really look at them, even though they're in a splint practically right under my face.

For the rest, there wasn't a lot they could do. They gave me blood, I guess. They cleaned me up, bandaged everything, pumped me full of IV fluids and antibiotics. They taped my ribs and sewed me closed with a lot of stitches. They reinflated the lung, which did its thing afterward without incident.

Lucky.

I'm not dead. I'll survive. If this is the worst thing that ever happens to me...

The doctor is holding up an X-ray and explaining all of this to me, but I'm in and out. I don't know what the hell she's talking about, and I wince in pain when I try to sit up straighter.

"Get me off of these painkillers," I think I say. I can't think straight. I look around, but only the doctor and a nurse are there.

I ask her if I'll ever play guitar again.

She says I'll have to talk to the hand surgeon.

I ask her if I was assaulted.

She looks at me like I'm insane, and for the first time, I notice how young she looks. Obviously. I was obviously assaulted. "You were beaten very, very badly." She sounds as if she's talking to a child.

"That's not what I mean," I say. "I need to get out of this bed. Is everyone else okay? I have to pee."

"I'll call the nurse to remove the catheter," she replies. "But you need to be careful. That—"

"No, I want to hear it. Before anything else." I steel myself, bracing for the worst thing I can imagine. "Is anyone else hurt? Did he rape me?"

I fill in the silent space with horrible, horrible thoughts.

"No," she says after too many seconds go by. "No, he didn't sexually assault you. And as far as I know, no one else was involved."

That magic word. No. I never really liked it before, but now it sounds like hallelujah.

I try to get out of bed. She tells me to stop, to be careful with my leg, and to watch that IV and the catheter. She says the lung is going to take some time to heal, and until I have PT, I need to use that cane, and be careful with the hand, and this and that and the other thing. I keep trying to get out of bed, but then it's too hard and I fall back, defeated, feeling small and impotent against the pillows.

I start to feel woozy and strange. *I need to eat something. I need to get off these painkillers.*

Goran appears in the doorway, looking like he's been crying.

That can't be real.

"Liz, holy shit." He approaches the side of my bed.

"Are you real?"

He squeezes his eyes shut and gently takes my good hand. "When you're back from this, I am going to kick your ass into next week for not telling me what was going on."

I manage a chuckle. "What happened?"

He knows what I mean. "We think Gibson, Mattioli, and Maxwell were all working together. We're trying to figure out motive, but method and opportunity are clear as day. It's too soon to tell for sure, but we're holding both of those shitbags and working it as hard as we can. The FBI is involved now because of what happened to you."

"We did it." My eyelids are just so heavy.

"Liz, I—"

But then I'm asleep again.

After he's gone—*was Goran really here?*—a nurse clad in hot-pink scrubs brings me some weird yellow soup, red Jell-O, and a big jug of water. I devour the tasteless soup and the Jell-O, chug the water, and fall asleep again after muttering that I want to go home.

IT'S STILL DARK, AND I can't tell how much time has passed. I need to call someone to pick me up. I feel all right now, other than the throbbing. Let's get these tubes out of me so that I can walk around. I can't lie here forever. I press the button on the side of my bed to call the nurse, but the shadow that appears in the doorway isn't a nurse.

"You're awake," Fishner says. She smiles, but I can tell I don't look good. That thing that pulls at the corners of her eyes as she crosses the room—that's concern.

She comes closer, drags the chair over, and sits next to me.

"Hey, boss," I say. "I didn't die."

She chuckles, but it's for me, not her. "No, you didn't. And you did a great job, Boyle. Really great job. We got them. We got Mattioli, Gibson. You did it. Incredible work."

"I want to go home. Someone needs to feed my cat."

When I look at her, I see tears on her cheeks.

"Hey, don't do that," I say. "I didn't die. Was Tom here, or did I dream that? Was I—"

"Goran was here for two days. And technically, you did die," she says.

Oh, right. The ambulance.

"You died twice."

The gas station and the ambulance? I can't remember. Everything is so addled in my throbbing, swollen, sunburned brain. I reach for my water, and Fishner hands it to me then helps me get the straw between my lips.

"What happened?" I ask.

"Heights received a nine-one-one from one of your neighbors. She called when she saw him shove you into a van. It was too late. You—"

"Ah, shit. Right, he smashed my phone. I lost all my pictures. Maybe they can recover them from the cloud." The weird things we say, the things we think right after we die twice. I lick my lips and taste metal, but I can't tell if it's blood.

Neither of us talks for a couple of minutes. I want to know what happened. Maybe I'll remember eventually. *The black baton.*

"Were they working together?" I ask. "Gibson and Mattioli?"

"Sims got some tech evidence suggesting that Gibson was communicating with Grimes and Householder," she replies. "It's unclear whether Gibson was involved with the Heather Martin murder, but we're tracing the connections. So far, we don't see a direct connection to Maxwell, other than Mattioli, which is circumstantial at best. Gibson said a few things when we recovered him from Geauga County about avenging Grimes and maybe himself, given Mattioli's book. He came after you because of Grimes." She runs a hand across her head. "It's twisted."

"Yeah, he and Mattioli seemed to hate each other."

"They still could have been working together—and we'll find out if they were. But Gibson gave us a bunch on Mattioli's misbehavior years ago. The FBI is taking over and opening a full investigation." She laughs sadly. "Carrothers hasn't come out of his office for two days."

I nod, but it hurts. "Let the feds have it. Get it the fuck away from us." I swallow, and it's too dry. "Holy fuck. But why? Why go to all these extremes?" *Why beat me within an inch of my life?* I close my eyes and drift off for a minute but snap back pretty quickly, all things considered. "How long have I been here?"

"Four days," she replies.

I let that sink in for a minute.

"Did they recover my gun, my shield? Where are we now? What day is it?" A wave of panic overtakes me. My gun—he pistol-whipped me with it. I remember that now. *Maybe I'm dead, and this is some kind of, I don't know, some kind of death thing. Or maybe I'm still hallucinating and no one has been here and I'm in the dark woods, alone. Why don't I know?* I start to get up, but my lieutenant holds me back with a firm but gentle hand against my good shoulder. *That basement. Gibson laughing as he brought the gun and the baton down on me, again and again, saying something about not wanting to break my pretty face. Fuck this. Fuck him.*

I have to get out of here.

"Liz, stop. The nurse will come in and unhook some of this, okay? Your friend Josh will be here to take you home tomorrow, assuming the doctor clears you. He was here yesterday with your other friends and family. He says you're in good hands."

I sit back and breathe. My ribs ache like hell, and I try not to wince. "What other friends and family?"

"Cora Bosch brought you some pajamas," she says. "Your mom and brother were here too. And Gillian Swift wants you to call her when you're able."

Everything hurts. *Friends and family.* I only remember Goran. "Gun and shield?"

"Yes. In evidence right now but recovered. You—"

A different nurse comes in and asks Fishner to give us a few minutes.

Once he's taken out all of the tubes and needles, he shows me how to use my cane, which is hard because my shattered hand and mangled leg are on the same side, so I have to use my right hand to help my left leg. He guides me to the bathroom and instructs me to pee while he waits outside. I do as I'm told, and no, there's no blood in it anymore, so thanks, now please leave me alone. Then he helps me out of my sling and tells me not to get my left hand wet. He hands me a toothbrush, toothpaste, a bar of soap, a washcloth, a towel, and the T-shirt and pajama pants that Cora brought for me. I set them on a shelf next to the sink.

I hesitate in front of the mirror. I wash my face and my right hand, the one that's not in the splint, without looking. I dry everything without looking. I brush my teeth twice, without looking. But then I can't help it.

Oh. Okay, then. Wow.

The theme is swollen and vivid violet. My face is ghoulish—the left side is purple all the way from the eyebrow to below my cheekbone, where it fades to yellow, which stretches to my jaw. I have a vertical cut through my eyebrow with what looks like five or six stitches holding it closed. My lips are dry and cracked and swollen. There are bruises on my neck from the choke hold.

The fingers on my good hand search through my hair. I feel three staples in the back along with a big knot and a thick scab. My body is doing what it can to heal itself.

Bruises line my arms. My wrists are bandaged. When I remove the pathetic hospital gown, I gasp. My entire torso is purple and red, angry and mottled, and bisected by a bright-white bandage that I peel off to reveal the long gash between my breasts. It's not stitched—it looks like they glued it. Maybe the scar won't be too bad.

Another bandage covers the hole where the chest tube was. There's bright-white tape on my ribs and a cut on my hip that I hadn't noticed, with three stitches there. My left leg, save for the white gauze covering the pulsing wound—I don't mess with that bandage, not yet—is purple and red to the knee. I turn around and strain my neck to look at my back, where there's more of the same. Horizontal bruises cross my spine, where he must have beaten me with the black baton that broke me.

Lucky.

I wash my face, bend over the sink, and run water through my hair until it's clear. I bathe my battered body as best I can, trying to erase the stink of my own blood and tears and fear, trying to remove the rusty, musky stench of it all. I'd pay a million dollars for a shower, but I'm not allowed to do that right now. So I just do my best with the sink then dry myself off. I wash my face again, just because, then gingerly don the soft, clean-smelling clothes, feeling grateful for them and for Cora.

I limp out of the bathroom and back to my boss, who's still all teary-eyed and serious-looking next to my hospital bed. The nurse is gone.

"Hey, I'm okay," I say. "I'll be okay. What's the status?"

She looks up at me and tries to smile. "Boyle, don't worry about it anymore. It's done. Goran just texted to tell me he fed your cat. He hates that he's not here right now."

I ease myself into bed. *But he was here. He was here for two days.*

The nurse comes in with three gigantic pills in a paper cup. "You have to take these," he says.

No BS, that one. I perch on the edge of the bed and take them all at once with the rest of the water.

"I'll bring you more water," he says. "You need to drink all of it." He casts a glance at Fishner. "Make her drink all of it."

"Shit. Fine, I'll drink it all," I mutter.

"Boyle, I can't tell you enough. What you did. I knew they were bad guys. I knew it back when they were playing those games in the nineties. I knew Gibson had lost his shit—if I'd known you were going to talk to him, I would have stopped you... I was just a dumb little rookie who thought she meant a lot more than she did." She rubs the side of her neck, searching my face. "There was nothing anybody could do about it then, anyway. And I almost wanted to stop you. But there's no stopping you, I guess."

"Which one hurt you?" I ask.

She grimaces.

"But they did. They hurt you," I say. "Gibson and Mattioli and Grimes and their boys. They were the guys. The ones that did that shit to women cops. Was it Gibson?" I don't ask whether Carrothers was involved. I'll find out eventually.

She looks down at her lap and nods. "Forgive me for this, but I'm glad he beat you instead of raping you," she whispers. "I regret with every fiber of my being that I didn't report them twenty years ago. None of this would have happened."

I regret it, too, but I don't say it. I blink several times.

"But he's going to prison now," she says, sitting up a little in her chair. "For what he did to you. We're going to look at him for Anna Mattioli, too, and my guess is that the FBI will uncover that Gibson was solidly involved in Heather Martin's homicide."

"But not for what they did to you. No one is going away for that."

"It doesn't matter now." We both know she's lying.

Friends and family showed up here for me. I glance at Fishner, who is staring out the window, into the darkness of night, and wonder whether she's a friend or if she's family.

The nurse brings more water, and I take a couple of sips and set the cup on my tray, but then Lieutenant Fishner makes sure that I drink it all.

Acknowledgments

Thanks to my editors, Alyssa Hall and Angela McRae, for filing off the rough edges, for seeing the dark humor in this book, and for laughing with me about things that others might not find funny.

Thanks to the whole staff at Red Adept for the good work that you do and to Streetlight Graphics for the fantastic cover.

Thanks to Claire Anderson-Wheeler, my amazing agent at Regal, Hoffman & Associates.

Thanks to my parents for instilling a love of dark, demented mystery fiction in me at a very early age.

Thanks to my writing partners, Kate and Sarah, for keeping me honest and on task.

Thanks beyond words to Malia, the love of my life.

All characters and events in this book are figments of my imagination. I am not Elizabeth Boyle any more than you are, though I like to think that she and I have an understanding of sorts. The Cleveland Department of Police does not have a Special Homicide Division. Therefore, the squad room, the ranking system within the unit, and some of the procedural aspects of the book are, like the characters and events, fictional. It's tremendously likely that I've botched several facets of how real police would investigate this crime, and I've definitely taken creative liberties with the city itself. In short, *none of this really exists or ever did*, and any similarity to actual places, events, or persons, living or dead, is a coincidence.

Any mistakes are my own.

Don't miss out!

Visit the website below and you can sign up to receive emails whenever Kate Birdsall publishes a new book. There's no charge and no obligation.

https://books2read.com/r/B-A-ALUE-DFCEB

BOOKS 2 READ

Connecting independent readers to independent writers.

Did you love *The Heights*? Then you should read *Warped Ambition*[1] by Debbie S. TenBrink!

[2]

When the battered body of a teenage girl is found in a dumpster, Lieutenant Jo Riskin is called to take the case. Investigating with her partner, Detective Lynae Parker, Jo uncovers secrets, loyalties, and ambitions that give motives to a surprising number of suspects , including a boyfriend from the wrong side of the tracks.

While immersed in her current case, Jo is battling her own personal demons. After two years, she is still grieving over the loss of her husband, who was killed in the line of duty. New information that could help solve his murder, and let her move on with her life, is within her grasp.

---

1. https://books2read.com/u/mYRqJd

2. https://books2read.com/u/mYRqJd

Barricading her heart, Jo is determined to solve both cases and bring the killers to justice.

Read more at debbietenbrink.wixsite.com/author.

Also by Kate Birdsall

A Liz Boyle Mystery
The Flats
The Heights

Watch for more at www.katebirdsall.com.

About the Author

Kate Birdsall was born in the heart of the Rust Belt and harbors a hesitant affinity for its grit. She's an existentialist who writes both short and long fiction, and she plays a variety of loud instruments. She lives in Michigan's capital city with her partner and at least one too many four-legged creatures.

Read more at www.katebirdsall.com.

About the Publisher

Dear Reader,

We hope you enjoyed this book. Please consider leaving a review on your favorite book site.

Visit https://RedAdeptPublishing.com to see our entire catalogue.

Don't forget to subscribe to our monthly newsletter to be notified of future releases and special sales.